The Dream of AO

JAMES POLUS

BALBOA.PRESS
A DIVISION OF HAY HOUSE

Copyright © 2021 James Polus.
Editor: Larry Kenna

All rights reserved. No part of this book may be used or reproduced by any means, graphic, electronic, or mechanical, including photocopying, recording, taping or by any information storage retrieval system without the written permission of the author except in the case of brief quotations embodied in critical articles and reviews.

Balboa Press books may be ordered through booksellers or by contacting:

Balboa Press
A Division of Hay House
1663 Liberty Drive
Bloomington, IN 47403
www.balboapress.com
844-682-1282

Because of the dynamic nature of the Internet, any web addresses or links contained in this book may have changed since publication and may no longer be valid. The views expressed in this work are solely those of the author and do not necessarily reflect the views of the publisher, and the publisher hereby disclaims any responsibility for them.

The author of this book does not dispense medical advice or prescribe the use of any technique as a form of treatment for physical, emotional, or medical problems without the advice of a physician, either directly or indirectly. The intent of the author is only to offer information of a general nature to help you in your quest for emotional and spiritual well-being. In the event you use any of the information in this book for yourself, which is your constitutional right, the author and the publisher assume no responsibility for your actions.

Any people depicted in stock imagery provided by Getty Images are models, and such images are being used for illustrative purposes only. Certain stock imagery © Getty Images.

Print information available on the last page.

ISBN: 978-1-9822-6824-4 (sc)
ISBN: 978-1-9822-6825-1 (e)

Balboa Press rev. date: 04/29/2021

To my wife Noreen for her valuable input and loving encouragement and my children, Caitlin, Matthew, Meghan and Sarah who believed in me and provided the momentum through four months of writing. A special thanks to Larry Kenna, who gave freely of his time and his intellect to edit the manuscript. I am also appreciative to George Deyman, Ann Grosz, John McGhee and Tracy Baldwin for their valuable comments and encouragement.

Contents

Introduction ix
Prelude: The Life and "Dream" of AO xi

Chapter 1   The Plight of the Varagans 1
Chapter 2   Wild Storms of Destruction 10
Chapter 3   Lessons of The Terrible Conflict 15
Chapter 4   The Wall of Deceit 19
Chapter 5   Devi's Warning to the Nivasi Council 23
Chapter 6   The "Granary" 27
Chapter 7   Betrayed Trust 31
Chapter 8   Devi's Terrible Dream 35
Chapter 9   Seeds of Doubt 38
Chapter 10   Crisis in the Nivasi Council 41
Chapter 11   The Strike of the King Cobra 45
Chapter 12   The Story of the Varagans's Defeat 49
Chapter 13   Romantic Strolls in the Greenlands 59
Chapter 14   The Horse Warriors Cross the Great Stars River 63
Chapter 15   Urgent Preparations 71
Chapter 16   Lies, Deceit, and Perceptions 76
Chapter 17   War Strategy Decisions 82
Chapter 18   The Final Month 87
Chapter 19   The Invasion Begins 92
Chapter 20   The Anger of the Shore People 99
Chapter 21   The Epic Battle Begins 104
Chapter 22   Day One of the Battle 110
Chapter 23   Day Two Battle Surprises 115
Chapter 24   Day 3 of the Battle: Revenge of The Woodlands 121
Chapter 25   Saisha's Terrible Dilemma 128
Chapter 26   Arian Confronts Pratham 136
Chapter 27   Rishaan's Dream and Oath of Revenge 140

Chapter 28	New War Strategies to Break the Stalemate	144
Chapter 29	AO interprets Rishaan's Dream	149
Chapter 30	Zeba and The Way of AO	156
Chapter 31	The Eve of the Decisive Battle	163
Chapter 32	The Poisoning of Zeba	167
Chapter 33	Day of the Epic Battle	179
Chapter 34	The Trial of AO	191
Chapter 35	Days of Mourning and Love Lost	205
Chapter 36	Obsessions of Love and Revenge	212
Chapter 37	Threats to Rishaan	219
Chapter 38	Civil Unrest in Desa	225
Chapter 39	AO's Recitation of the Ancestral Hymns	235
Chapter 40	Anya's Anguish	238
Chapter 41	War Plans and the Delights of Rishaan	244
Chapter 42	Jai's Terrible Fate	249
Chapter 43	Beautiful Revenge	254
Chapter 44	Nature Intervenes	257
Chapter 45	Love Fulfilled	263

Postlude: The Legacy of AO 265
Characters 267

Introduction

Some people have persistent and intense dreams every night, while others cannot recall any of their dreams. Everyone dreams, and those dreams can be very consequential for individuals and society.

History shows when powerful people dream, especially those with a troubled spirit, the consequences on vast numbers of people can be impactful, often devastating. There are many illustrative cases of dreams by political and military leaders which preceded some of history's most decisive battles and wars. The Greeks were fond of deploying the medium of a dream in which they used humans as pawns in the epic quarrels between the gods. In the Iliad, Homer employs such a ruse by Zeus, inspiring a dream in Agamemnon's deepest sleep, stimulating a vision of the ultimate conquest of Troy.

The dream state and reality often overlap, causing the dreamer to believe the dream is true, most times, predictive. In most religions, dreams have inspired prophets, such as Muhammad, the founder of Islam, to preach a major change in religious doctrines. Another person of immense significance was The Buddha.

Cultural writings explain the five dreams of Siddhartha Gautama, on several eves prior to becoming The Buddha, one of which tells of four different colored birds from the four primary directions, falling at his feet, turning pure white, signifying the release of people from the four castes, principally laborers. Buddhism preaches all people are equal, a radical idea and a threat to the privileged classes of India, chiefly the priests and brahmins, dominant in Indian society well before the rise of Rome.

Dream interpretation was a cultivated skill, rewarding many people with power and influence. For example, the dream interpretation of Joseph in Egypt warning of coming famines. Shamans and mystics, highly intuitive and intelligent, were held in high esteem, gaining power through shrewd interpretations with outcomes favorable to the dreamer.

The setting of this story is in East Asia several millenniums ago. History in this period witnessed four magnificent civilizations: in China around the Yellow River, the Mesopotamia River Valley, in the Nile Delta in Egypt, and the Indus River region occupying lands currently in Pakistan, India and to a smaller degree, Afghanistan. Within the Indus River Valley, there were dozens of major cities, of which remarkably preserved ruins exist to this day. Unfortunately, there is no elaborate writing system to rely on and the symbolic language, clear on pottery, remains untranslated, despite major efforts by linguists.

An imaginary historical tale set in the historic civilizations of East Asia, "The Dream of AO" depicts the challenges of a moral and ethical life, the fight for equality and the human drive for purpose. The backdrop is the clash and convergence of four vastly different peoples, each claiming cultural superiority. It is also a romantic tale of the genuine love of three couples who bridge these cultural divides. At the heart of the story is an epic mental battle of survival between two leaders of warring peoples, one led by a woman of superior intelligence and insight versus her deadly opponent, a man of extreme cunning. The fictional events and characters convey classical themes of courage and treachery, love and hate and the power of redemption as well as deep motivations of revenge.

This story of creative and fanciful imagination is the detailed recitation of a "dream" by a young man called "AO" who lived on the south-eastern edge of the Indian subcontinent. The "dream" was told through the words of professional storytellers, itinerant preachers and mystics with powerful memories and magical verbal skills. Audiences would sit quietly for hours, even days, absorbing every word of the tale.

Epic stories memorized and recited for centuries in the oral tradition eventually appeared in writings. The narrator of this story, called Akshay, a distant descendant of AO, assumes the task to write the entire story in precise detail, faithfully reproducing into a written manuscript every word as spoken by trained storytellers for hundreds of years.

Prelude: The Life and "Dream" of AO

May I introduce myself? You may call me Akshay.

I am of no importance to this famous story, recited by hundreds of itinerant storytellers for countless years. I am merely the first scribe, accepting the honorable duty to record for posterity the exact words of the story called "The Dream of AO". As a distant descendant of AO, I can claim no exclusive insight other than the countless references to our ancestors passed down from generation to generation.

Do not think it was simply a dream. The seeds of the story arose from the dream experienced by my ancestor, AO, but it was an elaborate morality tale, espousing the personal philosophy of AO. Of course, AO embellished his "dream" taking liberties, poetic license so to speak, to ensure resounding acceptance of his messages.

Please, if you permit me, I will tell you about AO, the man with the strange name, and explain how his dream occurred. I must spare no details; my duty is to write every word I learned, as a humble storyteller. I am Akshay, the scribe, not the author.

I mentioned his name as AO, although it is more correct to say "AO" only as his true name was unknown, even to himself. He was born into a small village bordering on a crescent peninsula of fertile rice fields on one side and the sea on the other. When he was a small child, some say two years old, a gigantic flood caused by a typhoon of historic proportions, engulfed his parents, leaving no trace. The typhoon was so devastating all the other people in the village perished.

The child swept into a watery grave along with all the villagers somehow washed onto the shore, remarkably close to his last breath on this earth. No one knew anything about this boy, not even his name. Some survivors from a neighboring village swore they saw the boy lifted from the waters by a gigantic octopus.

Priests who adopted the boy practiced a form of spiritual naturalism and lived a private life in cloistered monasteries. The priests named the boy "AO" which was a shortened version of octopus boy in their local dialect. The priests believed ocean creatures, above all the octopus, infused primordial spirits in certain humans. Although these people ate fish, they would never eat an octopus as they believed the legends fostered from one generation to another that human descended from them.

The people in this region were spiritual, although not in a religious sense. They followed a code of ethical behavior blended with the belief one must be in harmony with the natural rhythms of their universe, meaning everything around them, both animate and inanimate. Even the winds and the clouds spoke to them.

The priests taught AO about the soul within humans, the embodiment of their values and their fundamental character which expressed through one's spirit. All people required harmony between mind and body for the soul to prosper. An ethical embrace of society underpinned relationships between people. Personal honor and courage were most admired if the person also showed humility and empathy for others.

Over time, the priests noticed unique characteristics of AO. In particular, he spent most of his time walking near the ocean shores, deeply steeped in thought. He learned the art of wood sculpturing, using only wood he found on the beaches. Random driftwood became beautifully crafted figurines of sea creatures. None was more exalted than a magnificent sculpture of an octopus which he gave to the priests in deep appreciation.

The people in this region near the ocean depended on ocean life for their livelihood and sustenance. Sea life was precious. Villagers witnessed the wonders of life from the majesty of dolphins and whales to the meanderings of sand crabs leaving momentary traces in the sand.

Among the magnificent creatures of the ocean, they treated the octopus with reverence. The people did not believe in gods;

they believed in the divinity of nature. Of all the creatures of nature, the octopus occupied the highest echelon. They seemed to have intelligence in every tentacle, exhibiting behavior not seen in any other animal species. No one doubted the octopus had high emotional intelligence endowed with crafty skills.

Octopuses engaged playfully with divers who frequented the coastal reefs. The villagers witnessed the shifting behavior of octopuses toward certain divers. Some divers like AO seemed to swim in harmony with the octopuses, while they squirted others with clouds of ink and chased away. Most unusual was the fact AO seemed to attract communities of octopuses, normally solitary creatures. Some divers suggested he was holding court with his ocean friends.

The priests taught a purposeful life required a deep commitment to natural law which governed human behavior with all animate creatures and inanimate objects. Personal behavior gauged the quality of your spirit and inner core values.

People may understand the teachings, but people are not perfect. In fact, the more one recognized imperfections and limitations within their soul, the more liberated they became. Wisdom was not an absolute state. It was an attribute of people who discerned their own limitations through acquisition of knowledge, intuition, self-reflection, and experience. Humility was evidence of wisdom in people.

AO was once a very humble young man, highly influenced by his natural surroundings. He valued simplicity in life; his pleasures emanated from nature, especially from the ocean waters. As his reputation as a sculptor grew and demand for his sculptures increased, his ambitions grew as well. Creating magnificent art was no longer sufficient. He craved wealth and material goods, ensnared by human envy and ambition which consumed his waking thoughts. Happiness slowly drifted away.

Pervasive darkness shaded his soul, and his spirit hardened with jealousy and envy. He said to himself; *I am a good man, but I am not a great man.* He falsely thought only a famous man achieved great things. The more he wanted to be great, the more aggressive and domineering he became.

AO's spirit grew more troubled, his soul imprisoned by desires. His ambitions were of wealth and power. His behavior changed for the worse on each successive day as he became more critical of everyone. He did not realize people began to despise him.

Then he had the dream. That changed everything,

AO had powerful mystical abilities heightened in his nightly dreams. One night, AO experienced the most intense dream ever in his life. It was not, in any sense, a normal dream which most people experience. The dream was unusually long and vivid, following through tangled webs of sub-conscious thoughts. As AO often ate wild mushrooms and natural herbs, perhaps his deep dream state was because of some unusually potent mushrooms, wild chilies, rice wine; more likely caused by deep spirits rumbling and agitating within his soul.

Every night, dreams engulfed AO's mind. The dreams were often repetitive and mundane, but this dream was different. He saw an octopus floating in his imagination, gently advancing, then receding, the tip of one tentacle gently probing him. Another tentacle touched, inducing AO further into a dreamy dance with the octopus. His mind sensed the octopus was speaking to him, not in words, as we know them, but in some form of energy. He perceived the octopus was speaking to him with images.

AO's dream grew more intense, more fanciful, deeply intuitive. Moment by moment, he became more spiritually intoxicated, and the dream passed into deeper states of awareness and clarity. The skin of the octopus continuously transformed from one color to another, each shade sparking further twists in the mind of AO, seemingly more fuel for the dream. The octopus drew AO deeper, wrapping him within all his tentacles. Bodies merged, sinking further into the ocean depths. Although the dream was exceedingly stressful, AO did not resist.

Finally, AO emerged from his sleep, drenched in the exhaustion, and sweat of personal renewal.

AO sat quietly, thinking of what to do next. He decided he would go to the priests, people he had long neglected. When the priests saw him approaching, they smiled among themselves. They had expected for some time AO would return looking for a mix of redemption and spiritual renewal. AO approached a small gathering of priests who were working the earth for summer planting in their gardens. One priest looked up; his hands covered with soil. It shocked AO when the man said: "AO, tell us about your wondrous dream with the octopus."

Most shore peoples, expressly the priests, believed deeply in the folklore that the octopus possessed creativity, high intelligence, and solitary freedom. They rejected the folklore perpetuated by others that the octopus was dangerous and evil. Sailors would tell tales of gigantic octopuses and squids which snatched humans from the ship's deck.

Some people speculated if a person dreams of being wrapped helplessly by the many twisting arms of an octopus that symbolized entanglement in their own fears. These people live in a state of anxiety, trapped by worry and lurking dangers, obsessed with uncertainty.

The priests thought otherwise, believing if you dream about an octopus, that was incredibly lucky as these creatures are a spectacular species, complex, resilient, and most different from humans than any other large animals. They believed it meant the dreamer dared to be different, self-reliant, very intuitive, and cool-headed.

AO retold all the details of his dream to the priests who had raised him. They listened intently for hours. They perceived this was no ordinary dream. When AO finished, the priests gathered in meditation, sitting quietly in a small circle. They exchanged few words. To them, the meaning was clear. The wisest of the priests told AO that, although the dream seemed like a fantasy tale, it was a clarion call for the peoples to heed the wisdom of the dream.

The chief priest interpreted the dream as a fable of morality and love, a parable of individuals, from four different peoples with unique customs and values, challenging conventional beliefs. At its core, the dream was about the soul of a people, the quest for equality and purpose, anchored by reverence for universal, natural law.

The chief priest informed AO, "Fate has chosen you to renounce your current life of ambition and material greed and to pursue a purposeful life as a messenger." AO would follow in the long lineage of gifted, mesmerizing storytellers valued for tales of wisdom, intrigue, and messages of morality.

This is the "dream" story, embellished by AO's imagination and sagacity. AO, forsaking materialism, inspired by a new purpose in life and endowed with an extraordinary memory, traveled from village to village far from his home. AO excelled in the recitation of his "dream", gaining a reputation as a master storyteller. Listeners sat entranced for hours, hanging on every word, appreciating the dream as a fanciful tale, a story for the human spirit. Some people were simply curious, lessons of morality motivated others; some sought to glean insights into wisdom. Everyone loved the myriad imaginary details, unable to resist falling captive to the array of fictitious characters, many heroic and admirable, a few detestable, even wicked and vile.

Master storytellers recited AO's dream for timeless ages, each using various oral techniques, but every recitation of the dream of AO remained true to the originals words as first told by AO, faithfully repeated from one generation to another.

I, Akshay, the humble scribe of minor talent, testify to complete accuracy in the following chronicle, each word faithfully captured, as originally recited by AO, and cherished by expert storytellers throughout the ages.

This is the story, always beginning with the Varagans, a people in retreat from a devastating military debacle.

PART 1
The Plight of the Varagans

The initial group from the west slowly came into sight, spotted by some sheep herders who had grazed much further to the west than was typical. A long line of carts was scarcely discernable in the distance. Low clouds of dust, like a morning fog, gradually rose as the barely visible caravan came into view. The sheep herders headed back quickly to their principal city, Desa, two days' journey away, as any approach of strangers was rare. Whether these people were peaceful or warlike was not their primary concern; conveying the news of the strangers was paramount.

These strangers were from a distant land to the north, on the vast grassy steppes. A few people rode on oxcarts, but most of the weary migrants, called Varagans, were trudging along, a few stumbling, barely able to walk in the heat of the summer day. Two men walked alone out in front of the first oxcart, apparently acting as reconnaissance for the rest of the stragglers.

Neither spoke. Words were meaningless as thoughts occupied their long, hot days and cool nights. Since food and water were scarce, these two men, the senior leaders of the Varagan military, had given their meager rations to the older people, many on the verge of death from sheer exhaustion and starvation. The commander of the Varagan military, named Arian, accompanied by Veer, his second in command, had not eaten in days, partaking of only water to survive the summer heat.

In the first oxcart, two men and several women rode in modest comfort, their food and water provisions sufficient for the "Primary", a title accorded to Pratham, the ruler of the Varagans. Next to him in the cart sat his younger brother, Jackal, and several women whom Pratham referred to as his advisors or shall we say consorts. Their advice always coincided with sexual pleasures.

Occasionally Arian would glance back, trying not to gaze on the lead oxcart. He was more concerned about the stragglers, especially his soldiers, many with grave injuries, suffered in the long, deadly retreat from their land. Arian could not shake the images of his enemies, fierce warriors on horses who swept into their lands motivated by an insatiable conquest for land and booty.

Pratham, egged on by his brother Jackal who had never served a day in the military, had committed many tactical errors. Worse yet, Jackal had foolishly struck Axam, one of the most preeminent leaders of the invaders, called Horse Warriors. The cowardly act occurred in the palace of Pratham during peace negotiations. Lacking common sense and endowed with a mean spirit, Jackal had incurred the wrath of these invaders, provoking the undying hatred of Axam.

The "peace" emissary, Axam, also the chief military strategist, was the brother of the Supreme Commander of the Horse Warriors, an aggressive people with vast territories gained through unrelenting military expansion. These ferocious men who lived by their own strict code of conduct considered insults and personal abuse of emissaries as the basis for the complete annihilation of the offender, including members of his ruling class.

Arian pushed on mile after mile, devoid of emotions, numbed by ghostly memories of the slaughter of thousands of his fighters, senselessly sacrificed over several days of battle because of incredibly stupid battle tactics, inspired by Jackal's hatred of Arian. Jackal had persuaded the arrogant Pratham, the Primary of the Varagans, to launch bold attacks against the Horse Warriors, dismissing the vehement opposition of Arian.

These ill-planned, undisciplined attacks exposed hundreds of courageous Varagan fighters to a massive counterattack by the Horse Warriors. Virtually every Varagan attacker died, most the victim of long lances, skillfully employed by the Horse Warrior's heavy cavalry. Any Varagans, surviving the initial counterattack, fled in disarray. The Horse Warriors slaughtered them, as they did not believe in taking prisoners, considered as a dishonorable fate for any warrior.

Through the sheer skill and bravery of Arian, Veer and their military forces, the Varagans escaped by executing a daring retreat through a mountain pass until coming to a vast river. Countless brave soldiers died fighting off the persistent Horse Warriors, delaying their advance to provide enough time for the Varagan survivors to reach the river. The current was too swift and the water too deep to escape with the horses so the Varagan stragglers abandoned their horses and used oxcarts to cross. The Horse Warriors appeared as the last of the Varagans crossed. Not willing to risk losing their prized horses, the Horse Warriors halted at the river's edge, seething in anger and hatred as their prey escaped.

After days of retreat, the exhausted Varagans from the northwest arrived, dirty and somewhat crude in manner and speech. They had an unusual appearance featuring a skin complexion darker than the inhabitants of the local region. They arrived in dribs, a long line of oxcarts extending far into the distance. Most noteworthy was the absence of horses, most unusual, as horses were the primary means of transportation. Some people rode on oxcarts pulled by oxen, but most were walking, as if in a trance.

The new arrivals settled warily outside Desa, the most prominent city in the region. They did not know what to expect from the local inhabitants, but their sunken eyes and windblown faces betrayed their desperation and despair. Their clothes, torn and shredded, hung off their bodies like the last falling leaves of autumn still clinging to branches. There was no fear in their faces, just the stare of complete exhaustion.

Pratham climbed off the first oxcart, advancing slowly toward the gate. Standing stoically, with an air of nobility, summoning all his strength, announced, "I am Pratham, ruler of the Varagans. I request to speak to your king." The watchmen on the walls did not understand what he meant by the words, "ruler" or "king". They looked at each other with quizzical expressions.

The local people of Desa called Nivasi had for centuries governed themselves through a representative body called The Nivasi Council. Nivasi men and women were equal in status, sharing the same rights to vote and hold elected office.

They held Nivasi Council meetings in the Assembly Hall, a plain room with no distinguishing features, art, or sculptures. No elevated sitting areas marked rank or privilege. Seating comprised of sparse benches which circled the hall. Speakers would rise and address the council participants from an elevated stone platform in the center of the hall. Addresses to the Nivasi Council were brief, as the members valued listening and reflection more than speaking. Brevity and the neutral, deliberative manner of the speaker judged the wisdom of a person's words. Emotional outbursts signaled lack of thought and judgment.

The Nivasi Council, led by Gandesh acted in an administrative role as all authority emanated from the Nivasi Council, decided they would help these weary and troubled people. The wisest of all the Nivasi Council members, a very elderly man of timeless age named Mandeep, spoke on this matter. Standing in the center of the hall, his brief speech echoed these prescient words:

"We, the Nivasi, bound by our ethical beliefs, must welcome all people into Desa. This is our duty. These people are unknown to us. We do not know their culture or their values. We must welcome these people but must not delude ourselves that they share our ethical codes. They may be ethical and spiritual people. We do not know. We must peer into their souls. Observe the flow of truth, not the torrent of words."

Mandeep, without expression, returned slowly to his seat. No other citizens spoke, as no one felt additional comments would serve any purpose. Gandesh, judging he was speaking for all, declared the Nivasi would welcome these people and provide food, water, and land for their tents. He called these people "refugees", a word unknown to nearly everyone in the Nivasi Council.

Mandeep, a wise personage skilled in human perceptions, specifically the language of the human body, felt uneasy with the blind optimism of Gandesh. Mandeep sensed the Nivasi Council was far from unanimous in the matter of the migrants. In particular, he studied Shanti, one of the senior leaders of the Nivasi Council. The slight twitches of her shoulders and subtle facial grimaces betrayed her discomfort, perhaps even opposition, to the welcoming of these "refugees".

As the Nivasi Council members spilled onto the street, an elderly blind woman, disheveled and ragged in dress, began screaming in an eerily shrill voice:

"A terrible danger looms in our midst. I have heard the screams of these strangers, fierce men on horses bringing death. I warn you they will bring destruction to Desa. I am not the one who is blind; your vision of your own greatness makes you blind to reality. You so reek of your own deluded goodness you cannot smell evil. Your senses and imagination dulled by conformity. Your sight is worth nothing because you only see what your mind has deemed important."

Everyone assumed the pitiful, senile woman was speaking of the Varagans, ignoring her reference to "fierce men on horses".

Shanti emerged from the crowd to comfort the poor soul, empathetic to her pleas. The others merely walked away, paying no regard to an insane person. Shanti also assumed the shrill warnings pertained to the Varagans. She was mistaken.

After a few days to allow the refugees to regain some strength, Gandesh invited the leaders of the refugees to a Nivasi Council meeting. Three men appeared. The leader, Pratham, leader of the Varagans, explained their homeland was northwest of the Great Stars River, on a grassy, semi-arid land of vast openness. Arian, the senior military leader of the Varagans accompanied Pratham, as well as a much older man, named Amura, announced as the senior counselor, a man respected for his wisdom and judgment.

In contrast to Gandesh, who was in his seventies, of slight build with wispy white hair, Pratham was a middle-aged man, tall and stout, his face weathered through years of conflict. His presence exuded authority. He explained to the Nivasi Council that his people had suffered from an invasion of the Horse Warriors. His people had fought bravely, but these invaders used new fighting techniques, being highly skilled in coordinating attack maneuvers on their horses.

Pratham's speech described the brilliant battle tactics of the Varagans, which only failed because of an overwhelming number of invaders. The Nivasi did not know these claims were lies; soon, they would find out firsthand the devious nature of Pratham. Arian was not shocked, knowing full well Pratham was a master of lies and false claims. Arian said nothing, wisely judging time would soon unveil the truth.

Arian agreed with Pratham that complete surrender would mean not only loss of wealth and land but also total subjugation of the Varagans, widespread slaughter of the citizens. Not even children would be spared. Women would enter a hellish life of complete submission to the enemy. Yes, Arian thought, *We had no choice other to retreat but the fault was entirely due to the arrogance of Pratham and the wicked treachery of his brother, Jackal.*

Pratham related the sad story. As their numbers dwindled, it compelled the Varagans to move to the southeast toward the land of the Nivasi. They traveled for days, plagued by a lack of water and food, fighting a rear-guard action until a massive river halted them. The Varagans crossed the river with just oxen, leaving their horses behind as there was no workable way to get the horses across safely. Many people drowned, adding to the misery of the Varagans.

On the opposite side of the wide, treacherous river, the Horse Warriors halted, frustrated in their plans to inflict ultimate destruction on the Varagans. Exhausted and desperate, the Varagans continued their slow trek southeast, following down an extensive river valley.

Neither the Nivasi nor the Varagans realized their people were of vastly different cultures. Pratham promised his people would be perfect citizens and obey all laws. In fact, he asked the Nivasi

Council to give him a written parchment of laws. It surprised the Varagans to learn there was no set of written statutes, critical to the Varagans who lived in a very hierarchical, feudal, legalistic society.

Every day, more and more Varagans appeared, but the Nivasi were not a bit concerned. Prejudice had long ago disappeared. Timeless traditions had trained the people to believe all peoples regardless of geographical origins shared a universal set of human values.

That evening, Pratham gathered his senior advisers, including leaders from each of the aristocratic families. Unlike the Nivasi, the Varagans believed in a rigid class system with three distinct groups of people: the army, the farmers and cattle grazers, and the administrators. Heredity was the prime determinant of rank, although movement into the military class in times of war provided opportunities for ambitious and skilled men. One man from a powerful military family inherited the title of "Primary", a designation which endured for life.

The Varagans had long ago learned life in semi-arid climates meant the continuous dangers of marauding attacks by nomadic tribes, and their constant search for arable lands. As a result, most of the people were farmers, herders, or soldiers. Naturally, the soldiers occupied the ruling class although the Varagan professional army led by Arian served nobly even if many of the "retired" military class, like Pratham, had become corrupt seeking power and wealth.

Not surprising, the Varagan language did not have a word for "ethics" as that concept did not fit a feudal society. Among the military class, honor and duty were held in high esteem. For all others, the rules of behavior were clear. Fear of punishment ensured adherence to the law. The people did not conceive of natural rights as universally applicable, only inherited through one's family.

Pratham understood his position as Primary was at risk because of the devastating defeats at the hands of the Horse Warriors. Rival aristocratic families had their own clan leaders, many of whom secretly waited for the right opportunity to seize the role of Primary.

Pratham recited to his senior advisers and leaders of the aristocratic families the terrible events which led them to flee to Desa. He recounted all the benefits which the aristocrats enjoyed in his long reign as Primary. He was astute not to blame anyone above all the military. Everyone was silent.

He concluded the evening with this oath, "I swear we will return to our homelands. Our misfortunes are because of providence, not to any of our failings. Our military fought bravely. We were skilled in fighting off bands of nomadic tribes. No one could have predicted the invasion of the Horse Warriors who descended upon us in massive numbers, using small, fast ponies, unknown to us. We had no experiences with such blood-thirsty people with no concept of honor or justice."

Pratham continued, "The Nivasi are a soft people without strong leadership or even an army. They do not understand the terrible dangers and suffering the Horse Warriors will inflict on them. We must absorb their men into our infantry ranks as the only way to defeat this evil horde is through a vastly increased army."

No one would dare to question the dictates of the Primary. However, it was a time-honored tradition within the Varagans to permit the wisest person the opportunity to speak without prior approval. A quiet hush filled the air; people waited to see if Amura, the wise man of the Varagans, would even speak. Pratham was respectfully silent, cautiously waiting, as he also had no idea what the old man might say. Amura arose from the edge of the gathering and moved with the slow deliberation of age and experience.

The words of Amura flowed in a steady stream of wisdom, insight, and caution, radiating exhortations of challenges, stirring doubts and discontent, "It is right and just we regain our lands. People cannot be denied their rights. It is the correct path to rebuild our peoples and to nourish their minds and bodies. To defeat the Horse Warriors, we must rebuild and strengthen the character of our people. We must inspire greatness in the people of common rank, the backbone of our society, whose labors enable our aristocratic families to attain the privileges of pleasure and comfort. All people, including the Nivasi who have welcomed and nourished us, deserve our respect, even if their values differ from ours. You, the leaders of the Varagans, must adopt these ideas, otherwise we will never return home."

Stunned silence followed. These were radical ideas which would, if adopted, change the role of women and men, not originating from the aristocratic ranks. People with power in feudalistic societies usually derive their authority from ownership of land. The common people who made up most of the population provided the sweat and labor, and in times of war, foot soldiers. The aristocratic families from military backgrounds ruled through an alliance of privileged clans, sharing power among themselves on the backs of commoners.

Pratham and Jackal had absolutely no intention of changing anything. In fact, Jackal had often counseled Pratham to eliminate Amura, a man more aligned with Arian and Veer. This was true, as Amura harbored contempt for Pratham and Jackal, both utterly lacking in wisdom. Pratham's best days evaporated years ago. Jackal never rose above his scheming role as chief sycophant.

Amura had recognized the Horse Warriors were an egalitarian society in which action in battle was most highly valued, even above native birth, effectively absorbing conquered peoples into their societies. They deemed all men equal, the differentiation among men depended on leadership and skill on the battlefield. The only condition was absolute fidelity to the supreme commander and adherence to the strict codes of military conduct.

To Amura, the contrast between the Varagans and The Horse Warriors was striking. The Varagans lived in a repressive feudal society led by men who would use any means to maintain their privilege. Arian, Veer, and a substantial number of the military class served nobly, watching with growing alarm the crass abuse of power by the aristocrats.

PART 2
Wild Storms of Destruction

The land of the Nivasi benefited from a pleasant, temperate climate. Storms in the summer were infrequent. However, thunderstorm and hailstorms struck suddenly with strong winds and heavy rains causing minor damage: more of a nuisance than a threat.

That fateful day in July began pleasantly. Most people perceived no sign a powerful storm was brewing. Nature, however, produced some signs. The birds became still. The woods were dead silent. A few people noticed the air had become eerily calm. People on the eastern edges of Desa began hearing a dull roar which increased in loudness. Winds swirled; flying debris kicked up, the clouds thickened and blackened the sky.

People said after the freak storm occurred, the only real clue was a deafening roar gaining in intensity before any storm clouds were visible. Soon, the sky developed a massive, greenish-black wall of thunderheads. A tremendous number of small ice stones bombarded everything. The roar of the wind and the sight of the twisted cone of intense twirling winds overwhelmed everything in its path.

Nearly everyone thought the world was ending. For many, it did. Life ceased for many humans and animals. The storm swept away all life in its path into a tumult of suffocating dirt. Breathing was not possible. It struck many people with tree branches, bricks, stones. Visibility was zero, the noise beyond comprehension. People in their root cellars were the most fortunate. Ferocious winds smashed anyone in the open into stone walls, their necks snapped like dry twigs. The few survivors caught out in the open described horrible pain as their clothes shredded, exposing their skin to a merciless ordeal of thousands of pricks on their naked bodies from the sharp-edged shards of sand and grit.

The twisting wind funnel cut a path through the eastern side of the city, wreaking indescribable destruction. Many homes vanished, leaving only a dirt cellar devoid of life and once-precious objects. The granary suffered total demolition, and all the grain vanished in clouds of dirt and dust. Now, much of the city lay in rubble. The Varagans were on the western side of the valley, so their tent camp did not receive a direct hit. Also, their tents were of a spherical design which seemed to deflect the winds.

The storm disappeared in ten minutes. Ten minutes of sheer terror and massive destruction, notably of the crop fields and fruit trees. Everything became incredibly still, and, once again, the sun shined as if it would be a pleasant day. Horrible sounds quickly filled the air; the wailing and moaning of injured people pervaded every space. Worst of all were the voices of the living, searching, and calling out for their loved ones. A bereft mother, holding her dead child, sat on the ground dazed, too distraught to cry; she was so severely injured herself, moments later she died clutching her little girl. Small, crying children wandered aimlessly, searching for a parent or any family member able to provide comfort.

The wild storm injured and killed innumerable people, either by flying debris or the merciless pounding of the ice stones. It would take days to determine the number of dead. The most immediate task was to canvas the damage to the crops and farm animals and to bury the countless bodies strewn everywhere, some embedded in the thick of trees branches, hanging like ghoulish decorations.

Gandesh called together the Nivasi Council to assess the crop damage, number of injuries, and deaths. It was urgent to ensure all babies and small children had caregivers. Report after report was grim. The numbers of injured and dead as well as physical damage to the city were staggering.

Last, Priya, Chief of the Office of Agriculture, presented her report. She stoically outlined the status of each major crop. Most of the wheat fields with small tender shoots recently planted for the summer growing cycle were destroyed. Vast quantities of legumes such as lentils, peas, mung beans were the hardest hit, torn to tiny shreds and buried in the mounds of dirt. Walnut and fig trees would take years to replant. Worst of all, the city granary suffered extensive damage; the grain either swept away or too wet for consumption.

In just ten minutes, the Nivasi lost a vast amount of their food supply for the year. Fortunately, vast stocks of root vegetables stored in stone wells near each home escaped damage. Most of the farm animals survived, their feed boxes did not. There would not be sufficient food for the cattle, chickens, and goats. This created a moral dilemma for the Nivasi as they rarely ate meat and now clearly did not have sufficient livestock grain to keep the animals from starving. Normally, farm animals, raised only for their by-products such as eggs, cheese, and milk, were not consumed. With insufficient grain to feed the cattle, the only choice was to cull the herds, providing desperately needed food.

The question arose, could the devastating storm have been predicted? Would more storms quickly follow? Gandesh invited a man of the forests named Vidya to the Nivasi Council for his opinion. Vidya lived all his life in a small cabin in the heart of the deepest woodlands. Rather than say he was antisocial; it would be more correct he was too intuitive a man of natural wilderness to enjoy social life. The ethic of the time was not to criticize or to state an unfavorable opinion, respecting the rights of people considered strange. Vidya, considered as very strange but respected as the people of the forests, lived in self-reliant harmony with the deep woods.

Vidya explained he sensed danger was approaching as the golden-winged warblers took flight in the hours preceding the storm. Next, he felt the eerie silence of the woods. The normal sounds of birds busily chirping stopped; all the birds disappeared. Danger seemed to ooze from every tree and bush. Vidya's dog, Aarush, an alert black combi, whined, growing more fidgety as the moments passed. Suddenly, Vidya realized in a flash of enlightenment he must take shelter in the deepest recesses of his cabin, which had a dirt cellar for food storage. The massive storm roared through moments later. Fallen trees pummeled his cabin. Good fortune was with Vidya that day as he and Aarush emerged from the deep cellar uninjured.

Everyone listened intently to Vidya in awe of this minimalist man from the forests. Then, Mandeep, the wise man of the Nivasi, spoke these prophetic words:

"When the woods are silent, the dogs are whimpering and the birds no longer singing their melodious tones, the skies will reign terror on us to remind humans of their frailty and shallow understanding of natural forces. Listen to the woods, listen to the birds, listen to the dogs."

The Nivasi asked the Varagans to join in a collective meeting to discuss how to manage the dearth of food. Gandesh said everyone would get the same amount of food. No other method would be fair. To the Varagans, this seemed ludicrous. Surely, some people were more important than others. Pratham asked for a short adjournment and huddled with his senior advisors.

When he returned, Pratham explained he had a plan to provide food for everyone. There was no need for the children and old people to die or for mass starvation to afflict the people in sixty days when all sources of food would be exhausted. Pratham said he could ensure new food stocks before the people had exhausted current supplies.

The Nivasi, amazed, if not incredulous, thought the boasts of Pratham were meaningless. They failed to imagine unknown sources of food except for some date and fig trees still standing. No, they said to themselves, this is not possible.

Knowing his people were still weak from the ordeal, Pratham asserted achievement of his promise hinged on additional food rations for a new army, composed of both Nivasi and Varagans. He also required additional land tripling in size of the land currently occupied by the tents.

The Nivasi could not imagine alternative sources of grains and vegetables. The planting season was in summer and fall dedicated to harvesting. Now, there was nothing to harvest. The Nivasi did not object to these requests as a sense of dread and desperation was pervasive. The Nivasi, convinced all people believed in natural rights, did not perceive the deception underlying Pratham's proposals. Surely, the Varagans shared these values. How could they not?

The most troubling issue was the request for additional land, which included a vast part of the "Greenlands". These were the spiritual, forested lands, protected by strict rules of usage. The Nivasi were sure if the Varagans understood this, they would seek other locations. In that opinion, they were gravely mistaken.

To understand the ethics of the Nivasi and their intense belief in societal passivity, one needs to understand their history.

PART 3
Lessons of The Terrible Conflict

The land of the Nivasi had evolved over the last two hundred years to a peaceful kingdom. It was not always so. Stories had passed down from generation to generation of wars and conflicts, the worst of which was called "The Terrible Conflict". Suffering and devastation affected everyone. Disputes, normally solved peacefully, grew more and more tense. Groups with different opinions splintered, and then those groups splintered even further. It was soon apparent two major groups, the farmers, and the grazers, grew in power and numbers. The anger mounted between these two groups and tensions reached a feverish pitch.

The simple issues, originally resolved through reasonable debate, escalated into more strident and opposing positions. The primary source of most disputes were conflicts concerning land and water rights. Disputes between crop farmers and cattle ranchers fomented much of the tension as a growing population placed more demands on wheat and barley crops at the same time meat consumption was rising faster than supply. Grazing lands became scarce and demand for water grew exponentially. Legal conflicts became more contentious, and emotions reached a feverish pitch, threatening to spill over into outright violence.

The epicenter of the most contentious dispute involved the two largest landowning families in Desa who lived adjacent to each other and who owned vast tracts of the pastures. One family achieved attained wealth and power through cattle grazing while the other grew powerful through large-scale wheat and barley farming. Grazing depended on access to vast land tracts for free-range herding methods. To add more stress to the situation, an increasingly drier climate squeezed available arable lands for both the farmers and cattle grazers. Farm workers and family members from each side clashed in the streets. Injuries to body, ego and reputation flamed the tensions to a boiling point.

To unite their respective people and to win more support from the other farmers, the leaders of each group labeled the other group as cheaters and deceivers. Both sides gained adherents as these issues threatened many small farmers and sheepherders. Ideologies replaced class and wealth distinctions. The cattle grazers praised the open lands, available to all, while the farmers spoke of the rights of the small landowner toiling every day on the edge of poverty. They convinced both groups the other side was a threat to their liberty and way of life. Truth was a collection of beliefs supporting the rights of one group over another, no connection to reality need exist.

Each organization declared their ideas were the true ideas, while they labeled the other group as the "Falsifiers". Pamphlets appeared showing grazers as people looking like fat sheep, caricatures with ugly little faces marked by oozing sores. The grazers did not spare the farmers, pictured as scarecrow types creatures with drooling mouths. People started wearing different colors, marking their affiliation. The grazers wore red while the farmers favored blue. Each organization published their ideas in small parchments called the "Truths". Oddly. each side claimed the same name, so each parchment marked in colors became known as the "The Red Truths" and "The Blue Truths".

Each set of parchments clearly outlined the ideology of their organization. Simple phrases permeated like," We believe in peace, they believe in violence" or "we believe in justice for all, they want to steal our rights". Most alarming and believed by both sides: "We believe in freedom; they strive to enslave us". Years later, well after The Terrible Conflict was over, people realized the beliefs in each parchment, the ones dyed in red and opposing one dyed in blue, were precisely the same.

Leaders of each group taught that dialogue was useless, and you must not, under penalty of death, share the contents of "The Beliefs" with your enemy. You only had to know they were different, terrible, and evil. Soon the members of each group started paying dues, which were, of course, mandatory. Each side exhorted their followers to "volunteer" increases in dues.

Artisans tried to remain neutral but could not avoid being dragged into the conflict on both sides. People complaining found their doors marked with a gigantic F, extended each day with another letter until the word "Falsifier" appeared; at which time, enforcement squads seized your property. Some people resisted; others beaten when they refused to choose sides. No one seemed to notice when they vanished. Best not to ask too many questions or risk being labeled as agitators.

The artisans spoke out in public. One potter named Dharma, respected for his age and wisdom, asked the two sides to meet in a peaceful assembly. On that fateful day, the tense assembly of farmers and grazers gathered in the main square, glaring at each other.

Dharma, in white dress, stood on a high rock in the town park and spoke in a calm but firm voice, saying: "We the people of Desa must stop this ever-increasing rise in hatred. I urge everyone to wear white and disband their organizations. We must heal the divisions. Let us revive the loving spirit of this community and solve our differences as honorable citizens."

Dharma spoke on, urging peace and reconciliation, but a few men became more agitated as they realized their power as senior leaders of their respective groups was in jeopardy.

One farmer shouted out, "No one will trample our rights."

Without hesitation or thought, a woman from the powerful grazing family yelled in the farmer's direction, "Sit down, ignorant scare-crow, and stop the foolish words drooling from your mouth."

Dharma tried to regain control of the unruly crowd. He continued by condemning such talk, urging calm. Then, a rock hurled from the edge of the crowd struck Dharma, piercing his temple, drawing a spurt of blood. He stumbled forward semi-conscious; the sharp edge of the stone visibly lodged in his skull. After a few moments, he crumbled and lay still. He was the first casualty. Then the serious violence began.

These events occurred a long time ago. No need to dwell on those terrible times.

Anxiety arose in the Nivasi as days passed, but no additional food materialized. Meanwhile, Pratham directed Arian and the army to levy a small tax on the Nivasi. Arian realized this would be disastrous and ill-timed, so he deliberately stalled the actual collection. Arian thought to himself, *We need these people to help us regain our strength so we can retake our homelands.*

Besides, the ethical and caring attitude of the Nivasi impressed Arian, traits long ago lost by the Varagans. More Varagans trickled into Desa. Their numbers grew alarmingly, and their tactics took on an aggressive and sinister character. The Nivasi quietly whispered doubts.

Then she emerged from a respected but quite average Nivasi family. At first glance, she did not have the demeanor of a powerful person; people would soon discover this woman "Devi" would define fierceness, true leadership, and courage. She was the first to speak out against Pratham.

PART 4
The Wall of Deceit

Most of the homes in Desa were quite modest, normally suitable for a small family plus the occasional visitor. As the primary occupation was farming, numerous families owned land and livestock. They only used fences for corralling the family animals and not for land ownership demarcation. Of course, farming was free-range, so families eagerly shared grazing lands. Due to the vegetarian diet adopted by the Nivasi in the many years since The Terrible Conflict, Desa did not lack for good grazing and farmland. An area of supreme natural beauty known as the Greenlands held a privileged status. The Nivasi citizens enjoyed walking, hiking, and the general enjoyment of a pristine natural setting. Natural picnic settings dotted the serene landscape.

Soon after the reconstruction of the army, consisting only of Varagans, as no male Nivasi could understand the need for an army and would not think of joining a military force, Pratham went to the Nivasi Council with new requirements. Wisely and shrewdly, knowing his hand was still weak, he adopted a very respectful demeanor which, of course, was fake as Pratham was an arrogant and deceitful man. He respectfully requested additional portions of the Greenlands for development of new farming techniques, and training of an enlarged army, which was still quite small.

This request raised a lot of consternation as the people of Desa considered the Greenlands to be sacred, not in a religious sense but in a natural sense. Harmony with nature and respecting all life was of paramount importance. Parents taught their children to revere nature, especially the Greenlands. Above all, children learned about the high natural value of trees. The Nivasi prohibited any unnatural cutting of trees in the Greenlands, aiming to preserve the wild nature for timeless generations.

The Nivasi Council discussed this issue with much fervor, even hints of frustration and resistance to aiding the Varagans. Many Nivasi Council members, such as Shanti, warned the use of the Greenlands by the Varagan army would inevitably lead to irreparable damage. Gandesh called Pratham back into the Nivasi Council chambers and informed him the Greenlands would remain an exclusionary zone.

"Pratham, the woods of the Greenlands are sacred and not available for your purposes. I will make other acreage available."

Pratham rarely heard the word "no". His mind grew more and more angry. *How dare these people question me, he thought to himself?* He had surveyed all the locations. None were suitable. Only the Greenlands would suffice. Multiple favorable features existed in the Greenlands, principally the plentiful trees for construction, streams as a fresh source of water, and best of all, the highest point in the area with strategic advantages over any foe. What to do, he thought? Any material possession including gold will not influence these people, he correctly assumed.

Then Pratham realized how to convince the Nivasi Council. Pratham explained how the hillsides could develop new types of vines unknown in Desa which would provide a whole alternative source of food. Better yet, the mashed fruit of these vines offered a delicious and intoxicating type of nectar. He called this nectar "wine" which contained many natural substances, vital for health.

These types of plants were only indigenous in the small hillsides near the Shore People, an area a long distance south of Desa. Pratham omitted vital information pertinent to the health of the streams. The vines required prodigious amounts of water, notably in the early phase of development. He deceitfully promised to respect the Greenlands and to take every precaution to guard against damage.

With intrepid reservations, the Nivasi Council granted the

temporary right to use two hundred acres with the provision the Varagans replant any trees or wildflowers inadvertently damaged. Strict property measurements were not used to mark precisely the two hundred acres granted to the Varagans, as this would be too impolite a request. It was critical to avoid the slightest appearance of an insult. Mandeep, the Nivasi wise counselor, remained silent even though his heart warned him of impending treachery.

When Pratham returned to the tents, he ordered the immediate construction of a wall around the land. His construction team, unsure where to erect the wall, requested Pratham's guidance. He and his senior advisers walked the perimeter, selecting the best parts of the Greenlands. Pratham boldly appropriated an extensive tract of land, indifferent to any size conformity granted by the Nivasi Council. Not only did the tract exceed the dimensions permitted, the shape of the selected acreage was also irregular in form to encompass a stream which flowed through the center of the lands. He selected a spot on the highest hill. He jokingly said to his men, "This will be the site of the 'Granary'".

The work began immediately to build the wall, which was quite high, more than sufficient if the only purpose was corralling livestock. In fact, the wall was sufficiently tall to obscure observance any of the activities within the enclosed area.

Word of the wall quickly reached Gandesh. He listened intently to the reports of a tall fence, really a wall, being constructed. Nowhere in Desa was there such a wall, except surrounding the city of Desa, as it would serve no purpose. Gandesh said, "I will go to see this wall for myself."

As he approached, Gandesh was very alarmed. The size and extent flabbergasted him; the walled area was more extensive than 200 acres and fully encompassed the stream, a primary source of the natural life in the Greenlands. Stunned, Gandesh remained calm, but the veneer of trust subtlety cracked. Mandeep saw the wall as full confirmation of his suspicions.

Pratham greeted Gandesh at the gate of the new wall and warmly embraced him. He invited Gandesh for tea to discuss any concerns he might have. Gandesh spoke first. "Pratham, this wall and your seizure of the stream violates our agreement."

Pratham interrupted him, speaking in soft and smoothing tones, referring to the wall as a fence. "This fence is solely for the betterment of all the people. This fence is only temporary, to train the army and develop new farming techniques. I promise I will restore all land disrupted and remove the fence in due time. Please be patient with us, as we shall provide Desa with the greatest surplus of food ever. The people will be happy and think, we are a powerful people with hefty surpluses of food."

It would never occur to the Nivasi to think of themselves as "great", so this boast was meaningless to Gandesh.

Gandesh left foolishly satisfied there was a good purpose to the wall. Watching with consternation from a short distance was Devi. Although Devi did not benefit from a privileged education, available to certain families aided by personal tutors, she excelled in her studies, being particularly gifted in the study of Philosophy. She was highly intelligent, shrewd, and extremely perceptive.

As a keen observer of human behavior, words or promises could not deceive Devi. She heard Pratham laughing and joking with his inner circle, mainly family and sycophants. Devi was sure she heard him say: "That old fool Gandesh, he will soon learn who we are." This was all the confirmation Devi needed.

Pratham would soon learn she was no mere slavish female subject to manipulation and abuse. It never occurred to him or his inner circle that any female required respect; no people would choose a female as their leader; and if so, she would be no match for him. Pratham suffered another mistake of human insight, just as he had underestimated Axam.

PART 5
Devi's Warning to the Nivasi Council

Desa was in the truest sense a simple but elegant democracy. The political structure comprised two layers; each neighborhood had a Nivasi Council of nine elected by the all the citizens above the age of 16. This group had the authority to plan and implement laws pertaining to local matters. The next level was a Nivasi Council, of which there were 99 members. These people were advisors and philosophers whose primary duties were to discuss all aspects of life in Desa and to promulgate position statements in a document called "The Insights". This document contained the cumulative wisdom of an ethical life, harmonious with nature and natural rights.

Every month, new "Insights" were posted on display in the city square. There were no laws in Desa equivalent to a normal legalistic society. Before The Terrible Conflict, laws proliferated every week as conflicts and disputes over land, business affairs and ordinary life, even marriage, rose fueling the increase in tensions. Every dispute led to a new law. Unfounded, wild claims asserting systematic violations of the law led to citizen teams, initially designed for meditation, but soon evolving into violent enforcement squads. Those days were long gone.

Memories of The Terrible Conflict faded, the last survivors of the bloody ordeal long deceased. The lessons of that time, however, did not die and there was a group of citizens whose only task was to study current events and write essays for "Insights" drawing parallels back to the days of conflict. This group was a sort of "tripwire" to warn people in studied essays of certain perceived behavior causing rising tensions. People read the essays and adjusted their behavior as everyone believed from birth natural harmony was the primordial principle of life.

Devi was not an elected member of the Nivasi Council. To speak to the Nivasi Council, she was required to write a statement asking for a time slot in the day's agenda, needed for orderly conduct of business. Most people did not know Devi. Among those who did, she was considered precocious and highly gifted with a quiet, if not passive demeanor. She had recently secured the highest professional distinction, awarded to only a few of "Research Fellow".

To gain acceptance as a researcher, an individual had to show the senior members a deep understanding between the natural environment and the expression of the human spirit, whether through social ethics or artistic discovery. Acquisition of knowledge, fostering the connection between the inner spirit and the external human and natural world, was the highest purpose. Although of high distinction, the research fellows maintained a private existence and low profile as a reputation was not desirable.

The research profession required deep analytical skills and insight, capability to think in complex and abstract terms, and unwavering dedication to truth, regardless of implications. All data and concepts fit into frameworks of thought. If the data gained through study did not systematically fit, then the frameworks were challenged and subject to change. They permitted not a hint of personal bias.

Devi specialized in a form of human philosophy addressing the issues of moral dilemmas, tough choices facing individuals and societies. Both individuals and societies have an ultimate purpose which finds expression through the "soul", embodying the core values of each person and the collective whole. How individuals and societies resolved moral dilemmas, living true to their souls, was the essence of life itself.

She wrote a provocative and unusual essay called "Live Your

Purpose" which, as usual, was unsigned by her actual name. Since nearly everyone was unfamiliar with these concepts, most people ignored the essay. However, some very conservative citizens, imprisoned by traditional thinking, found these new ideas irritating or even dangerous. The traditionalist believed that individual creativity and purpose was detrimental to a tranquil society. Most troubling was this statement in the essay:

"It is not sufficient to only study and adopt the collective wisdom of society. Society cannot flourish without unleashing individual creativities derived from honor, discipline, and moral strength. It satisfies the best interests of society when personal expression is in harmony with the collective, cosmic good. The only way to unleash true human potential is to foster each person's true purpose in life, balancing individual expression with collective purpose. True equality demands this condition."

People who believed in a homogenous, traditional society failed to see the point. Mandeep, the Nivasi wise person thought otherwise and anxiously awaited to know the author behind these prophetic words.

As Devi mounted the perched rock in the council hall, she was a bit nervous. She started in a low, barely audible voice as she was not aggressive by nature, rather a more intuitive person. She recalled the long tradition of ethics and morals in Desa emanating from the end of The Terrible Conflict, when from the ashes of destruction and sheer exhaustion, the leaders of the grazers and farmers united in a solemn pledge to banish conflict and prejudice forever. Devi described the ethical values of the Nivasi, ingrained in every child and reinforced throughout their lives.

Her voice grew stronger, her energy intensifying as she laid out in plain terms the fundamental ethical beliefs of the land: respect for people, respect for nature, and respect for individuals without distinctions of class or birth.

She hesitated for a moment, drawing energy from every fiber of her body, then continued, "I fear the Varagans do not understand or share our values. They represent a threat to our land. We are too trusting, too gullible. We are being deceived."

Her words completely stunned the Nivasi Council, as no person would levy such a charge in a public meeting, most believing such behavior was unthinkable. Some senior members protested, denouncing Devi as ill-mannered. Others joined in, deriding such irreverence to the rules of hospitality.

However, some members, coalescing around Shanti, had harbored suspicions among themselves, believing the Varagans represented real dangers. Although very suspicious of the Varagans, they remained quiet for the moment, even though they believed Devi had underestimated the threat. Shanti reasoned the time was not right for stronger resistance.

Suddenly, a messenger burst into the Nivasi Council room, covered in perspiration, his hair matted with dust and grime. Silence filled the chamber. The messenger uttered these words, which shocked everyone to their core.

"They are cutting down the trees in the Greenlands!"

PART 6
The "Granary"

The Nivasi constructed houses of fired brick, never from wanton cutting of trees. The people cultivated trees primarily for the wood required to fuel the kilns used to make bricks. People were constantly planting new trees of all varieties, each variety serving a specific role. Some were date trees which along with jujube red berries were a primary source of food and nutrition. Other trees like the majestic oak trees were natural habitats for birds and squirrels and to connect humans to nature, and to provide shade and beauty. If any wood was available because of pruning or natural reasons, they gave it to wood artisans for furniture and other artifacts, each piece a jewel in design and beauty.

When the Nivasi Council heard the Varagans were chopping down trees in the Greenlands, a shock wave reverberated around the Assembly Hall. Some people started weeping, others seething in anger. The Nivasi Council immediately dispatched a delegation which included Gandesh, Shanti and Devi.

Meanwhile, Pratham had in previous days summoned Arian, leader of the military; a man universally respected among the Varagans for his courage and honor. One should not assume the Varagans were evil. Most upheld their codes of honor. Since Arian was not a member of the family of Pratham, the clan members held him in high suspicion, especially Jackal who complained Arian placed duty to the people above fealty to Pratham. Any trust in Arian stirred jealousy and hatred in the darkened soul of Jackal.

"Arian, I need you to embark on a sensitive mission. You must travel to the land of the Shore People and barter for some grain. Perhaps, the Great Storm spared their lands. Bring back ten wagons full of grain. Also, barter for sufficient vine plants to cover the hillsides next to the Granary. You must return within a week." Pratham instructed his gold keeper to give ten bars of gold, which essentially depleted their gold reserves.

The Shore People did not greet Arian with joy but misgivings. Arian arrived as the personal ambassador of Pratham, a man held in contempt among the Shore People. Over the past decades, relations between the Varagans and the Shore People were anything but cordial; in fact, they had fought several minor wars over territorial boundaries in the past year. On a personal note, they perceived Arian as a man of courage and honor, someone worthy of trust.

They negotiated terms for ten wagons of grain: the bargaining lasting well into the night. By morning, negotiations halted as the Shore People declared ten bars of gold were insufficient as payment.

Arian asked to speak to Rishaan, the ruler of this benevolent seacoast kingdom. Arian retold the story of the invasion by the Horse Warriors and the subsequent travails suffered by the Varagans in retreat. He then described the devastating storm and imminent starvation faced by both the Nivasi and the Varagans. Although there was only limited contact with the people of Desa, the Shore people judged the Nivasi as a peaceful people with strong humanistic values.

These misfortunes moved Rishaan. He did not have any animus toward the Varagans; it was only Pratham, the Primary and his brother, Jackal, whom they held in contempt. Arian summarized his plea: "I pledge our people will repay you with an additional five gold bars. I give you my word." Rishaan accepted the word of Arian, not bothering to require a written contract.

Rishaan summoned Arian to walk with him in his garden while Shore People workers loaded the wagons with the desired grain. Rishaan and Arian approached a small canvas, propped up by a wooden frame. Arian noticed the painting seemed suspended in time, patiently waiting for the artist's brush to bring completion and fulfillment. Rishaan paused in front of the easel, inquiring whether Arian had any experience with the joy of watercolors. Arian, somewhat embarrassed, honestly answered that he had none as military duties took precedence, the word joy causing him hesitation as he never thought of his life as joyful.

"Arian, life is like this watercolor, always in some phase of completion. I have finished many such watercolors capturing different shades of light, leaves and trees in various seasons, flowers in bloom and decay. I use a variety of brushstrokes, adding or deleting details, altering colors, using varied brush stroke techniques to capture minor details or bolder splashes of color. Each stroke is equal, in fact the smallest touch of the brush, capturing the glint of a bee flickering from flower to flower, is as significant as the bold, blue strokes of the sky.

"Today, we can say we represent these strokes of white and spots of yellow radiating from the heart of this flower nestled in a sea of green leaves and vines. The "star jasmine" is of extraordinary significance: a symbol of peace and friendship. I will not complete this painting until we meet again. If that day does not arrive, the painting, like our friendship, will remain frozen, just as you see it now. Only time, fate, and circumstances will determine what becomes of this painting, as with our own lives."

Arian returned to the Greenlands just hours before the Nivasi delegation arrived. Pratham again greeted the delegation warmly, feigning respect for the Nivasi. He only spoke to Gandesh, ignoring the other members of the delegation, specifically Devi, whom he assumed was there for some administrative task. But Gandesh did not speak. It was Devi who stood in front of the gates of the wall and with a stern voice and steely eyes spoke these words:

"When the Varagans arrived, we realized your people needed food and shelter. As our culture embraces physical differences and places the highest value on hospitality, we provided you with every need. Perhaps you did not fully grasp our culture. In this land, we revere nature and all aspects of the natural world. We promote the highest standards of ethical behavior. This is the essence of our moral code. You have violated the agreement for 200 acres, and you have taken the stream completely for your own purposes. You have built a wall of stone higher than needed for agriculture. Now you have chopped down trees which are sacred in the Greenlands."

The powerful simplicity of this woman, not discernable from her unimpressive physical appearance, amazed Pratham. Clearly stunned by her forthrightness, he was momentarily lost for words. He gazed at his senior advisers, some with subtle smirks on their faces. Arian was not smirking but biting his tongue as he had no idea the Varagan builders felled the trees in the Greenlands, disrespecting the trust placed in them by the Nivasi.

Pratham turned his gaze solely back to Devi. Gandesh no longer seemed significant. "I gave the order to cut only the trees, diseased and in stress from the wild storm."

Devi thought, *This is patently false as many great oaks had easily withstood the storm, now cut apparently for no purpose other than to construct a great wooden house.*

"By chance we may have cut too many, but I assure you we needed these trees for the new granary now required. We have grain for the granary."

This seemed laughable as there was no harvest to produce grain. In disbelief, "How is it possible you have surplus grain?" Devi asked.

Jackal responded, "We have developed new farming techniques behind these walls." At that moment, the gate swung open and five wagons full of grain rolled out. Jackal with the pretense of a poor actor said, "This is a gift from us to your people." To the side, Arian muttered to himself the word "liar" as he withdrew behind the wall.

Later in the evening, there was a grand celebration in the "Granary" which had no grain, and which appeared to be the first floor of an impressive house. Pratham envisioned in the coming weeks a magnificent house, perfect for a leader of his stature. Pratham smiled and joked with his dinner guests; yes, he thought, *things are looking up.*

PART 7
Betrayed Trust

Villagers were joyous when they saw the oxcarts full of grain. It had been several months since the epic storm, and they exhausted all the food stocks. There was no widespread starvation as the people were exceptionally skilled at foraging in the wild fields and woodlands. Walnuts, wild leeks, lettuces, and hackberries abound in the woodlands and forests. Wild rice previously used as a feedstock for the farm animals, now consumed by the people as well. They stored root vegetables in sheds, cellars and virtually any available space.

They rarely ate chickens, prizing their eggs as a key ingredient of nutrition. The people did not consume meat as a daily staple as they considered it not only crude to eat animals, but research professionals had showed it was more land-efficient to minimize meat consumption. The Nivasi did not morally object to meat consumption; they thought protein sourced from grains, milk, and vegetables as more efficient and nutritious.

The people realized in the past when meat was a primary source of food, cattle, pigs, and chickens required vast amounts of water and land. Inevitably, conflicts arose over land and water rights. People used ruthless techniques to build extensive ranches, giving rise to wealth disparity. Disputes over land and wealth were the underlying issues behind The Terrible Conflict.

Diseases pertaining to obesity did not exist as there was none in Desa. Diseases and bodily disorders of the lungs, kidneys and heart were rare. People with mild heart conditions utilized a specific diet consisting of mung beans, mashed chickpeas, lentils wrapped inside layers of rye bread. Grapes, figs and walnuts, jujubes and mangos were the "deserts' of the day. Daily markets flourished everywhere.

It is a common belief population growth requires a growing stock of animals. This belief is categorically false. Food researchers in Desa had long ago determined it was twice as efficient to use land for agriculture derived from consumption of plants and some byproducts of animals such as milk, eggs, and cheese as supplements to plant-based diets. They raised all animals as free-range, which placed a ceiling on the quantity of these animals as arable land was in short supply. Occasionally, cooks used free range animal meats, mainly in stews in which the primary ingredients were vegetables. All the animals died a natural death, so consuming their remains was a sign of respect. Stews containing these meats followed strict preparation practices.

The Nivasi had no idea the celebratory banquet hosted by Pratham featured hares and wild birds freshly procured, so to speak, from the once serene bramble bushes. Nivasi children often kept hares as pets. It was ironic. The Varagans were now consuming the natural pet of the children!

Over the next several days, the Varagans utilized two shifts of laborers to complete "The Granary". Pratham directed the tree cutters to seek their building materials far from any prying eyes. They felled, in hours, magnificent trees which stood for decades and hosted many birds and other wildlife. The Varagans deployed every ruse to hide this destruction, but unknown to the builders were the Forest Dwellers who witnessed the widespread plundering of the land.

The Forest Dwellers, also of the Nivasi culture, lived deep in the forests, savoring their private lives in the dense, tangled woodlands. They were more comfortable, experiencing inner peace with animals and trees than with people. Forest Dwellers shared the same humanistic values as the villagers, except they valued their solitary life in the deep woods more than anything. They took no joy from materialism, the fewer possessions, the better. Forest Dwellers did not need the comforts of a spacious house with water from community wells and kitchens, well-stocked with several cooking utensils and an array of pottery of intricate designs. They ate from plain brown bowls and used few cooking pots.

The Varagans had posted guards ringing the construction site. They escorted any wandering villagers away with gruff warnings. The Varagans never realized hundreds of tearful and angry eyes were watching. Vidya, the leader of the Forest Dwellers, watched the rape of the land. He stood perfectly still, his spirit trembling, growing angrier as each tree tumbled down.

Pratham was pleased. His new home was nearing completion. It would be only a matter of time before he would have to change his tactics with the Nivasi. Yes, they were a good people, but weak and naïve. They lacked strong leadership and had no army or military skills. They were skilled in talking; he was skilled in action. He laughed to himself as he thought about that woman, Devi, who seemed to be his major opponent. How ludicrous, he thought, as he pictured a mere, wimpy, slightly built, plain looking woman as his opponent.

Vidya found Gandesh sitting eerily silent in his small garden behind his modest home. Gandesh sat deep in thought, looking without seeing. His attention turned to a black-throated bird with distinctive markings of golden yellow wings, which was perfectly still on a branch. Both the bird of the woodpecker species and Gandesh seemed frozen in a time warp. He imagined the bird was also deep in meditation. He tried to imagine himself in the bird's consciousness. It is true both Gandesh, and the bird were feeling and connecting.

Unlike Gandesh, the bird was fully sensing every aspect of its natural surroundings, aiming for more utilitarian purposes; perhaps, waiting for an insect to appear or watching warily for other birds. Most definitely not lost in a dreamy state. For animals, their senses are always in a keen state of awareness and absorption, even in sleep.

Gandesh eased out of this moment and began listening to

Vidya. He felt sadness and disappointment. He thought back to the warnings of Mandeep reflecting on these words: "We must peer into their souls. Observe the flow of truth, not the torrent of words." His mind quickly conjured up that fateful warning from Devi: "We are too trusting, too gullible. We are being deceived." He had not wanted to believe these warnings. Now, faced with the truth, he had no choice.

PART 8
Devi's Terrible Dream

By late evening, all the villagers had heard the whisperings of the Forest Dwellers. Stunned and angry, the Nivasi people could hardly comprehend such treachery. Families and friends gathered to share opinions. Feelings of helplessness, even submissiveness, underlined their fates.

As full darkness slowly descended over the land, Devi fell into her nightly dream state. Devi did not wish for dreams, nor was it possible to control them. Many times, her dreams were unpleasant, even frightening. The next day, she continued with her life with no apparent impact from her prior dream escapades. This night was different.

In Devi's dream, she saw a distant cloud of dust, a brownish haze, perhaps an approaching windstorm? Another tornado? Swirling dust kicked up by horses became clearer. As the wave of dust came closer, the blurred images gaining sharpness, she discerned warriors on horses. Their numbers expanded, revealing a massive army, images of ferocity and terror on countless faces. She had never seen such fierceness, such determination. Some Nivasi ventured out, thinking displays of friendship would engender a friendly response. Then shockingly, in a flash, she saw them all slaughtered. The Horse Warriors suddenly halted. One man emerged. He started speaking in a language, understandable but clearly of distant origins.

"I am Khander, leader of the Horse Warriors. You must follow my commands, or we will destroy everything in our sight. Every person will be slain. I will spare no one. If you swear allegiance to our rule, I will not treat you as my enemy. If you resist, your lives will end quickly. I know the Varagans are hiding here. They must surrender to us immediately. I demand Pratham be brought to me. To be clear, just bring me his head, feed the rest to the dogs."

Gandesh, with enormous courage, slowly proceeded forward. He spoke directly to Khander, carefully choosing his words, explaining the Nivasi were peaceful. He did not even finish one sentence when Khander jumped down to the ground, grabbing Gandesh by his wispy, white hair. He dragged him right up the Nivasi, who watched in horror and disbelief, refusing to comprehend the brutality in process. Khander easily overpowered the helpless, limp body of Gandesh, powerful hands twisting his neck upwards, exposing the victim like an animal being slaughtered. Khander deftly pulled a sharp knife from his belt, slicing Gandesh's throat, killing him instantly.

Devi suddenly realized she was panting and sweating, Devi made her way to the outside door and collapsed in her garden. Just a dream, she thought as she fell back to sleep.

Devi awoke to the realization her dream was a foretelling. In past years, some mystics had misled the people into believing their dreams were predictive. On one noteworthy occasion, a young woman with a powerful imagination feigned seizure, babbling wildly. Then she suddenly became silent. She pointed to the west, predicting an extreme dust storm would soon emerge which would destroy the vulnerable, young, fragile seedlings. She convinced the farmers to delay summer planting to build a strong wall facing the west. Day after day, the people waited, and the lands lay fallow. Then a thunderstorm erupted, which cleansed the land and the people's minds. No massive dust storm appeared.

Devi sought the advice of Mandeep. She found him sitting quietly in a small corner of his home. Mandeep had long ago learned the skill of meditation. He found wisdom through his ability to clear his mind of extraneous thoughts, while seeking calm and understanding. Mandeep did not live a structured life. He simply rose at daybreak and followed the opposite routine at sunset.

He was the oldest man in Desa, a fact of no concern to him. Mandeep did not fear aging or growing old. Some late middle age people think their best days are behind them. With minds afflicted by exaggerated memories of past glory or joy, these people cannot grasp that the future will soon become moments in the past. Mandeep took solace and inspiration from the waning flowers in his garden, surrendering to their fate to serve as winter homes for birds and insects. These dead flowers still had purpose and would be reborn in the spring. For the ageless Mandeep, life was more than beliefs about life and death, rather it was about each day of life, purposeful and precious.

Mandeep listened, without interruption, as Devi described her "dream", ensuring she covered every detail, even the horrible scene of the brutal slaying of Gandesh. Devi searched Mandeep's face for some hints, hoping the sage would assuage her anxieties, conjure up some fragments of hope. Both remained silent. Devi understood well enough not to ask questions of Mandeep. She waited and waited. Neither person moved. About an hour passed, gauging by the sun passing over the house. She thought to herself: *Am I being tested? Why doesn't he say something?*

Mandeep then spoke: "You did not have a dream. You had a horrible vision of what will confront our peoples. Every part of your "dream" will occur and not so distant into the future. Currently, our people think the Varagans threaten their liberty. In fact, this is true, but the apocalyptic threat will come from the Horse Warriors who have already defeated the Varagans. The Varagans will seek to dominate us; the Horse Warriors will seek to destroy the Varagans. They will destroy us along with the Varagans as these Horse Warriors will think because of our values and passive lifestyle, we do not deserve to live as a free people. They will regard us with contempt, as in their culture, excellence through battle reigns supreme. They would rather die nobly than fail their fellow warriors."

Devi, scarcely comprehending what Mandeep was saying, thought to herself: *How does Mandeep know these things? Anyway, the Horse Warriors cannot cross the Great Stars River, so we are safe.* She was more concerned about Pratham, who gave her every impression he sought to dominate the Nivasi. *We may not die, but we will lose our liberty*, she thought.

PART 9
Seeds of Doubt

❧

Arian stared at the new "Granary" with barely concealed contempt. Pratham and his brother, Jackal, along with their families, now enjoyed much of the trappings of privilege they had previously had on the prairies. They were not in the least bit concerned the vast majority of the Varagans still lived in make-shift tents. Fall was approaching, followed by the frosty nights of winter. Food supplies were still in short supply. Worse yet, Pratham had made a mockery of his promises to the Nivasi. He openly mocked Gandesh as a fool in meetings with the senior advisers and family leaders. Oddly, he did not mention Devi, keeping any opinion of her to himself.

Arian admired the frank and feisty spirit of Devi, a woman unlike any of the Varagan aristocratic class. Most of the Varagan men admired women for their skills in the kitchen and sleeping chambers. Women of beauty and fine stature, from the best aristocratic families, were betrothed or married to men based on the power of their families. Marriage based on love was a foolish idea embraced by only the commoners.

No woman among the Varagans had any outward political influence, although several of the men of the powerful families had consulted with their wives in private. Few doubted their matriarchal power. A few of the aristocratic men, above all Pratham, enjoyed the excellent advice of beautiful consorts, adorned with precious gold necklaces. While all aristocratic women wore beautiful jewelry, only the consort advisers to Pratham wore these magnificent gold and pearl necklaces. After a good night's sleep away from his wife,

Pratham would often change his ruling on some matter when, just the evening before, his mind seemed closed.

Arian did not yet have a wife, but at age thirty, the urgings of family and female fellowship were growing more intense. Arian combined an excellent physique with a handsome face, the object of desire for numerous Varagan women. He laughed to himself, reckoning he could have any unmarried woman (and married, as well, if he so desired) with the mere utterance of a few words. Even a playful and inviting glance or a subtle gesture of his hand would be sufficient. Having experienced the pleasures of several beautiful women, these empty, momentary trysts left Arian devoid of meaning.

Images of Devi occupied his mind. Even though she was rather plain in physical appearance, wore few adornments, and clearly did not value clothing to enhance her physical attributes, he found himself oddly attracted to her.

It also troubled Arian by his pledge to the Shore People to deliver another five gold bars. When he returned to the tent camp, he informed Pratham of his commitment. Jackal burst out in laughter as Arian proclaimed his honor was at stake. Pratham was clever enough to just sit and smile. He assured Arian the Varagans would pay off their debt to the Shore People.

Arian pushed the matter with more persistence. Pratham snapped at him and proclaimed: "I am the Primary and I will decide when and if." Arian remained silent but the word "if" kept repeating in his mind. That moment, both Pratham and Arian crossed a line. The quiet tension between the men reached the breaking point, seemingly on the verge of erupting.

These were the two most powerful men among the Varagans. Pratham was the Primary and had complete authority, but Arian was head of the military and revered among his men. He said nothing, nor showed any emotion; now was the time to remain quiet. He also appreciated a basic fact of military discipline- every soldier was indoctrinated from youth to follow the command of the Primary. No one could disobey his orders, no matter how distasteful.

The meeting concluded with no further words between Pratham and Arian. Pratham and Jackal walked away, whispering to each other. Pratham's face noticeably reddened as Jackal began gesticulating wildly.

Arian, alone in his thoughts, said to himself, *Things must change.*

PART 10
Crisis in the Nivasi Council

Gandesh summoned the Nivasi Council to an emergency session. He also invited Devi and Vidya, an honor, as neither were members of the Nivasi Council. The actions of the Varagans clearly shook Gandesh. Only Mandeep knew in the preceding hours, Mandeep had described to Gandesh all the terrible details of Devi's dream. For Gandesh, it was nearly too much to endure. Mandeep had warned him the dream was a foretelling of the evil which awaited them in the next few months. "But what about the Great Stars River?" exclaimed Gandesh to Mandeep out of desperation.

Mandeep responded that the annual rains were much lighter than usual and a dryer than normal climate pattern had persisted for years. Mandeep said to Gandesh: "Our land is changing, becoming drier and drier so the Great Stars River will soon be passable by men on horses. The Horse Warriors halted their pursuit of the Varagans at the river's bank, but whether solely due to the risk to the horses or other factors, we cannot know for certain. The Horse Warriors value military prowess and excellence in battle. Devi's "dream" is true, they will consider us weak, passive people, not worthy of life."

Gandesh stared blankly at Mandeep. He was devoid of any spark of life. He quizzed Mandeep, "What we should do?"

Mandeep responded firmly, "We will need the Varagans as our ally, but we must develop fighting skills within our people or they will dominate us when the Horse Warrior threat is blunted, if we can defeat them. If not, we all will perish or live in true abject slavery."

Reaching deep into his inner spirit and mustering strength and clarity, Gandesh outlined the two threats facing the Nivasi. He told the Nivasi Council an existential threat faced them, their culture and way of life was in grave danger. "We must plan several actions to build the fighting skills of all Nivasi men and woman while negotiating with Pratham who will be happy to soothe temporarily our anger with minor concessions."

Shanti, reflecting the time-honored values of pacifism, mounted the speaker's dais to question this plan, arguing the Nivasi values did not support military or aggressive actions toward any peoples. She fervently believed with enough time, the Varagans would see the worthiness of the Nivasi way of life.

She concluded her appeal by saying, "This is the time to re-enforce our traditional values, which do not support violence in any form. We must inspire the Varagans through our continued passivity and commitment to peaceful relationships at any price. This is the bedrock of our culture. I don't have to remind anyone in this Nivasi Council of the disastrous conflicts in our history when violence and force ruled over reason."

Mandeep retorted: "The Varagans cannot and will not change. If we do not adopt a fighting spirit and adapt defensive tactics which suit our strengths, our culture will cease to exist within two generations. We can choose not to train our bodies and mind for conflict or choose alternative methods of military defense. We can choose submission."

Gandesh realized a significant number of the Nivasi Council members endorsed the traditional views of Shanti. Tension within the Nivasi Council chamber permeated everywhere. With no additional words being spoken, it was easy to see the Nivasi Council was split. Gandesh asked Shanti, Mandeep, Devi and Vidya to join him in the garden for a peaceful stroll.

The Nivasi believed good and wise decisions could not be made in the moment's passion; only a tranquil mind provided the basis for clarity of thought and action. They chose a pleasant spot surrounded by bushes and tall grasses. The fragrance of jujube trees and the rustling of its leaves was slightly intoxicating. In fact, jujube fruits combated anxiety and induced a calming effect, mitigating life's stresses.

Devi did not dare to speak first. She thought it best to listen and only speak when asked. Surprise took her when Gandesh turned to her," Devi, please give us your thoughts." She glanced over toward Shanti, implicitly asking for her consent. Shanti did not betray any sign of her feelings. Tradition had taught people to guard their genuine feelings.

Although Devi's mind was racing, she was well-schooled in the methods of composure. She knew a few poor choices of words or the wrong tone of voice or even a twitch of her face could sabotage her advice. "We can never forget our cultural history. Our values have served us well for over two hundred years since The Terrible Conflict. We will fail if we try to change even in the face of danger." She did not sense any expression from Shanti.

Devi continued, "We know the danger from the Varagans is real in this moment. We have seen the first indications of the drought Mandeep spoke about. The land is changing. That is the way of Nature. The Horse Warriors could arrive in a few short months. We still face food shortages. We cannot turn a blind eye from the Varagans. We know they are dishonorable. Unquestionably, they violated our trust. However, we should not think of them as evil people."

She stopped, fearing chastisement for continuing when others may wish to speak. Shanti said to her: "Devi, please continue, give us your best advice. What should we do?"

Devi reminded herself what her mentor always said about advice. She heard the wise counsel reverberating in her mind: *Devi, remember advice is not truth, as only a person's soul perceives truth. Advice is an opinion, a judgment of certain information. You may strongly believe it is true; you may even think you have factual, objective proof of your advice. You may question the wisdom of someone who seeks your advice, only to reject it. Remember, some people who pretend to seek advice, do not really want your advice. If you take responsibility for your advice, and speak it without duplicity or bias, you have answered that duty.*

Devi outlined three key points which seem to flow from a well-organized plan in her mind:

"First, we should engage the Varagans in peaceful dialogue to persuade them of the need to respect our values and rights. They will willingly agree, as they also are seeking to buy time for their own purposes. We should not show outward hostility but continue to be firm in our rights and their responsibilities as guests. We should learn from them about their farming techniques and the possibility of new crops. We should seek information as to all the facts underlying their defeat and learn their military strategies, especially those of a defensive nature.

"Second, we should motivate our people to enhance their physical capabilities by launching athletic contests to develop physical skills, primarily in distance running, archery, javelin, and martial arts. All men and women must take part and master these disciplines.

"Third, we should position some of our people along the Great Stars River to gauge its depth and to monitor for any signs of the Horse Warriors."

Mandeep was pleased. Devi's advice showed she was truly one of the wisest people in Desa. Everyone including Shanti nodded their agreement. Gandesh directed Mandeep, Shanti and Devi to begin discussions with the Varagans. Gandesh, despite being quite elderly, would organize the athletic games, including three months of extensive training. Gandesh also took the task to inform the Nivasi Council, as respectful communications were part of his leadership style.

PART 11
The Strike of the King Cobra

The Nivasi delegation arrived at the Varagans compound the next morning, asking to speak to Pratham. Devi was selected as chief spokesperson, although that did not confer any authority. The chief scribe to Pratham informed the Nivasi Pratham was inspecting the tree damage to determine how to best restore the land. Pratham had the opposite intention as he was rummaging through the cut forests with his chief builder to plan the next expansionary phase of the "Granary".

Devi said firmly and abruptly: "It is urgent we speak to him immediately." The scribe scurried off to find Jackal, who was lounging in his newly planted garden with one of his favorite consorts.

Noticeably irritated by this interruption, Jackal reluctantly agreed to lead the Nivasi to speak with Pratham. As they approach the Pratham group, they suddenly heard a loud scream of pain and horror, the group scattering in sheer panic. One man lay on the ground thrashing in pain. Devi immediately realized the man, the chief builder, had been bitten by a king cobra, an olive-green snake with bands of black and white, further marked with orange specks. The king cobra latched onto the leg of the victim with a bite so powerful the snake's fangs remained deeply imbedded in the twisting victim, writhing in pain on the ground. Devi skillfully grabbed the king cobra's tail, bending it up and backwards, causing the snake to release its victim.

The poor man immediately started vomiting, his face severely distorted in agony and fear, his arms completely numb. In addition, another king cobra had bitten Pratham. The Varagans had inadvertently stumbled on a cobra's nest, disturbed by the number of trees felled in that area. Vidya would later say Pratham had provoked Nature's revenge.

The Nivasi had a lot of experience in dealing with cobras. Dozens of Nivasi suffered bites each year with virtually no survival rate. Normally, the bite was fatal with an agonizing death occurring within thirty minutes. The amount of venom from each bite can vary, but a direct bite of the king cobra was always fatal. Pratham, stumbling backwards, was lucky as the bite of a second cobra only struck him with a glancing blow, quickly releasing its bite before injecting a lethal amount of venom. Even a partial bite caused death without quick mitigating actions.

Devi screamed at the scribe: "Quickly, bring a bowl of sour milk." Instead of wearing jewelry around her neck, she wore only two necklaces, one a gift from her mother, the other a "snakestone" made from ground pieces of a dried cow bone. Soon, the sour milk arrived. Pratham was already experiencing the first stages of his impending death, exhibiting the same symptoms as those of the chief builder, now stiffened by muscle paralysis, enduring the last minutes of life, unable to breathe. Devi dunked the snakestone in the sour milk and skillfully applied the snakestone sponge to the wound on Pratham's hand. She continued this method for several minutes. Slowly, Pratham showed some signs of recovery, slowly edging back from the precipice of death.

Several days later, Pratham had recovered to an extent his life was no longer in danger. He asked the Nivasi to return, being careful not to meet them in the "Granary". Pratham greeted them warmly, with sincerity, which was for the first time quite genuine. Arian, Jackal, and Amura flanked him. He approached Devi with a bowed head, gently clutched her hand, softly kissing it, saying," Devi, I owe you my life. My medical advisers have never witnessed such a brilliant feat of medicine. Only you had the skill to save my life, as we have no means to cure the bite from this type of serpent."

Devi and Mandeep both realized it was not only a matter of skill but also chance or fate, as the cobra had missed a direct bite onto the hand of Pratham. Although the bite secreted the deadly venom, apparently only a non-lethal amount penetrated the skin. Even though most men would have died within an hour or less, but Pratham was no ordinary man, possessing unusual strength and determination.

Both stunned and flattered, Devi quickly regained her composure, responding, "I thank you for your gracious gesture. I acted as I did out of duty and as a reflection of our values to savor all life. I am deeply sorry I could not save your chief builder."

She paused for an instant, savoring the moment of good will. "Pratham, we know full well you have seized more land than granted by the Nivasi Council, and you have violated the serenity of the Greenlands by cutting so many trees. These woods and forests are home to many wondrous animals, including the king cobras. Nature always finds revenge, not always so immediate as evidenced by the king cobras who were only defending their home, a natural right of all living creatures."

Pratham who just moments earlier gushed with the spirit of gratitude noticeably hardened his demeanor. He could not endure the criticisms from a woman, even one as extraordinary as Devi. He remained calm, for the time being, asking, "Devi, what would you have us do? We are indebted to the people of Desa." Meanwhile, Jackal was predictably ill at ease as his mediocre character always reflected the worse in the Varagans. Arian also remained quiet, sizing up the situation, eager to understand how this discussion would end. He had already decided he would not allow the Varagans to destroy or subjugate these fine people.

Amura, equal to Mandeep in wisdom and moral judgment, interrupted the perceivable tension slowly building in the group. As usual, he kept his words terse. "Our mutual fates have thrust us into this situation. We are separate peoples, only loosely bound by a common language. Our values are unique but not irreconcilable. We must find common ground so we can nurture the minds and bodies of our people and their respective sufferings, you from the great storm, we, from the slaughtering of many of our peoples at the hands of the Horse Warriors. We do not seek revenge; we seek to regain our homeland."

Pratham thought to himself maybe Amura did not seek revenge, but most surely, he did. Besides the personal humiliation experienced, Pratham's desire to recover the riches his family would realize upon their return further amplified his hatred of the Horse Warriors.

Now was the time in the discussions which Mandeep had waited for. Mandeep always believed it was not how much you spoke, but when you spoke. Too many words muddled the minds of most people, he thought. "The words of Amura are highly worthy of our consideration. He speaks to the souls of our respective peoples. He speaks the universal truths which govern all of us."

Mandeep continued, shifting now to his principal argument, "Desa is becoming drier, the rains are arriving later and leaving sooner; they are shifting south and east. The Great Stars River will become shallower. Soon, maybe in the next few months, crossing by horse will be possible."

An electrifying shock rippled down the backs of Pratham and Arian. They had witnessed the bloody brutality and superior battle tactics of the Horse Warriors. Pratham despite his earlier dispute with Arian turned to him and said," Arian, seek the finest warriors among the Nivasi and construct a battle plan. Return in one week along with Gandesh and his senior advisers."

To everyone's surprise, Shanti swiftly responded that Devi would lead the battle plan discussion on behalf of the Nivasi. Arian and Amura immediately understood the reasons for Devi's selection, but it dumbfounded Pratham. Jackal tried to protest, betraying his ignorance of Devi's skills, but Pratham quickly interrupted, nodding his consent. "I trust Devi will conceive a shrewd plan. Use the next days wisely and return with a brilliant plan as nothing less will save us."

PART 12
The Story of the Varagans's Defeat

Warfare in Desa had not occurred since The Terrible Conflict. The benefits of geography contributed to this phenomenon as extremely high mountains to the north blocked access to Desa, while The Great Stars River was nearly impassable for much of the year, making crossing by wandering peoples exceedingly difficult. Also, the expanse of the vast lands to the northwest provided sufficient grazing lands and favorable climates for all peoples. These favorable climate conditions were slowly changing as more prolonged dry spells occurred with greater frequency. The rainy season in the summer and winter was shorter, causing conditions for farming and grazing to degrade and become more unpredictable.

The Varagans had a long history of military conflict as the vast region occupied by the Varagans and many nomadic peoples was becoming more arid and less sustainable. The Varagans were continuously under siege from marauding peoples, moving from location to location, in search of water and arable lands for grazing. Conflicts became inevitable. Tribes unable to defend themselves suffered devastating defeat and vanished or swallowed up by the victorious. The Varagans fostered martial skills among the male children from an early age and maintained a professional army.

The Nivasi did not value military training as there was no need because of the peaceful nature of the peoples in Desa. Political systems had evolved to create an egalitarian society. The people practiced several sports and valued expertise in sports, such as archery and running. Female children engaged in every sport like their male counterparts. Annual competition events fostered competitiveness; the winners treated like heroes.

The small group of Nivasi and Varagans found a calming spot in the gardens. Devi spoke first, trying not to look only at Arian: "We are honored you have embraced us in common defense. You know we have no military experience. In fact, I cannot say how our people will summon up the fighting spirit which we will desperately need. We, the Nivasi, love our freedom, as do you. I believe not one person would choose slavery over death."

"All our people are highly skilled in archery and in the construction of bows from the finest wood materials. Our bows are wood composites of yew and teak, trees readily available in our forests. We only use the wood from these trees for composite bows, weapons valued as objects of art. We have bows and arrows designed for different purposes; our finest bows are constructed for long distance accuracy. Even though we do not need them for defense against other peoples, we need them for protection against some wild animals, especially the tiger who often attacks and kill our livestock and some of our sheep herders."

An archer handed a long-distance bow to Arian. His eyes widened with amazement as he had never seen such a bow. He rubbed his fingers across the teak section of the bow, his heart pounding as he immediately realized the properties of length, flexibility, and strength of the bow, would make terrific weapons against the Horse Warriors. Arian mulled over the principal advantages, specifically, the capability to double the normal range of archers and the increased penetration power of the arrows at shorter ranges.

Devi then said to Arian, "Please tell us, if you will, everything you know about the Horse Warriors. We need to know every detail, no matter how small." Arian stepped back, his mind reaching back to the earliest moments. He stared, emotionless, for a few minutes without speaking. Mandeep wondered if Arian could speak, speculating to himself that maybe the experience was too painful. Mandeep quickly discarded this notion as Arian launched into a long monologue.

"At first, only a few of the Horse Warriors appeared, about ten in total. They seemed more inquisitive than threatening. We approached them cautiously as we had never seen people with their facial characteristics, strikingly their eyes, which were narrower than ours. We did not fully comprehend their language, although after a few days, they quickly learned many of our basic words. Axam, their leader, was most polite, amicable, and soft-spoken. They said they are peaceful and were seeking to establish trade with us. Before long, we extinguished our suspicions; trust replaced caution. That was our first mistake.

"After a week in which they enjoyed our hospitality and had presented gifts to Pratham and other family heads, we bid them farewell in the hopes they would return with more items for trade. They returned, this time with a vast army. They sent three emissaries forth, one of whom was Axam, the leader of the group who had enjoyed our hospitality only a few months before. Axam said curtly, without a hint of the false politeness he had previously shown: 'I require you bring me to Pratham.'

"Axam was very blunt and aggressive in his attitude toward Pratham and me. He said our only choices were to surrender or face annihilation. Pratham seemed more amused than angry, laughing, feigning fear, and shaking. He looked over to me seeking support, but I stood silent and stolid. Jackal jumped up and grabbed Axam, threatening to kill him on the spot. As Jackal walked away, he spun around suddenly and struck Axam, drawing blood from his nose. Axam did not even blink, as if he expected it to happen. Striking Axam was our second mistake, as he was the younger brother of Khander, their supreme chief."

Arian explained that Pratham angrily dismissed the three emissaries with insults. 'Axam, go back to your leader and tell him Pratham spits on him; they are not worthy of any respect as he and his people reek of cow dung.' Axam showed no fear, no anger, only confidence as we escorted him back to the army of Horse Warriors."

Arian hesitated for a few moments to drink some water and then continued, as if telling a story of two distant peoples, unknown to him. Arian continued, "The Horse Warriors withdrew from sight. I was relieved, but Pratham and Jackal rejoiced in their ignorance, drinking deep into the night, and congratulating each other's toughness."

Arian recounted how in the next morning, about 1,000 Horse Warriors re-appeared on the horizon. With the hubris of a petty, ignorant dictator, Pratham gave the order to attack them with no reconnaissance or forethought. Arian explained how the Horse Warriors cleverly sucked the Varagans into a trap.

"We launched our best cavalry in a group numbering over 2,000. As soon as the Horse Warriors spotted us, they slowly retreated, which only lured us into more complacency and over-confidence. We held our formation but quickened the pace. Then, behind the Horse Warriors, we saw the long lines of archers. Within seconds, arrows filled the air, which struck us with deadly accuracy. Our men dropped by the dozens. Chaos reigned in our lines; then a second line of archers unleashed another deadly volley, ensuring the complete collapse of our formation.

"Then, from nowhere, formations of Horse Warriors appeared on our left and right flanks and split our group in half. Caught in the vise, our men panicked. Horse Warriors with long lances quickly slaughtered our men. Our surviving calvary pivoted and fled wildly back to our lines where we had positioned most of our army. The Horse Warriors ceased their attacks and drew back out of sight. In a few quick minutes, we lost over 200 men with another 105 wounded. Not an overwhelming defeat, but they bloodied our nose, referring to the cowardly strike by Jackal.

Arian recounted the sheer fury of Pratham. "He screamed at everyone in his presence, insulting all of us as fools and cowards. Although Pratham had served bravely in battle, he had no idea this enemy was different. I had seen the ferocity in their eyes, felt their evil in their hearts. These were no ordinary warriors."

At this point, the group broke for some dates and mangos. Devi wondered whether Arian had the strength to continue and relay the disastrous facts of the battles. She approached him with some nuts and fruit, softly urging Arian to sit and eat some dates. Devi felt the tension and bitterness ooze from Arian. He had been seething for months, but this was his cathartic moment to expunge his spirit.

"Later in the evening" continued Arian," Pratham summoned Amura, the leaders of each family, my chief lieutenant, Veer and me. Pratham demanded we immediately launch a major offensive the next morning."

Amura, the wise counselor, politely interrupted him, 'The Horse Warriors use different tactics than anything we have previously experienced. They blend unique elements of their army in a very disciplined manner. If we rush out tomorrow morning as today, we will meet the same fate."

Arian described how Pratham muttered to himself while Jackal foolishly argued for swift and immediate revenge. Jackal had never experienced actual combat. He claimed his crucial role was military intelligence, of which he had none. Pratham called on me for my opinion. 'Pratham and clan leaders, Amura is correct. These warriors are unlike any we have ever faced. They are not only fierce and skilled, but they also have excellent battle tactics. Their fighting spirit dominates their physical body. They show no fear, only the ecstasy of victory."

Arian said the Horse Warriors soon showed their shrewdness. Arian explained their timing was perfect. At the critical moment of debate, a group of soldiers appeared with a "captured" Horse Warrior whom we recognized as one of the ten who had originally visited us, pretending to be traders. "We knew him by the name 'Jangi' which later we found out meant 'brave' in their language. He said the leader of the Horse Warriors, Khander, did not care for human life, having in the past sacrificed enormous numbers of his people in vain, worthless military campaigns. His soldiers thought him crazy but were too afraid to resist, as any soldier who did rebel met death along with his entire family.

Arian described Jangi as a highly skilled actor reciting lines of false sincerity, he had used many times before, informing he had no family and no fear deserting as he faced certain death at the hands of the Varagans who were superior to the Horse Warriors. These lies seduced Jackal who took encouragement from Jangi, as did Pratham. Pratham's mind, absorbed in dreams of glorious victories, fixated on the increased opportunity to further strengthen his grip on power. Pratham took the bait and commanded his troops to launch a major offensive the next day.

Arian explained to us he was not at all fooled by this man, Jangi. "I urged caution, 'This man is a liar, an actor, sent to lure us into a trap.' But the senior leaders, urged on by Pratham and Jackal, started chanting 'attack, attack'. Our third fatal mistake; we listened to a spy, not to Amura."

Arian continued with his story, which was obvious and predictable to everyone in attendance.

"The next morning, under direct orders from Pratham, we marched out in battle formation to confront the enemy. Knowing the mistakes of the previous day, we led with our archers equipped with heavy shields to deflect the expected onslaught of arrows. Several hundred Horse Warriors launched a feeble attack and then fled in retreat upon meeting the least amount of resistance.

"Our leader of the cavalry, a nephew of Pratham, eager to please his uncle, immediately launched a major counterattack. I intercepted him and commanded him to pull back the cavalry, but he sneered at me, saying his last words, 'I only take orders from Pratham.' Moments later, the foolish lad lay dead, his body trampled to pieces by hundreds of Horse Warriors in full attack."

Arian continued to relate the story, perspiration of sweat visible as he relived those terrible moments.

"The Horse Warriors continued their retreat, which encouraged the Varagan cavalry to speed up, breaking disciplined formations as cavalry unit commanders were vying with each other to spearhead the victory. Suddenly, the Horse Warriors wheeled around in unison and launched a counterattack. From both flanks came light cavalry who rode up close enough to get off an arrow shot at close range. No other warriors had their mastery of horsemanship; the capability to turn their horses in a split moment of time and regroup for a fresh attack.

"After several of these maneuvers, lancers on bigger horses bore down on our center and tore us to shreds. Now, the entire cavalry was in full retreat and the panic of death eliminated any sense of order. With the cavalry in shambles, the Horse Warriors advanced on our archers and foot soldiers, who also panicked and fled in all directions. Some Horse Warriors carried short swords, while others carried lances. It was not a carnage of uncontrolled madness; it was a slaughter of highly disciplined madness as the Horse Warriors trained from childhood to put their minds into a state of sheer ferocity."

Arian said he and Veer had prudently held back an elite corps of cavalry and archers who launched their own surprise attack on the Horse Warriors, blunting them momentarily, to allow some Varagan ground troops to survive, at least for one more day. The Horse Warriors pulled back and regrouped. They believed the next day would finish the Varagans.

Pratham finally realized his folly and listened to our advice, finally discarding the babbling nonsense of Jackal.

I told Pratham. "We are now too weak to resist the Horse Warriors. We must retreat toward the Great Stars River. Veer and I will stay back to fight a rear-guard action as you lead the people out of the city under cover of darkness." Within hours, everyone evacuated, heading southeast toward the river.

Pratham may have been foolish, but he was not a coward, unlike his brother, Jackal. He said to Arian, "I will take a stand with you even if it means my death."

Questioning both Pratham's sincerity and bravery, I responded, "Pratham, if you do not lead the people toward the river, they will panic, and all will perish."

Veer and I devised a plan to provide enough time for the people to get to the river. We collected the remaining soldiers and placed them in various hiding spots along the trails heading southeast. The Varagan leaders selected a strategic spot for defense, a narrow pass with step canyon walls which posed several challenges for the Horse Warriors. If they tried to march around it, it would take days. If they entered the pass, the narrow road would force the invaders to stretch out and severely hamper maneuverability, completely emasculating the superior battle tactics of the Horse Warriors.

The Horse Warriors sent a detachment of scouts into the city, entering with ease. Jangi appeared, smiling at the city's gate. Khander embraced him with joy, praising him for his spectacular success as the "deserter", a mission which had often ended badly for some unfortunate brave souls, now with the ancestral spirits. After several hours, it was clear to the Horse Warriors the city was abandoned. Khander gathered his senior officers as he was wise enough to consider many viewpoints. Some officers argued the city was the prize and there was no need to pursue the fleeing Varagans. Others argued it was dangerous to leave any foe intact, no matter how badly defeated.

Khander settled the discussion, "Pratham and Jackal not only insulted us, but Jackal struck Axam, which violated the honor code protecting emissaries. We will send 4,000 warriors led by Dhanur to destroy the remnants of the Varagan army. Their orders are straight forward: bring the heads of Pratham and Jackal to me. You may take any women as desired but leave the old people. Capture all the young children and integrate them into our society."

Khander entrusted his older brother Dhanur with the mission. The military code of the Horse Warriors was clear: mission entrusted, mission executed, no matter how long it may take. Dhanur could not return without his objectives accomplished. The Horse Warriors marched off the next day. Within two days, they approached a massive pass. Dhanur, accomplished and shrewd in all aspects of military tactics, did not immediately enter the pass. He sent scouts to explore the pass who reported back the fact the terrain was very narrow, marked with rocky outcrops, capable of hiding hundreds of archers.

Arian was aware of the geographical features of the pass. Holding the pass for at least two days would allow the Varagan people the required time to trek to the river. He selected the best places to hide his troops. These troops believed they were literally fighting for the lives of their families. Dhanur also understood these motivations elevate soldiers to the highest level of consciousness and bravery. Unlike Pratham, he understood the soul of a warrior. The Varagans he faced on the grasslands were different now; they were much more dangerous. Purpose filled their souls and energized their spirits.

Dhanur instructed his unit commanders who operated in units of ten to capture the cliffs, fighting primarily at night. That night, he sent out his first wave of Horse Warriors who were as deadly on foot as on a horse. The next morning, the unit commanders reported heavy night casualties but had progressed well. It took three nights and heavy losses, but eventually the Horse Warriors either killed or forced a retreat of the Varagan defenders. There were no prisoners taken. The pass was now secure.

The Horse Warriors could ride fifty to seventy miles in a day, about ten times faster than a caravan of oxen carts. The Varagans were extremely fortunate as they had now reached the river just as the Horse Warriors appeared on the horizon. Seasonal rains swelled the depth and flow of the river, causing powerful turbulence. Pratham and Arian had no option but to leave all the horses behind as a crossing with horses was inconceivable. Only the oxen and the drawn carts would attempt to cross. The Varagans plunged into the river as the only other choice was annihilation by the swords of the Horse Warriors.

Dhanur watched the Varagans cross with their oxen. He

witnessed many people drown in the strong currents, sadly the old people too weak to battle the raging waters. People of all ages washed back onto the shore where the Horse Warriors swiftly ended their lives or took them captives as directed by Khander.

Dhanur setup a temporary camp on the banks of the river to plot his next moves. The Horse Warriors were very patient people. They did not think of setbacks as failures, only as obstacles. Just as water flowing down a mountain will always find a way through the rocks, the Horse Warriors will always find their way to victory. Living with failure was not conceivable, victory or death, the only options.

Arian finished leaving his listeners exhausted and fearful. Arian himself showed no emotion or fatigue. In fact, he seemed stronger, more resolute, more determined to change the course of history. Of course, changing history is impossible if one thinks of time as sequential, flowing only in one direction. The truth perceived by wise people is time flows in multiple dimensions, like the seasons. Summer rains follow a climatic pattern with some variations. Trees follow the cycle of growth until life is no longer possible. Natural life follows predictable patterns and is a source of knowledge, if one heeds attention to the smallest details. Nature speaks in a myriad of ways, but most people do not listen; they are too busy talking.

PART 13
Romantic Strolls in the Greenlands

༺❦༻

Arian's story touched Devi. She saw Arian and the Varagans in a different light. She tried, in her mind, to reconcile the deceit of Pratham with the honor and courage of Arian. She sensed Arian was a good man, a leader worthy of trust. She experienced some emotional twitches, unsure exactly what she was feeling other than an attraction to a man, feelings she had never experienced before.

Devi approached Arian, gently encroaching, "Would like to be alone? I am sure your fateful retelling of the battles has exhausted you."

Arian responded quickly with enthusiasm, "No, I am fine. Perhaps a walk would suit me well."

Devi took the hint and responded, "May I show you a path through the Greenlands which I hope will refresh you with wild scents?" Devi did not need to hear the words of agreement from Arian, his eyes spoke for themselves.

A substantial part of the Greenlands was still undisturbed by the Varagans. Many paths wound through the woods, exposing nature's secrets to a discerning eye, or rather to a discerning nose. Devi and Arian meandered into the woods, taking care to keep a friendly distance as neither wanted to disrupt the harmony between them. There were no words of war or the threat of the Horse Warriors. They walked along various paths, breathing in the scents of life on every branch, on every blade of grass, and from an array of dazzling flowers.

Wondrous jarul trees treated Devi and Arian with magnificent expressions of white and purple flowers; the scent of myrtle enticing the bees and butterflies in a dance of primacy. The birds seemed to serenade them, perhaps only wishful thinking as the birds had their own business to attend to; the mating season was approaching.

Devi stopped and turned to Arian and said, "There is an incredibly beautiful place just ahead, the home of the largest tree in the Greenlands called the banyan tree." Arian saw a splendid, immense tree with many twisting branches and shoots emanating from the ground. It was difficult to know whether this was one tree or several trees, intertwined to appear as one. The tree, crammed with scurrying monkeys and chirping birds, was alive in every sense. Gusts of wind swirled through the leaves, creating the image of a magical world. Arian, transfixed, said he had never seen such wonder.

"Arian, this tree is also uniquely important as a source of medicines from its barks and leaves. Most important, this is the place to come when you need to free your spirit from the ravages of life, when meditation is your only desire, or I should say the cure for any desire."

As Arian looked at Devi, he thought the part about desire could not be true as his desire for Devi was growing by the minute. Then Devi saw an intricate spider web nestled in the lower branches of the banyan tree. Intrigued, she said, "Arian, look at this spider's web." It was an elaborate design with radial spokes overlaid on silk strands creating a web which was as twisted as the tree itself. Then a tiny insect made the unfortunate choice of climbing onto the web, not sensing the sticky coatings on the silk strands. Trapped, the unfortunate victim would not escape, its destiny now certain.

Devi turned to Arian, "Are you thinking what I am thinking?" Arian had two different thoughts contending for space in his consciousness. He was sure Devi meant the spider's web represented a novel defensive tactic.

"Yes, we can lure the Horse Warriors into the Greenlands and trap them with massive nets created from jute."

Devi's face sparkled with excitement. "Yes, exactly what I was thinking."

At that moment, with excitement in both of their hearts, they brushed into each other, slow to move away. Arian gently grasped Devi's hand, peering directly into her eyes, saying, "Devi, your people have been truly kind and welcoming. We have not rewarded you with honor and respect. Now, we both face a terrible enemy who will not relent until they destroy us. Although your people do not have a military, you are resourceful and ingenious. Our people are brave but stuck in old ways which will lead to defeat and annihilation."

Devi gently pulled away, not of her own volition but simply out of a sense of propriety, saying, "Arian, we will join as one force and develop a new way of combat to defeat the Horse Warriors as they will disrespect our values and find no reason for our continued existence. The expression, "one force", stuck in his mind. Of course, Devi was simply referring to the military alignment, nothing else.

Arian only replied, "I pledge my honor to you." Devi was not sure exactly what he meant. She wanted to believe he was speaking of her, not just of her people.

The cries of owls pierced their solitude.

Devi said, "There are many legends of owls in our culture. Small owls can mean babies. People are joyful when they see small owls, thinking of newborns. They mistakenly see big owls as dangerous and possessing magical demonic powers. People conjure up myths of animals who thrive in the night. They believe the sighting of a large owl means impending disaster. This is wrong, as one can learn from all animals, even the king cobra. Owls are masters of disguise, blending into tree branches, perfectly aligned with the colors of the bark. They expertly hunt at night, endowed with keen eyesight and hearing and extreme patience. The methods of Nature can teach us how to defeat the Horse Warriors."

They meandered down the path. Then, they spotted a pair of great owls, blended onto a branch, their feathers and the tree bark forming a continuous visual image. Devi said, "It is bad luck to only hear the owl, but it is good luck to see a male and female owl together, especially if they do not flee." Then she shyly added, "Any couple spotting owls together are in harmony with each other and bound by special emotions."

Somewhat embarrassed by her romantic allusion, her face slightly blushing; she was happy to have expressed these sentiments. Arian, without hesitation or shyness, quickly replied, "Devi, I believe the favorable omen is true for us."

PART 14
The Horse Warriors Cross the Great Stars River

Dhanur sat motionless on the banks of the river, staring but not seeing. He was deep in thought as he found the flowing river to be hypnotic. The Varagans were off into the distance, barely visible, slinking away on a dusty road leading from the river. Dhanur always reserved time for meditation, which was essential to each horse warrior for spiritual revival. Dhanur elevated meditation above food and sleep as the quandary he now faced seemed daunting. How to cross the river with sufficient men and horses, including supply wagons? He could take some solace knowing the Varagans had to leave their horses behind, giving his army additional horse reserves.

Dhanur's men encamped in a shady woodland near the river. Rest and recuperation were their purpose as the order to mount and ride continuously for hours, though extreme temperatures were always possible, even imminent. Each man followed their own physical and spiritual recovery. Recovery did not mean only going to sleep or some form of meditation; it also meant getting prepared for battle.

The horses required attention. The warriors tended to them before tending to their own needs. Each warrior required several horses, so securing water and feed, and a ritualistic set of massages, took precedence and time. The men treated their horses with the same respect as a fellow warrior. The Horse Warrior code of discipline was very harsh on men who failed to revere their horses or treat them improperly. Each Horse Warrior remembered the cautionary words of the military commander, "A majestic war horse is more perfect and valuable in battle than any human warrior."

Before long, a small distant object interrupted Dhanur's meditation, slowing moving down the river. The Horse Warriors were not familiar with boats as their homelands were mainly semi arid and lacked rivers of any significant size. As the small boat appeared, Dhanur noticed it carried two men, one of whom was manipulating a long pole apparently for steering. The boat had a flat bottom with curved wood planks on both the front and back. Carvings of birds adorned each side.

Dhanur summoned the two men to steer close enough to shore. The Horse Warriors often traveled with interpreters, as local dialects often created communication problems. Through an interpreter, Dhanur inquired as to the destination and purpose of their voyage. Dhanur learned the boatsmen were traders from the land of the Shore People, which was down river nearly three sailing days away. Dhanur asked many questions about the river's width and depth.

The boatmen explained the waters were deeper than normal as the summer rains and melting glaciers in the high mountains had swollen the river's banks. The helmsman advised patience to cross the river, possibly in three months if dry conditions persisted. He also warned Dhanur freak thunderstorms occurred without warning, causing surges of river water, trapping soldiers in mid-river.

Dhanur stared at the boat for a while and then asked: "How big can you make these boats?"

To which the helmsmen replied, "We could build these boats to carry ten men and their horses, but not more. I should warn you boats of such size become unstable and capsize, if the horses panic and shift positions."

Dhanur summoned two men and their horses to board the small boat. The helmsman tried to protest but quickly realized silence was his best option. The two warriors tried to soothe the anxiety of the horses, stroking them, and urging them onto the boat. The breathing of the horses intensified as their fear of the boat increased. Oddly, it was not the water itself; it was the sense of floating which triggered the horse's agitation. Just as the boat was about to launch from the shore, Dhanur said, "Stop, I have seen enough."

Dhanur immediately realized small boats would not work to transport horses and men across the raging river. It required a unique solution. He turned to his chief lieutenant and said: "Summon Jung-Guo". Khander had long ago secured the services of master builders from the Middle Kingdom, which was far east of Desa across the mountains of the gods. The master builder Jung-Guo was most renowned for massive wooden siege machines. He had invented complex catapults designed to hurl massive stones and firepots against enemy fortresses.

"Jung-Guo, I need you to solve the crossing problem. The river is too deep and the current too fast for either men or horses to cross. Heavy oxen can cross, but without the warriors and their horses, no good purpose would result. Bring me the best solution in three days."

An efficient crossing meant very simply that every man and horse reached the other side with no losses. Jung-Guo spent the first day measuring the river for several miles north and south of the camp. He also directed his men to explore all the woods and forests within one day's travel to determine availability of the perfect trees for boats and rafts. They examined several species of trees for strength and buoyancy. Wood from the bamboo trees had the desired features and was available in sufficient supply. Further tests showed combining bamboo with the wild jack tree would be the best solution, as it was equivalent in quality with teak but more readily available near the camp.

The next task was to determine length, width, and materials for bindings. The solution required rafts fifty feet in length, sufficient to carry ten men and horses along with supplies. The biggest challenge was to secure wooden and rope enclosures to assuage the natural fears of the horses. Jung-Guo built a small prototype within the three-day period as commanded by Dhanur.

Dhanur had never seen such a boat before. It was a combination of a boat and raft, as it had to be of sufficient size to carry at least ten men and their horses. In addition, sturdy sides, fashioned like a horse corral, had to be both pragmatic and visually comforting to the horses. Bounded bamboo poles added ballast to prevent tipping from one side to the other. They fashioned a large oar out of teak wood for guidance. Finally, the raft had a long rope managed by several warriors to pull the raft back to the river's edge. Jung-Guo also explained a long guide rope would stretch across the river to prevent loss of control while crossing.

Dhanur said to Jung-Guo and the other builders, "Now we must test your boat." Of course, any of Dhanur's men including the builders would have stepped forward, if ordered. Dhanur thought for a moment and said, "Come Jung-Guo, you and I with our two chief Lieutenants will take the first voyage". None of them had any experience in managing such a boat. Instead of horses, Dhanur ordered the raft-boat loaded with enough rocks and heavy objects to simulate the weight of the horses.

Jung-Guo and his chief assistant learned from long service to Dhanur not to show any fear or anxiety, as in the cultural world of the Horse Warriors, any display of anxiety would incur a beating with repeated episodes of fear and anxiety resulting in death. Everyone was equal and subject to the oral laws of the Horse Warriors which had endured for many generations. Horse Warriors prohibited tribal or racial loyalties or discrimination of any kind. They accepted peoples from other regions as "brothers" if they swore allegiance to the Warrior Codes. In time, these peoples learned from experience the Horse Warriors were true to their word and faithfully followed each precept of the Warrior Codes.

The selection of the boat's crew did not surprise Jung-Quo. Dhanur selected his best unit commander, another builder and Jung-Quo, and of course himself. The four men boarded the vessel along with the "horses". Everyone had an assigned task. Dhanur assigned to himself the most dangerous of the duties which was to maneuver under the raft-boat should it get lodged. The boat proceeded down river at a rapid rate, careening from side to side as control of speed was not possible. The rope from the shore extended further and further as the raft veered out into the middle. Several men on shore anchored the stretched rope, but it was becoming clear by the moment the use of ropes had limits which were quickly being reached.

Dhanur signaled the men to pull the boat back to shore, which required oxen kept in reserve as a precautionary measure. Slowly, with the ropes stretched to their limits, the boat inched closer and closer back to the river's edge. Finally, with the boat safely ensconced on the riverbank, relief swept through the men. Dhanur jumped out of the boat and spun to Jung-Guo, who was stoically standing at attention, awaiting his fate.

"Your boat solution is excellent", Dhanur exclaimed. "We will work on some improvements, chiefly with the rope mechanism. Also, in a month, the river will be calmer. Jung-Guo, I want you to build ten more, twice as big with stronger ropes able to reach across the river. Have the first one ready next week for another test voyage." Jung-Guo did not flinch. The harrowing experience served him well, education by a close brush with death! He silently thanked his creator because he was still alive, as he was sure he would not survive when trapped in the middle of the river.

The next morning, a commotion awakened Dhanur. He glanced from his tent to see a group of warriors headed toward him with two women lagging in the rear. Sudhir, the unit commander, led one of his finest warriors by the name of Balashur, who had a rope wrapped loosely around his neck. The rope was not a preventative measure but a symbol of shame as it showed the man in tow had possibly committed a serious violation of the Warrior Codes. Sudhir stepped forward; everyone else waited back.

"Dhanur," said Sudhir, "This man has possibly violated the laws concerning rape." Balashur looked straight ahead, expressionless. "He apparently raped the woman, Omisha, taking her into the woods against her will."

Omisha was unmarried, which was important as rape or adultery of a married woman carried a death sentence with no question. Strict prohibitions existed against sexual abuse of any female within the Horse Warrior culture. In cases of a willing relationship, protocols proscribed physical relationships. Sexual union before marriage was unknown and taboo.

"Omisha, come forward" said Dhanur. "Is it true Balashur raped you?" With her head lowered, she softly said Balashur had forcibly dragged her into the woods and pulled off her top shirt, but had not violated her, as Omisha's sister who had followed them into the woods interrupted him. Dhanur asked Omisha's sister to relate every detail of what she had witnessed. Dhanur then asked if any man had witnessed any of this violation. To this point, Balashur was still silent.

Omisha and her sister both concurred to the fact there were no other witnesses, as the time in the morning was still early and most people were still asleep. "Do you have anything else to add?" inquired Dhanur. Omisha said she was sure alcohol affected Balashur's judgment, as if to offer some explanation of the unlawful behavior. Intoxication violated the codes, although not normally serious, no mitigating rationale for molesting Horse Warrior women.

According to the Warrior Codes, Balashur could have simply denied these charges as there were no male witnesses. Dhanur asked Balashur to speak without prodding him with questions. Balashur, a warrior of renown, only said, "The words of Omisha are true."

No one expected him to say he was sorry, as it was self-evident. Every warrior memorized each word of the codes, notably those provisions pertaining to the behavior of men designated as warriors. Any violation brought shame. Dhanur told Sudhir to appear at noon with all the warriors of his command, which numbered exactly 1,000.

At noon, Sudhir, Omisha and her father, Balashur and all the troops in the unit command gathered in central camp. Rape was punishable by death; any other sexual abuse of an unmarried woman also carried the same fate. They discarded intoxication as an excuse. Balashur understood his fate but stood stoically. Sudhir positioned himself next to Balashur with the execution sword at his side. Everyone waited for Dhanur to issue a simple command, "Die with honor". Immediately, the victim would kneel and extend his neck forward. The deed would be swift.

Dhanur raised his hand and said: "Does anyone wish to speak?" This question was not intended to find mitigating circumstances, but simply as a courtesy to anyone with important information. Even though Balashur was a celebrated warrior, that fact could not save him. No one including Balashur would ask for mercy, an act held in the highest contempt.

Omisha's brother stepped forward and said, "I am Omisha's brother", a fact already familiar to all men in the unit command. "This man, Balashur, saved my life in the last battle with the Varagans. He did so by incurring severe injuries to himself with no regard for his own life."

This was useful information but not compelling since the warrior ethic expected bravery of each man. Then Dhanur summoned Omisha to speak. "I have known Balashur for many years now. He is a good man and has been kind to my mother and father. Early this morning, as I was doing my morning chores, he approached me nervously. He told me he loved me and wanted me for his wife. Balashur asked for my affections, which cannot happen before marriage. He said he failed to control his passions; his aggressiveness aggravated by his intoxication. Although not harmed by his assault, I am now afflicted by a troubled spirit."

Then, Balashur asked to speak. Dhanur nodded consent. "If my life as a Horse Warrior continues, I would like Omisha to be my wife. I will also provide items of gold to her family and a gold necklace for Omisha to honor our lives together. I will dedicate my life to Omisha and her family."

If Omisha's father consented, then Dhanur could spare Balashur's life. This was the moment of destiny, as any failure to nod would mean the immediate execution of Balashur. Dead silence ensued. Moments later, Omisha's father nodded his consent.

Dhanur spoke again, "Balashur, I will marry you to Omisha. You must honor her always and her family. Your life is indebted to any member of Omisha's family. Now, you must go into your tent for seven days of fasting. On the seventh day, you can marry Omisha."

In the following week, Jung-Guo and his men met Dhanur at the riverside. Dhanur seemed to think the river was calmer but likely a wish, he thought to himself. As ordered, the boat met all the criteria as directed by Dhanur. Extensive ropes, at least a half mile long, were ready. The boat launched with Jung-Guo, Dhanur and eight other men and their "horses". This time, the crossing went smoothly as the boat was bigger and the currents not so swift. They also guided the boat with more skill. The boat reached the other side, maybe with luck and some additional skill by the builders. Unknown to Dhanur, Jung-Guo had already crossed several times in the day before, as practice, and had become skilled as a helmsman.

The only remaining task was to build another nine boats and start the tedious crossing, being careful not to leave one side or the other unprotected. Dhanur dispatched scouts across the river with orders to search a radius of at least one mile in all directions.

PART 15
Urgent Preparations

Sheep herders were prevalent in all regions. They traveled with their sheep in small groups, proceeding through the countryside. Superbly trained, the Horse Warrior scouts examined everything, even the smallest details. The scouts headed in the direction the Varagans had taken weeks before. They soon encountered the "sheepherders", also Nivasi scouts. Both sides practiced the art of deception as each falsely stuck to their scripts, the Nivasi scouts as sheepherders and the Horse Warriors as traders in search of new trading routes.

The advantage was with the Nivasi as these men were sheep herders and scouts. The Horse Warriors were unsure if these claims were accurate. The sheepherders were certain the men in search of trade only desired knowledge of the Varagans. The sheep herders listened in amusement to Axam, leader of the "trading" group, spin his tales. They were peaceful and humble people, he said.

Axam asked lots of questions for which the sheepherders were well-prepared. How far to the nearest city? How many people? Were the people friendly or warlike? Each question designed to get a kernel of information. Meanwhile, they gave small gifts to these poor "sheep herders" who seemed to live in a subsistence world.

The leader of the sheepherders, Simran, skillfully played his role. He pointed to a path which would lead the Horse Warriors off to the east, well off the direction to Desa. He said the people in the east were aggressive and unfriendly and considered all strangers as enemies. "A terrible and evil people who attack without warning. I told this to the Varagans who passed by here, but they ignored my warnings."

The next morning, the Horse Warrior scouts carefully examined the road heading east. They scoured the ground looking for evidence of oxen. Slowly, they made their way eastward, still uncertain whether this road showed sufficient evidence of heavy use by the retreating Varagans. They continued for two days through arid lands into the woodlands. Axam saw plenty of evidence that someone well used this road, but did it lead to the Varagans? Then a sudden late summer thunderstorm swept the area, forcing the scouts to take cover. Now the road was too muddy for clues and leery of potentially aggressive people further east, the scouts returned to the river shore.

Axam would not consider returning to the base camp without more definitive information. As an insurance policy, he captured a small group of sheepherders who in fact were truly desert people with no allegiance to any other people. They had learned over time that the best way to ensure survival was to say nothing to anyone, appearing dumb as a ruse for clever survival.

Axam questioned each of the pitiful souls while they were staked to the ground still asserting, they knew nothing about the path of the Varagans. Axam appeared to gently probe them until he announced that he did not think that the sheepherders needed all their fingers. In unison, the Horse Warriors sliced off the smallest finger of each man. Screaming in pain, the men cried for mercy asserting they knew nothing. Then a moment later, the three men lost another finger. Before each man endured painful separation of a third finger, Axam had the information he desired and released the men to their sheep. Axam was certain that the original sheepherders were indeed spies and had intentionally misled them from the true direction.

Meanwhile, Simran, the lead Nivasi scout, started his journey back to Desa. Leaving most of his fellow "sheep herders" behind to continue their monitoring. After five days of riding, Simran finally reached Desa and immediately requested a meeting with Gandesh and the most senior members of the Nivasi Council, including Devi. It surprised him to see Arian and Amura in attendance, unaware of the new relationship between the Varagans and the Nivasi. Warily, he glanced over at Arian as he began his report.

Many of the Nivasi Council were in shock, some in disbelief. Mandeep explained that because of the waning of the summer rains and the growing signs of a perpetual drought, such a crossing was entirely workable. Simran relayed the shocking information the Horse Warriors had discovered the means to transport horses on their "boats", essentially large rafts. The Shore People had mastered boat construction and had vessels which crossed the vast seas, but transportation of horses on rafts was another matter. Mandeep predicted late summer thunderstorms could make the river too treacherous to cross, which would pose only a temporary delay.

Gandesh asked Arian to comment on this recent information. He rose quickly and starting speaking, his words carefully crafted although with hints of optimism. "The Horse Warriors attacked our homeland with over 10,000 soldiers. We know they continued their attack on our retreating columns with about half that number. They base military organization of the Horse Warriors on legion sizes of 1,000 soldiers with a specified mix of cavalry and foot soldiers and defined numbers of archers and lancers. In addition, each legion has a certain number of horses, usually three assigned to each rider, and defined support personnel and wagons with full supply of weapons. Based on losses incurred in the pass, I estimate only four complete legions are available."

Based on descriptions of the rafts used to cross the Great Stars River, Arian estimated a complete crossing of four legions, numbering 4,000 men, would take several weeks depending on river conditions. Then the march to Desa would take at least five more days, as the area was unknown to the Horse Warriors. Arian also said Dhanur would not be foolish enough to attack with four legions unless he was sure of success.

Amura added the Horse Warriors would send an emissary whose only purpose would be for military intelligence. He added, "Their primary purpose is to gauge the total forces deployable, assuming the

Varagans still had the equivalent of three legions, although without the benefit of war horses.

Mandeep waited for Amura to finish and then offered his advice: "It would be to our advantage to display a meek and pacific culture. The Varagans should stay behind their walled encampment. The Horse Warriors cannot have access to the eastern part of Desa where evidence of the Varagans is discernible."

While these events were unfolding, the Nivasi under the tutelage of Gandesh, a champion archer in his youth, were undergoing strenuous training. Gandesh organized all the citizens between the ages of sixteen to sixty into archers and javelin throwers. Archers were further divided into two sections, short bow and long bow, each group with unique skills and purpose. All citizens underwent distance running and personal training in karate and other related forms of martial arts.

Most important was mental training. Groups of fifty would gather each morning and undergo active meditation, including various forms of visualization. When the day of battle arrived, each Nivasi had to be mentally and spiritually prepared for engagement with an enemy, unimaginably fierce and skilled.

An elite group of Nivasi men and women formed the core of the defensive force, each selected for their physical and emotional skills. One young man by the name of Dhira excelled above all. Even his name was propitious, as it meant "fierce". Gandesh selected Dhira as leader of the elite force. Gandesh selected women, also highly skilled with steady nerves, critically important to archery combat. Mishka excelled among the woman and above nearly all the men. Her choice as chief lieutenant to Dhira brought a smile to everyone as her name, Mishka, meant "gift of love". People who knew her first-hand remarked her gift to the Horse Warriors would be anything but "love".

Despite this training, it would have been foolhardy to imagine the Nivasi able to stand up to the Horse Warriors in battle. The Varagans were worthy opponents, but their numbers were deficient, and their morale still stunted by successive defeats. Arian and Amura believed success required different tactics. The Nivasi had no experience in matters of war, but they offered a unique energy and high intelligence. They established a War Committee comprising Mandeep, Devi, Dhira, Vidya and Mishka from the Nivasi along with Arian, Veer, Amura from the Varagans. The best estimate was one month, perhaps two months, before the Horse Warriors would appear in force.

A few weeks later, to the shock of everyone, the emissaries from the Horse Warriors appeared at the city gates.

PART 16
Lies, Deceit, and Perceptions

~~~

The visitors did not mask their intentions as traders in search of new markets. The Nivasi invited the Horse Warrior emissaries into a small room in which only Gandesh, Mandeep and Devi were present. It surprised the Horse Warriors to meet with two old men and a woman of slender build. Axam introduced himself as the Chief Emissary of the Horse Warriors. The Nivasi showed no emotion to this introduction, only asking Axam to explain further the culture of his people and the purpose of his visit.

From the onset, Axam became more forceful and blunter. "We are looking for renegade people called the Varagans who have committed crimes against our people. We believe these people are here, in your land, or have passed by. If you are truthful and provide the information and location of these people, we will reward you with gold. If you use the slightest amount of deceit, then everyone in this land shall die at the hands of our warriors." Axam's eyes were sharp and piercing, his words deeply ominous.

Trained in meditation, the Nivasi could maintain a calm demeanor as their minds were in a semi-trance state, hearing words but not listening or comprehending. Devi said, "We do not know of these people you refer to."

Axam, extremely skilled in body language, searched her face and eyes, scanning her body primarily her neck muscles. The slightest amount of tension, any subtle bulging of veins betrayed lies. Although Devi was looking straight at him and hearing every word, her mind was only visualizing the great owl, deep in a pleasurable state as to her tender moment with Arian. His words meant nothing to her, so she showed no tension or stress.

Axam eased up and portrayed a friendlier demeanor. "I believe you", he said with a smile, shifting his body to become more open and accepting.

"Perhaps, you would grace me with a tour around your city so I can be more appreciative of your culture." Gandesh responded it would be his pleasure to do so and planned the tour for the next day. The Nivasi were incredibly careful. They would allow no one except people with the most advanced meditation skills near the emissaries. Even a house assistant might unknowingly say something which would be important to Axam. Everyone possibly meeting Axam was thoroughly prepared to answer any question, no matter how inconsequential.

Gandesh sent two women to the sleeping chambers of the Horse Warriors to inquire as to their needs. These two women were meditation teachers, although they appeared to Axam as plain, peasant women. Axam thanked them for the water and small dishes of food. As they were leaving, he stopped them. "Yes, I have a question. What types of sporting events do your people practice?"

One woman turned and responded, "We do not have any organized sports or a military organization. We do not value physical fitness, only training of our minds. Work strengthens our bodies." Axam thought to himself, *These people are soft*.

After a few tedious days of very boring discussions concerning philosophical matters such as the purpose of life, Axam decided he had heard enough. Despite his best efforts, he could not discern any evidence of deceit.

The lack of personal possessions surprised him, most noteworthy, the complete absence of gold and jewelry, either worn by the people or in any public spaces. He had never seen women devoid of gold rings or necklaces, the booty of war and the primary way to show appreciation for the women in their culture.

Livestock was plentiful, so Desa would be an excellent source of food should the army march through these lands. Meanwhile, the lack of additional information pertaining to the Varagans frustrated Axam. He had found no clues.

One detail puzzled Axam. When visiting the Greenlands, he noticed a tall fence enclosure off in the distance. Immediately suspicious, he asked to visit that area. Gandesh told him the area was the sacred lands of priests who practiced an extreme religion which forbade interaction with non- believers, meaning practically everyone in Desa.

Priests greeted Axam at the door and invited him inside for tea, which was the only interaction permitted for their religious order. As he left, he turned back at the enclosure, described as a fence for tending of livestock. He thought to himself, *The height of the fence exceeds the requirement for cattle raising. It looks more akin to a wall, not a fence for animals.* Devi saw the quizzical look on Axam's face; they just smiled at each other, but Devi understood the tall "fence" ruptured their ruse.

The next day, Axam and his fellow scouts left, thanking Gandesh and Mandeep for their hospitality and honesty. Devi remained back in her house as she felt the energy with Axam was negative. Both were incredibly suspicious of the other. At first, Axam did not respect Devi, but as their time together passed, he instinctively grasped she was exceedingly gifted. Most important, he believed Devi was the most intuitive person he had ever encountered, making her the most dangerous person among the Nivasi.

Axam excelled in his profession, as he was a master of a very intuitive thought process, a quality lacking in most people who rely on physical skills or sheer bravery born out of deep ideologies. In fact, Axam mused, the more you believed in something, the worse your skills of intuition. Other people may refer to this quality as critical thinking; yes, he thought to himself, but with the added dimension of a sixth sense, a reading of a person's vibrations and energy flows. Axam did not handicap himself with preconceived beliefs or opinions. An outstanding memory characterized his superior qualities.

The Nivasi Council quickly started discussions, analyzing and replaying every detail. Axam's charm had seduced some people like Shanti. She said Axam was a man of good intentions who deserved trust. Amura, the wise man of the Varagans, reminded everyone, "We know this man Axam, brother to Khander, Supreme Leader of the Horse Warriors. He is a master of deceit and lies. He is an actor sent to consume as much information as possible, even the smallest morsel might be valuable. It appears you all did well, but we should assume Axam detected some minor detail creating doubt as to our veracity."

Devi then decided the moment was right to take the floor. "Yes, we did exceedingly well in our ruse. But we must scrutinize not only what Axam said but also what he did not say."

She paused, hoping to stimulate a response. It puzzled everyone how to respond. "Please Devi" said Gandesh, "explain what you mean."

Devi continued," Axam showed remarkable interest in the "priests" enclosure. He engaged in small talk, knowing the "master priest" would not provide any truthful information. He asked only basic and trivial questions about the religion but was more interested in asking about the type of livestock the "priests" raised.

Before leaving, Axam stood in front of the teahouse and slowly gazed from one side of the corral to the other side. Perhaps he did not smell the animals or see any signs of animal droppings. He asked nothing about this. Upon exiting through the main gate, he scanned the entire length of the "fence". He did not ask why the fence was so tall, much taller than required to keep cattle inside, but tall enough to be a barrier to anyone outside. Our gazes locked, each knowing what the other was thinking."

Devi's observational capabilities impressed Arian. On each occasion in which they met, his feelings for her increased, even to the point of suggesting to himself they would be good together as man and wife. *Stop those foolish thoughts*, Arian said to himself. *Our cultures and peoples are too different. The Nivasi would never accept a Varagan into such an arrangement.* Arian could not know or let himself believe Devi was having the same thoughts. She was sure Arian would never be interested in her as he had many beautiful women to consider.

The Nivasi Council agreed they must speed up the war plans. A month, no more, was all the time available. Several Nivasi Council members led by Shanti, not a tiny minority, had severe misgivings. She chose not to speak, but she was sure disaster lay ahead, maybe extinction; a deal with the Horse warriors could save the Nivasi. As to the Varagans, she was thinking they had over-extended their stay. She believed they represented the primary threat.

Shanti believed it was inconceivable to kill another human being. She held firm to the principle all human beings were inherently good and would not kill another person. Shanti did not grasp the fact that in many cultures, notably the Horse Warriors, the essential principle of life centered on continuous excellence in every aspect of life, including military life. She failed to understand the Horse Warrior's belief in the world of nature, the primary drive for survival and procreation, killing of another life essential for existence. The Horse Warriors believed their actions were in harmony with natural law, providing a justification for domination over others.

Shanti believed higher, humanistic principles which differentiated humans from animals guided the Nivasi. She adhered to a moral code: all life was sacred, and humans could choose not to kill animals or each other; the intellect of humans created a higher order of existence underpinned by human rights. She had argued this point of view with Devi frequently. In her heart, Devi wanted to believe Shanti was right, but her mind told her such idealism had to be tempered with reality. The problem, Devi reasoned, is there are multiple realities just as there are different opinions. The reality of the Horse Warriors and the reality of Shanti's world were irreconcilable.

Upon returning to the river, Axam lost no time in briefing Dhanur on his mission. Two weeks had passed, during which time they constructed additional rafts. He entered Dhanur's tent and commenced with his briefing. Axam spared no details. The Horse Warriors regarded patience as a military virtue, so Dhanur and his senior legion leaders sat and listened with no interruption. Axam recounted every fact, his report unfolding like a treasured story similar to oral traditions of endless length, memorized and told over the generations by seasoned story tellers. Most people crave certainty, but the Horse Warriors understood the best military intelligence was often subtle and seemingly insignificant.

Axam finished, concluding, "The Nivasi are hiding the remnants of the Varagan army."

Axam had two reasons for his conclusion. First, the priest's enclosure had no evidence of animals; the ground looked untouched, no animal dung was noticeable, and the area did not smell like cattle; and, of course, the fence was really a wall. Second but more subtle, all the rehearsed answers by each Nivasi to his question impressed him as too stilted. The Nivasi knew their lines but did not deliver the recitation with energy and passion. In short, they made no mistakes, but their performances lacked credibility like actors in a play, emotionally exhausted from far too many ritualistic performances.

Axam failed to discern anything about the military capabilities of the Nivasi. He determined the leaders, above all Devi, were very shrewd and cunning. Axam advised extra caution in their battle tactics. Dhanur, amazed at the brilliance of Axam's report and the fact a woman appeared to be the leader, responded, "We cannot know with any certainty who the leaders are or their military capabilities. For sure, they do not have the foolish arrogance of Pratham and the stupidity of Jackal."

Dhanur thanked Axam and his men saying, "Although these people treated you with respect, they are a dangerous and uncertain foe. You warned them not to lie, but they chose a different path. Now, they we will treat them the same as the Varagans." Everyone grasped this meant the extinction of the Nivasi people.

PART 17
War Strategy Decisions

"One month" kept resonating in Devi's mind as she entered the War Committee chambers. They had been training for several months, which was a blink of an eye compared to the Horse Warriors who never stopped training from the earliest age. Everyone in the War Committee knew they could not defeat the Horse Warriors with traditional tactics. No one understood this better than Arian.

Keeping his thoughts to himself, he promised he would never let Pratham and his cowardly brother, Jackal, dictate the battle tactics. Pratham was personally courageous, but his arrogance and ego would overcome good judgment. Any outward disobedience would fail, as the army had sworn loyalty to Pratham. Many of the army officers were from the powerful aristocratic families who had their own motivations to keep Pratham in power until it was their time to move against him. Then, Arian had a brilliant insight, the flash of clarity as to the right action.

As the War Committee members were gathering, Arian asked Devi to step out in the garden. They walked silently together, Arian in deep thought, pondering if and how he should propose his plan. Devi was walking with an air of expectation, secretly urging Arian to speak his mind. Finally, they stopped and looked at each other. Both knew this was not a moment of love but a critical moment of trust which would forever bind them.

Arian finally summoned the initiative to speak, "Devi, if our forces fight in unison but under separate command, the Horse Warriors will defeat us at the most critical moment of battle. Even within the Varagans, there are too many commanders whose first loyalty is to Pratham, not to our people. Pratham is a courageous but foolish man. He has led many successful military campaigns, but he is not capable of change. He will stubbornly keep insisting his tactics were correct, but the battle execution was flawed. Any admission of error on his part would mean he was a personal failure."

Arian stopped speaking, searching her face for any clues to what she was thinking. "Continue", Devi said.

"We need one integrated army under a single command, but Pratham and his clan will never agree to this idea for several reasons, one of which is they would not trust the Nivasi in battle. Therefore, we should join the elite forces of the Nivasi with elite counterparts from the Varagans under my command. This force shall number 1,000 male and female soldiers, selected by us, from both the Nivasi and the Varagans. They will live and train together and undergo visual meditation which you will direct."

Devi reached for Arian's hand, her mind occupied with the new plan, but her heart burning with a different desire. She kissed him on his cheek, only saying: "I have been waiting for you to propose this plan. Together, we will either prevail or die."

Arian, overcome with emotion, gently kissed Devi on her lips, a daring act in any situation. She willingly embraced the solitary kiss and softly whispered, as if unwelcome ears were listening, "Let us return to the war planning meeting. Then we can stroll together later."

As Arian and Devi walked back to the meeting chamber, they spoke no words. Arian and Devi, lost in their own thoughts, separate when, just moments before, intertwined as one. Thoughts of Devi dominated his mind, embedded in his soul. His darker thoughts took over his mind. He did not think there was any way to defeat the Horse Warriors. He thought of his last hours either slain on the battlefield or executed together with Devi. Then he realized their lives would not end that way. They would drag her into slavery, tortured for hours if not days. Sweat was pouring down his forehead.

He turned to Devi, in a sober, if not desperate tone, said: "We must not lose."

Devi opened the discussion strangely by saying, "Let us outline all our weaknesses and all their strengths. "People in the room did not know if they should be amused or irritated. Arian realized the brilliance of the question. Next, she would ask to list all our advantages and their disadvantages. The Varagans suffered overwhelming defeat because they focused only on their strengths and their advantages, more chest-pounding than strategy. They did not think like Horse Warriors, so they were outclassed and outmaneuvered at every critical instance.

Mandeep said the Nivasi did not have the psyche of a warrior, nor the battle-hardened skills. The Varagans did not have enough trained war horses, all their best horse left behind at the river. Amura said: "The Horse Warriors fight as a coordinated force with one integrated plan for all phases of the battle and an aim with one purpose, winning at all cost. They will die for their purpose as losing is an unbearable shame."

Arian began listing the disadvantages of the Horse Warriors. They will be strangers in this land, unfamiliar with the woodlands and forests of Desa. They like to fight in cavalry formations on the prairies but will be hampered by the unusual terrain of Desa. They do not know about the animals of this region, especially the elephants. They use short bows for short range and flexibility of motion on horses, but their bows do not have the range of the Nivasi bows. Most likely, they will come with three legions comprising 3,000 men, a force less than normal. Although of superior fighting confidence, they will not be expecting a vigorous defense. As to their advantages, "They never lose in battle, never accept defeat and are the most complete warriors imaginable."

Unintentionally, the last comment purged the War Committee of any latent optimism; the mood turned grim. Then, Arian said," Devi and I have a plan to win; we think we can prevail over the Horse Warriors." It was the perfect setup. The plan combined three core fighting forces: the Nivasi Forest Dwellers, the integrated "elite" archery core, and the Varagan cavalry core supported by attack foot soldiers. The Forest Dwellers, both men and women with hawk-like camouflage making them indiscernible from the trees themselves, would also use new tactics. Vidya loved this idea, as the hawk was a favorite hunting bird of the Forest Dwellers.

The War Committee approved, mesmerized by the daring and innovative tactics. Arian and Devi did not delve into the details of the training of the "elites". She referred to the arduous physical and mental training, requiring group isolation for one month; even excluding visits from family members and spouses.

Pratham and Gandesh listened intently to the war plan outlined by Arian and Devi. Pratham stared at Devi, refusing to take her seriously. Jackal seemed to snicker repeatedly. The senior leaders of the family clans were more receptive, as they had already lost sons and nephews to the disastrous and impetuous tactics of Pratham and Jackal. They held Jackal in the highest contempt as he fashioned himself as a strategist, although never in the front lines and always the first to run.

True, Devi and the Nivasi had not seen battle, but Dhira and Mishka from the Nivasi and Manbir, a very highly respected warrior from the Varagans, would lead the "elite" forces. They looked formidable, especially Mishka, as she had a very tenacious and noble demeanor which impressed the clan leaders.

Pratham looked around the room among the Varagans, slowly gazing from face to face, searching for clues and signs of disapproval. Pratham did not like this war plan as he believed it would dilute his power and weaken the feudal culture of the Varagans which had served his family for generations. Then the unthinkable happened.

Samarth, respected for his administrative capabilities and righteous judgment, spoke, "If we try to fight the Horse Warriors with our traditional military tactics, they will destroy us as a people. We have also brought mortal danger to the Nivasi, whom we have mistreated and disrespected. They could have signaled their cooperation with the Horse Warriors and saved themselves. The Nivasi fight for freedom, we fight for family aggrandizement. This is our moment to unite with the Nivasi and fight together as one force led by one superior commander."

Samarth then courageously proposed Arian as "Supreme Commander". The next moment was extremely tense as Samarth had invoked an ancient custom, not used for over a hundred years. If the clan leaders voted to approve the title of "Supreme Commander", Arian would have unquestioned authority on any matters pertaining to war sidelining Pratham and Jackal. If most of the clan leaders voted no, then Samarth would have no choice other than to leave the Varagans and adopt a hermit's life as he would have so dishonored his family. Even though this proposal was a vote of non-confidence in Pratham, it did not mean the end of his rule as "Primary". Pratham, by custom, had to remain silent. Jackal was twisting in his seat, helpless to blunt this affront to the authority of Pratham and himself. Pratham remained stoic.

Voting by the leaders of the clan proceeded without haste. Several of the clans requested a brief break for private discussions, which extended the tension even more. Most unusual was the fact the leaders of the five largest clans met as a group with each clan chief speaking his mind. It did not take long to decide as the situation was dire.

One by one, each clan leader said the same thing, "Arian should be Supreme Commander and Pratham should remain as Primary." The entire military would now only take orders from Arian, with absolutely no interference from Pratham and Jackal. Arian did not gloat or take any satisfaction. He was humbled. Devi and Arian looked at each other, their eyes speaking volumes.

PART 18
The Final Month

At the heart of the war plan was the motto, "Every person a soldier". For the Nivasi, this was a tremendous challenge, as generations of people had learned the virtues of non-violence. Some people led by Shanti could not alter their pacifist views. Devi and Arian treated them with respect, compelling no one to fight. Some people like the Forest Dwellers adapted quickly and naturally, as they viewed violence as inevitable in the natural world. Vidya, leader of the Forest Dwellers and a fierce advocate for their unique form of independence, revealed he commanded about two hundred highly skilled archers, including both men and women. They would also control the use of nets designed to trap the Horse Warriors. They did not need the customary training, only instructions as to place and timing.

Related to the Forest Dwellers were the elephant trainers. They had perfect mastery over the magnificent jungle beast. They also had their role to play, a weapon of surprise and shock which would blunt any frontal attacks by the Horse Warrior cavalry. Professionally trained elephants were extremely fierce and effective, attacking and trampling enemy soldiers and wielding their tusks as an additional weapon.

Arian selected the toughest and most skilled archers from the Varagan ranks. Together with the Nivasi, the Elite Force was 1,000 in number, including 200 Nivasi women and 50 Varagan women. The Varagan women buried all their fine jewelry, swearing they would wear no adornments until the defeat of the enemy. The Varagan women treated the female archers like heroes as no Varagan women had ever served in a direct military role. When

Pratham realized Varagan women would serve in combat, he was furious, but powerless. As the days passed, the number of Nivasi and Varagan women who wanted some combat role exploded, most held in reserve. The Elite Force grew to 1500, at which point Devi and Arian capped the number. If the battle plan worked, that number would be sufficient.

Training of the Elite Force focused on archery, running, and visual meditation. These fighters lived together away from their family. Ultimately, small units of fifty trained together. This would create thirty waves of elite fighters who trained in unison with other units. Logistically, the biggest challenge was production of thousands of arrows along with 1,000 long bows and another 500 short bows. The Forest Dwellers had no need for any supply using their own unique weapons, including poison-tipped arrows for additional effectiveness.

The elite forces underwent extensive visual meditation. Normally, meditation calmed a person's soul, but, in this case, visualization in a meditative state had a different purpose. The meditation instructor, also skilled in martial arts, asked each person to sit, eyes shut, guiding them through a subconscious trance.

"You are in a field with a child. The wind is rustling through the tall grasses, everything is alive, everything is moving. The sun is intense, so intense you are squinting. You can barely see as the child drifts away, partially out of sight. You are carrying a bow with only a single arrow, the other arrows used moments earlier on an old tree stump. You become very still. You listen to the grasses, you realize the child is being stalked by a wounded tiger, too sick to hunt for normal prey. You watch the tiger crouch; you hear the child singing school songs completely unaware. You have one second to aim, you have one shot. In a split moment, you pause, focus, aim, holding steady. Your timing must be perfect and your aim true. You release the moment the tiger leaps. Your shot is true, and it saves the child."

Every morning, they rehearsed these types of visualization

practices over and over. The "child" represents the people, specifically those who cannot fight and who completely depend on the fighters. In another sequence, trainers invoke the image of a Horse Warrior in a pose ready to strike the elite fighter. Through each exercise, it is the same process: pause, focus, breathe, aim, thinking only of the purpose of the moment. All elite fighters endure painful exercises which command silence and poise. The message is clear: you live in the moment; you fight in the moment.

Every day, the warriors learn to endure a bit more pain for longer periods. The archery sessions are endless, shooting from multiple positions. Each elite fighter required to run miles upon miles in the afternoon. The days are hot; the mind grows numb, the instructions from the unit leaders cascading. "What is your purpose, what is your purpose?" One drill requires a long sprint over the grassy meadows; the incessant commands being screamed, "Stop, pause, focus, breathe, aim, release". The drills drive each person to the breaking point. The most skilled of all is Mishka, the Nivasi elite leader. She got stronger with every drill, her intensity boiling within her. She lived within her purpose, every moment of every day.

In the last week of training, the fighters went through the same ritualistic drills, but this time, as they stood still, Varagan cavalry appeared over the horizon. The instructor yelled," Stop, pause, focus, breathe, hold still". The mounted warriors kept coming, swinging sticks wildly in the air. "Hold, hold, hold, drop" just as the mounted riders swept by. Some who were too slow to drop received a painful slash on their backs as a reminder to do better in the next drill.

On the sixth day, there was rest but no talking, only 24 hours of meditation, aimed at calming the spirit. After three weeks, the Elite Force was ready. Meanwhile, the training of the elephants continued. The Horse Warriors were in for a surprise, a special "treat", as they had never seen elephants in battle before.

Five days' distance away, Dhanur was pleased to see the last of the rafts, water tested and ready for use. He had to decide how to split his forces. Clearly, one legion remained to protect the supply lines. In the interest of speed, he decided not to cross with the typical logistics support. Crossing the river was still tricky, as a sudden thunderstorm could dump several inches of water in a matter of minutes.

Long campaigns required heavy logistics support, but quick thrusts designed for surprise attacks or short campaigns used light logistics. Dhanur weighed carefully both options, opting for the light approach as speed was his most important criteria. Perhaps Dhanur was also overconfident, as Axam did not see any evidence of battle-hardened people. Axam said everyone he encountered looked soft. Dhanur kept thinking of Shanti, described by Axam as a starry-eyed visionary burdened by beliefs in the fundamental goodness of people.

The river conditions had to be perfect. The invasion force comprised 3,000 warriors along with just 2,500 horses and 500 infantry soldiers, serving primarily as archers. The total force would cross in a day. Matching just one horse with each mounted warrior was a major deviation, as military doctrine required at least two horses per warrior. Another fateful decision was to leave behind the heavy cavalry, eliminating the contingent of lancers who normally served as a battering ram to crush the enemy's front lines. These were all critical decisions; Dhanur knew well this plan was perilous but would bring the fastest results.

Because of overconfidence or faulty strategies, Dhanur made mistakes. He badly split his forces and exposed his supply lines. Solutions were never perfect, viewed in advance; after a brilliant victory, his senior commanders would laud his strategic genius. One last check was to discuss his plans with his younger brother Axam, considered the shrewdest of all Horse Warriors. Axam questioned the decision to omit the heavy cavalry but agreed speed and agility of forces were of primary importance. Axam thought of the sheepherders, who would no doubt try to warn the Nivasi of the advancing army. They did not have any horses, at least he had not seen them. Without horses, the sheep herders could not provide warning.

Dhanur and Axam concluded the odds of a surprise attack were low, but the warning would be at most a few days. They decided; no change to Dhanur's plan. Both Dhanur and Axam were confident of a quick victory, perhaps within a day or two. Supply lines supported five days of battle, well more than requirements.

PART 19
The Invasion Begins

Dhanur was delighted, thinking: *The heavens must be with us as the river is the calmest in months, a very favorable omen. Everything is ready; the warriors itching to go.* Dhanur gave the order to start the crossing. Axam embarked on the first raft. Dhanur would wait until everyone was across safely. He sent riders back into the Varagan territory to provide the latest status on the crossing. As Khander trusted his senior commanders to determine the best timing and mix of forces to optimize expected battle results, he did not influence Dhanur. Of course, Khander understood all details about the invasion, including the scrutiny of the emissary report from Axam.

If Khander had any doubts, he did not express any of them as tradition dictated Dhanur would have total control. Commanders rarely failed, as it would bring shame on themselves and their families. Normally, if a senior field commander suffered defeat incurring exceptional losses of warriors, honor demanded suicide, the only means of redemption for their families. The Horse Warriors considered tactical retreats with minimal losses acceptable if on the way to ultimate victory. Outright defeat was so rare, the current set of commanders had only experienced victory.

There was one addition to Dhanur's plan which Axam suggested. Later in the day, under cover of darkness, ten elite warriors known as the "Assassins" crossed with their horses. The crossing was challenging in the best of conditions; impossible, if not suicidal, under darkness. These were not ordinary warriors. They were blessed with exceptional horses, perfectly trained to be calm under stressful conditions. If the raft turned over, the best trained horses in the world could well perish. Their mission was simple: eliminate the sheep herders and any other unfortunate travelers on the trail to Desa. Since there was no quick way to discern the true sheep herder or travelers on trade missions from the spies, they would treat everyone as a spy.

The crossing was nearly perfect. The Assassins quickly and quietly spread out in pairs. They sauntered their horses, stopping every few minutes. Listening and hearing in the dark of night was most critical. First, they listened for the sheep, then stealthily moved toward their prey. For these men, the art of killing was not exciting or joyous, it was simply duty. The first to die were common prairie people who lived their entire lives on the prairies. Next to die were three men in a small camp decorated with the trappings of traders and merchants. They quickly killed the men, sparing two women and two young children around age 12 who offered no danger. Any survivors were gagged, tied up and warned to stay perfectly quiet until dawn. The Horse Warriors did not spare the women and children out of empathy or any regard for life, they were following the honor code of their people, which did not allow wanton killing of people without some military purpose. The exception would only apply if any people had insulted the Horse Warriors.

The five teams moved methodically through the night. Two Nivasi scouts, masquerading as sheep herders, awoke, stirred by the anxious horses stationed nearby. They tried to mount a defense to no avail; their necks sliced skillfully, as if the carcass of tribal animal butchers. Within the space of six hours, the Horse Warrior assassins slaughtered twenty men, including four men from the Nivasi and Varagans sent as scouts. Working diligently through the night, by dawn, mission completed. Then, the Assassins freed the women and children from their bondage and allowed them a few hours to bury their men in shallow graves. Normal burial rituals required several days of mourning, but the Assassins did not concern themselves with their customs.

The Assassins sent the remaining woman and their children off to the river to face their fates in the Horse Warrior culture. If they resisted this fate, immediate death occurred where they stood. The Horse Warriors left their bodies to rot, as they had just insulted the benevolence of the Horse Warriors. Only one woman challenged, informing the Horse Warriors in a loud voice they were from a royal family and would not submit. Immediately, the unit commander grabbed her by the hair and slit her throat, her eyes frozen in fear, her shirt quickly stained red in a spurt of blood.

The other woman, clearly the mother with her children cringing at her side, quickly bowed, and said, "We will obey your commands and thank you for our lives."

The unit commander just moments before, a heartless killer, smiled and said to one of his men, "Take this family to a private tent and ensure they have proper food and water."

Within five days, the invasion force had crossed the river and in position to advance to Desa. Axam advised Dhanur they could cut the normal five days to three if required, but would exhaust the horses, especially as the days were hotter than normal. Dhanur reasoned since the outer ring of Nivasi scouts were likely eliminated, there was no reason to push the horses and the riders. He thought it wise to send his own scouts ahead for reconnaissance as the terrain encompassed rolling hills. Also, he wanted the tension for battle to build within his own forces. Let his men dream of the booty awaiting them in Desa.

Not lost in his thoughts was the intense hatred he felt for Pratham and Jackal. He dreamed of the day they captured Pratham and Jackal alive. The Horse Warriors would "invite" them for a unique victory dinner, ending in their very cruel and agonizing death. He envisioned the last hours, Pratham and Jackal begging for mercy, screaming in pain, crushed under the weight of a huge wooden banquet floor. What a memorable celebration dinner!

Arian had posted Nivasi and Varagan scouts in three concentric arcs between Desa and the river. Mandeep's warnings about the diminished rains and the dryer climate had proven correct. The Great Stars River was passable, although no one could imagine the Horse Warriors and their master builders had constructed such sizeable rafts. Even more stunning was the fact the Horse Warriors solved the challenge of horse transportation on these rafts. Earlier scout reports showed the various test crossings were successful, so the Nivasi Council realized it was just a matter of time.

The first reports back to Desa were still shocking to the War Committee. The Horse Warriors were advancing with three legions numbering 3,000 men. Arian knew the Horse Warrior strategy comprised coordination of the three legions in orchestrated and time-honored tactics. Horse Warriors practiced movements best described as "The Fountain" in which streams of mounted warriors on light, fast horses would follow a specific pattern of attack and withdraw, attack, and withdraw, in the same way water flows up through a fountain and then recedes back into the pool, drawn up in repeated, predictable patterns.

The basic attack unit was ten men aggregated into intricate attack patterns creating a swarming effect, like frenzied hornets protecting the nest. Given the mental toughness, horsemanship, and physical endurance combined with superior archery skills, the Horse Warriors could destroy much larger forces and wear them down physically and emotionally with repeated surges from both flanks. The ultimate attack featured the lancers on bigger horses, which shattered the remaining resistance. Slaughtering the retreating enemy, now paralyzed with total fear, was the easy part. These methods of battle had yielded enormous success for generations.

Arian addressed the morning session of the War Committee. "The Horse Warriors will be at the city walls in three days. This morning, we will review our battle strategy." The War Committee had expanded to include Vidya, the natural leader of the Forest Dwellers, including the elephant warriors, Mishka, Manbir and Dhira as senior leaders of the Elite forces. Realizing the Elite Force needed a single leader, Manbir and Dhira jointly proposed Mishka as their sole commander, an incredible honor, as no female had ever served in such a role in the histories of either the Nivasi or the Varagans.

Also, in attendance was Samarth, the elder leader of the Harara Clan, second in size and power to the clan led by Pratham. With Samarth as commander of the Varagan cavalry, Mishka as commander of the Elites and Vidya as commander of the Forest Dwellers, that left Arian as supreme commander with Veer as his second in charge. They selected Devi as leader of the War Committee, a new title and position unknown in the history of either people.

Devi called for a short adjournment to brief Gandesh and Pratham on these leadership changes. Of course, neither man wielded the authority to over-rule these decisions, but respect for tradition and the need for unity was paramount. Arian found Pratham sitting quietly in his garden. Arian was not sure what to expect, but the mellow and calm demeanor of Pratham surprised him.

Without his brother, Jackal, to agitate him, Arian hoped Pratham would offer active support. To Arian's surprise, Pratham endorsed the war plan, saying, "This is a most unusual but creative war plan with a very odd collection of leaders. I do not know Mishka, but I am told she is as fierce as any Varagan warrior. You are wise to avoid open combat on the grassy, open lands. Your challenge is simple, luring the Horse Warriors into the forest. At any rate, the biggest risk is, they lay siege to the City and dominate the surrounding countryside. Starvation will set in."

Arian thought these comments were wise. Perhaps Pratham, now a humbler man, had shorn his spirit of arrogance. Doubts surged in his mind; his intuition warned him to be careful, mainly as Jackal would never change his character. Pratham was still vulnerable, as once a person experiences absolute power, true transformation was not possible without a traumatic life-changing event. Arian bowed upon departure, leaving with only polite and ceremonial words to show his respect.

He needed to consult with Devi. Before the War Committee reconvened, they strolled together in one of the more isolated parts of Greenland. Devi listened intently as they walked stride in stride at a slow, methodical pace. They paused and sat on an oddly shaped rock; a bench fashioned by nature.

Devi took Arian's hand and said, "You cannot be distracted by any possible treachery by Pratham and Jackal. They have no choice other than to step aside, hoping our forces win. The best outcome for them is victory and your death in battle. Your people remain divided by rival clans. Samarth is trustworthy, but the smaller clans may turn on you. If victory is achieved, your life will be in mortal danger; more correctly, our lives will be in mortal danger."

Devi's cautionary words were prescient, but her warnings aroused deep feelings, urges he could no longer resist. The dangers melted away, replaced by passion. He gently slid his arm around Devi's back and kissed her with intense fervor. Devi responded with her own pleasurable murmurs and kissed him back, signaling a deeper commitment. Arian then whispered: "I love you Devi and want you for my wife."

Devi paused, not from doubt, but to enjoy the pure happiness of the moment. She kissed him again and said, "I am honored and pleased to be your wife. I love you more than my emotions can express." As they walked back, they tried to keep a professional demeanor, but each had a glow which happens so rarely in life.

The War Committee convened, following the briefings of Gandesh and Pratham. Arian outlined three phases to the war strategy. In the first phase, the Varagan cavalry, at barely one third of normal size because of losses in the prior battles and a shortage of trained war horses, would launch a weak attack. This would incite a counterattack from the Horse Warriors eager for a quick victory. The rolling hills would provide perfect cover for three spaced rows of archers from the Elite Force. The barrage would shock the Horse Warriors as they would not expect arrows launched from long distances.

Arian referred to this phase as "stirring up the hornets". The next phase would take place as the archers "fled" from the battlefield, seemingly in disarray as the Horse Warriors launched successive counterattacks. It was critical to lure the attackers into the forest. Arian believed the Horse Warrior force would number around 500, with most of the 3,000 men held in reserve. Arian emphasized the need to slay all Horse Warriors, sparing no prisoners. This statement shocked the Nivasi, causing rumblings and undertones of disagreement. Arian sensed he would have to relent and take prisoners.

The ultimate phase would include an all-out assault. Deployment of the elephants would take place in this phase of the battle. The key task would be to capture Dhanur and Axam and negotiate a ceasefire and peace treaty. Of course, everyone understood not to trust the Horse Warriors. Khander would agree to any terms to achieve the release of Axam and then return with a massive force to destroy Desa, leaving virtually no traces of an enduring civilization.

The Nivasi and Varagan defenders would require some other act of luck or chance. The next morning, Ekavir from the Shore People arrived. Devi and Mandeep rarely believed in divinity, but they both had to concur. This was an act of Providence!

PART 20
The Anger of the Shore People

❦

Ekavir and his small group of five well-armed men arrived at the city, immediately hosted by Gandesh. Devi and Mandeep sat with Gandesh while his staff served the five men some food and tea. Gandesh provided the Shore People delegation with the opportunity to retire for the evening. "You must be exhausted. Would you like to sleep for a few hours after which we can host you for dinner?" Truth be told, it relieved the Nivasi when Ekavir declined, saying he was on an urgent mission from Rishaan, the wise ruler of the Shore People. Out of both respect and devotion, all Shore People referred to Rishaan as the "Wise Ruler".

Ekavir referred to his people as the Shore People, an extensive kingdom with a vast shoreline. The people were extremely skilled in fishing and boating with a small seaport from which its sailors had navigated vast distances. The people held all ocean creatures in high regard, although certain villages to the southeast corner of the land deeply worshipped the octopus, a creature of superior intelligence with a spiritual connection to the local people.

Ekavir told the Nivasi the Shore People men who navigated the long Great Stars River had met the Horse Warriors. The helmsman said although well treated, he clearly witnessed the militaristic atmosphere surrounding the camp. Clearly, the Horse Warrior army was keen to cross the river. In particular, the helmsman sensed the intensity of Dhanur, the camp general who seemed driven by some very acute purpose, perhaps motivated by revenge or some other nefarious reason.

Then Ekavir became visibly angry as he described the purpose of his trip to Desa.

"I am the nephew of Rishaan and oversee all military operations. Unlike yourselves, we have found the need to develop and maintain powerful land and naval forces as our kingdom extends along the ocean shoreline, far to the south of Desa. We have traveled peacefully in the wild lands north of here and often camped along the shorelines as we pursue trade negotiations with the people from the northeast. My uncle and his family and several relatives were on a trade mission when they disappeared. We believe the Horse Warriors killed or captured them. We want them returned or avenged."

Complete silence filled the room. The Nivasi believed the evil fate of these people was in the stars. Hope was futile.

Devi instinctively spoke on behalf of the Nivasi, explaining the incipient invasion by the Horse Warriors and the fate of the murdered Nivasi scouts found near the river. Devi explained the Nivasi scouts had found no bodies in the area, but evidence of shallow graves was noticeable.

"Ekavir", Devi said, "We have no information as to your uncle and his family. It is true no violence of this nature has taken place in Desa or in the lands to the north up to the Great Stars River. It is highly likely the Horse Warriors committed the evil deeds, currently only a few days away with an army of at least 3,000 men. We offer you our comfort and protection for the next few days, as we believe the Horse Warriors will not attack without sending a delegation seeking our surrender. We can inquire as to the mystery of your relatives."

Later that evening, Simran, the leader of the Nivasi scouts who had been traveling to bring supplies to his four comrades, burst into the room. Exhausted from three hard days of travel, Simran muttered, "I arrived at the camp of the Nivasi and Varagan scouts early in the morning following the night they were slaughtered. I saw some woman burying men, also victims of the Horse Warriors. They seized two women and two young children and transported back across the river."

Devi and Mandeep knew Ekavir's uncle, the brother of Rishaan, was likely in the shallow grave and his family enslaved by the Horse Warriors. Mandeep sadly murmured to Devi, his voice laden with a mix of despair and anger, "These people, the Horse Warriors, do not value human life aside from their own people. They do not care about the grief of other people related to the men randomly killed. They are below the dignity of the most aggressive carnivore animals, such as the tiger who will normally only kill for food and to protect a territory. The Horse Warriors dispassionately killed the Shore People, considering any innocent men caught in their kill zone as collateral damage. We must inform Ekavir right away."

Ekavir was grief stricken but even more angry at the thought of the dead men improperly buried in shallow graves as the Shore People believed in cremation. Trembling with anger and burning within his soul for revenge, Ekavir pronounced, "Our men did not receive the normal burial rites according to our customs. We must find their bodies and cremate them according to our law, otherwise their spirits will not find peace. We must allow humans to mourn for the dead and obey the burial rituals of their culture. Many noble creatures of the animal kingdom, notably elephants, mourn for their dead. The Horse Warriors violated these elementary rules of decency."

Devi thought to herself, *few people could achieve the nobility of elephants*. Widely distributed within Desa and the land of the Shore People, elephants commanded respect as a very empathetic and intelligent species who communicated through complex vocalizations, formed strong clan bonds, and showed reverence for their dead.

Devi could not grasp how the Horse Warriors sustained such an austere culture with incessant motivations for domination well beyond their natural homeland. It seemed disrespect for other people made them devoid of empathy. Devi would later learn the Horse Warriors tolerated other cultures and religions, but submission to Horse Warrior domination and payment of tributes was the price for this "freedom".

Ekavir was hopeful he could still save the family. He departed immediately, accompanied by Simran, to inform Rishaan of the terrible news and to request an auxiliary cavalry force of 500 men deployed to Desa as soon as possible. A more substantial army would take weeks to organize, so a light cavalry operation would have to suffice. He ordered Tarak to stay in Desa to coordinate a new war plan with Devi and Arian.

When Rishaan received the terrible news, he wept uncontrollably for Kalpit and the other murdered men. He falsely took solace from the belief the abductors spared the women and children. His mind failed to imagine a worse fate than immediate death. He immediately summoned his senior advisers, including Harnish, responsible for military planning and intelligence. During war, it was customary for each side to allow sufficient time for burial or cremation services as the spiritual life continues after the physical demise of a person. Stunned by these dastardly acts combined with the utter lack of civility deepened vows of revenge.

There was the matter of the kidnapped wives and children. His brother's wife, Saisha, and his two children were of royal blood, members of the ruling family of the Shore People kingdom. In Rishaan's delusional mind, he believed their elevated status of royalty accorded them privileged status. A large ransom negotiated with their captors would secure their release in due time.

Rishaan had never been more angry or inconsolable in his life. Dying in battle in protection of the homeland was an honorable way to die. In that case, the cremation service was celebratory as living and dying with honor was of paramount importance and considered the most noble of all deeds. The Shore People believed the good deeds you performed when living within a physical body determined a person's standing in the spiritual world.

Rishaan told Ekavir and Harnish, his most important military leaders, to construct a war strategy to destroy the Horse Warriors and to find the "hostages" and secure their safe return. It did not occur to Rishaan the captured women and children were not hostages, but as chattel forced into a life under terrible conditions. He could not have known they would treat captured women as the lowest servants, subject to repeated beatings. Worse yet, a horrible fate awaited young girls when they reached reaching the age of thirteen, eligible for "purification" by many warriors, then assigned to the older men who did not have a wife. The female child, named Anya, was twelve, about to turn thirteen.

As for the boys, separation from their families was immediate and contact forbidden with their families. Forced to go through extensive and harsh indoctrination and extreme physical training, the chances of survival for captured boys were low. Those who survived took on the cruelest personality features of the Horse Warriors. Their ultimate test was to kill a captured soldier with their bare hands. If they failed that test of toughness, their unit commander executed them.

Ekavir chose Harnish to lead fifty of the royal guard to depart for the riverbank to find the slain men. Simran, who knew the exact location, would guide them. They had only one mission. Prepare the bodies for cremation and return them to their homes.

PART 21
The Epic Battle Begins

Unfortunately, as predicted, a significant army of Horse Warriors appeared in three days. The strategy was always the same. Surround the city with enough forces to enact a blockade. All movement in or out of Desa ceased. Tension would rise within the city as a few days passed with no additional contact. Then, a lone rider emerged and rode slowly to the gates. Devi immediately recognized Axam and ordered the gates open to allow him to enter.

Gandesh respectfully invited Axam to enjoy some tea with Mandeep and Devi. They sat in a small circle to show inclusion and civility, although the Nivasi were not misguided. Axam had only one reason for his visit.

Gandesh spoke first, "Axam, what do you wish from us? Why did you return with a massive army? We explained on your prior visit we are a peaceful people who treated you kindly and with respect."

Axam did not immediately respond, searching in his mind for some logic which would convince the Nivasi to surrender without bloodshed. "Yes, Gandesh, you were generous and respectful to us. I only wish you had spoken the entire truth."

Gandesh feigned surprise at this accusation. "We have no idea what you mean. We answered truthfully all your questions and allowed you to visit any part of Desa you desired."

Axam deftly responded, "You did not allow full access to the priest's compound. We believe the Varagans are hiding there. If you permit me to search all the woodlands within the property of the priests, the truth which you claim can be verified."

Gandesh, mustering sincerity with tinges of spiritual reverence, declared, "We cannot violate the property of the priests or encroached on their sanctity. Such an intrusion would be sacrilegious, dishonorable, a crass religious insult."

Devi then asked, "Axam, why do you seek to destroy the Varagans?" Axam promptly responded the Varagans were dismissive and insulting of the Horse Warriors and would not surrender. "Also, Jackal, the brother of Pratham, struck me when I appeared before them in their court."

Devi immediately saw the trickery in the way Axam phased the question. Quizzically she asked, "Who is this person, Pratham, whom you speak about?" implying she did not know of the people referenced by Axam.

Axam clarified the identities of Jackal and Pratham asserting, "Of course, you know exactly who these people are." Continuing her game of thinly veiled deception, obvious to both, Devi questioned, "Why is it proper for the Horse Warriors to invade our land if, in fact, the Varagans have fled from their lands leaving you with an excellent prize?"

Axam said, "Because they insulted our leader, Khander, by refusing to surrender and further aggravated the situation by striking me as an emissary which violates the norms of the peoples who live on the vast plains."

Devi pondered for a moment. Axam tried to stay calm and stoic, but Devi noticed a slight amount of perspiration. "Axam, you are saying the noble Horse Warriors who live by a strict code of behavior would attack a peaceful land such as ours and cause the death of hundreds, if not thousands, because of an insult?"

Axam, now a bit flustered, rendered his memorized answer, "Turn over Jackal and Pratham to us and we will spare your city and people from destruction."

Devi parried by saying, "Axam, you know we do not have a military force, so we have no means to compel the surrender of the men you seek, even if they were in our lands. How is it honorable in your culture to kill peaceful people who have never threatened or insulted the mighty Horse Warriors? Your army can search the countryside as you wish but cannot enter this city or the priest's property in the Greenlands."

Axam said the Nivasi had until the next dawn to concede to his demand to search any part of Desa as they wished, including the Greenlands where the priests live. His parting words could not have been more ominous, "When dawn lifts and you have not formally surrendered, we will destroy the city."

Axam reported back to Dhanur every aspect of the discussions. Dhanur brusquely furnished the order, "One hour after dawn, launch the first wave of attack."

Devi convened the War Committee after Axam departed from the city. The initial phase of the defense plan would be initiated in the morning once it was clear the Horse Warriors were launching their offensive. Arian asked Tarak, who was now an integral part of the War Committee, "When can we expect your soldiers to arrive?"

Tarak responded, "Some light cavalry shock troops, numbering about five hundred, will be here in four days." Arian thanked him for the information, as they would require additional cavalry. He only hoped they could sustain the battle by then.

In the evening's calm, Arian and Devi strolled quietly in a secluded path in the Greenlands. Normally, the woods seduced her with beauty and natural scents. Overcome with anxiety, Devi sobbed, "Arian, do you think we have any chance to holdout until the Shore People arrive, if they arrive"?

They stopped and Arian took Devi in his arms and said, "Yes, we can prolong the battle at least four days, perhaps a few days longer. Maybe the Horse Warriors will decide the casualty numbers are too high and withdraw or hold back awaiting reinforcements."

He wanted to believe his own words, but he poorly disguised his doubt. Devi sensed the truth and clutched Arian as tightly as possible. Feeling the palpable tension, he gently kissed her on her neck, then moved to her cheek and her lips. Soothing actions beneficial to both. Pressed together, two bodies intertwined, passion intensifying by the second Devi whispered, "Arian, I want to join with you, but we must wait until our marriage evening."

Arian whispered back his words interrupted by passionate kisses. "We can ask Gandesh to marry us this evening. The war will start tomorrow, and I will lead the first cavalry charge."

It stunned Devi to hear Arian would be in the front lines, thinking the Supreme Commander would not see immediate battle. "Devi, I know what you are thinking, but I must lead the men; it is my duty." Watching from a distance, out of earshot, were two spies beholden to Jackal. Watching the two spies were two Forest Dwellers. Vidya would always assert, "There are no secrets in the forest." Vidya, convinced Devi and Arian of the need for additional protection from the treachery of Pratham and Jackal. The new protector would soon arrive.

Gandesh was happy to perform a brief ceremony witnessed by Mishka and Veer. Then, to the surprise of Arian and Devi, Mishka asked Gandesh to marry Veer and her. Everyone, for the moment, was happy. At least both couples could fully consummate their love and find happiness together, if only for a few hours.

That evening, Devi and Arian spent the happiest hours of their lives. Neither had been content with the world they lived in. A twist of fate had brought them together. For the moment, they did not think of the terrible days which lay ahead. As they slid into bed, each with anticipation and desire, their bodies and spirits joined in the most pleasurable harmony. Time seemed meaningless as the sensual enraptures of the moment, heightened by deep spiritual love, sealed their lives together.

A short distance away, the last preparations for the attack were in place. Dhanur said to his senior officers, "Something is not right. Axam, you say the Nivasi have no army. You say the people look soft. You also say a woman named Devi is the actual leader of the Nivasi. We also know the Varagan army was in tatters. They left behind all their war horses; maybe half their forces are intact, as we know they suffered extensive casualties. Why would the Nivasi defy us?"

The same questions mystified Axam. The Nivasi had nothing to gain by siding with the Varagans. Perhaps some Nivasi were being held as hostages. Could it be this abstract sense of freedom and a naïve hope the Horse Warriors would honor their nonviolent values?

Axam slowly edged his way around the room, contemplating these questions, mulling in his mind some deeper explanation, "It is true the Nivasi claim their culture does not permit violence, but they are hiding the Varagans for reasons we do not understand. We cannot assume they are being compromised by hostages as there are no royal families in Desa. They would have to hold all the peoples as hostages! Devi is extremely savvy. She would have found means to signal that information to me, if true. They would welcome us as their saviors."

The senior officers listened intently, unsure of the direction Axam was taking with his logic. Axam continued, "There can only be one answer. The Nivasi have some military capabilities. They allied with the Varagans, believing we are the greater threat, as we would enslave them as vassals. We should attack with one full legion of 1,000 men and a full complement of archers, as I suspect they will not give up easily."

Dhanur concurred with this assessment primarily as he thought of his brother Axam as a strategy genius. Axam was not only a strategy genius, but he was skilled in the psychology of people, possessing keen powers of observation. No detail was too small to assess. As a boy, an old man, a wise former celebrated warrior, mentored him. One day, the mentor said, "Axam, you have excelled in military skills, but now you must learn the true lessons of life. We will walk in the woodlands and observe the hawks. The old man chose the hawk, especially the golden hawk, as they were fierce and intelligent hunters.

Axam and the old man walked and walked, occasionally the old man would stop and listen. Axam tried to speak, but the old man told him not to utter a word. They continued for hours spotting many birds of prey, but the old man just shook his head and said,

"Keep walking and do not say a word". Axam was tiring and grew very thirsty, but the old man kept walking and stopping. Axam thought to himself, the old man is lost, as each time they stopped, he lifted his nose and sniffed the air. Then they stopped and were still for a long time.

The old man then asked Axam, "What do you see?" Axam answered with a tone of slight irritation, "I see a hawk."

The old man looked contemptuously at Axam and repeated, "What do you see?" Confused, Axam hesitated, "I see a hawk sitting on a branch on a tree."

Slowly the old man grabbed Axam by the neck, squeezing tightly. It shocked Axam to feel the strength in the man's hands. The old man firmly repeated, "What do you see?"

Axam said, "I see a golden hawk surveying the surroundings from a short branch near the top of the tree. I see his talons firmly gripping the branch." Axam felt confident he finally satisfied the old man, but, unexpectedly, the old man struck him to the ground, angrily repeating, "What do you see?"

Dazed and bleeding from his nose with blood streaming down his face, Axam stood slowly to regain his composure, his mind now emptied of any extraneous thoughts, only the sharp image of the hawk pervading every part of his mind, "I see a warrior preparing for battle. I see the golden hawk observing every detail of the sky, every rustling of the grasses and bushes, detecting any slight movements. I see the neck of the hawk, tension rising, the only actual sign of an imminent attack. I perceive the spirit of a superb hunter who pursues his objective relentlessly. I am witness to a patient, majestic warrior who attacks only when the timing is perfect. I see I am a humble, stupid boy who knows nothing about the ways of the true warrior."

The old man said, "You see well."

PART 22
Day One of the Battle

The rising sun was just a sliver of itself, slowly climbing to occupy its rightful place in the sky, casting away darkness. The Horse Warriors judged the most opportune time for attack was with the sun to their backs. They recognized how the glare of the sun and the angle of its rays presented an advantage. They choreographed everything. Time and time again, the Horse Warriors succeeded in battle, often against overwhelming odds. The unit commanders instructed their men to visualize the enemy as demons. "You must summon all your strength and energy", they would say, warning against any complacency.

The typical attack pattern was to launch a foray with five hundred mounted warriors armed with short, highly flexible bows designed for quick release at a short distance. Then they would retreat, expecting the enemy to counterattack. True to script, five hundred warriors slowly approached the city over short rolling hills which were not ideal for battle tactics. As the horses used were short and squat in build, with strong hooves suitable for any terrain, these rolling hills were no impediment. However, such terrain offered perfect spots to hide enemy archers. Arrayed against them were about the same number of Nivasi mounted warriors.

Unsurprised as Axam had concluded, the "Nivasi" would, in fact, consist mostly of Varagan warriors. Their horses of a larger size were a different breed which Axam thought would be a disadvantage when battle favored speed and agility.

The Nivasi arrayed foot soldiers in odd patterns not usually observed in these types of military engagements. Dhanur rode next to Axam and commented," A very unusual arrangement of fighters. What do you think?"

Axam, pondering the situation, did not immediately answer. "Let's lure them out." They gave the order for a limited attack with three hundred men.

Even three hundred mounted warriors attacking at top speed is a chilling sight. As they got closer, the Nivasi forces drew to the left and right, occupying flank positions. Two hundred archers appeared with their new recurved, composite bows which allowed a longer, more potent shot. The command, "breathe, pause, focus, steady, hold, hold, hold" repeated. The attacking forces kept coming, determined to destroy the motley group.

Mishka was right in the center. She was issuing the commands. Some men were sweating profusely, the tensions in their bodies so intense their arms were shaking; but not Mishka. She was enjoying every second. The Horse Warriors neared closer and closer, now about 100 yards away, then fifty, sparking the right time. "Now", shouted Mishka. They released three hundred arrows in unison. Unlike the typical pattern in which flights of arrows would fill the sky, landing randomly among the targets, these arrows aimed for each charging rider as if each of the Elite fighters had their own personal target.

The defending archers struck over one hundred Horse Warriors in the first volley, their leather protection of little value as these arrows were heavier and more impactful being released from the recurved, composite bows. The first archer line dropped flat on the ground and the second line appeared, immediately firing off a second wave striking another fifty Horse Warriors. Most of the attacking force suffered direct hits in the chest with such force they rocked back off their horses, falling in the dust.

At this point, the Varagan cavalry led by Arian and Veer launched their counterattack from both flanks. The remaining Horse Warriors retreated while a fresh legion of 1,000 men prepared to shut the trap on the attacking Varagans. In the meantime, Nivasi men collected any riderless horses now scattered around the battlefield. Wounded Horse Warriors left on the battlefield felt the cold steel of the Varagan swords pierce their necks The attacking Varagans halted their counterattack within five hundred yards, knowing full well what the Horse Warriors would do next.

The elite archers ran to a series of rises to occupy two lines arrayed on each flank. The Varagans retreated, stopping one hundred yards in front of the archers, now flat on their stomachs. Sure enough, the Horse Warriors attacked with 1,000 warriors, a frightening sight assured to demoralize most soldiers. The attacking forces closing rapidly to within three hundred yards of the archer's line. Suddenly, a long volley of unexpected arrows blunted their attack.

This was a complete shock to the Horse Warriors, as they had no experience or knowledge of these powerful bows. Arrows were coming from their left and right flanks with uncanny accuracy. Horse Warriors were dropping everywhere. Then the second line of elite archers launched their arrows, halting the counterattack. Dhanur had seen enough; he called for a halt to regroup. The Horse Warriors withdrew a sufficient distance to regroup and treat their injured.

The archers sprinted back into the city and into the neighboring woodlands, as did the Varagan cavalry. The battlefield was quiet. Incredibly, no Varagan or Nivasi suffered any fatalities. Arian estimated the Horse Warriors lost at least two to three hundred men, which under any conditions would be a shock. Equally important, the Nivasi captured over fifty horses herded to the walled compound. Four hours had elapsed, and high noon was approaching, so Dhanur ended the attacks for the day. He and Axam, bloodied from the day's engagement, had gravely underestimated the Nivasi and the Varagans.

The Nivasi and Varagans were pleased. Day one had been good. Day two would be a lot more challenging. Arian thought to himself, *Another day to live, another day with Devi.*

That evening, the War Committee convened to plot their next

steps. The course of the battle overjoyed everyone except Arian and Veer. They were cautious, knowing Axam and Dhanur would work straight through the night to adopt a new strategy. Arian counseled, "Yes, it was a good day, but the Horse Warriors will assess today's battle in excruciating detail. They will not make the same mistakes. In fact, they are even more dangerous!"

A few miles away, Dhanur, Axam and the senior commanders were doing exactly as Arian had described. Axam realized the Nivasi had a new bow construction much more powerful allowing longer arrow flights with greater piercing power. Many Horse Warriors suffered lethal wounds, the leather chest protection failing to stop these new, more potent arrows. In addition, the Nivasi archer tactics were very impressive and novel, clearly more deadly as each archer seemed to have their own dedicated target. Axam outlined a new set of battle tactics which would "change the game".

Earlier in the afternoon, Arian and Veer had examined the agitated horses captured from the Horse Warriors. Naturally, these fine war animals wandered restlessly in their fenced pens. Arian selected one of the finest, no doubt ridden by a unit commander killed in the morning conflict. Arian was very skilled around war horses, knowing it would take a long time to seduce these horses to permit a strange rider to mount it. War horses and riders trained together and remained bound by smell, touch, sound, and personality.

Some believed the loyalty between the warrior and his horse was so strong no foreign person could even mount them. The Horse Warriors considered losing horses in battle such a terrible loss Khander would say a war horse is more valuable and majestic than the human rider and more difficult to replace.

As Arian slowly approached, the horse reared up, refusing contact. Arian did not mount him, knowing such an attempt would be futile and counterproductive. Arian offered some hay, gently stroked the horse's side, careful to touch just in one spot, speaking in a soothing voice. Arian named him Chatresh, implying the horse was more of a divinity than an animal. He softly repeated his name, Chatresh, over and over, gently stroking the horse and offering handfuls of hay. After a short while, Arian withdrew slowly, walking backwards, still facing Chatresh. Soon, he would come to love Chatresh, second only to Devi.

PART 23
Day Two Battle Surprises

Arian woke early, well before dawn. He walked over to the Greenlands to pay his morning visit to Chatresh. Arian spotted him in the corral's corner. Arian expected little a change from yesterday, but he could hope. Chatresh was a veteran of many battles and still beholden to his former master. The traditional method of domesticating a wild horse was to show control and domination of the horse, essentially a test of wills. Arian grasped this method would fail, as Chatresh would never bend to another rider's will.

Gingerly approaching the war horse, Arian thought to himself, *No, Chatresh, you are too proud and majestic. Patience is the only answer.* Arian would have to settle with feeding and stroking, walking along with Chatresh, using a loosely tied guide rope.

Meanwhile, a hundred miles away, Simran led Harnish and his men to the place of the slaughter. They found several shallow graves, partially exposed with arms and legs chewed down to bones with scantily hanging flesh. What the animals and vultures had not eaten was now the purview of insects crawling on the bodies inside every crevice. Most disturbing to the Shore People were the hollow cavities of the eyes, now crawling with maggots. Even the most battle-hardened fighters vomited at the sight of the dead, nearly desecrated beyond recognition. They wrapped each body inside funeral cloths and repeatedly applied tight layers to control the stench for the journey back home.

Hours before, in the deep darkness of a cloudy night, hundreds of Horse Warrior archers were creeping forward, moving on their stomachs across the rolling plains. A mass of two hundred archers, positioned in multiple formations, were ready. Time for stillness, time for meditation, as no Horse Warrior would ever enter battle without completing a ritualistic meditation routine. They could lie in place for days with only a small amount of water for nourishment.

Shortly after dawn, the Nivasi and Varagans occupied similar positions as the day before. However, the attack maneuvers would be vastly different. Axam would not repeat the same disastrous tactics again. Mass attacks would not work as the Nivasi and Varagans had too many archers with superior bows. Axam was certain this morning would hold surprises for the enemy forces.

Arian arrayed his forces, mimicking the same defensive pattern as the day before. He also assigned a force of fifty archers to supplement the various entry points into the Greenlands. Arian would protect even the narrowest path. The major road into the Greenlands leading to the walled compound was most heavily fortified. Arian correctly judged that today would not be the epic battle of the war. "Today, the Horse warriors will seek to intimidate us", he said to Veer. "They will inflict casualties as a psychological blow."

The Horse Warriors appeared over the horizon, a low-level dust cloud gently rising as they walked their mounts slowly forward. Veer estimated the number to be about five hundred. "We can handle five hundred", opined Veer. "They do not know the correct size of our force so they will continue their attack ruse, mainly to probe our forces."

Arian said, "You are right, hold back the lancers and half the mounted fighters."

The Horse Warriors were getting within range of the archers deployed in clusters to increase the intensity of the volley. Today, the long bows would increase the range, although with reduced accuracy. The Horse Warriors closed within five hundred yards, at which point Mishka's archers launched a wave of arrows, hundreds in number, an orchestrated movement of beauty, then descending like a massive hailstorm into a flight of death.

Concurrently, over two hundred arrows filled the sky headed directly toward the Nivasi and Varagans. The Horse Warriors had hidden many archers in the tall grasses; now it was their time to wreak havoc. One of the most terrifying scenes of battle unfolded on both sides. The arrows crossed each other in flight, a few even colliding as two waves of arrows sailed past each other. The arrows would strike in clusters, but the random nature of the launch technique meant everybody, and everything was a target. The Nivasi and Varagan forces carried the heavier shields which would help deflect some arrows, but many landed with such direct impact a shield would not save the victim.

Arrows rained down on Arian and his men. Dozens of fighters suffered mortal wounds to their chests, often to their heads. They struck some looking upwards in their eyes; cries of pain and death erupted everywhere. Random arrow struck the horses, causing them to stampede. An arrow struck Veer in his arm, another Arian on his left wrist, the arrow piercing through his wrist like a carpenter's nail. Arian and Veer stayed upright and awaited the charge of the Horse Warriors.

The Horse Warriors and foot archers suffered as well, incurring countless numbers of mortal strikes and severe injuries. This time, the horses suffered terrifying wounds which added to the confusion. The wounded lay strewn on both sides of the battle lines. Horses shrieked in pain. The wounded Horse Warriors tried to muzzle their pain, but some injuries were so painful even the most disciplined warriors expelled uncontrollable cries.

On the Nivasi side, the casualty rate was extreme as the Horse Warrior archers launched a second wave which caused absolute panic among the Nivasi who were now experiencing war for the first time. Mishka emerged unhurt, which was good fortune, as arrows pierced about half the defensive forces. In a space of a few hours, one hundred thirty-six Nivasi and Varagan fighters died while another ninety suffered crippling injuries.

The Horse Warriors regrouped and attacked. The Varagan's well-trained cavalry regained formation. Mishka regrouped a mass of archers who steadied their nerves. The archers, splattered with blood from human and equine sources, fixated on Mishka's commands. She gave the order at a slow pace, "Pause, breathe, focus, aim, launch!" Another hundred arrows headed right into the center of the attacking Horse Warriors.

Seconds later, the two armies clashed in hand-to-hand combat. Both Veer and Arian fought like tigers, no thought other than to strike, bob, weave, strike. Swords slashed at arms and necks. A unit commander of the Horse Warriors spotted Arian and headed toward him. Their eyes met first, then the clash of swords. Arian struck first, slicing off two fingers of his opponent. Then it was Arian's turn to suffer a blow which he partially deflected with his arm. He felt the pain in his left arm and saw the blood spurt; even more focused, he drove his sword into the neck of the unit commander, his eyes and mouth squirting blood and phlegm from the force of the blow.

Both sides wheeled back. The Horse Warriors heard the horns signaling to retreat to their lines. Dhanur had seen enough for the day. *A much better result than yesterday*, he thought. *I must admit the tenacity and bravery of his foe deserved admiration.* Normally, Dhanur held his opponents in contempt.

The Varagan forces retreated to the city gates. The worst news awaited Arian. Manbir among the most celebrated Varagan warriors and a senior leader of the Elite Force was dead. The casualty rate was stunning. Over two hundred men and a few women of the Elite Force were dead or gravely wounded and incapable of further combat. Arian's multiple injuries shocked Devi. She muttered to herself, *How is it possible for Arian to persevere with a severely damaged wrist and a slash wound to his arm?*

Arian with his wounds wrapped returned to the corral. Chatresh slowly approached him, sniffing the wounds. He rubbed up against Arian, seeming to say, "So, you are a noble warrior." Both walked aside each other, gently stroking mixed with soothing words from Arian. And, of course, some hay for Chatresh.

Veer's wound was not as bad as feared as the major arteries were not directly hit. However, bone damage was substantial, meaning he would fight in tremendous pain. Mishka did her best to bind the wound and to give some local remedies for the pain. Similarly, Arian's condition was about the same, recoverable if infection did not set in. It was not unusual for the use of human or equine feces-tipped arrows. Therefore, it was vital the wound was completely clean the wound and applied with special medicines. They summoned Vidya to apply a paste made from honey and ghee, fortified with barley and designated herbs. All the wounded fighters received this treatment as it was common for the Forest Dwellers to have ample stocks of the materials required to make such a paste.

The mood at the War Committee was grim, a huge change from the evening before. Devi addressed the group saying, "Our forces suffered many losses today, but we still have freedom. More Nivasi want to volunteer in any way possible. Our dead are being buried, and the wounded treated. Hundreds of women from both the Nivasi and Varagans are joining in work groups to make more arrows, shields, leather chest coverings and bandages. The Forest Dwellers have mobilized their forces to make honey paste to treat the wounds and bark scrapings for pain relief. In addition, Vidya has a group of nearly two hundred skilled fighters, both men and women, ready for combat."

Mishka reported of the 1,000 elite fighters, about 700 remained combat capable. Samarth counted 174 Varagan mounted fighters as either dead or gravely wounded. In addition, several hundred suffered wounds of some fashion but could continue to fight. Mishka then spoke of the warring spirit of Manbir, the finest Varagan elite fighter slain in today's battle. Both the Nivasi and the Varagans held him up as a hero, a warrior deserving emulation.

Then, Mishka announced Lajita, one of the Nivasi female members of the Elite Force, had succumbed to her wounds. There was a gasp in the room as everyone was aware of how this quiet woman, named for her modesty, had risen to become one of the most skilled archers. Lajita was the first woman of either peoples to die as a soldier in combat. Many generations in the future would respect her name, given to many female babies in the years to come.

In her heart, Devi mourned, shocked in just two hours of battle, Arian had suffered such terrible injuries; all of this to protect Pratham and Jackal, two depraved cowards who were far from the battlefield. She corrected herself. *This is not about those two men; this is about the freedom of people to live without the threat of tyranny.*

In the Horse Warrior camp, there was no talk of casualties, no discussion of freedom. The Horse Warriors lived for one purpose, their destiny and fate to rule over all peoples according to their laws and command of Khander. Whereas it was true, the Horse Warriors did not repress the chosen religion of the conquered peoples. It was also clear these people had no choice but to submit, in any way Khander required, as he was their new god and supreme ruler. And on these two fateful days, many of these former conquered warriors met their ancestors in the divine world of spirits.

Dhanur smiled at his brother Axam, saying the day had been successful as the enemy now understood the meaning of death at the hands of the Horse Warriors. Axam's response was plain enough and neutral in tone, "Dhanur, I suggest you send messengers to Khander to request two additional legions."

Dhanur's smile eroded to a glare, saying, "That would amount to an admission of failure. With four legions, 4,000 supreme warriors, I will crush the Varagans and any enablers. I will do my duty. You do your duty."

Axam was clever enough not to show any subtle signs of disagreement. "My lord, it was foolish of me to even suggest such defeatism." Both knew the use of the title "lord" meant submission to the will of a superior, even though both were brothers. They discussed the tactics of the next day as Axam's "foolish" words evaporated like wisps of smoke from a nightly campfire.

PART 24
Day 3 of the Battle: Revenge of The Woodlands

Arian awoke in terrible pain as the day following battle injuries were always the worst. With the adrenalin long dissipated, the throbbing pain of the injuries increased in intensity. At least his right arm was healthy and usable, but his left arm from wrist to shoulder required tight bandages, causing some immobility. He walked over to the corral to visit Chatresh, whose ears suddenly pricked forward upon glimpsing Arian. Arian wondered, is Chatresh excited to see him, maybe only in anticipation of his morning breakfast? After feeding, he ambled alongside Chatresh, who willingly proceeded without hesitation. Arian ruminated the question, would Chatresh accept Arian as a mount? Chatresh had already permitted Arian to stroke any part of the horse's body.

He stood in front of Chatresh, gently stroking his head, softly asking, "Do you want me to ride you?" Tuned to the sounds of horses but still wary as Arian understood pedigree war horses were different. They know they are superior and want the world to know as well. Arian looked for any sign. Was Chatresh neighing? Did Arian detect a deep sigh? Chatresh started inhaling quickly, puffing out the air. "Perfect, Chatresh, you want to go out of the corral."

He carefully mounted Chatresh, who was a bit nervous as the body and smells of Arian were different. Arian convinced himself Chatresh was honoring him by saying, "You are worthy." It did not take long; soon, horse and rider were one.

Arian arranged his forces in a distinct pattern so that any flight of arrows could be better blunted. He also re-enforced the number of elite fighters in the woodlands, convinced the Horse Warriors would probe multiple entry points around the City. The first two days of battle had taken place in this area. To the west and southwest lay the woodlands, including the Greenlands. Due to the devastating attack of the enemy archers, Axam worried the lack of war horses would hinder his capability to launch attacks. A top priority was the recapture of the horses lost to the Nivasi in the first day of fighting.

He convinced Dhanur to open multiple attack fronts, hoping to splinter the defending forces and capture the compound in the Greenlands. Three separate coordinated attacks would take place, but first he thought it wise to send his scouts into the woodlands. He had to be sure no traps awaited them. An hour before dawn, the Horse Warrior scouts were in position at multiple entry points on the edge of the woodlands. Shortly after dawn, the Horse Warrior scouts carefully and methodically entered the woods in five designated spots, including a major path leading directly to the priest's compound where they believed the captured horses were being held.

Each scout carried a short sword, more like a long knife and a short bow ideal for quick arrow release. These scouts proceeded cautiously, needing to ensure they remained undiscovered. The leader of one group of ten, skulking in a dense area of the woodlands where the paths were narrow and covered with vines, suddenly cried out in muted pain. Then a second man near the back suffered the same fate. King cobra snakes had bitten both. They fell to the ground, exhibiting all the telltale signs of a fatal snake bite. The men trapped in the middle panicked as they may not have feared human enemies, but they considered snakes a deadly evil, a terrible omen for people susceptible to superstition. The two victims were writhing in pain, their bodies contorted by uncontrollable muscle spasms. Within five minutes, the snake venom paralyzed their faces in a horrific pose, their eyes glassy and cloudy.

The remaining eight men froze, not so much in fear but more in confusion. Their duty was to carry the mortally wounded warriors back to the camp. They did not spot any enemy fighters, so the Horse Warrior scouts concluded the snake attack was just an unfortunate act of nature. They failed to imagine the king cobras were one of the myriad weapons the Forest Dwellers unleashed on intruders. Hundreds of eyes watched every move of the marching forces; the Horse Warriors saw nothing unusual. Each of the scout forces reported back to Dhanur and Axam they found no enemy defenders. Only the unfortunate snake attack marred the morning probes.

It delighted Dhanur to hear these reports. Axam was not smiling. Like words not spoken but whose absence speak to the skilled listener, the lack of enemy sighting also spoke to him; it was a bad sign. Also, Dhanur was not interested in the unfortunate snake incident, but Axam asked many questions. Axam recognized snakes are shy and will normally retreat at the sounds or vibrations of the earth. The scouts were sure they had disturbed no bushes on the side of the path. If the mounted warriors did not disturb the snakes in their nests; something else motivated them to attack.

Dhanur remained convinced a large attack force could successfully occupy the woodlands which would threaten the Nivasi and Varagans on multiple fronts. He directed a force of 500 men to invade the woodlands and seize the compound. Little did they realize that a successful capture of the compound would yield a greater prize, Pratham himself. They selected three different entry points. Only mounted warriors, numbering 300, would invade via the main road, whereas 200 soldiers on foot would invade via two other smaller paths.

All three forces entered on command and within thirty minutes were deep into the heavily forested part of the woodlands. Each group preceded by scouts tasked to signal danger of traps. Meanwhile, another force of Horse Warriors guarded each entry point to protect the rear from attack. Dhanur also gave the order for 1,000 mounted Horse Warriors to inch forward toward the Nivasi and Varagan forces. The Horse Warrior force slowly appeared on the horizon, an ominous sight to any opponent, no matter how courageous. Axam kept his forces out of range of the long bows. The primary aim was to distract the defenders, forcing them to maintain a substantial defensive force to prevent deployment to the woodlands.

The main attacking force was nearing the open space of the compound when a loud rumbling shook the ground. The horses of the attackers showed the first signs of anxiety. They sensed these loud rumblings were natural sounds of other dangerous animals.

The noise got louder; all the Horse Warriors halted and deployed their weapons. The war elephants appeared with mounted warriors with long spears. The elephants would dominate the horses through sheer size and the height advantage and long spears of the mounted warriors would easily out match the mounted Horse Warrior. Plus, there was not sufficient room for the Horse Warriors maneuverability. They squeezed twenty Horse Warriors across the road, limiting defensive tactics.

Copper adorned plates covered the elephants, so thick as to be impenetrable to enemy arrows. The Horse Warriors launched a wave of arrows, wounding only one elephant. The rest rumbled on, well trained to attack with no regard for fear. The first set of elephants smashed through the front wall of mounted Horse Warriors, creating massive disruption as the horses reared up and wheeled around from sheer fright. The long spears carried by the elephant warriors stabbed the mounted Horse Warriors. A spear thrust through enemy neck was most effective, as the spear quickly jabbed and retracted. Some elephant warriors struck the opponent's stomachs, a death blow which sometimes caused the spear to get stuck. A few fighters fell off their horses with long spears stuck upright in their stomachs, an odd sight as they lay dead on the ground.

Simultaneously, an array of arrows from a myriad of trees and bushes struck many Horse Warriors in the middle of the ranks and near the back of the invasion force. The Horse Warriors responded with their own arrow launch, but most of the arrows struck trees or empty ground behind bushes. The Forest Dwellers were invisible.

They had slinked behind many bushes and positioned high in the trees, a complete surprise to the Horse Warriors. There were at least fifty women fighters who were as adept as their male counterparts in archery and tree climbing.

One of the unit commanders realized the high trees were harboring attackers. As he gazed up, a well-aimed arrow penetrated the left side of his cheek, protruding through the other side of his face, creating a bizarre image of a man with an arrow perpendicular to the vertical shape of his face. High in the trees, the slight smile of a female archer was undetectable.

Meanwhile, along one of the other narrow roads, the fate of the Horse Warriors was no better. They strung the marching fighters out in a long line with men positioned two abreast. At the point where the road narrowed the most, the unit commander halted his men. He was shrewd enough to realize narrowing roads were a tremendous disadvantage for his men. He sent twenty-five men down the road to ensure the road was safe.

These men had only marched ten steps when a huge net dropped across the roadway. It was a double hexagonal design, imitating the intricate design of a spider web. Like certain silk strands on a spider web, the hemp strands of this net slathered with a very sticky substance made penetrating exceedingly difficult. A torrent of arrows launched, striking Horse Warriors in sizable numbers. Another disaster ensued as a net of equal size and complexity dropped near the back. The Horse Warriors realized it trapped them!

Horse Warriors tried to slice openings in the net, but their swords quickly became stuck in the sticky strands. Other fighters struck with arrows fell into the net, making an escape even more challenging. Just as it appeared hopeless for the trapped fighters, a Nivasi emissary appeared unarmed, wearing all white, the sign for negotiations. The Horse Warriors counted twenty-two dead and more wounded, but surrender was not thinkable for these men. Arian had warned against taking prisoners, but the Nivasi could not stomach the idea of slaughtering all the men. "We will never surrender", yelled the force commander.

The Nivasi emissary disappeared into the woods. Another volley of arrows filled the air, each foot soldier a target. The Horse Warrior commander who just a minute before had defiantly rejected negotiations now lay dead on the ground, a gruesome sight as an arrow was protruding from his neck causing a gurgling sound as blood poured out. The reality of ten more dead and gravely wounded convinced the remaining force to surrender their weapons. The Nivasi emissary reappeared, this time meeting with success. Of the original force of one hundred, only half survived unhurt or with minor injuries.

They instructed the Horse Warriors to discard their weapons and walk one by one through an opening on the side portion of the net. Twenty-five Varagan warriors processed the prisoners. Within seconds, another hundred well-armed Forest Dwellers emerged from the woods, encircling the captured warriors. A couple of foolishly brave Horse Warriors attempted to attack, pulling short knives from their back vests. The fully armed Varagans immediately slew them. No other captured fighters repeated that foolish act of defiance.

By noon, the only action had been in the woodlands, which proved to be disastrous for the Horse Warriors. The attack of the elephants had blunted the major force. In disarray, the Horse Warriors retreated, suffering casualties all the way back to the open prairies by hidden archers firing from camouflaged sites. Every tree, every bush seemed to hide an archer. An unlucky number of the Forest Dwellers lost their lives, but fatalities were less than ten.

Dhanur was furious with the results of day three. The enemy killed or captured one entire unit of 300 men, their fate unknown. The other unit of 100 men trekked around the outer woodlands accomplishing nothing for their efforts. The reports shocked Dhanur. The major force retreated because of an attack of elephants! He angrily sent messengers back to the river to inform the remaining legion of heavy cavalry to cross the river as soon as possible. Dhanur concluded he needed an overwhelming attack force, even if casualties would be high. In the meantime, he would isolate the city of Desa, enforcing a strict quarantine.

The outcome of the day relieved Devi. Arian did not have to engage in battle, providing another day to ease the pain. When Arian arrived at his home, he greeted Devi, who was sitting next to Vidya. Between them lay a hefty dog, mainly white but with a striking splash of black surrounding one of his eyes. Vidya jumped up to greet Arian. Arian was quick to hug Vidya, congratulating him on his magnificent victories in the woodlands.

Vidya thanked Arian but added grimly, "Arian, your life is in grave danger from assassins working for Jackal. We have been tracking their movements. We know Jackal's men have been monitoring you and Devi. I think both of you are in imminent danger. I have brought you a new warrior named Kutta. He is a superior watch dog and fiercely loyal to his masters. He is a gift to you from the Forest Dwellers."

Arian stooped down to pet Kutta. Arian and Devi delighted with a new family addition! Arian kept stroking Kutta's head and rubbing his side. Between Devi, Kutta, and Chatresh, Arian's life was nearly perfect. The birth of a child would complete the circle of perfection. He did not consider the imminent dangers of war, the quest for raw survival, ignoring death in battle as an option. Another danger threatened; he thought, *I have neglected to consider my real enemies*. He fell asleep thinking of how to exact revenge on Jackal.

PART 25
Saisha's Terrible Dilemma

~~~~~

Every night was the same for Saisha, marked with streaming tears of deep sadness on her face. Captured by the Horse Warrior Assassins over two weeks ago, vivid memories of her dead husband, Kalpit, were never absent from her thoughts. She had not seen her son, Jai, or her daughter, Anya, since that horrible morning. The vision of her screaming kids forcibly separated haunted her day and night. Dhanur assigned her to the household of Balvan, an older former unit commander whose fighting days had long passed. Balvan was in his late 60s and still in good health despite nagging injuries which would never leave his body. He lived with his loyal wife, impaired by a breathing affliction, her days winding down like an afternoon sun, slowing sinking to a predictable end.

This night was different. Shortly before dawn, Saisha felt the chilly edge of a knife on her throat. Startled, she heard Balvan say as he leaned over her, "Do not make a sound." Terrified, but not confused, she resigned herself to her fate. Slowly, Balvan used his knife to slit an opening in her nightshirt. She tried not to scream or cry but could not control her trembling. "Lie still", Balvan ordered, "or your life will end right now." She thought of her children, not freedom, or her own life, as she had given up hope of ever returning to her homeland.

She forced herself to lie still. As he clumsily forced himself on her, she drifted into a trance. Her spirit floated above her body. She felt nothing, only hearing the grunts of her rapist, her mind far away. The ordeal did not last long. Within seconds, he slid off her, not sure what would happen next. Balvan understood he had just violated the laws of the Horse Warriors, which did not permit the joining of a man with any woman except his wife. Saisha did not realize her status as a house servant did not empower Balvan to rape her at will.

Balvan, betraying guilt and a bit of shame, said, "Saisha, you must not speak a word about this, or they will take you from this household. We have treated you well and have spared you from beatings, which are normal for servant women, not of our people."

Yes, she thought to herself, *This is true*. Finally, she said, "What do you want of me?"

His answer shocked her. Balvan said, "I want you to submit willingly to me."

Saisha was an astute woman. The picture became clearer in her mind. She was thirty years younger, endowed with desirable features; she had to reorient her thinking. If she resisted, the nightly rape would continue; her risk of violence increasing. She had an over-riding aim. "Balvan, I will willingly submit to you and keep silent about your passions until the passing of your wife if you do two things for me."

Balvan's mood lifted, asking, "What do you desire?"

"You must bring Anya to live with us under my care and promise never to touch her. She is approaching her first days of womanhood, yet she is still so young. Also, I want Jai released from the army."

Balvan reflected for a moment and responded, "Jai will become an equal member of the fighting force once he completes training and passes his last test. I cannot alter his fate." He was careful not to give any hint as to the meaning of the 'final test'.

"As to your daughter, she is being secluded from any men, as her woman guardian has not confirmed her passage into womanhood. No man can take her until her guardian releases her. I am a former senior unit commander with much influence and will seek custody of your daughter."

Saisha smiled to herself, realizing she had some womanly leverage over Balvan. A slight shimmmer of optimism diluted her dense pale of sadness, fueled by the thought of being reunited with Anya. She faced a dilemma. If she sacrificed her dignity and honor by being the concubine of Balvan, it would reunite her daughter Anya with her, sparing her from the ravages of men lusting for a young girl. Saisha quickly concluded with her husband dead, murdered by these savages, she had to survive by any means and protect her daughter. Saisha softly said, barely a whisper, "Bring me my daughter Anya and I will share my bed with you and maintain absolute silence."

Concurrently in Desa, another set of evil deeds was about to occur. Three men crept silently through the city, approaching the intended target. Jackal had waited for this moment for years, as he had always hated Arian for no reason other than insane jealousy. He convinced himself he was serving the best interests of his brother, Pratham, but his logic made no sense as it was Arian, not the slimy coward, Jackal, who risked his life on the front lines.

His spies had monitored Arian for several days, preparing their plans. Jackal was so sure of success, that he wanted the pleasure of slicing the throat of Arian. Of course, they would murder Devi to eliminate any witnesses. In addition, in his own mind, Jackal had added Devi to his list of people marked for elimination. His capacity for hate was unbounded. The Nivasi would blame agents of the Horse Warriors as Jackal planned to leave obvious clues pointing to them.

As usual, the Varagan killers were unaware they were being watched by Vidya and two other Forest Dwellers, men moving stealthily, hidden by fluctuating shades of moonlight, created by passing clouds. The Varagan assassins quietly entered the dwelling, cautiously moving into the night room where the victims slept. Arian, who always slept with a long knife at his side, imperceptibly grasped the handle as he heard Kutta's growl increase in tone. Just as the assassins attempted to launch their attack, Kutta leaped on Jackal, tearing at his throat, viciously ripping flesh. Jackal screamed in pain, not expecting the sharp teeth of a ferocious dog in his throat.

Arian drove his knife into the chest of a second assassin, swiftly shifting the knife to the man's throat to ensure the deed was complete.

Two Forest Dwellers entered and seized the third assassin, slicing his face with several knife strokes, sufficient to cause pain, but not death. His purpose shifting from assassin to witness. Bleeding profusely and dazed, the Forest Dwellers used cloth bandages to cover both his eyes, halting the flow of blood, further rendering the man helpless.

Devi had rolled out of bed, falling to the floor, sliding away as quickly as possible, staying down until out of the room. Arian firmly warned her, "Devi, do not defend yourself as the well-trained assassins will be ruthless in their mission." He instructed her to escape through the side entrance, which was not visible to people outside the house.

Jackal was screaming on the floor as Kutta had bitten off one of his ears, leaving a bloody stump of mangled flesh. Arian, unsure whether to kill Jackal or take him prisoner, called off Kutta, now controlled by one of the Forest Dwellers. Jackal's eyes looked up to Arian, feigning the look of defeat and surrender.

"Arian, I surrender", Jackal muttered slowly, rising both in genuine pain and with an exaggerated pretense of exhaustion. In a quick move, Jackal pulled a small knife from his belt and thrust it toward Arian's neck. Wheeling to his left, Arian's right hand intercepted the blade a mere inch from his neck and certain death, as a major artery would have been deeply lacerated. Arian squeezed Jackal's hand, methodically crushing each finger as Jackal begged him to stop. Jackal screamed, "I surrender, I surrender."

Arian ignored the pathetic, hollow cries of a coward, thinking for the moment how Devi was nearly slain by Jackal and his traitors. He twisted Jackal around out of brute strength and kicked him with his right foot, the blow landing in Jackal's scrotum. Arian then jammed the knife into Jackal's stomach, slowly twisting for maximum pain. In a few minutes, it was quiet except for Kutta, growling and lunging, desperate for another piece of Jackal; any part would do.

Devi appeared and ran to Arian, ignoring the blood and dead bodies strewn around the bedroom. They spoke no words as they hugged for minutes. They were both safe, but the harrowing experience terribly shook Devi. Arian, sweating profusely, was still in a heightened state of violent rage, his attention shifting to the morning showdown with Dhanur's forces.

Pratham would be furious, but the facts of Varagan law were clear. No one, not even the Primary or any of his relatives, could enter a person's home without permission. Under Varagan law, the defender of the home could use any means, including killing the intruder, especially if the intent was to cause harm. Arian decided the inevitable confrontation with Pratham would have to wait. It was time for the morning alignment of both forces in front of the city gates.

As usual, the Nivasi and Varagan fighters assumed their standard defensive positions. Arian and Veer were sure there would be a lull in the offensive while Dhanur and Axam awaited reinforcements. Nivasi scouts had reported seeing a sizeable contingent of riders headed toward the river.

Arian had earlier concluded Dhanur would mass the largest possible attack force and launch a last offensive. Arian and Veer both believed such an attack would eventually succeed. The rest of the day featured small skirmishes aimed at increasing the anxiety of the defenders. In Dhanur's mind, time was on his side as a full blockade would choke off food supplies to the city and another 1,000 fighters would be available.

Satisfied no attack was imminent, Arian returned home, leashed Kutta and headed for the corral. They fed the horses in the morning as usual, but Chatresh was becoming a bit spoiled; he wanted Arian to feed him. No other person would suffice. Chatresh would trust only the hands of Arian. Kutta was used to being around horses, so he offered a few small barks just to let Chatresh know Arian had more than one love.

Arian led Chatresh out of the corral. He cantered slowly, allowing Kutta to run along with them. Arian returned shortly, as he had business with Pratham to attend to. Chatresh was none too happy, as he wanted a lot more action; his days were becoming too boring for a war champion!

The evening War Committee meeting was buzzing with excitement. Ponmudi accompanied Gandesh. Ponmudi earned fame within Desa as an unusually creative man who had invented several innovations in horse-drawn plows, leading to dramatic agricultural yield improvements. Devi invited everyone to walk with Ponmudi and Gandesh to a barn discretely located in a secluded section of Desa City. Ponmudi proudly stood in front of a strange platform contraption, which at first brought some laughter to the Varagans.

The odd construction was a platform on two wheels connected by a long pole called an axle, attached to a horse also through a long pole fixed to the horse by leather straps. Still confused, most of the War Committee did not immediately see the value of the strange cart. Devi, sensing the confusion, said, "Ponmudi, your invention is a war platform, able to carry one warrior to drive the cart and a second warrior with a spear or bow. Is that correct?"

Ponmudi perked up with a quick response, "Yes, Devi, correct." Devi then said, "Gandesh and Ponmudi will now demonstrate how this war cart works."

Everyone filed out of the barn. Devi said, "We call this war cart a chariot". Clearly in charge, Devi directed Ponmudi and Gandesh to step into the chariot, the most immediate task to control the horse and position themselves on the small platform, just big enough for two warriors. Arian watched in amazement as he had no idea Devi led such a project, still not sure whether a foolhardy endeavor or a work of genius. Ponmudi controlled the horse while Gandesh brandished a short composite bow favored for maximum flexibility and accuracy. The chariot started out slowly but soon picked up speed, the horse in a slow gallop. Devi was quite confident in the outcome, as Ponmudi had been practicing with Gandesh for several days.

The twin figures of Gandesh and Ponmudi might not strike fear in the hearts of the enemy, but what came next was nothing short of amazement. The chariot suddenly turned and headed for two straw figures previously arranged in position to imitate enemy fighters. Gandesh fired off two quick arrows, striking each target, and then immediately release a third arrow into a third enemy straw figure a few yards from the first two. The handling skills of Ponmudi and the marksmanship of Gandesh stunned everyone.

Arian, Veer and Mishka looked at each other in unison, realizing the power of this new weapon. A fleet of chariots could wreak havoc on any attacking force. Ponmudi maneuvered the chariot back to the barn, an attendant controlling the horse. Devi, beaming with pride, told the group within five days, they would train twenty-five teams for combat.

Devi showed the War Committee a map she and Gandesh had constructed, illustrating how the chariots would be a new decisive force in battle, providing mobile archers in mass formations with triple the fire power as compared to mounted archers. Devi summarized the advantage succinctly, saying, "The chariot provides the speed and maneuverability of mounted horseman and the firepower of archers in flexible formations."

Arian was extremely proud of Devi and quite impressed with her. He knew she was a political genius, but now he saw her mind was extremely capable of military strategy as well. He hugged her, whispering, "This chariot can alter the course of battle, if we can survive the next five days."

In the camp of the Horse Warriors on the banks of the Great Stars River, the sun was nearing the end of another day, its task completed for the time being. Now, it was the moon's turn for duty. Saisha heard the steps of a person approaching, someone light, as the steps were barely audible. Saisha looked up to see the most beautiful sight in her life; it was Anya in the doorway. Both mother and child sighted each other, first with wariness, then absolute delight, as neither could imagine such a moment of joy. They rushed to hug, smothering each other with tears of happiness and relief.

The mother's instinct took over as Saisha asked Anya, "Are you well? Were you hurt by anyone?"

Anya meekly replied, "No mama. No one mistreated me. My guardian was very protective." Saisha looked over to the doorway, glimpsing Balvan watching her with a mix of empathy and lust.

PART 26
Arian Confronts Pratham

A messenger arrived at Pratham's residence after the deadly intrusion into the home of Arian causing the death of Jackal. Pratham always had his personal guards, either with him or close by. Guards searched the messenger and told him to wait until further notice. The commander of the guards approached Pratham, who was quietly sitting in his garden. "Sir, a messenger is eager to speak with you. He says it is urgent." Annoyed but curious, Pratham reluctantly agreed to see the messenger.

Although prostration was not customary, the bearer of terrible news felt the urge to show the ultimate humility. The messenger bowed but found it difficult to speak any words out of fear for his life. "Speak up", commanded Pratham impatiently; his morning routine disturbed. Glancing behind Pratham, the messenger saw several young women in the garden, scantily dressed.

"Sir, it is my duty to inform you of sad news. Your brother, Jackal, is dead." Pratham thought to himself, *What did the fool do to get himself killed?* Pratham looked up at the trembling messenger and responded, "What happened and who did this to him?"

Arian then appeared, directing everyone to leave. The relieved messenger quickly obeyed the command and darted from the room. The beautiful young female attendants reluctantly departed as well. They would return at another time to vie for the benefits accorded from an old man's passions. Only one loyal guard remained who refused to leave when ordered by Arian. Pratham signaled with his hand that the bodyguard should also leave. Arian waited for

Pratham to speak first. Pratham took the initiative, staring at Arian, asking, "Tell me what happened."

Arian relayed the details of the attack, leaving out some finer points like the bone crushing grips and the last method of death.

"Pratham, Jackal, along with two other assassins entered my home early this morning, an hour before dawn and tried to kill me and my wife, Devi. The Forest Dwellers had warned me Jackal's men had been tracking us for days, waiting for the opportune moment.

They did not know just hours before; I had secured a watchdog who alerted me to their entry. Jackal came at me with a long knife, while the other two tried to kill Devi. Jackal never saw the watchdog's attack, which quickly immobilized him while I fought off the other two assassins with the help of several guards working for Vidya. After we called the watchdog off, Jackal lunged forward, screaming curses. He pulled a small knife from his cloak and tried to stab me. I had no recourse other than to defend myself, which ended in his death. One of the attackers, who survived the ordeal, is outside your chamber."

Pratham hardly responding with any force but more with an air of resignation said, "Bring him in". It surprised Pratham to see the deep gashes on his face reserved for traitors before their execution. "Yes, I know the man. Speak the truth," Pratham commanded. The traitor, judging he was a few hours from execution, corroborated all the details of the event, wisely omitting any details as to Jackal's ultimate death. The testimony was sufficient for Pratham, who dismissed him from the room. "Arian, come, sit over here."

Arian, alone with Pratham, not being sure of his intentions, maintained extreme vigilance. He accepted the invitation to sit beside Pratham, still alert to any treachery. Pratham said, "Arian, how are your wounds today?"

This question shocked Arian, doubting its sincerity. "Much improved, but the pain in my wrist is intense, but we all have to live with pain. The most important point is to keep going, keep fighting."

Pratham seemed to express a bit of guilt, not an emotion natural for him. "Arian, I know you could have saved yourself and Devi by turning me over to the Horse Warriors, but you know the Horse Warriors did not deserve trust to honor any agreements." Arian thought of the broken agreements with the gullible Nivasi. *How ironic for Pratham to speak of trust!*

Arian, without malice, said, "You are our Primary and we owe allegiance to you so the promises of Axam, meant nothing to me."

Shocking admissions from Pratham surprised Arian. "As for my younger brother Jackal, he could be shrewd, but most often his vanity got the best of him. I had to protect him as my brother, but his hatred for you, in view of the injuries and personal sacrifice you are making for all of us, was not worthy of our royal family. I felt he wanted to harm you, but I did not know of his diabolical plot to enter your home with assassins. He also broke one of our fundamental laws by attacking your wife. I have one request. I would like you to spare the life of the prisoner as he is a cousin. He must repent, live in silence and wear the scars of treachery forever." Arian nodded consent.

"I have some important news, which no one else knows. I am going to tell you because I need your help." Arian listed intently. Pratham continued, "I have the illness of the stomach which slowly destroys the body causing a slow, painful death."

Arian knew this disease was a terrible death sentence, reducing victims to a shriveled sack of protruding bones before death mercifully took them. "I am sorry to hear this news", said Arian with empathy.

"Arian, I am going to join the battle against the Horse Warriors and die nobly for my people. You can tell no one of my disease except Amura. He is already knowledgeable of my condition. I require nothing more about Jackal. We will give him an honorable funeral and no one in the clan will know exactly the circumstances of his death other than caused by unknown assailants, possibly Horse Warrior spies. Can I have your trust on this matter?" Arian gave his word, only saying it would honor him to have Pratham fight at his side.

On the battlefield, an eerie false calm settled like morning dew following several days of inaction. Arian and Veer could not determine exactly how many Horse Warriors were still available for battle, but they were sure the number was substantially less, perhaps down as low as 2400 fighters. Less clear was the fact they spotted no lancers on the heavier horses. Axam and Dhanur had dispatched groups of riders back to the Great Stars River, indicating additional forces and supplies were being secured.

Veer advised Arian and Devi saying, "Dhanur failed in his aim for a quick victory and has suffered serious and unpredicted casualties. We inflicted psychological damage to the confidence of the Horse Warriors. You know what this means?"

Arian nodded, "Yes, it means extreme motivation and resolve. Failure only serves to mobilize more fanaticism and determination. We must get help from the Shore People to achieve ultimate victory."

Devi added, "We should send scouts to intercept the forces of the Shore People and convince them to divert sufficient soldiers to the southern banks of the river to prevent additional crossing from the encampment."

For several more days, the battlefields remained calm, because of a self-imposed temporary truce by the Horse Warriors. Dhanur and Axam clearly understood an outright victory with the forces on hand could not succeed, or, if successful, would cause many additional casualties. Khander would be extremely critical of a successful campaign with an unusual number of casualties. He would conclude poor generalship was the primary problem; Dhanur's fate would be a demotion, if fortunate, but outright banishment or execution was more likely.

Days lumbered on, the Horse Warriors waiting for the imminent arrival of reinforcements, primarily the heavy cavalry equipped with long spears and more archers. The Nivasi and Varagan forces waited for a miracle.

PART 27
Rishaan's Dream and Oath of Revenge

❦

For weeks, Rishaan endured the same nightly dream. He is walking alone in the desert, a strange place, far from his home. He is searching for his brother, Kalpit, unsure where to go or where to look. He plods on, increasingly bewildered, an occasional dust swirl momentarily blinding him. Day is falling into darkness. Suddenly, a twisting funnel of wind and dirt lifts him a few feet off the ground and drags Rishaan along, tumbling, pummeled by rocks and debris. Then it is calm; he finds himself in a shallow hole. Dazed and injured, he cannot move. Silence prevails for a few moments, then Rishaan sees his brother's shadowy figure hovering over him. Kalpit is trying to speak to him, but his mouth spews maggots, not words.

Rishaan hears laughing men on horses, mocking him, saying. "Get up old man, you need to finish your grave." Rishaan tries to muster enough strength to rise but stumbles, slumping to a kneeling position. He sees strange men with odd features, wearing strange leather vests. Their faces are dry, brittle, and weather beaten, as if their skin is about to shrivel away. He notices their hands appear grotesquely swollen, faces marked by lacerations, their bodies lean, tight, long muscles shimmering in the twilight.

One man jumps off his horse and strikes Rishaan above his right ear, knocking him flat on his back into the shallow grave. As he slowly drifts into unconsciousness, he hears one of the mounted riders say, "Rishaan, join your dead brother to rot together in the dark universe where the maggots are your rulers. We are the rulers now in this earthly domain, your people subject to our will and bidding."

Rishaan slides to the ridge of a dark, deep pit. Just as his body was about to breach the edge into death, a magnificent hawk of immense proportions snatches him. Rishaan felt long, sharp talons digging deep into his arms; no pain, only salvation as he was lifted away from the darkness.

Sweating profusely, Rishaan awakes and summons Vedant, the senior priest from the nearby monastery and a close adviser. "Vedant, help me escape from this nightmare. Is this dream because of my dead brother who has not been properly cremated?"

Vedant was shrewd enough not to interpret dreams, above all dreams of death. He cautiously advises Rishaan, "Sire, I am not gifted enough to inform you of the meaning of your dream, but there is a mystic who lives at the very southern edge of your kingdom. They say he is more than a human, borne from the sea with dominant skills of intuition."

The idea of a notable mystic intrigued him. "Bring this man to me as soon as possible. What is his name?" Vedant replied, "Sire, he has a strange name. People call him AO."

Later that morning, Harnish arrived with the remains of the men brutally murdered a few weeks earlier. Rishaan greeted the funeral carts at the main city gate. The sight of his dead brother triggering uncontrollable cries of tears as he draped his body on the linen-shrouded corpse. Harnish with lowered eyes out of respect for the grieving ruler simply stated, "Everything the Nivasi told you is true. Simran led us directly to the shallow graves. Also, our scouts detected an extensive encampment across the Great Stars River. We have no information as to Saisha, her two children and her house servant."

Rishaan turned to Harnish, asking, "How many fighters have we deployed so far?"

Harnish responded, "We dispatched a force of 500 light cavalry led by Ekavir several days ago. They should reach Desa tomorrow."

Rishaan quickly commanded, "Harnish, prepare a full invasion force, ready as soon as possible."

The military officers departed, leaving Rishaan alone with his grotesquely decayed brother to begin the mourning and cremation process. Rishaan draped his body over the corpse and swore an oath of revenge: "Kalpit, may your tormented soul find sanctuary and last peace when your ashes blend into the sea whence you came. I swear I will exact revenge upon your killers, their wicked bones crushed into dust, their souls banished to the darkness beneath our feet."

Since Kalpit's body was in a desecrated state, it was vital to begin the cremation service immediately; in fact, they had already built a pyre on the shores of the ocean. Normally, the Shore People would cast the residual ashes into the sea, considered as the source of life for all living creatures. The ashes carried the essence of each person, and absorption into the water was the ultimate act required to release the soul to its natural state.

Revenge of Kalpit's murders remained unaccomplished. Therefore, custom required the storage of Kalpit's ashes in an earthen jar, painted with decorative pictures of various sea creatures, especially the octopus. They buried the funeral jar on land at a depth proscribed by law and would remain buried until completion of the revenge oath.

It was vital to get the bodies of the killers, especially the skull bones, the shell containing the killer's spirits. Mourners would crush the skull into bone dust and place the remains in a separate jar decorated with demons and evil spirits. Kalpit's ashes would then be scattered into the sea to symbolize the final liberation of his soul and reunion with the primordial elements of life. They would bury the demonic jar containing the bone dust and fragments of the killers in the same spot, but a foot deeper, to symbolize the eternal banishment of the killer's souls into a hellish world.

A few chosen members of the families performed the actual cremation of the three men since the bodies were in an advanced stage of decay and considered unclean. Before the ceremony, Rishaan bathed and anointed his own body with sacred holy oils. Tradition required the placement of the deceased on the pyre with the feet facing south toward the sea. Normally, mourners would place rice in the mouth of the deceased, but the body remained tightly bound as exposure of decayed flesh was extremely sacrilegious. Thus, each mourner cast a handful of rice onto the corpse, chanting the customary prayers.

It was now Rishaan's duty to light the pyre and loudly announce his oath of revenge to the witnesses gathered:

"Kalpit, may your tormented soul find sanctuary and last peace when your ashes blend into the sea whence you came. I swear I will exact revenge upon your killers, their wicked bones crushed into dust, their souls banished to the darkness beneath our feet."

It was clear in the customs of the Shore People any revenge oath, uttered, but not fulfilled, would require the suicide of the maker. Upon completion of the service, custom required each mourner to undergo a prescribed bathing process and a full day and night of meditation without speaking, eating, or sleeping.

Just as Rishaan was about to enter the obligatory meditation period, Vedant appeared with a strange figure. "Sire, I have brought you the man called AO, whom you seek. I found him in the priest's compound just a short distance away." Rishaan was very curious to speak with AO, but he had to be sure he complied with the mourning process.

Vedant assured Rishaan a short delay to discuss the dream would not be disrespectful, but AO deftly interrupted, saying, "Lord Rishaan, I suggest you abide by the wishes of your spirit which seeks a period of meditation and union with the soul of your noble brother, Kalpit. I can return tomorrow at your bidding." Vedant, a bit embarrassed, meekly agreed.

Rishaan muttered "Thank you" and slipped away into his private chamber, still overcome with grief but with his curiosity piqued, pleased AO had referred to him as "Lord Rishaan".

PART 28
New War Strategies to Break the Stalemate

Ekavir had traveled to within a day of the gates of Desa City, encamping at a spot on the river which was far downstream from the camp of the Horse Warriors. He had not diverted any forces to the north to halt the crossing of additional Horse Warrior forces as information showed the crossing had already taken place. Boat people who made their living by a perpetual journey up and down the Great Stars River had witnessed the last remnants of the crossing.

These boat people, although Shore People by birth, were citizens of the river, earning their meager wages by transporting trading goods along the entire river. They survived by adopting neutrality, avoiding any disputes, pledging no allegiance, and paying bribes as required to survive each trip. Information pertaining to the crossing by the Horse Warrior leaked through a random comment by one helmsman revealed vital information.

Soldiers brought several of the boat people before Ekavir. Knowing in advance the wayward comment which brought a rebuke from the other boat traders, Ekavir approached the young man with the loose tongue, "Please tell me what you saw?"

The boatman in question would not lie, but he could be vague. "I saw a few men and horses on the southern bank of the river."

"Were they Horse Warriors?" asked Ekavir.

The boat traders held their breath, knowing a lie would likely bring immediate trouble, but the truth a betrayal of their neutrality. "I cannot be sure" was unfortunately the wrong response.

Ekavir turned to one of his unit commanders and said, "The Wheel", meaning little to the boatman but correctly perceived as ominous. Soldiers seized all four men and tied them to the enormous wheels of a supply wagon. Some men endured this torture for hours, even days, but most men yielded quickly. The wagon lurched forward, slowly turning the pitiful bodies rotating with each turn of the wheel. Ekavir gave the signal to the oxcart driver to increase the speed.

Mercifully for the helmsmen, the oxcart turned back after a few hundred yards, stopping in front of Ekavir who approached the helmsman in question. "What did you see?", Ekavir asked again with the tone of an avuncular relative. This time, the answer satisfied Ekavir, and the men released, not seriously injured, as Ekavir reasoned they would speak the truth confronted with a short, practical lesson in persuasion.

In severe cases, such as an assassination of a member of the ruling family, "The Wheel" was a death sentence preceded by excruciating pain, as the alleged criminal suffered beatings and broken legs. More torture ensued. Mounted and stretched on the oversized wagon wheel; days of agony on a rotating wheel followed until death provided a merciful end.

After a full day's march, the Shore People cavalry reached the southern gates of the city, an area not blockaded by the Horse Warriors as they lacked sufficient forces to completely envelope the city. It delighted the Nivasi and Varagan defenders to see Ekavir and his force of five hundred men. The good news was their arrival, but other news quickly dashed spirits. The Horse Warrior's reinforcements would arrive in a few days.

Late in the evening, in the Horse Warrior's encampment, Balvan appeared at the door of the small sleeping quarters Saisha now shared with her daughter, Anya. Saisha took her cue and arose quietly, not wanting to awake Anya. Balvan led Saisha to another small room, speaking gently to her, asking how Anya was doing. Saisha questioned the sincerity of this question, thinking it was Balvan's way of reminding her of the "bargain".

In their prior engagement, Balvan had been rough and crude, more voracious with lust than any desire for a meaningful engagement. He looked at her differently, more like a suitor needing to deploy convincing and persuasive charm. She was gratified he did not demand she remove her clothes, understanding some modestly was in order. Like a nervous man on his first encounter, he kissed her tenderly on her neck and proceeded gently, as if needing approval to move to the ultimate act.

Later, she tried to convince herself she found no satisfaction in the act, but a brief twitch in her heart belied that notion. After all, Balvan was still of fine build, treating her with respect and gentility; he had quickly fulfilled his promise to bring Anya to her. As she reclined next to Anya, she thought of Jai and sadness returned. Balvan claimed Jai's fate was beyond his control; all captured boys had to survive the ordeal and "final test". As she drifted off thinking about Jai, her mind turned to Balvan, wondering if an adopted boy would receive different treatment.

If Balvan sought pleasure in his evenings, matters near Desa were dramatically different. Within a mile of each, entrenched in their camps, the deadlocked opposing forces, following several days of intense fighting, remained in an uneasy stalemate. The Horse Warriors had vastly underestimated the resilience and tenacity of the Nivasi and Varagans, and their innovative tactics.

Dhanur still kept his swagger as he marched around the campsites of his fighters, exhorting his men and promising gold and other riches he was sure awaited the worthy invaders. Within two days, the heavy cavalry would arrive, and he would launch a full-scale attack to wipe out the pesky resistance that had frustrated him. He could not conceive of any outcome other than total victory; in his tenure as field commander, he had only feasted on success.

Axam was far from confident. Everything he surmised about the fighting spirit of the Nivasi was wrong. His only solace was the fact of the limited number of mounted Varagan fighters, battle elements critical to success in war. He took comfort knowing the Nivasi, although skilled in archery combat, had no experience in the wild, intense, hand to hand combat which was inevitable. "Yes", he advised Dhanur, "they will collapse when confronted with our major onslaught, but we must destroy Arian and Veer as soon as possible, then the rest will surrender or run. Either way, we will slaughter them."

Axam wisely exuded confidence but kept the nagging doubts to himself. Dhanur sensed Axam was concealing some concerns said, "Axam, what other defensive tactics should we consider?"

Forcing a stoic look, especially in his eyes, as experienced soldiers understand the eyes of a man can reveal secrets, Axam responded, "You were very shrewd to bring in the heavy calvary and I am certain of the soundness of your new plan, but…".

Dhanur turned on Axam, glared into his face, only inches from Axam's face, screaming, "But what?" It was not a question. Axam, trained since youth in mind control, did not flinch. "I was about to suggest you send news of your impending victory to Khander and ask him to meet you at the base camp in a week."

Dhanur stepped back a bit, smiled, contented, "Yes, exceptionally good idea. Besides, we don't want our camp on the northern side of the river to remain unguarded with only two hundred fighters for any long period."

Axam thought to himself the two hundred fighters mentioned by Dhanur were mainly men of the reserve force typically over the age of sixty whose finest days had long passed, and the young boys in training to be warriors. Nevertheless, they could fight off marauding bands, if needed, as the intense dedication of a Horse Warrior was the last emotion to depart from a dying man or boy born into the Horse Warrior culture. Even some captured Varagan boys, and a few outsiders, including Jai, would fight tenaciously if attacked.

In Desa, the War Committee was listening to Ekavir, who had returned as promised. Ekavir thanked the Nivasi, notably Simran, for the excellent help to find the bodies of the murdered Shore

People. Couriers had briefed Ekavir on the funeral services and the mental disposition of Rishaan, including his oath of revenge and the decision to send an army to destroy the Horse Warriors. Unlike the Nivasi who had no army and the Varagans whose army core of professionals was quite small, the Shore People with a larger population, more land to defend, and a sea trading system to protect, had a comprehensive professional army and a small navy.

The only other peoples with a professional army of comparable size were the Horse Warriors in which every man was a professional warrior. They had no need for tradesmen or farmers as everything they required, including food accrued through battles. They treated conquered peoples as vassals obliged to pay high taxes in goods and food supplies. They tortured captured tax dodgers for days, as setting "good" examples for other tax avoiders was the hallmark of Horse Warrior administration.

The essential elements of the new coalition of Nivasi, Varagans and Shore People would center on surprise counter attacks by a much larger light cavalry force. In addition, they planned to deploy the new weapon, the "chariot" in limited numbers. Fleet footed Nivasi using javelins would complement the elite archers, a combination so far not introduced into battle.

Ekavir asked, "What is our defense against the heavy cavalry? Forces armed with lances can crush any size mass of light cavalry." Devi and Arian looked at Vidya, who simply spoke one word, "elephants".

Puzzled, Ekavir ruminated, trying to comprehend the use of elephants in battle. Ekavir jokingly responded, "Next, you going to tell me king cobras are in your arsenal." Vidya, deadpanned as usual, pronounced, "Yes, we use king cobras. They are excellent weapons when deployed properly."

PART 29
AO interprets Rishaan's Dream.

Rishaan's meditation and fasting period ended the next morning. When Rishaan emerged from his meditation chamber, he found AO exactly in the same place he sat earlier. He wondered if the man, AO, had ever left. AO was of slight build, green eyed with a light complexion unlike most of the Shore People who were darker in complexion. He also had blond hair, most unusual in the kingdom. Vedant had explained AO lived in the furthest southeast corner of the kingdom, an area of tiny fishing villages.

"AO," said Rishaan, "What is your actual name?"

AO responded, "My name is AO. I have no other name."

The odd answer dissatisfied Rishaan, but he sidestepped this minor detail for the moment. "Lord, I believe you would like me to provide my understanding of your dream. Please tell me every aspect of your dream; no detail is too insignificant." Rishaan thought the manner of AO speech devoid of emotion, but he relayed the full contents of the dream.

If AO, heralded by Vedant and other spiritual leaders, cannot adequately explain my dream, thought Rishaan, *This so-called mystic will find enlightenment in "The Hole"*. Reserved for difficult and unruly prisoners, the "Hole" motivated dread. Men squeezed into the narrow pit, unable to move, forced to stand for days. People convicted of the most heinous crimes would suffer a lingering death of unusual cruelty.

Rishaan went into all the details of the dream. AO listened

dispassionately, asking no questions. AO sat quietly, pondering everything Rishaan spoke. He did not need to ask Rishaan to repeat any aspect of the dream, as AO had a superb memory. Upon completion of the dream recitation, it seemed everyone just stared at each other in silence, Rishaan in a state of anticipation, AO in a state of deep meditation, Vedant, icily stiff in a state of poorly disguised fear. Vedant, cringing in anxiety and reciting prayers to boost the prospects for a favorable outcome, visualized himself cast out of the kingdom, banished for foolishly bringing a false mystic to Rishaan.

Unsure how to break the impasse, Rishaan inquired, "AO, what does my dream mean?"

AO began speaking in a trancelike voice, his words flowing like water over a fallen tree in a gentle stream. Rishaan watched AO's hands drift in a circular, repeating pattern. AO himself seemed to speak as if separated from his body. AO repeated the dream in incredible detail, accurately recounting every word spoken by Rishaan. AO's impressive recitation of each word of the dream and his extremely calm demeanor was reassuring to Rishaan, who was mentally and physically exhausted from his meditational fast.

"Rishaan, your dream is a vision of your kingdom and its ultimate salvation from wicked threats. The men on horses are mocking you and your kingdom; the blow to your head is an arrogant strike against your people. These men from distant lands exalt in greed and lust for domination. They do not have any regard for other cultures, convinced they have the superior culture. Their world is solely about conquest, their ambitions only momentarily satisfied by subjugating other peoples. They direct their evil intentions at you, Lord, as you are their principal obstacle. They mock you because they fear you. They fear your oath of revenge. The dream is testing your resolve to rise from your grief over Kalpit's murder and lead your people to salvation. The men on horses want you immobilized by your brother's spirit; a troubled spirit seeking revenge, proper cremation, and reverence. Until you satisfy your brother's spirit, you will continue in despair and guilt.

The maggots are troubling as they symbolize rot and decay. In your case, the decline of your civilization. The maggots expelled from the mouth of Kalpit are dead; his spirit destroyed them. Kalpit is warning you the horsemen find an ally in the inevitable decay of cultures. The magnificent hawk is a symbol for you of a stronger civilization imbued with new spiritual values to strengthen the will of your people and lift them to victory over any enemy. Your salvation in the dream means your people will find salvation through you, their Lord."

Mesmerized and enchanted by AO and his interpretation. Rishaan stood excitedly, exclaiming, "Yes, AO, that is exactly what my dream means! You have opened my eyes and mind to the task I must undertake. You have shown me the way. I am naming you my spiritual adviser. Engage with my daughter, Zeba, to instruct every person in this kingdom in your beliefs and practices." Vedant, stunned and relieved, visions of banishment dissipated, darted off to fetch Zeba.

In Desa, the momentary lapse in fighting brought an uneasy and false sense of normalcy. Daily routines had to proceed. Arian took his inspiration from Kutta, a dog with an indomitable spirit, his best friend in life along with Veer and Chatresh. It delighted Kutta whenever Arian showed him the leash, twisting, turning, nuzzling up to Arian. "Ah, Kutta, afraid you will miss your time to frolic with Chatresh? I know, this is your time."

Arian enjoyed his time with Kutta and Chatresh, but tonight was going to be a bit more exceptional. He approached the corral, admiring the black sheen of Chatresh, his majestic pose and the way he stood seemingly taller than the other horses, although they were all similar in height. None of the other captured horses, each an experienced war horse, would concede anything to Chatresh; they had their pride as well.

Kutta and Chatresh bonded as well, each playfully nudging the other. Chatresh's ears pricked forward, Kutta excitedly responded to any sign of encouragement. Arian enjoyed the two of them, but now the playtime would end. Arian held his full battle saddle in his hand, showing it to Chatresh whose demeanor changed. In earlier forays, Chatresh and Arian were bonding as friends, but now was the moment to elevate to warrior status.

The war saddle on the back of Chatresh changed everything. Arian carefully mounted Chatresh, now as master, the next step in an orchestrated process between rider and man, both noble warriors. Each had a role to play; both understood the purpose. Both men and horses could experience fear, the horse more attuned to the rider's body, tension in his muscles, throbbing of blood through his legs. The rider's courage had to match the courage of the horse, not a simple task when confronted with death in battle.

Chatresh and Arian executed a series of battle maneuvers with Kutta chasing from behind, barking, running, and dodging. Kutta, highly spirited, would not be excluded! Satisfied. Chatresh was nearing readiness, Arian headed back to the waiting arms of Devi. This time, Kutta would have to wait outside. Despite the looming tension and awareness that each night may well be their last night together, Devi and Arian could relax, commingled in a unison of genuine love and sharing. Both laughed, joking about Kutta being left outside with strict orders to guard the house.

Several miles away, Dhanur found a different way to relax, sipping a concocted boiled milk, containing dried crushed leaves of cannabis mixed with nuts and spices. Dhanur reached for a small earthen bowl, dipping his fingers into a resin, crafted from the fresh flowers of female cannabis plants. He slowly rubbed the resins between his hands, a hypnotic act contributing to the state of semi-consciousness Dhanur sought.

The Horse Warriors believed human will did not arise from the conscious state in which logic and reason diluted the power of the spirit. Commanders designed all training of Horse Warriors to push humans to physical limits when the rational mind is desperate to stop, urged by tormented cries of the flesh. The subconscious mind, fearing failure or humiliation, commands the body to continue, disregarding pain, no matter how severe.

Although the union of warrior and horse was sacred, the Horse Warriors relied on training methods the ageless veterans, survivors of countless battles and fierce hand to hand combats, claimed would bring one's courage and will to match the perfection of their war horse. You were garbage, pathetic scum, not worthy of your horse until you reached the ultimate state of human will. The veterans used a unique and self-serving logic that all young warriors had to hear countless times. Screaming at the untested young warriors, nose to nose, foul breath, matted hair, and spittle exuding from a vile mouth stinking of sour milk and cheese, the words were always the same, "Do you know why I am here, alive, while others are dead?"

Of course, every young warrior knew the answer. The dead warriors, praised and exalted for their courageous deeds, had momentarily faltered, sometimes a quirk of fate. The Horse Warrior creed was simple: every battle a victory, every warrior a survivor, every day a glorious chance to serve. Defeat on any level was unthinkable. Death, although noble in battle, was a defect of the human will. The "Walk" would fortify the will to a point where momentary lapses of the body or spirit were not possible.

Dhanur, reveling in his hypnotic state, enjoyed reliving the "Walk", an ordeal experienced by all Horse Warriors and the subject of many macabre jokes by the veterans. The "Walk" followed a one-mile course through the desert, each recruit wearing a sack, initially filled with a rock about one pound in weight. Upon completion of each circuit, senior leaders added another rock to the sack. Organizers always selected one of the hottest days for the "Walk"; occasionally an expected rainstorm would mercifully cool the suffering recruits. Circuit after circuit, they trudged on, their sacks becoming more unbearable. Besides the intense aching pain, thirst soon tormented each young man. Hour after hour, circuit after circuit, they marched on with long gaps in distance between the young men.

In these hours, one learned the true art of meditation, the

method to separate your mind from the body. The mind commands the body to keep moving, ignoring cries of pain and fatigue. The warrior's spirit infuses the mind with purpose and a mysterious energy, creating motivation to far exceed the normal limits of the body. One can harden the body, but the superior warrior must develop the superior mind propelled by the warrior's ethos. The mind is the weak link, easily seduced by the body, yielding to physical pleasures and comfort. The mind can play tricks on your will or even sabotage your spirit, obsessing over worries and doubts.

Mental weakness undermines the body and the spirit, rendering both as empty, vacuous shells. The "Walk" is about the simplicity of a task and the training of the mind to keep going, no matter what. The Walk teaches failure is not an option, quitting is choosing death. The young men know there are only two choices for the mind, keep going or die. The body has no vote, no say; we cannot trust it.

Well into the afternoon, now with dozens of rocks weighing down their sacks, some young warriors fell. Veterans would jump off their horses and whip these boys, commanding them to rise. No one failed to rise; they continued. Deep fatigue gave way to hallucinations as they endured another circuit, another rock. The young men were stumbling, often barely moving, which only resulted in thrashes to their heads, knocking them down, more whippings. The veterans were screaming, "Just quit. Your pain will go away." No young warrior would yield to these taunting words.

The ordeal kept going on and on, most falling, unable to get up. The whippings intensified, the curses of scum radiating from all directions. The will reverberated, silently urging, "Just keep going, crawl, keep moving." Ten hours into the ordeals, the sacks crushing the backs of the young warriors, their stomachs raw from crawling; no one quit. They no longer felt the whips on their backs.

The veterans continued their verbal attacks, sometimes pretending to befriend the young men. "You don't need to continue, you can quit. Nothing will happen to you. Why go on? I will vouch for you." The taunts and lies continued nonstop.

Completely dehydrated, nauseous from heat and fatigue, the young warriors kept crawling into the night, their movements slowing to a virtual halt. Now the ultimate test arrived. No more rocks could fit into the sacks, no more movement, the last ounce of willpower deleted. The senior leader ordered each recruit to stand to attention. A few slowly rose to their knees, then a mighty effort to stand. Others made it to their knees and collapsed back to their stomachs. This time, the veterans screamed encouragement. "You can do it. One more effort!" Eventually they all made it to their feet, except for one young man. He lay dead from complete exhaustion.

Dhanur smiled to himself, reminiscing about "The Walk", a fine moment in his life.

PART 30
Zeba and The Way of AO

Vedant did not have any difficulty finding Zeba, knowing she was tending to her flower garden, a place of striking beauty with a magnificent variety of plants and flowers and trees like the banyan tree, the epitome of nature itself. The garden featured varieties of champas, scented yellow cream flowers perfect for soliciting solitude inside temples. Zeba's favorite, and that of her father, was the lotus, blooming each day, rising with the sun, following suit at night, closing its leaves for ritualistic sleep in the moonlight.

The lotus adorned the palace home of Rishaan and Livia, wife, and mother of his children. Rishaan and Livia had a splendid marriage as each brought intelligence and strength to the family. Rishaan was perhaps more pragmatic and tactical in his thinking, whereas Livia, through her charm and graceful persistence, ensured music, art, and philosophy proliferated. Unfortunately, she suffered an illness common to middle-aged women; she died after several months, always a model of courage and grace as she endured tremendous pain. Her last words to Rishaan were barely audible, which added to the grief. Rishaan was sure she said, "My spirit sleeps with the lotus and will awake tomorrow, alive in the gentle pink blossoms. Dream of the lotus and you will see me."

Rishaan was so heartbroken he did not leave his bedchamber for months, drained of any will to live. It was Zeba, the youngest of his three daughters, who nursed her father and slowly reawakened him to life. Zeba serenaded Rishaan with melodies from her flute. She arranged the lotus stems facing the morning sun, timing her melodies to create the illusion of the rising sun and the blossoming lotus moving in unison, solely at the bidding of the flute. Cheerfully, she always selected a flower with pink petals, saying, "Good morning, Mother, I hope you have a delightful day."

Zeba grew into a woman of unpretentious, but stunning beauty, happy to live in her garden for endless hours, nurtured by the flowers. She enjoyed hosting men of philosophy, but with a sharp mind, she probed them with unanswerable questions. She was fond of questioning the purpose of men and women in the natural world, asserting women were more gifted in metaphysical matters because of deeper levels of consciousness and sensibilities. The philosophers argued the spirit was intertwined with the mind, whereas Zeba claimed only the soul speaks to nature, and it is the mind which is untrustworthy.

The most senior philosopher in the kingdom was Viraj, chief advocate and protector of the dominant religious beliefs. At first, he considered Zeba as an odd, if not pampered, child of Rishaan, but as Zeba grew in age and wisdom, he began viewing her with increasing alarm. Viraj taught divine fate destined all people to live their entire lives in the class into which they were born. Yes, Zeba should receive exclusive treatment as royalty of noble birth. The chief priests and philosophers were also of noble birth, entitled to a set of privileges, protected by these same doctrines.

Zeba argued beliefs and doctrine trapped the mind into a rigidity which leashed vast numbers of people to poverty and servitude. According to Zeba, the civilization of the Shore People would reach additional levels of prosperity if they banished societal restrictions. The mere thought of this heresy made Viraj cringe. If Zeba did not live in the protected bubble of royalty, Viraj would convict her as a heretic!

When she first saw AO, she immediately sensed this man, much younger than the spiritual leaders of the kingdom, was different. The senior spiritual leaders, like the men of the military or political leaders of high rank, wore distinctive clothing, specifically adorned to signify status and privilege. AO's plain white shirt reflected the dress worn by people of little or no distinction. He was handsome but of plain physical presence, causing observers to underestimate him. He approached Zeba and slightly bowed, reaching gently for her hand, gazing at her palms, remarking," You have the hands of nature." It was a polite gesture which garnered brief notice from Rishaan and Vedant but felt more intimate to Zeba.

Rishaan quickly commanded everyone's attention, informing Zeba AO would become a spiritual adviser because he had brilliantly interpreted his dream. "Zeba, I am aware of your talents in the ways of nature and the philosophies of our peoples. I would like you to learn everything AO can teach. Take your time to probe his views and return to advise me of your thoughts."

AO and Zeba walked together to the gardens, finding a serene spot. "What is your proper name?" Zeba asked, thinking "AO" was a shortened version of his actual name.

"I am known to everyone as AO. I have no other name, nor do I wish one. Does each animal in the forests, each fish in the ocean, have a name?" Zeba thought for a second and then responded, "But you have a name if you answer to AO. Did you select that name?"

"No, the priests who raised me called me AO, the name referring to the divine octopus." Deterred for the moment, Zeba pursued collecting information of her father's dream. "AO, what is the interpretation of my father's dream?"

AO answered with a question, "Zeba, what is beautiful and what is ugly in your garden?" Zeba gazed slowly around the garden. It was easy to pick the magnificent lotus flower, an object of sublime beauty. She could have selected a gnarly bush with twisted brown bark lacking the natural grace of the lotus but selected a centipede as her example of ugly. Surely, AO would agree it is an object of ugliness.

"Zeba, what is the purpose of the lotus flower."

Zeba quickly answered "to bring beauty to humans."

"What about the centipede?" AO asked. "Why is it unworthy of your respect?"

Zeba caught herself before answering, reflecting on how AO

might consider the centipede useful. "I guess they eat other harmful insects, but they look slimy to me."

AO thoughtfully responded, "Centipedes have multiple medicinal uses. They are a source of food for snakes and small rodents and keep spiders and other insects in check. Lotus flowers are a fundamental source of food for humans and insects, notably lotus seeds, which are prolific in quantity. We extract potent medicines from the lotus flower; however, these flowers are toxic to women bearing babies. I fear you judge the centipede as ugly and unworthy of life because its physical form did not please you."

Zeba, somewhat chastened, snapped back, "But the lotus flower is so beautiful, and the centipede is disgusting."

AO responded in a calm voice, "Did your soul inform your opinion or was it your mind speaking?" Startled, she realized she had used a similar argument in her previous discussions with Viraj.

Zeba stood up and beckoned AO to walk out of the garden, remarking, "You are teaching all life has a place in the natural world, each life form, no matter how insignificant to humans, has a purpose. It is our mind which makes judgments often with little connection to the reality of the natural world. We are the arrogant species, violating the fundamental principle of natural harmony."

AO smiling, simply added, "And?" Zeba intuitively replied, "We must respect life, its full expression in nature embraced. Judgments about beauty or usefulness are subjective expressions of the human mind, not an objective fact of reality." A slight tinge of satisfaction was noticeable as AO continued, "What about humans?" With no hesitation, Zeba answered, "They are all equal and have value."

"You are an extraordinary young woman. Many spiritual people, claiming to live in a state of wisdom, cannot achieve such insight. Shall we meet in the morning?"

Zeba, still marveling, haphazardly said, "Tomorrow morning? Yes, tomorrow, can we meet here in my garden?" AO bid his farewell, nodding consent to meet in the morning.

Zeba tried to be serene, emptying her mind, but she could not shake the image of AO. He said little in contrast to Viraj and the spiritual elders who preached continuously on the rules, obligations, and duties of life. Most fascinating was an odd comment from AO. "Those who know, do not speak; those who speak, do not know."

Back in the base camp of the Horse Warriors, Saisha anointed her body with fragrant oils, preparing for her nightly ritual. First, she attended to Balvan's wife. Savita, growing weaker each day, her illness accelerating the decline of her body. Saisha was kind and patient with Savita, who in return showed no resentment toward Saisha. Savita with waning energy and consciousness, moaned, "Saisha, come closer to me as my strength is failing."

Saisha bent down, close to Savita, to hear the whisperings of a dying woman. "Saisha, I have only a little time left. Balvan has been a good man to me. I know how he feels about you, how desirous of you. After the customary mourning period, he will ask you to marry him and adopt your children. You are not obligated by our laws, but I think it would be the best for you and him."

As Saisha departed, she thought of how Balvan now treated her with respect and, yes, love. She thought of all the advantages of adoption, but she was not of the Horse Warriors and she did not embrace their culture and values. She did not want Jai to become a Horse Warrior who thrives on war and violence. The question remained, would they ever reunite with the Shore People, her people?

A nagging demon embedded in her soul. Balvan had raped her through unbridled lust with no concern for her feelings. *Can I ever forgive him?* She thought. Tonight, she went through the ritual motions with Balvan, playing her role, bringing him the expected pleasures. Upon completion, with drops of sweat clinging to their faces, Balvan said, "Saisha, I love you." Hours later, breath departed from Savita, leaving her body lifeless, freeing her spirit to join her ancestors in the realm of eternity.

AO rose early at the break of dawn. He enjoyed a cup of tea and some rice cakes while sitting quietly, gradually sliding into his meditative state. AO sat quietly, meaning he permitted not a hint of a curious mind nor casual glances around the room. He did not ask himself what the day would bring, not contemplating some future experience, whether imminent or in the distant future. He sought nothing. He experienced emptiness. The morning calls of birds welcomed, the rustling of the trees acknowledged, the rays of the morning sun noted. Another cycle of day begins.

As AO walked to the dwelling in which Zeba lived, he saw her peering from underneath an arching roof, offering some protection from the morning gentle rain. Zeba welcomed AO with an air of regret, "Good morning. Too bad it is raining so we cannot use the garden. We can sit here, protected from the rain, if you like."

AO looked a little surprised; he had not realized it was raining. "Zeba, it is a good morning, so we should sit in the garden as we planned." Zeba chided by her own recognition a rainy morning should not matter, a natural occurrence, no different from a bright sunny morning.

"What are you thinking about?" asked AO.

Zeba thoughtfully responded, "I am thinking about what you said to me yesterday. It was very enlightening."

"You are referring to experiences of the past. I am asking about now, this moment."

Zeba, a shrewd thinker, retorted, "What is knowledge if we do not keep it in our minds. How do we change the future without the experience of the past?"

AO responded, "How do you experience the moment if you anchor your mind in the past or find seductions by musings of the future?"

Zeba wisely discerned, "It depends on the purpose of the moment. Here, in this moment, in this place, thinking of past or future interferes with the sensory experience of the moment causing disharmony with nature. You would agree, however, in other circumstances, it is wise to think about the future?"

AO smiled, pleased in his thoughts, continued with the dialogue, "What do you wish for your people?"

Zeba answered, "I wish them prosperity."

AO asked, "Is prosperity defined as material comforts, or do you wish for more?"

Zeba hesitated to grasp the complete sense of the question. Rainwater dripped off her face, a fact she had not previously noticed. She loved the rain, feeling the rainwater soaking her hair, running off her skin; somehow, she felt a sunny morning would have dulled the moment. "I wish for all my people to fulfill their purpose, in harmony with natural law, not under the doctrines of men, no matter their purpose. Every person should blossom like flowers in the garden, each in their own way, each based on their own natural qualities."

"How can society thrive if each person can do as they please?" AO quizzed.

Zeba walked over to another part of the garden, picked up a banana from a low-hanging branch and replied, "The banana tree must have the right soil, the right amount of rain and the capability to endure insects. Given the right conditions, banana trees can flourish. So, it is true with people, it is about creating the right conditions which is the primary duty of the ruler. A wise ruler inspires his people to greatness as individuals and as a valued part of society. He is the garden keeper, tilling the earth, nurturing each plant, each tree, not the house master who never soils his hands."

AO said, "Zeba, now you know how to interpret your father's dream. His dream is calling him to be the master gardener to cultivate the people of his kingdom to a life, unshackled by other people's domineering beliefs. It is also a vision of wicked men who want absolute power over this land. They live by their own codes of law and conduct and believe themselves to be superior to all other men."

Zeba thanked AO and said, "I am ready to advise my father."

PART 31
The Eve of the Decisive Battle

The arrival of the heavy cavalry pleased Dhanur, delighted with the men armed with long thrusting spears. Their horses were much larger, a breed designed to serve as a mass of battering rams. The heavy cavalry complemented the fighters who, on their short squat horses, could accelerate and maneuver rapidly, perfect for the tactics of attack, retreat, counterattack, and swarm. The Horse Warrior tactics would not be a surprise to Arian and Veer, who structured their forces for defensive maneuverability, spiced with surprise ambushes.

Ponmudi had not only designed the war chariot but was pivotal in the development of copper shields, which were more rugged and impenetrable to deflect the lighter arrows used by the Horse Warriors. The surrounding hills blessed Desa with vast amounts of copper in nearby mines, normally used in household items and jewelry. Devi and Mishka had consulted with Ponmudi and the metal workers to design a shield, perfect in stationary formations. The copper shields, oversized for one individual, would offer protection for the archers on either side. Everyone would move in tandem, ensuring continuing protection from the overlapping shields. Ponmudi called it the "Turtle" formation, which seemed like a perfect name.

A week had gone by since the last engagement, which helped heal the non-fatal wounds typical of this type of attack and retreat warfare. The clash of armies was inevitable; the terror of showers of arrows replaced by hand-to-hand combat in which sheer ferocity of the fighters and their sword skills would dominate. The heavy cavalry would add an enormous advantage to the Horse Warriors. Dhanur and Axam were counting on a different motivation. Their men were angry, having lost lifelong friends, boiling in hatred, expecting the complete destruction of the defenders. They believed no finer warriors existed anywhere. Imbued with a deep, fanatical fighting spirit, they did not think defeat was possible. Scores of devastated armies over decades of warfare justified this confidence.

On the defensive side, Arian was happy to have the additional light cavalry of the Shore People. He worried the true number of professionally trained soldiers were few compared to the Horse Warriors. He was commanding a citizen's army against the most professional and motivated army force in the known world. "Yes", he said to Veer, "we will again have the element of surprise and some new weapons." Veer quickly responded with a sly smile, "Don't forget the elephants!"

The Horse Warrior strategy would initially launch a storm of arrows which would momentarily darken the sky. Concurrently the light cavalry with a force of five hundred would attack, launch their own arrows, retreat, before the heavy cavalry would lead the counterattack. The light cavalry, now twice as large, would swarm the disorganized and demoralized enemy forces. This tactic was always successful because the opposing forces were overconfident, thinking they had the Horse Warriors on the run. Secretly, Axam worried Dhanur was not being innovative enough, relying on old methods. He thought, *Devi, not trained at all in classical military tactics, will be extremely dangerous, as she is very inventive and unpredictable.*

That evening, Arian visited Chatresh. He brought Kutta with him, admonishing him that tomorrow he would need to stay home and protect Devi. Kutta loved his primary duty to protect the home, but he also loved to hear the word "go". Kutta's love in life was running, even challenging Chatresh to various imagined contests as they went through drills on the practice field. Poor Kutta never guessed Arian used him to practice enemy maneuvers with

Chatresh. Kutta enjoyed the games, but he was a poor loser, always seeking another chance to best Chatresh. "Yes, Kutta, you are a fine competitor, a true warrior, like your friend Chatresh."

In the evening's embrace, Arian drew his body close to Devi, with more passion than the other nights. Devi sensed this time was different; she wondered, *should I be alarmed?* Arian was always caring, loving and very attentive to Devi, especially in her moment of pleasure. He had experienced other women, but he thought sex without love felt empty. Tonight, Arian kept repeating, "I love you; I love you." It was not rote, thought Devi; it was almost an act of desperation. They lay exhausted. The moment of relaxation when the physical passions extinguish, and emotional love fills the void.

"Devi, Veer, and I think tomorrow will be the epic day of this war. The Horse Warriors will do everything, no matter how many losses they incur, to demolish us. They will be unmerciful with any survivors. I do not fear for myself; I fear for you."

With tears streaming down her face, she nuzzled up to Arian and whispered, "We have made love on many nights. I am certain on one of those wondrous evenings, the time was right for your essence. I do not know for sure, but I suspect a baby will be in our future."

Arian's eyes welled up with pride, love, and fear. "Devi, you are a remarkable woman and will be a splendid mother. I swear I will never let you down, nor will my love falter for the briefest moment."

Devi stiffened slightly, "Arian, be the leader you must, live your purpose in life. Lead our peoples to victory, it is your mandate. I shall never live without you, so come back to me."

The next morning, Arian awoke early and headed for the corral, leaving a disappointed Kutta behind to tend to his duties to protect Devi. He saw Chatresh alone, quiet as if meditating and preparing for the day of battle. "Chatresh, today, we will ride into battle, two soldiers following their duty as noble warriors." Arian took several moments to caress Chatresh's back and sides, gently massaging to create an energy flow between the two of them.

Great warriors understand and experience fear. They do not

run from fear; they summon the courage of the elite warrior spirit. They understand courage is not foolish belittling of your opponent with rash displays of arrogance and bravery. Courageous warriors stay disciplined and cool-headed. Courage is a deep conviction, emanating from one's soul to follow one's duty faced with fear and death. Successful completion of duty requires execution of the perfected skills of both horse and rider; neither can allow fear and anxiety to diminish the practiced union of body and mind. Regardless of courage and skill, chance can strike down any courageous warrior, whether from a random arrow, a spear thrust or an unseen sword slash from behind.

PART 32
The Poisoning of Zeba

❦

The morning of the epic battle was also pivotal in the future of the Shore People. Zeba had notified Vedant she wanted to consult with her father. Only Vedant, whom she viewed as loyal to her family and AO, could attend. None of the other senior spiritual leaders of the kingdom, notably Viraj, would know the discussions. Rishaan was charmed to see Zeba, greeting her with a fatherly hug and a kiss on her cheek. "You are back so soon, Zeba, it has only been three days."

Zeba confidently responded, "Yes, father. I saw no reason to delay as I understand your dream and our course of action. My soul comprehends the genuine needs of the people." Vedant tried not to wince at these words, hoping her advice would be more poetic and not interpreted as polemics on society and political structures. Vedant may have been loyal to Rishaan, but the rage of Viraj made his spirit tremble. Any change to the current class status which weakened the power of the priests would be dangerous. Viraj would hold him accountable for any rash actions taken by the royal family, meaning actions disadvantageous to Viraj.

"What have you learned, Zeba?" Being careful in her choice of words, Zeba began with a positive approach, as a forerunner to the advisory messages which would be controversial. "Father, our peoples have prospered for many generations due to your wisdom and that of your ancestors who have ruled. Your benevolence and love pervade the soul of each person in the kingdom. You have inspired harmony within our society."

Rishaan laughed and interjected, "So, you tell me I am perfect." Zeba respectfully answered, "We are all imperfect; it is the desire for perfection which impels our souls, serves to ensure our humility and motivates our mind to good actions and self-improvement."

Vedant was sitting perfectly still, forcing a blank expression, but he feared Zeba was crossing critical boundaries. "Self-improvement" could not apply to Viraj and the priest class and could undermine social stability among the working poor. Rishaan, sensing some discomfort from Vedant, said, "If the people are prosperous, why is self-improvement required? Is it not sufficient to work hard and follow the teachings and rituals of the chief priests? Are the people unhappy?"

Zeba continued, "In your dream, you saw men on horses who treated you with scorn. You saw maggots, which are symbolic of decay. A magnificent bird symbolizing an uplifting spirit and freedom from the bondage of your tormentors swept away you. You did not escape by running away; you did not have the strength to defend yourself. It was the collective souls of your ancestors who plucked you away and who now are speaking to you in a plain message. Through the mystical powers of the great hawk, they are exhorting you to unleash the full energy of all people in the kingdom to mobilize against an enemy which seeks your destruction."

Rishaan squirmed uncomfortably, "Are you saying I need a bigger army?"

Zeba drew closer to her father and said with a mix of firmness and love, "No, I am saying anyone can be a soldier, anyone an artisan, anyone a farmer or fisherman, anyone a priest. Their birth or family status cannot define people's lives. Everyone should fulfill a life purpose, limited only by their talents and efforts, not by doctrines and beliefs. An enduring civilization, never conquered nor subject to the will of foreign peoples, relies on the moral strength of individuals."

Rishaan turned to AO and asked for his advice. AO, head slightly lowered as usual, said, "Zeba speaks the wisdom which lies hidden in our souls as we are all creatures of this living world. Within each soul are the seeds waiting to erupt and mature to its ultimate purpose. The acorn is a small insignificant seed from which springs a mighty oak tree. Our souls contain the seeds of the spirit, which under the right conditions can foster a majestic life. Just as the acorn can wither, failing to reach full maturity in growth, so too can a mind trapped in doctrines, beliefs, and rituals stunt the growth of the soul."

Turning now to Vedant, Rishaan invited him to speak his mind. "Rishaan, I am not qualified to comment on the wisdom espoused by AO."

Rishaan abruptly snapped, "Vedant, I am desirous of your opinion. It is not acceptable to decline my request."

Vedant, choosing his words carefully said, "I appreciate the insights Zeba and AO have offered for your consideration and completely agree living creatures have their purpose to follow natural law. I fully embrace the need for individual harmony with their natural world to achieve the greatest social welfare. Perhaps, it is wise to consult Viraj and the other chief priests for their views."

AO remained silent as he understood Vedant had chosen many words to say nothing. Vedant was faithfully echoing the prevailing religious doctrine of the priest class, asserting all people belonging to a specific social class should remain fixed in time to benefit the natural harmony of the current world. Any change could bring disharmony, possibly destructive civil wars. The common people should accept their predetermined state in life, no matter how harsh or limiting.

Rishaan ended the discussions saying, "I will meditate for the day to discern my wisdom on these matters." Everyone melted away, Zeba disturbed by the lack of action, AO fully understanding the dilemma posed to Rishaan which prevented action, Vedant relieved nothing conclusive emanated from the meeting. Vedant reasoned to protect the royal family and the priesthood, the priests must banish AO from the kingdom, and discredit his ideas. As for Zeba, perhaps, a temporary illness, a coma caused by poisonous plants would keep her bedridden for a while, sidelined while Viraj ended this intellectual rabble.

As Vedant and Viraj intended, Zeba took ill that very evening, beginning with stomach cramps, vomiting and diarrhea. Within hours, she slipped into a coma. None of her doctors determined the cause, although some suspected mushroom poisoning, which was usually fatal within a few days. Vedant consoled Rishaan, who was in near hysteria, sobbing and trembling from the mere chance Zeba could die. Vedant repeatedly assured Rishaan of Zeba's recovery, but it would take several weeks, and it would impair her memory for a long period.

Rishaan said, "Vedant, pray to the Spirits she recovers, and if your prayers succeed, I will give you a just reward." Vedant was very certain Zeba would ultimately recover as he had not used the most toxic flowers, a mix of less toxic and well-chosen azaleas in a wine compote was sufficient for his purpose.

The next day, Zeba's condition stabilized, although she showed no indications of regaining consciousness. AO, upon hearing of Zeba's condition and feeling confident as to the reason for her illness, planned his return to his home village, a few days' travel to the southeast. He would consult with the natural healers and the priests who were skilled in all the various forms of poisoning, defensive knowledge against murderous acts toward unsuspecting victims.

As he packed his sack for the journey, he felt many eyes monitoring every movement. He anticipated the fate they planned for him, as Viraj had already decided AO should disappear, lost on his journey, perhaps killed by roadway thieves. *Yes,* AO thought, *associates of the high priesthood shall entertain me. I must ensure they receive a proper welcome when they befriend me on my journey.*

AO began his journey after morning tea and meditation. He also performed his morning self-defense exercises, taught by the priests who raised him in his childhood. His regimen, developed at from an early age, combined rigorous physical training, mental exercises to simulate calmness in life-threatening situations, and hours of meditation to empty and relax his mind of fear, anxiety and desires, each set of actions following a prescribed sequence. AO was also taught the mysteries of the forests and neighboring jungles. He mastered the simple rhythms of natural life expressed through the wondrous complexity of the countless animal and plant species.

The most important lesson of all was respect for natural life, the awareness of each animal species, each tree, each plant. The priests constantly reminded AO that he was a guest, a humble visitor, no better and no worse than any life form. One did not consider snakes as demons or owls as harbingers of poor fortune or tigers as dangerous carnivores. Each living creature required respect and knowledge of their habitats and behavior learned through experience. Very few humans can survive long in the deep recesses of the jungle, if ignorant, inexperienced, and worst of all, arrogant. The most important survival skills were listening, seeing, smelling, only valuable if the mind was clear of entanglement.

"Move slowly, stop, listen, feel and absorb your surroundings", advised by Kalpesh, the most gifted of the natural teachers, as if reciting a mantra from a sacred text. Kalpesh emphasized your senses are your friends, your cluttered mind, the enemy. Oddly enough, Axam learned similar skills in his youth.

Similarly, the martial arts instructors echoed the same approach. The physical skills of self-defense are only valuable to ward off attacks. Attackers with aggressive intentions cannot match the well-trained master of self-defense because the mind of the attacker is filled with the negative energy of a defective spirit. The most able practitioner of martial arts is the one who does not rely on the mind or emotions. When attacked, the spirit directs all bodily actions which rise out of trained instincts of survival and defense. The mind is idle, the spirit, emanating from the soul, dominates with no conscious effort by the defender. Just like the most skilled gardener, archer or wood carver, there is no need to "think" how to do the task, your total person, undirected from the mind or some deep ambition for accomplishment, proceeds in perfection.

After a long day, dusk beckons the sun to defer to the moon as the sun's task was complete and now the moon must fulfill its purpose. People like to describe dusk in term of colors or as a transitional time of day. A person of the natural world might understand dusk as the beginning of the day for many creatures of the night. Owls, leopards, and wolves all are nocturnal; for them, their day is about to begin. For some humans, with darkness, deeper shades of night slowly appearing, dusk signals the transition to another phase of the day, no better, no worse than the hours of light. Some people of evil intent welcome the dark night, tempered with the right amount of moonlight, an opportunity to strike the unwary target.

For AO, dusk brings danger. He cannot be sure how many assassins are tracking him, perhaps two or three at most. He does not concern himself with this question or their weapons or when they may attack. His natural allies are the night creatures who will warn him when the time is at hand. AO's natural friends did not fail him at the peak of moonlight. Birds nervously rustled; the bushes swayed gently, even though there was no wind. He had selected a spot to rest for the night with shrubs housing skittish birds which would take flight at the first signs of an intruder. The assassins sought the advantage of night, but not the impediment of sheer darkness, so they carefully chose the time of their attack.

The first attacker came from his right, lunging at him with a knife recently sharpened for the task at hand. AO leaped up with lightning speed and launched a kick with his heel to the chest of the attacker. The man wanted to scream, but the blow had knocked the breath from him, cracking his sternum, the shock to the heart immediately causing the attacker to collapse. AO instantly turned just in time to deflect the second attacker. AO's elbow caught him across his jaw, slamming the attacker back, off balance, at which point AO kicked him in the groin, causing the attacker to double over and fall to the ground. The final blow, with the full force of his heel, directed to the man's throat, caused the sounds of crushed bones and gushing of blood through his nostrils. Unnatural sounds disturbing the solitude of the night.

The third attacker, deliberately left out of the initial attack, had the mission to head off any attempt by AO to escape by running away. Locked in fear, he stared at AO. AO advanced toward him in a protective stance. The unfortunate, distraught young man, seemingly too young to be a professional assassin, ran into the jungle, thrashing wildly, escape his only thought. Perhaps it was good luck the young man did not get too far into the deep recesses of the jungle where certain death awaited. He stumbled into quicksand. Seized with panic, he struggled to lift himself out, which only sucked him down further. Realizing his situation was extremely dire, he called out to AO for help.

AO appeared moments later and asked, "May I be of service to you, my young friend? What is your name?"

"My name is Manan", the young man, in fact more a boy, said frantically. "Really?", AO replied, "I believe your name means 'thoughtful', am I correct?"

The boy, increasing frantic, started thrashing again, only sucking him down further. Soon the quicksand would trap his arm, then only a minute would remain before the muck would ooze above his mouth and nose, causing suffocation. "Do you think it was thoughtful to join the other assassins?"

"I swear, they forced me. My family is extremely poor and indebted to the assassins. They coerced me to join them as the means to relieve my family of their debt obligation. I swear I am a good boy from an honest family. I did not know our mission was to kill you. I will owe you my life if you save me."

AO replied, "You owe yourself a better life. To me, you owe friendship." AO extended a long stick, which Manan, in panic, urgently clutched. "Don't move, just hold firmly." AO warned. He gently pulled the boy from the quicksand, taking pains to keep a firm grip and warning the boy to keep still.

Within a minute, he extracted the boy who immediately prostrated himself on the ground, imploring AO for forgiveness. "Rise Manan, you are now reborn to fulfill a more noble purpose in life than to cause harm to others." Manan was joyful beyond words. This man, the target of his malevolence, just saved his life, revealing the power of forgiveness and belief in redemption over revenge.

Feeling enlightenment, Manan changed his name, asking for acceptance as a trusted disciple. "Lord, I do not know your name, may I know how to address you? I would like you, lord and master to call me Sachiv, as I will follow you as your servant and disciple from this moment on."

AO could see this young man, Manan, now called Sachiv, meaning, 'friendship' transformed. "Sachiv, you may call me AO, as I am known by that name. You may share my life after you acquire the knowledge and experience to find your true purpose in life." Manan, now Sachiv, did not comprehend these words, wondering how to gain such knowledge.

AO and Sachiv disposed of the two assailants, both of whom suffered fatal injuries, one from cardiac arrest caused by the kick blow to the chest, the other from asphyxiation due directly to crushed bones in the throat. AO did not deliberately intend to kill these men, but, in the moment of attack, when a few seconds determines survival, the rational mind concedes control to the warrior spirit seeking freedom from death.

AO and Sachiv quickened their pace to reach the monastery of the naturalist priests who raised AO. Upon reaching the compound, AO quickly explained the symptoms of Zeba, her state of unconsciousness now being nearly three days in duration, assuming the purpose of the poison was not immediate death, but long-term incapacitation.

The most expert of the priests in the craft of natural remedies was Kalpesh, a devout practitioner and teacher of an ancient diet combining deep meditation with beneficial natural foods, especially herbs and seeds. He was also the most knowledgeable as to the various poison plants, including mushrooms. After listening to all the details of Zeba's symptoms, Kalpesh stated with certainty the culprit was not mushrooms, but more likely, the beautiful pink and red flowers of the nerium oleander plant or perhaps the common but toxic flowers of the azalea bush.

Kalpesh explained if the purpose was to incapacitate the victim, then mushrooms were not the right poison; a better solution was a wine concoction infused with a crushed compote of oleander or azalea. At any rate, he must leave immediately to begin treatment as time lost increased the odds against full recovery. If Zeba revived from the coma, she would face long periods of disorientation, depression, and fatigue. Time was most critical.

AO learned many species of flowers are toxic to humans and animals. Sometimes, the mere touch to better sense the full beauty of the flower would cause severe skin rashes. AO was sure various yellow and red oleander flowers adorned Zeba's garden, and she would fully understand which plants were toxic in any form. "Yes," AO said to Kalpesh, "it seems a gift of wine graciously received by Zeba was the agent of her illness."

AO and Kalpesh departed within hours, the only delay being the gathering of the necessary spices and herbs to resuscitate Zeba, if fate had not yet passed her body back to the spiritual world from which all life emerges. Turning to Sachiv, AO said, "You will stay here within this priestly community as you need the passage of time in meditation and natural living to rebuild your spirit and infuse your mind with the correct thinking of these men, who live in full accordance with their natural environment. When the priests determine the correct time, reborn with a soul cleansed from your bad choices in life, they will send you back to me. Sachiv, please understand the basic rule."

With humility but a terrible sense of timing, Sachiv interjected, "May I know the rule?"

AO wrinkled his face in a tone of slight admonishment, "Do not speak, do not talk, unless invited to do so; then reply only briefly a brief reply. Learn through sensory experience and listening, as words from your mind would be only gibberish. You will know when to speak; no one will need to inform you."

AO walked away, confident Sachiv would, in due time, realize when you have nothing to say, have no compulsion or need to preach, cajole, convince, or persuade, then you understand truth.

The journey back to the home city of Rishaan and Zeba was quicker as AO did not need to concern himself with assassins sent by Viraj. AO and Kalpesh arrived in the early afternoon of the next day and immediately went to the home of Zeba. Rishaan and several sisters surrounded her, and Viraj and Vedant who were performing rituals and prayer services to bid the protective spirits of the Shore People to breathe life into Zeba.

AO introduced Kalpesh as a holy man, highly skilled in all practices of natural medicines. Rishaan, weak from mourning and despair, his spirit increasingly bereft of hope, feebly greeted Kalpesh. The reception from Viraj and Vedant stood in contrast as they warily performed the required etiquette of politeness, signaling their genuine feelings through twitches in their faces. Kalpesh immediately understood the situation. They had taken no actions to cure Zeba, other than meaningless rituals foisted on people desperate for any shred of hope.

Kalpesh opened a small sack which contained a mix of spices, including several varieties of pepper and ginger. He turned to Rishaan and politely asked, "May I treat your daughter?"

Viraj slinked close to Rishaan and whispered in a loud enough voice so all could hear, "Sire, we know nothing about this man or his training and methods. We are precisely following the prescribed rituals which will bring Zeba back to full consciousness. I fear this man will anger the spirits who are being summoned."

Rishaan, with a spark of irritation and anger, icily admonished, "Viraj, your chants and poetic prayer rhymes have done nothing. Do not interfere." Then he turned to AO and asked," Do you trust this man?"

AO closed his hands and slightly bowed saying, "He is a father to me, and I trust him with my soul."

Kalpesh poured the mixture into a small bowl, applied fire to burn the substance, creating a wispy smoke. He then inhaled the smoke though a small pipe and immediately exhaled the smoke into the nostrils of Zeba who although in a coma was breathing normally. Rishaan perked up, stood right next to Kalpesh, who repeated the treatment of Zeba multiple times. Kalpesh then pulled a small flask from his belt and gently poured drops of the juice into Zeba's mouth. In addition, Kalpesh suggested various physical therapies, massaging of the limbs and chest area by a sister, as no man, other than a husband, was permitted to touch any part of Zeba's body.

They applied these procedures each hour through the night and early dawn. In the morning, Kalpesh placed Zeba's body to face the rising sun, warming the room with rays of sunlight. AO and Kalpesh stayed continuously throughout this medicinal treatment phase to ensure the precise application dosages and sequence. AO also watched carefully to ensure no one, from the servants to the chief priests, had any contact with Zeba.

In the late afternoon of the second day of treatment, Zeba slowly regained consciousness. It overjoyed Rishaan and her family members, whereas Kalpesh and AO showed no emotion, just persistence in the treatments. Upon hearing the good news, Viraj, on first impression, did not seem to share the joy. Catching himself, he quickly threw up his hands symbolically toward the sky proclaiming the spirits had heard his prayers.

Zeba gradually improved over the next hours, and by morning had sufficient consciousness to greet her father and begin the second phase of the customized diet designed to build her strength. With a quizzical and slightly accusatorial look, Zeba said, for all to hear, "Vedant, why did you send me the gift of wine?" Zeba immediately fell back into a sleep state which gave the high priests the opportunity to deny any involvement, pleading innocence and swearing absolute devotion to Rishaan and his family. And, of course, there was no damming evidence as Vedant had days earlier removed any traces of the wine.

Rishaan suspected the truth but wisely judged the time was not propitious to accuse the chief priests of this treachery. Yes, he thought, *I will exact my revenge in another time and place*, but he would never forget these false purveyors of virtue tried to kill Zeba. He vowed revenge. Perhaps they would spend their last days in the pit's darkness, more than enough quiet time to atone for their sins.

PART 33
Day of the Epic Battle

Although the rainy period of the summer months had passed, violent and unpredictable thunderstorms could strike bringing drenching rains, lightening and hail; exactly Axam's worry on the morning of the full-scale attack on Desa. The sky looked menacing as dark clouds billowed up, casting a dull haze over the battlefields. The battle plan for the Horse Warriors required full cavalry mobility, preferably on dry ground. By mid-morning, the air still misty and threatening, Axam and Dhanur decided on diplomatic tactics to better assess the fighting spirit of the defenders. Perhaps a wedge within the Nivasi could succeed if the Horse Warriors made appeals for peace.

With the array of forces lined up within five hundred yards of each other, Axam came forward alone on his horse to seek a peace discussion with Devi and Arian. Only Devi would ride out to meet Axam, halting him from reaching the defensive lines of the defenders. There was no doubt among the Nivasi and Varagans that whatever the intent of Axam, it was not to discuss "peace". Devi approached Axam, exchanging the courtesies of warring forces who deemed some polite formalities necessary to feel civilized. Axam's skill was hiding his true intent while feigning different emotions suited to the situation. Vidya jokingly quipped Axam changed colors faster than a chameleon. Diplomacy for the Horse Warriors always had a nefarious intent, although Axam sometimes regretted the failure of his brand of diplomacy as massive human slaughter would always follow.

"Devi, I bid you good health. I trust Arian is not ill".

Devi chose each word carefully, remembering it is more important to consider words not said than the words said. "Arian is in fine spirits and looks forward to a beautiful sunny day as soon as the morning storm clouds dissipate." Of course, Axam knew Arian had suffered serious wounds in previous battles. Perhaps Arian had succumbed to his injuries.

Axam responded with a level of insincerity surprising to someone as shrewd as Devi, "Devi, it is a shame we have shed blood over such minor issues. We should negotiate trade agreements, even mutual defense treaties, as we have profound respect for you and your people."

"Really?" Devi countered. "We have the same objectives, so how should we proceed?"

Axam responded on cue, "We would like to invite you and the senior Nivasi leaders to dine with us. I pledge we will guarantee your complete safety."

Devi answered with her counter proposal, "I propose all your warriors return to the banks of the Great Stars River. When we have verified your complete withdrawal, then each side will meet with a trade delegation of ten."

Axam, changing tactics, tried bribery, "Devi, we will provide you with gifts of gold which will enrich your peoples, if you honor us by turning over the senior Varagan leaders including Pratham, Jackal, Arian and Veer. What are these men to you? They are below your dignity."

Devi, hiding her rage, desperate to say Arian was her husband, held her tongue and curtly replied, "We have nothing more to say". She quickly turned her horse back to the city.

Axam rode up to Dhanur and uttered one word, "attack", which was exactly what Dhanur wanted to hear. Dhanur signaled to his light cavalry commander to move up five hundred mounted warriors. Another five hundred archers flanked them on either side with arrow range sufficient to barrage the defenders. Outside the city gates, the new copper shields previously hidden from sight now were arrayed like a gigantic turtle shell, each fighter protected by the overlapped shields. The timing was perfect as in the next moment, hundreds of arrows rained down, sharper, and more deadly than any hail stones from the most ferocious storm clouds.

The torrent of countless number of arrows, randomly landing on targets, is one of the most feared aspects of battle, as fortuitous chance is often the only salvation. Here, most of the arrows crashed down on the overlapping shields like small rocks of hail, causing a tremendous pounding sound but very few casualties. Splinters from the crashing arrows flew off in every direction, projectiles of shattered wood, causing a secondary effect of small flesh wounds. An unlucky hand or foot struck, causing some men to crumble, but the "turtle shell" held.

Next the light cavalry of Horse Warriors attacked, galloping in a frenzy toward the defenders, wheeling around and launching their arrows with limited effect. Ekavir and the Shore People's light cavalry launched their counterattack, joining several hundred of the Varagans led by Veer and Arian. The Horse Warriors completely outflanked retreated sooner than they expected, though retreating was a normal tactic to lure the opposing forces into the trap.

Arian had warned Ekavir not to penetrate too deeply into the field of battle to chase down the retreating Horse Warriors, knowing feigned retreat was a practiced tactic. Even very disciplined field commanders, intoxicated by momentary success, make critical error. So, it was with Ekavir who feverishly urged his men forward, thinking complete victory was at hand. Arian signaled to his men to slow the pace to provide additional cover for the Shore People warriors.

Within a short period, the Horse Warriors fanned left and right, revealing several hundred heavy cavalry riders, wielding heavy lances, plunging forward in a direct frontal attack, perfectly synchronized as a killing machine. The heavy cavalry horses were much grander and served as battering rams as they charged headlong into the light cavalry of the Shore People. Ekavir's bravery became a mere flash in time as a long spear penetrated directly through his neck, killing him instantly.

The Horse Warriors launched simultaneous flanking attacks which would have normally surrounded and destroyed the mounted warriors under Ekavir's command, but a well-timed advance by the Varagan cavalry led by Veer and Arian blunted each frontal attack, neutralizing the Horse Warriors offensive maneuvers.

The Varagans and Shore People's warriors reorganized and unite under Arian's direction, executing a disciplined retreat to the city gates. Meanwhile, the Horse Warriors now in an absolute frenzy, more ferocious than any pack of hungry lions and more deadly than the bites of hundreds of king cobra snakes furiously mounted an assault led by the heavy cavalry and hundreds of light cavalry riders. The Horse Warriors, sensing this was the ultimate moment to crush the enemy, their minds in a self-induced trance, believed the slaughter would soon begin.

The main gates of the city opened, and twenty-five warrior elephants emerged in full armor. These magnificent animal warriors were of superior training and able to fight as one huge unit of overwhelming weight and force. Out of the gates they rumbled, a sight never witnessed by any Horse Warrior as the previous engagement with elephants in the Greenlands resulted in either the death or capture of the Horse Warriors. The immediate effect was to shock the horses of the Horse Warriors into sheer panic, followed by confusion among the mounted attackers as to a method of defense since the elephants wore fully clad armor, fabricated with layers of copper. To add to the rout, the Nivasi archers and the Varagan cavalry, buttressed by the Shore People fighters seeking revenge, launched their attacks.

In a melee involving thousands of fighters on both sides, with the elephants trampling everything in sight regardless of friend or foe, the chaos was overwhelming. The elephants had initially blunted the attack of the heavy spear equipped attackers, causing numerous casualties but as the long spears of the Horse Warriors found exposed legs, sometimes eyes, causing the wounded elephants to throw off their handlers and madly plow through anything in their way. At these close quarters, swords were most effective.

Fighters on both sides were swinging wildly at each other, causing untold flesh wounds and mortal blows. Veer and a brother of Omisha, the woman previously assaulted by Balashur squared off in a vicious clash of sharpened metal. Each fought with tenacity and skill, but Veer sliced off the right hand of his opponent, which did not stop the Horse Warrior, despite a huge squirt of blood. The fighter jumped onto Veer's horse, stabbing furiously with a knife clenched in his left hand, completely oblivious to his missing right hand. The gravely injured Horse Warrior managed a backward slash, catching Veer in the neck, a severe but not fatal wound. Veer choked his opponent with both hands, the power of the grip crushing his enemy's larynx, inducing gasping and bulging eyes. Omisha's brother dropped to the ground, trampled by one of the injured elephants which was rampaging wildly through the battlefield.

Balashur having sworn to protect Omisha's brothers aimed directly at Veer. Insanely cursing and screaming, Balashur struck Veer's temple with his sword with such enormous force Veer momentarily blacked out, creating the perfect opportunity to inflict a deadly slash to his neck. With the last instincts of a great warrior, Veer pivoted to his right, striking Balashur in the mouth with such a force, the edge of the sword shattered Balashur's teeth, the blow penetrating up through his nose into his eye socket. In fact, this blow did not kill Balashur, but the blood squirted into his eyes, blinding Balashur, now swinging wildly at anyone in range of his sword.

Arian, glimpsing the attack on Veer and mad for revenge, charged directly into Balashur, the two horses colliding in their own contest but Chatresh easily bested his opponent and Balashur soon crumpled on his horse, his neck slit open with a gaping wound to match his bloody, shredded mouth. It was too late to save Veer, his neck bleeding profusely from a ruptured artery. Veer fell unconscious from his horse.

Both sides threw everything into the battle. Each side exhausted their forces, but Devi and Arian had held back the chariots. Dhanur, knowing the battle was at the most critical stage, launched his last force of light cavalry. Instinctively, the remaining Horse Warriors sensed the decisive moment. With a thirst for victory and a controlled madness seizing their spirits, the Horse Warriors with Dhanur leading the charge, plunged headlong into the battle.

Then the chariots emerged, and the last contingent of Shore Cavalry held in reserve, and a hundred Varagans led, not by Samarth as planned, but by Pratham. Pratham advanced directly toward Dhanur, but a group of four Horse Warriors intercepted and surrounded him.

Witnesses say Pratham was truly a king in his demise, a warrior of courage, nobility, and honor. Encircled by the four Horse Warriors, he viciously sliced at the first opponent with such force the man's head rolled onto the ground. Veering to his right, he attacked the second mounted warrior, driving his sword into the man's heart while taking a severe blow to his own chest. Gravely wounded, he fought on, gaining the respect of the Horse Warriors, one of whom decided a well-aimed arrow would stop him. The arrow struck slightly to the side of his neck, causing a horrific scene as Pratham continued his attack with an arrow lodged in his throat. With his last gasp of energy, Pratham hurled his knife at his killer, striking the man directly in his eye, thus ending his time on earth as well.

The chariots, although relatively few, caused more confusion and panic among the horses of the attackers, disrupting the disciplined formation of the Horse Warriors. The archers on the chariots, mainly women led by Mishka, closed within ten feet of their targets, launching arrows at point blank range. Simultaneously, hundreds of Nivasi ran onto the battlefield, hurling sharp javelins at any available enemy target. The element of surprise of the chariots, the attack by the javelin warriors in unison with the attack of the Pratham forces, routed the last offensive initiative led by Dhanur.

Axam and Dhanur both simultaneously realized a full retreat was necessary to prevent outright disaster. A powerful horn reverberated through the battlefield, sounding the retreat; all the Horse Warriors with the discipline of army ants collected and retreated without panic. Complete exhaustion afflicted the Nivasi and Varagans, so the organized retreat of the Horse warriors was an immense relief. Clearly the Horse Warriors could have persevered for hours, but Dhanur realized a complete victory would need to wait.

The wailing sounds of hundreds of wounded fighters permeated the killing fields. For the Horse Warriors, too wounded to escape, their wailings were not the moaning of physical pain but chants to prepare for the spirits of their ancestors who awaited them.

The battle scene was sheer destruction, the number of dead and wounded staggering for both sides. The Horse Warriors understood the inevitable. They would have to withdraw, their mission incomplete. For Dhanur, he understood his fate. Axam also understood the consequences for Dhanur, as half the original force was dead or gravely wounded. It would take months for them to recover. They had no choice but to retreat to the river and build fortifications to prevent any future counterattack from the Varagans or these new warriors called the Shore People. Despite his humiliating withdrawal, Dhanur had the duty to lead his troops back to a sanctuary.

Back in Desa, tremendous sorrow and unimaginable grief affected nearly every family. Throughout the day and night, the Nivasi, the Varagans and the Shore Warriors shared their grief and jointly mourned their losses. Arian and Devi tried to console as many families as possible, but their biggest challenge was Mishka, herself wounded in the battle, now in overwhelming despair having lost Veer, her bitter fate worse than death.

The defenders protected freedom, but at an enormous cost. People were in shock at the sheer carnage of dead and wounded on both sides. Families roamed the battlefield, stumbling numbly from one body to another, some fainting upon recognition of a loved one. Others vomited from the sight of sliced arms and hands, gruesome cuts of human flesh, mangled faces covered with blood, the dead, icy stare of the warrior's eyes. Among them was Shanti, a passionate advocate for pacifism, now even more sickened by the madness of war. For many, freedom seemed an abstract idea, meaningless in the reality of such widespread butchery.

As Devi and Arian consoled each other, both realized their freedom was only temporary. The Horse Warriors would return in massive numbers, having vastly underestimated the rugged determination of the Nivasi and Varagans. Arian assessed the Horse Warriors would study all the tricks and innovative tactics. The next time they would return with a force triple the size, with an army customized to complete the mission.

A Desa War Committee meeting convened that evening to plan the next steps. There was no certainty the immediate threat of renewed attacks had disappeared. Before attending to any other task, Arian fetched Kutta from the house, delighted at the prospects of going to the corral to chase the other big dog. Arian and Kutta spotted Chatresh in his usual resting place. Arian had to restrain Kutta, who was circling and agitating, "Kutta, Chatresh had a busy day and will not be interested in playtime. He needs to rest." For Chatresh, there was only one question, "Is it time again?"

Meanwhile, on the edges of the littered battlefield, lay a few select men, the "Assassins", artistically disguised casualties covered with blood and dirt. They had wagered the Nivasi would not systematically spear each enemy body, customary with certain armies such as the Horse Warriors. Five of them laid in wait, motivated for their mission, their own death not a concern.

At the War Committee meeting, there were no celebratory words spoken as the defense of their people had exacted a tremendous toll. Everyone believed peace was temporary. Amura, the wise man of the Varagans, echoed the dark sentiments lurking within each person, "We have repulsed the Horse Warriors. The dangers are now more elevated, as these people know only victory and are deeply vengeful in their souls. They believe death in battle is a path to a glorious eternity, and any defeat requires the most brutal retaliation. They will return in larger numbers with one singular mission, the complete annihilation of our people and the physical destruction of this city."

Devi, the most insightful of the leaders on both sides, warned the dangers were hiding in plain sight, "The physical prowess of the Horse Warriors is plain to see. Yes, we must be vigilant against assuming anything. Axam is extremely ingenious and will use myriad ways to probe and penetrate our spirits and lull us into a false sense of relief. Do not trust your eyes. Above all, do not trust your rational mind, which cannot see anything other than the futility of war and desperate hopes for peace. Vidya, what do your instincts say?"

It was wise for Devi to query Vidya. Normally, Vidya did not like to speak, believing talking distracted the senses, creating a momentary vacuum of the senses, sometimes fatal in the forests. Words should be sparse, mainly to create images for effective communications.

His words haunted the Nivasi Council members, "The tiger is a master of night hunting, with eyesight and hearing superior to its prey. I believe danger still lurks among us. Fear the night, do not let your eyes deceive you or words dull awareness."

Arian gave strict orders to protect the walls and all gates, emphasizing strict vigilance must be enforced. Vidya had already ordered his men to occupy strategic positions throughout the city, cautionary actions on the night of a day in which most of the inhabitants desired a respite from the anxiety of war and any method to calm shattered nerves.

Some Nivasi, either in search of loved ones or souvenirs of war, principally from dead Horse Warriors, exited the city through secret doors which were nearly invisible to anyone outside the walls. This was the opportunity the Assassins were hoping for. Like sick or lame antelope struggling to keep pace with the herd, they picked Nivasi looters off, their death quiet and sudden. The Horse Warriors stripped their bodies to disguise themselves as ordinary

Nivasi citizens. Within minutes, all five assassins were inside the city walls, fanning out in two teams, each with their mission. Trained in languages, these elite fighters, now dressed in Nivasi clothes, began their search.

Soon, two men appeared on a side street, walking aimlessly, perhaps their senses dulled by local intoxicants. The assassins snatched them from the darkness, covering their mouths, a sharp knife to their throats. "Take us to the house of Devi and Arian and we will spare your lives." One of the two Nivasi made the error of resisting. A sharp knife sliced through his neck, cutting off his blood supply, causing immediate fainting followed by death. The remaining Nivasi immediately agreed to cooperate.

Several streets away, they seized a young woman in the same manner, but she did not require any coaxing, leading the second team to the home of Gandesh. Upon reaching the home of Gandesh, the unfortunate woman also departed from this earth; no witnesses allowed. Gandesh's home was lightly guarded, for no one feared for the old man's life. A guard, more like a manservant, was quickly eliminated, making access to Gandesh in his bed an effortless task. Gandesh, now sensing the approach of evil, sat up only to encounter a vicious slash of the assassin's knife. Slowly, consciousness flowed out of his life, the pain of the initial thrust receded, no different from falling asleep. No one knows their last thoughts before sleep or death, and so it was with Gandesh.

The two assassins, satisfied with the ease of the task, slid warily out the front entrance, now in search of Mandeep. Perhaps overconfident, they made a fatal error. Both emerged quickly, barely noticing the growl of the dogs hidden across the way in the shadows. Two arrows released, the only sounds being the subtle "whoosh" of the arrows in flight, followed by "thunk, thunk" as the arrows struck the imaginary bullseye on the chest of each recipient. Enraged, the assassins attacked, but the Forest Dwellers were quick to launch another round of arrows, each finding their mark, dropping both men who madly tried to snap the protruding arrows from their chest. One last shot to their necks from five feet ended their resistance.

The other team, led by the traumatized young Nivasi approached, the home of Devi and Arian. Expecting the need to overpower guards, the wary assassins cautiously crept into the house. Two men entered, the third left behind to guard the entrance and to dispose of the traumatized youth. The assassin dragged the boy into a side alley where Vidya waited. Fate was kind to the young man. Vidya choked the sole assassin with sharp vines wrapped around his neck, squeezing so tightly no sound of pain or warning was possible. Vidya kept twisting and squeezing, not relenting his grip, watching the distorted and protruding eyes of a squirming body, blood seeping out the assassin's ears and nose, then speedily deploying his knife to ensure death. Vidya signaled to the Nivasi boy to keep quiet.

The two assassins stealthily entered the bedroom, spotting two figures lying still in the bed, apparently fast asleep under the covers. With hand signals, the two assassins each chose their victim. They simultaneously leaped on to the bed, furiously slashing the figures. They shredded the fake figures made of straw. From the dark area of the room, Kutta and Arian attacked. One assassin turned to face Arian, just in time to receive a fatal slash to his neck. Arian grabbed the stunned attacker and smashed his head into the floor, snapping his neck. Kutta had leaped on the back of the second assassin and was viciously tearing off his ears when Devi appeared from the dark shadows and thrust a long spear into the heart of the intruder. Falling back and slashing madly, the assassin's knife unfortunately struck Kutta, severing a main artery.

Seeing Kutta collapse to the ground, incensed Arian beyond control. He jumped on the wounded assassin, desiring to choke the life out of him. The assassin, although gravely wounded, flipped Arian onto his side and was within a blink of an eye from killing him with a knife when Devi cut off the assailant's right hand with a sword thrust. With his left hand, the assassin tried to grasp the severed hand with the knife still firmly locked in place. Marshalling every ounce of energy, Arian grabbed the knife and plunged into the assassin's neck, ending the struggle. Arian flung the assassin to the side, the severed hand with the clutching knife embedded in his neck. Arian noticed a strange tattoo, the image of a skull and knife.

Arian, stunned and nearly mad with grief, picked up the lifeless body of Kutta. There is no greater loyalty than that of a dog. Kutta was a noble warrior who attacked with no regard for his own safety, the only task to defend his masters. Arian and Devi decided the first-born son would bear the name Kutta. In one day, Arian had lost Kutta and Veer, but thankfully, he still could cherish Devi and Chatresh. It would take a long time for his grief to pass. The spirit of revenge and hatred for the Horse Warriors would never dissipate.

PART 34
The Trial of AO

Viraj thought Zeba's recovery was a miracle, clearly a result of the intervention from the spirits who watched over the Shore People, accessible only by the chief priests. The chief priests, dominant in the society of the Shore People, superstitious by nature, taught there were ancestral spirits of great deceased leaders who served the ultimate spirit only referred to as the "Original Spirit". It was not possible to communicate with the Original Spirit. One could only communicate through the lower echelon of the spirits, formerly distinguished war leaders, kingdom rulers and chief priests who were long deceased.

Ritualistic prayers and poems, memorized by the priests in oral tradition, were the only channels to the spirits who still roamed on earth, appearing to the chief priests, mainly through visions and seances. Occasionally, people, not of the priest class, would claim a connection to the spirits through dreams or visitations, often with the help of potent strains of cannabis. These claims were clearly heresy. Such people, daring or foolish enough to assert visitations with the spirits, faced execution or simply disappeared in the night, if of sufficient class distinction to avoid an inquisition. The power of the chief priests rested on their influence with the eternal spirits, a status they would allow no other humans to weaken.

As to the "miracle" of Zeba's recovery, Viraj ensured the total credit accrued to the chief priests. The actions of Kalpesh and AO were meaningless gestures, not significant. The gift of wine had disappeared; thus, it was easy for Vedant to claim it was a gesture of friendship, not in any way connected to Zeba's illness. Viraj was stunned a few days earlier when AO and Kalpesh had appeared at the home of Zeba. The private guard of the priests had assured him he would never see AO again.

Rishaan, suspicious about the illness which nearly killed Zeba, summoned Viraj, Vedant, Kalpesh and AO to his chambers. Viraj assumed the pose of piety, Vedant less confident, if not anxious, while Kalpesh and AO were practically stoic. Rishaan asked Viraj to explain the cause of illness and the miraculous recovery.

"Rishaan, sire, I am sorry to inform you Zeba had angered the spirits by questioning our doctrines, demeaning, perhaps unintentionally, their omnipotence in our daily lives. I tried with all my heart and love for you and your family to dissuade her, but she persisted."

Rishaan did clearly recall Zeba insinuated anyone could aspire to be a chief priest, her words still ringing in his mind, "everyone should be a soldier, everyone an artisan, everyone a farmer or fisherman, everyone a priest." Zeba's advice had troubled Rishaan, since social unrest would threaten his rule as well. Rishaan contemplated, *Why should he, or anyone from the royal family, be the ruler, if all people are equal?* Viraj was making valid points.

Rishaan recalled the fateful words of AO, "Our souls contain the seeds of the spirit which under the right conditions can foster a majestic life". Ruminating these words in his mind and influenced by Viraj, Rishaan realized the right conditions may well lead common laborers to seek a majestic life, his majestic life! "AO, please enlighten all of us with your thoughts."

AO briefly commented. "There is natural law and the law of men; both must be in harmony. There are spiritual forces in the natural world which require our respect."

Not sure what to conclude about the comments of AO, Rishaan turned to Viraj and said, "Viraj, do you have questions for AO?"

Secretly delighted, Viraj now had the opportunity he had been seeking. "AO, was Zeba cured by our ancestral spirits induced by our prayers and solicitations or by the hands of mortals?"

AO deliberately waited a few seconds, the tension building in the room. "The love and care of each person in this room cured her; our hands simply the means to bring natural cures into her body."

Viraj quickly pounced, "Wise AO, are you saying the spirits of our ancestors obliging our incantations were not of supreme importance? Should the ancestral spirits who guide everything in our lives share the credit with men with herbs and spices?" This was the ultimate trap, as the doctrines preach man is completely subservient to the ancestral spirits, to suggest otherwise is blasphemy.

AO, speaking with modesty and gentility, responded, "Humans should respect and honor the wisdom of the spiritual world which permeates all life and is the essence of nature itself."

More insistent, Viraj firmly asked AO again, "Do you believe the spiritual ancestors were the only force to cure Zeba?"

"There were many spiritual and natural forces in harmony which healed Zeba."

Viraj, somewhat satisfied, stated unequivocally, "I accept your answer as a no."

AO remained silent. Puzzled, Rishaan thought to himself, *AO did correctly interpret my dream and I believe AO and Kalpesh cured Zeba, but how could he align himself against Viraj?*

Viraj then asked for a moment alone with Rishaan. Without objection, which would have only worsened matters, AO and Kalpesh departed. Viraj, sensing a golden opportunity to strike, pronounced, "AO has committed blasphemy and must stand trial. The only resolution to please our ancestral spirits is death."

Rishaan, thinking he could take his chances with the ancestral spirits but not risk insurrection from the chief priests, responded "Proceed, but ensure the trial is in an open forum." Disgruntled by the requirement of an open trial, but hiding his feelings, Viraj bowed respectfully, and feigning subservience bid him farewell. The next act would be the arrest of AO.

It was no surprise to AO when four men, suspiciously dressed like the assassins sent to kill him, announced they were from the private guard of the senior chief priest, Viraj. AO politely submitted to the demands of the arrest squad. The guards escorted AO to the compound of the priests which contained a prison, a dingy small room secluded from the earshot of the public. AO smelled suffering and pain, urine, and dried blood, reeking from the walls and floor, as the small, dank dungeon had been the scene of various tortures.

Soon afterwards, a man appeared introducing himself as Dumurkha, a rising star of the chief priests. He explained Viraj had selected him to attempt one more time to clear AO of any charges of blasphemy. "I do not understand what crimes I have committed", countered AO.

With slight annoyance, Dumurkha recited the charges, in the manner of an actor on opening night mimicking a prepared script written by the scene director. This was exactly how the trial would play out, with the outcome already scripted and predetermined. "You have failed to acknowledge the supreme power of our ancestral spirits and have denigrated them by casting them in with all spirits, treating them as natural phenomena. If we do not rectify this slander, our peoples will suffer a calamity such as a flood or famine."

AO replied, "What would you have me do?" Since Dumurkha was expecting a denial, the apparent confession of AO caught him off guard.

Dumurkha quickly departed and sought the advice of Viraj. In his twisted, cunning mind, Viraj viewed AO was a gifted man who would easily manipulate the Tribunal in a public trial. Viraj smiled and offered the answer to Dumurkha, a priest of high rank with modest talents and low intellectual capability. Dumurkha's supreme talent was his unmatched capability to recite extraordinarily long passages of the sacred poems and scriptures, a feat of amazement and envy, a man of specific value to Viraj.

The poems and chants were the primary method to communicate to the ancestral spirits. The people considered Dumurkha a genius in awe of the sheer volume of memorized verses. Unknown to the public, Dumurkha was devoid of any other knowledge or mental faculties. Normally people used the word "idiot", referring to a person with extraordinary mental skill in memorization but lacking normal intelligence in all other respects.

"Dumurkha, perhaps you were a bit misinformed as to the charges. AO is guilty of undermining our society by preaching all humans are equal, which is not the case in our land as privilege in our society rests on the virtues of wisdom and high intelligence, common to the ruling families in the military and in politics and among the priests."

Befuddled and cowering like a small puppy dog who has soiled his master's home, Dumurkha meekly said, "I recited the charges exactly as you stated." Viraj grabbed him by the shoulders and proclaimed, "You did well Dumurkha, your information is most helpful."

Viraj set the trial time for the next day, judging a quick determination of guilt was ideal before potential defenders could call any witnesses to testify on behalf of the accused. Besides, Viraj reasoned, Zeba's illness prevents her from attending. Kalpesh, although a priest in his own right was not of his faith and Rishaan was too fearful of offending the chief priests to intervene. *No*, Viraj muttered to himself, *I will settle this quickly, and pronounce AO's guilt. Sedition against society was even a greater offense than blasphemy, and AO would spend his last days in agony in the hole.*

There was no trial notice, although it is unlikely anyone would have taken an interest with a mystic on trial for sedition or blasphemy. The only unusual part was the fact the trial was in public. Rishaan directed his other two daughters to attend the full proceedings and report back to him as to progress. He did not mention the word, "outcome", as Rishaan knew Viraj had already determined AO's fate; the only question remaining was whether Rishaan would alter that outcome.

Zeba was improving by the hour, although sleep filled most of her day. She hardly took notice when one of her sisters nonchalantly mentioned she planned to attend the trial. Barely alert, Zeba inquired, "Why are you going to a trial?" The answer shocked her when she heard the name AO and trial in the same sentence. In her heart, she understood full well the chief priests had poisoned her. Likely Viraj himself had directed Vedant to do the deed. She tried to rouse herself, only to fall back into bed; sleep was her master now.

At noon, the Tribunal comprising Viraj, Vedant and Dumurkha and a scribe, came to order. It surprised Viraj to see Zeba's sisters accompanied by Kalpesh. Nothing prohibited any of them from attending the full proceedings. It was tradition. Any direct member of the royal family could speak, although no one remembered any such occasion in the past.

Viraj began by reciting aloud the charges. To add formality to the proceedings, he farcically read the charges as if he were seeing them for the first time. "We have charged the man, AO, with sedition against the established kingdom of the Shore Peoples. This man has been preaching a set of beliefs undermining the spiritual values and stability of our people. Whereas the kingdom has entrusted the chief priests with upholding and protecting these beliefs, promoting harmony among the people, and fostering loyalty to the royal family, it is our duty to judge the preaching of the man called AO."

Viraj then asked AO to stand and state his position. AO said, "I plead only to the truth as defined by the natural laws of man and the divinity of nature which must coexist in harmony."

Viraj then questioned AO further, "Do you believe and accept the supreme role of ancestral spirits?"

AO answered, "I believe humans must cherish and respect their ancestral spirits and seek inspiration and truth from their legacy. I believe we all infused with the divinity of our ancestors, even those ancestors which inhabit the seas such as the octopus."

The mention of octopus was of enormous significance as many Shore People lived on the seacoast and made their livings by fishing, excluding the octopus deemed to be not only of a higher intelligent species but also the source of humanity. Viraj continued, "Do you believe in the natural law of man which bounds people to their class based on birth?"

The crux of the matter, AO thought, as he firmly answered, "No one can doubt the truth of natural law: all creatures of the wild are equal, meaning their purpose of existence is not inferior to any other creature. All life seeks to grow and prosper whether we speak of the vegetative seeds in the fields to the most majestic creatures such as elephants and tigers, from the meandering sand crab to the divine octopus, all endowed with natural gifts to fulfill its destiny and purpose. This is also true for all humans."

Viraj secretly cursed to himself as the mention of the octopus would raise spiritual sentiments within people. Viraj pressed as if dealing with a murderer, "So you are saying all humans are equal regardless of birth or class?"

AO responded, "Just as every acorn has the potential to grow to a mature oak to fulfill its purpose, so it is with humans. All humans are equal driven by the same forces to prosper and proliferate; nothing guaranteed, it is the potentiality, following natural law, to realize the purpose of human life. Humans cannot deny any other person their natural rights."

Viraj was now becoming incensed, "Do you believe only through the verses can humans communicate with their ancestral spirits?"

AO sensing the desperation of Viraj answered, "All humans have a duty to honor their ancestral spirits and respect those people gifted and knowledgeable in the verses. All people can find inspiration from the spiritual world; however, the greatest source of comfort and strength derives from the harmony of human and natural life, even the soil, waters of the seas and the very air we breathe require respect."

Switching his line of questioning to seek a clinching argument, Viraj asked his ultimate question, "Do you believe any human, even a humble laborer could be a high priest, an exalted military leader or even the supreme ruler, despite their lowly class?"

AO had no hesitation to answer from his heart in union with his mind, "Each person has the potentiality to achieve those positions you cite and any other in human society. Ideally, only those with a pure soul, high talent and good aspirations and respect for life will succeed, but no force can extinguish human potentiality and purpose. Most will never rise above their current condition, but each person has the spiritual seeds in their souls to realize their dreams."

Viraj snapped back, "Do you mean to include woman as equal to men?"

AO had broken one cherished belief of the chief priests asserting people are not equal, now, the ultimate challenge. AO stood, hesitating to amplify the tension, surveying the small crowd. To his surprise, he saw not only the sisters of Zeba but also Zeba symbolically clad in a white dress shirt, normally a sign of mourning; here, an obvious symbol of protest and resistance to the injustice of the chief priests.

AO gathered all his strength, and with eyes lifted toward the sky, his arms extended, spoke these words, "All women are equal to men as the ultimate potentiality of women is equal to men. You might ask me if a woman can strive to be the chief priest of the land. My answer is yes. Can a woman serve as ruler of this kingdom? Again, I affirm the answer is yes."

Viraj had heard enough. The next step would be a false private discussion of the facts leading to the rendering of the judgment. Viraj closed the trial, saying, "The Tribunal will now seek wisdom in this matter using meditation and a fair review of all words spoken by the defendant."

To the surprise of Viraj and Vedant, Zeba stood and defiantly announced, "I wish to speak". At first, Viraj tried to invoke procedural rules to stop her, but Zeba retorted, "It is my right as a member of the ruling family to speak. Do you wish to confront the authority of Rishaan and his direct heirs?"

Viraj, his mind contorted in anger, calmly said, "We are gratified to witness your recovery and, of course, fully embrace your right to speak." Dumurkha looked dumbfounded while Vedant felt a sense of dread. Zeba chose not to mention the poisoning, even though she was sure Vedant had executed the bidding of Viraj. Zeba also learned from Kalpesh that assassins from the guard of the priests had tried to murder AO. Kalpesh mentioned Sachiv would testify to these facts.

Zeba, summoning her spirit to provide clarity and lucidity, testified, "This man AO has slandered no member of our society nor advocated for any harm or disrespect. In fact, AO has emphasized the duty of all people to respect the laws of man and has repeatedly spoken respectfully of the need to uphold traditional values. His only crime is to argue for the harmony of the human spirit with naturalism. His only crime is to speak the truth: all humans have the potential for achievement according to their purpose. His only crime is he has advocated the freedom of all humans to pursue their aspirations and dreams, and to follow the purpose as expressed in those dreams. AO has stated it is against natural law to use violence or crimes of the soul to achieve one's purpose."

Further adding to the complexity of the situation, Zeba spoke these fateful words, "If you determine AO is guilty of any crimes against our civil laws, then you must find me guilty. I fully endorse the words of AO."

Viraj now faced a dilemma. Zeba was essentially challenging the power of the chief priests to judge on a wide matter of crimes invoking broad interpretations of religious law. The question was uncomplicated: was advocating for human equality and opportunity a crime, a seditious act against the state, or merely an affront to the religious order?

Viraj fully understood Zeba was beloved by her father, but even family members will turn on each other to gain or sustain power. *Would Rishaan fear the wrath of the chief priests less than the wrath of a daughter arguably deluded from her illness?*

The Tribunal adjourned for their meditative discussions, mainly a screaming lecture by Viraj against Vedant and fate itself. He had failed in his attempt to abolish the foolish notion of equality. He scornfully said, "Can you imagine a woman as a chief priest? How ludicrous is that notion?"

Dumurkha, as usual, sat dumbfounded but was of sublime purpose as he could recite every word spoken by AO. Vedant thought to himself, Zeba had proven her wisdom. He even envisioned her as a chief priest! Fearing for his own life and self-interest, he obliged Viraj, "Yes, a nonsensical idea."

Viraj called the Tribunal back together in the public session. It shocked him to see not only Kalpesh and the three daughters of Rishaan, including Zeba and Rishaan himself. Viraj initially panicked, as it was impossible to know what Rishaan would do. "Rishaan, sire", Viraj said, "May we consult with you in private before rendering our verdict?" Rishaan responded, "I don't believe trial law permits private consultations with members of the public, am I correct?"

Viraj, a quick thinker, responded, "Sire, as all priests, including the chief priests faithfully follow the guidance of the ruler, we consider you as a standing member of the Tribunal." Rishaan thought, *if true, such an interpretation of civil trials must exclude the ruler and include other citizens, not just the self-chosen priests.* Rishaan further reasoned if he waived the right of membership as articulated by Viraj without expanding the membership of the Tribunal, he could not legitimately stop a guilty judgment. He would have inadvertently increased the power of Viraj.

Everyone waited for Rishaan to articulate his response, but only Viraj and AO fully comprehended the significance of the decision Rishaan faced. Needing to think through all his options through the benefit of meditation, Rishaan said, "The Tribunal shall convene tomorrow morning shortly after tea and prayers."

The evening light flickered hazily from a few candles, perfect for the tranquility Rishaan sought. The warm evening temperatures were also a seduction to meditate under the fig trees with heart-shaped, gently rustling leaves, although there was no discernible wind. His mind shifted away from the matters of the Tribunal, his body relaxing from toes up to his head, the intention to empty his mind of Viraj and AO. He thought of the words of the meditation masters, *Return to the source to find the truth of your being, the source being your inner spirit, the origins of consciousness.*

Then, Tarak shattered the tranquility, standing in the twilight, exhibiting tears of anguish despite every effort to project calmness.

"Lord Rishaan, I must inform you of some terrible news." Rishaan responded "Come forward", barely audible, as his mind was somewhere in the murky transition between a meditative trance and full awareness of the physical world.

"What news do you have?", hoping perhaps the word 'terrible' might be too grave a description. Tarak, second in command of the military and a direct report to Ekavir. "Ekavir died heroically, leading our men in the battle against the Horse Warriors."

Rishaan slumped back, sadness and anger competing for control of his mind. "What about the rest of our forces?"

Tarak replied, "Our forces along with the Nivasi and Varagans were decisive in defeating the attack on Desa. At one point, an overwhelming number of enemy soldiers surrounded us, but Arian led a counterattack which repelled the Horse Warriors, saving hundreds of our fighters but unfortunately, it was too late to save Ekavir, trapped by enemy forces."

Rishaan still mourning the death of his brother now added Ekavir, his nephew and the future ruler of the Shore People, to his sorrow. Bitter tears and vengeful thoughts shattered the solitude of the last moments before the news from Tarak. He would need a bigger army now. Thoughts of the trial faded into annoyance in his moment of surging anger. Rishaan thought, *Later I will find a shrewd way to end the farcical trial of AO and embarrass Viraj.*

Tarak and Harnish had informed Rishaan that the Horse Warriors had invaded with a force of 4,000 fighters, of which at least 2,000 had retreated to the Great Stars River. Arian informed Tarak of an assured fact. Khander, the Supreme Leader of the Horse Warriors, who according to legend had never suffered defeat in battle, would return with a force at least 10,000. Such an army of overwhelming strength and capability would crush the Nivasi and Varagans in one day.

The key aim was to secure the southern banks of the river with sufficient men and fortifications to halt the crossing of such an immense force. Tarak added, "When the Horse Warriors come, they will march to our seacoast, subjugate our people, kill all the elites and destroy our land as we know it." Rishaan's thoughts turned to AO and his prophetic interpretation of his dream.

The next morning, the Tribunal reconvened with Rishaan in attendance. As rumors had spread of the trial and the intervention of Rishaan, noted by Viraj to be legal, curious observers jammed the tribunal meeting. Rishaan was careful to show the proper respect to the members of the Tribunal, a show for the attending citizens. Viraj was villainous and of evil intent. Rishaan suspected Viraj would seek any means to become ruler of the land, fulfilling his true motivation to transform the land into a religious kingdom, proclaiming himself as a god.

Viraj briefly read the charges against AO while the audience listened with a mixture of awe and curiosity. With his voice directed squarely at the populace gathered in the courtyard, Rishaan stated, "The members of the tribunal have conducted this trial openly, but have neglected to hear from an important witness, a high priest of a different religious order within the distant shores of our kingdom. He is a citizen of our kingdom bearing important knowledge of the man, AO."

A hush filled the courtyard as it was not normal practice to hear from religious witnesses from a different order, plus the coded expression, "important knowledge" implied Rishaan intended a dramatic shift in the outcome.

Rishaan asked Kalpesh to stand before the tribunal and identify himself, to speak truthful words.

Kalpesh said, "I have known this man AO for many years; in fact, I was the one who lifted his body from the sandy beaches near our village, AO being the only survivor of a wicked typhoon which struck his village consuming the lives of everyone. The young child, AO, swept into the deep of the sea along with his parents, should have shared the same fate as his family but the arbiters of life summoned the octopus to lift the boy onto a waterspout and gently place him on the beach. Does anyone doubt the plain truth of our origins? Is it not true the seeds of humans long ago derived from the life of the sea? We believe our ancestors who inspired the octopus to save the life of AO desired the survival of AO, a human uniquely infused of their spirit."

An amazing hush came over the proceedings. No one doubted the veracity of this testimony, believing AO possessed unique wisdom. Viraj faced a terrible dilemma as he realized the only option was the full acquittal of AO.

Viraj rose and pronounced the tribunal judgment. "The man called AO may not be fully aware of our teachings. We find him innocent of any crimes, but so determine AO must memorize the poetic scriptures of our land. The man, AO, must recite the mantras, within ninety days, pertaining to the rituals which govern societal behavior. If he cannot satisfy this task, then he must accept banishment from this land." Viraj was quite happy with himself as the ordered task was beyond the intellectual capacities of any person. Even Dumurkha, blessed with the most gifted memory of all priests, had taken one year to accomplish the same task. However, Viraj should have realized by now. AO was no ordinary person.

If such an outrageous task stunned anyone in attendance, they were all quiet except for Zeba who boldly said," Viraj, you know the sentence is unjust. You believe banishment is inevitable. You do not know the man, AO." Viraj, hiding his contempt, remained silent, mulling in his mind how to dispose of Zeba, his thoughts and motivations hidden to everyone except Kalpesh and AO who understood the depravity of religious intolerance and the arrogance of Viraj.

Among the throngs of attendees stood Daiwik, another chief

priest in the land of the Shore People. Daiwik's beliefs in civil law over religious law diametrically opposed the strongly held opinions of Viraj, a staunch adherent to the view religious law should reign supreme and the ruler should come from the establishment of chief priests, based on subjective qualifications such as divine reverence, wisdom and extensive knowledge of spiritual beliefs and practices. Of course, Viraj thought he was perfect in these qualities.

Daiwik modestly saw his own imperfections as a human being and considered his purpose in life to promote harmony and community between humans, not just a maniacal dedication to the spiritual ancestors. Daiwik remained silent for the moment. He would choose the time and circumstances to denounce Viraj and protect AO, whom Daiwik judged to be the harbinger of the spiritual renaissance destined to come. Any slight tinge of uncertainty evaporated when Daiwik encountered a peacock on his daily stroll through the local woods. The peacock exploded into brilliant, shimmering feathers, each marked with the eyespots of green and blue. It did not matter the peacock may have staged this magnificent display, solely to prove worthiness to a desired female; Daiwik was sure the peacock was a favorable omen inspired by the ancestral spirits.

PART 35
Days of Mourning and Love Lost

―⋅⋈⋅―

Devi could not stop thinking of the senseless death of Gandesh. She fixated on the gentle image of Gandesh, an elderly man of humility who represented no threat. Surely, Axam would have understood Gandesh was of little significance to the battle and wielded virtually no political power. Axam understood she and Arian were the primary architects of the war strategy, the spirit of resistance. What did Gandesh represent, and why have him assassinated?

Gandesh's body was wrapped in white cotton linen and carefully placed in a wooden casket, a plain box to ensure his body did not touch the soil. His head lay due north, his arms folded across his chest. He wore a beaded necklace, a unique design of jade, gold, and precious stones, the only symbol of authority granted to the leader of the Nivasi People. The ceremony was simple, a few musical instruments such as the flute and some cymbals pierced the melancholic stillness of the service.

Mandeep recited the long history of the skillful leadership of Gandesh, his mastery in the art of persuasion, best encapsulated with an ancient saying, "A leader is best when people barely know he exists."

The violence and death of the war sickened Shanti; in her mind, the evilest expression of the human spirit. She represented a significant number of Nivasi who thought it was foolish and unnatural to join with the Varagans against the Horse Warriors. Shanti believed in nonviolence as the correct way for the Nivasi to live, since their values, traditions and cultures were pacifist in spirit. Now aghast as to the sheer number of dead and wounded with no certainty of future security and prosperity, she became more vocal and more aggressive in her opinions. She also organized an impressive number of Nivasi, equally disturbed and motivated. Gandesh was her symbol of the insanity of war counseling, "We should hold up Gandesh as the rally point for nonviolence and the complete futility of future struggles. We must emulate Gandesh, the epitome of a gentle spirit."

Those words were the spark of insight as to the motivation of Axam. *Yes,* Devi mused, *Axam wants to make Gandesh a symbol of the futility of war. Shanti needed a rallying point, and Axam has cleverly delivered the perfect hero of pacifism. Peace at any cost is far superior to death.* Axam was already plotting the next invasion. He would leave nothing to chance, every move calculated. Shanti would raise the white flag of defeat and rally the Nivasi to yield to their fate, urging peaceful subjugation, preferable to death.

In contrast to the simplicity of the funeral of Gandesh, the Varagans buried Pratham in the most magnificent manner. Colorful purple robes shrouded his body, his neck adorned with an intricate necklace with a variety of precious and semi-precious beads of gold, ivory, and silver. Pratham's ear contained an earring decorated with diamonds, the most rare and precious of all stones, reserved only for the Primary. The common Varagan people passed by his body, gazing with respect but devoid of love whereas the privileged class who cared nothing for the man, focusing mainly on their next steps, calculating how the balance of power might shift. Arian paid his respects for the position Pratham had occupied, his respect for the man long ago diminished.

The contrast between Pratham and Gandesh was striking. Pratham wore the royal clothes of a king, his decorated coffin and body a shrine of jewelry and sacred objects, the illusion of greatness which had long ago vanished from his spirit. The Nivasi buried Gandesh wrapped in all white, devoid of garnishments of the body, his plain coffin and personage reflecting the reality of a humble man beloved by all.

Both the Varagans and the Nivasi held Veer in the highest esteem. His name symbolized bravery; a virtue Veer never dishonored. Veer lived only to serve the Varagan people, including each foot soldier, no matter how inconsequential the position or menial the man's duty. He loved Arian more than he loved himself. In fact, his greatness arose because unlike Pratham, he did not love himself; it was not an emotion fit to his purpose, which was to care more about his men than himself. His leadership emanated from his devotion to the practice of a noble life, an inspirational life of courage and duty.

Arian ensured Veer's burial received the highest military honors. A headband of gold with the inscription, "Live forever in honor" adorned his body. His coffin, also modest in design, contained his sword, and a few seals of lions and tigers. In his right ear was a black onyx pearl, only awarded to Varagan men of outstanding military distinction. Arian unabashedly shed his tears for Veer, unashamed to show the world of his deep and bitter sorrow at the loss of a great friend, forever gone.

Veer and Mishka were deeply in love, a true merging of souls. Two people of vastly different cultures found each other in the most unintentional way, on the archery training fields. Perhaps the truest form of love originates in the most obscure manner, when just a mere glance sparks something very pure. Veer's respect for the fierce spirit of Mishka quickly transformed into passionate desire, mellowing into enduring love and devotion.

Mishka, respected by both peoples, for her bravery and leadership had unleashed an intense spirit, magnified in both love and war, a woman of unlimited energy and passion. Mishka, true to her stoic personality, made a pledge never to marry again, as no man could ever fill the vacuum, cure the pervasive emptiness she experienced from the loss of Veer. Noted for her brevity, Mishka, draped over the body of Veer, prophesied their ultimate reunion, "Veer, our spirits will meet again, rekindling our love in different bodies. Watch for me, as I shall for you, united, we will know who we once were."

Arian and Devi dedicated the last burial service of the day to Kutta. They timed the small service at dusk to mark the transition of the day into night, then night into day, a cycle repeated endlessly. Perhaps a hopeful symbolic gesture even the spirits of dogs could live on? Kutta brought much joy to Arian and protection to Devi. Both loved Kutta in different ways. For Arian, Kutta's loyal and unwavering devotion was the essence of duty and friendship, his death in defense of his masters, the ultimate act of courage. Devi found a more philosophical side to Kutta's death instructive for her people; protecting loved ones was not an act of foolery, but defiance of tyranny.

They interred Kutta in a pot decorated with symbols of war and freedom. The pictorial images showed war horses and hawks and two owls on a branch, an unusual graphic of specific meaning to Devi and Arian. The inscription read, "A warrior in defense of freedom." If the death of Gandesh symbolized the futility of war for Shanti, the death of Kutta symbolized for Devi the opposite; death in the name of freedom and duty is noble and righteous.

Vidya, the man of the land, closest to the natural flow of life told Devi and Arian, "When you sealed the burial urn of Kutta and covered him in the soil of our land, I saw the spirit of a dog rise and join the spirit of a great Varagan warrior. Their spirits are now one." A small amount of joy crept into Arian's heart. He could only hope and dream Vidya's vision was true.

Arian thoughts of Veer and Kutta reminded him of the moments when Pratham, seeking eternal reverence from the people, would seek Arian's advice. "What can I say to the people? What can I give them?" It was really a pathetic question from a corrupt man, once a man of the people, leading soldiers into battle, believing it was important to earn the name, "Primary". Pratham recognized the ancestral list of men held in eternal esteem were few. Pratham also wanted his name added to the short, distinguished list, held in memory by succeeding generations, a legacy of wisdom and nobility from honored lineage. But he craved power, corruption and lies, not wisdom. He was not evil like his brother Jackal, but he tolerated evil and grew increasingly ignoble as the riches of his position made greed, not nobility, his principal goal.

Arian, sighing, thought, *Pratham wanted the secret words of wisdom, the magical mix of oratory which would provide the illusion.* Kutta could not speak and Veer did not speak of honor and nobility; they lived it every moment of their lives.

As Amura often said, "Mystical words from a master are not a sufficient source of wisdom. Wisdom derives from the act of doing. In the same manner, one cannot study honor; one must live an honorable life."

Arian recalled Pratham and Jackal seeking the answers from Amura, like learning an old recipe from a grandmother. "How can we get wisdom, what sources of knowledge can we seek?" Pratham would inquire.

Amura would humbly respond, frustrating Pratham further, "Wisdom is being". Exasperated, Jackal would scream, "Being what? Wise?"

Amura's answer was always the same, "yes". Amura chose not to say wisdom is the recognition of imperfection, the humility of self-awareness of weakness. Wise people would unpretentiously say, "Focus on the words not spoken, not the words spoken." Attainment of wisdom required no clarifications or expositions, no advice from pretentious peddlers of folk wisdom; only insight into one's soul would suffice.

It never occurred to Pratham and Jackal that awareness of weaknesses, not in a political or military sense, was the epicenter of wisdom. They wanted to appear wise and strong, equating self-doubt as weakness, the opposite of the illusion they sought. Jackal could not imagine courage as the absence of fear, it is proceeding with your purpose in the face of fear. He was cowardly because he always chose lies and self-deception over truth; he was too important to risk death in battle. Jackal was quick to demean, saying to Pratham, "Let Arian and Veer risk death, they are only soldiers, easy to replace."

If Jackal was a coward, Pratham was vain, as he believed no one could ever be as brave, courageous, or noble as he had been, long before his darkened spirit became a twisted, intertwined knot of lies, vanity and greed. Even Pratham's heroic death was suicide to escape the agonizing pain from an incurable illness. Arian thought it best to remain silent; let Pratham's secret die with him. People needed heroes; even flawed heroes were valuable. Amura often said all heroes are flawed, which makes them more admirable.

Despite the suffering and profound sadness, there was a budding sign of joy and happiness, as Devi confirmed a child would arrive within the next year. She believed, at least symbolically, in Vidya's vision of the spirits of Veer and Kutta rising from the graves and joining, waiting only for the right time to merge into the spirit of the unborn child.

Devi and Arian would teach their children the truth: words are not truth, actions are truth. Truth is doing. Hoping for honor, or wisdom, or courage, or success is meaningless. Doing and being, the actions of a spirit which values honor and wisdom, are the keys. It is easy to trick the mind, not the soul. Often the mind speaks gibberish, the soul speaks truth.

Devi reflected on the guidance from Mandeep, "Observe the flow of truth, not the torrent of words". Some people were prone to say, "Those are empty words", as if they can decipher words with accuracy. Devi also laughed at the description of someone as "a gifted orator", words which did not seem to have meaning on their own but required a person of physical or intellectual distinction. She thought of the story of a man so hideous in appearance, people believed his words must be truly from the gods. She could not deny the power of words to deceive or to seduce people into blind faith; and yes, some well-chosen words brought joy and comfort, other words stirred the spirits of men to battle.

Then her mind shifted to Mishka, who said little at the funeral service of her husband, Veer. *Did that mean she loved him less? Were words required to interpret the deep sadness and emptiness in her face and heart? Were the tears dripping from blood-shot eyes insufficient, or were words required as well?*

Sometimes, only words from the heart can suffice. Saisha was still waiting to hear Balvan utter three simple words, "I am sorry", followed by three more words seeking redemption, "Please forgive me." Saisha was still waiting for those words, only those words.

Balvan could say, "I love you", often in moments of passion, but deep love demanded more.

PART 36
Obsessions of Love and Revenge

※

Only a sliver of sunlight was discernible as dawn had not yet signaled the day to duty. Saisha lay silently. The sunlight pierced her sleep, shifting her consciousness from the nightly dream state to full awareness. She thought she heard the night sounds of an owl, but more likely it was her imagination, harkening back to days in the more luxurious land in which owls were unmistakably hooting to mark their territory. People say dawn is a welcomed fresh start to each day, ripe with hope. More suspicious people believe the morning light erases any fears of the demons of the night; what we cannot see, we often fear. Saisha loved owls and understood nocturnal animals thrive in the dark hours, endowed with keen senses of the night. In Nature, light of day and darkness of night are equal; the mind of humans ascribe value judgments to each, proving again the frailty of the mind to understand truth.

Saisha thought of the night just passed, the appointed hour when she would yield to Balvan. She wondered why the expressions of love coincided with his moment of release. During sex, he would constantly tell her how beautiful she was, how much he loved her. Afterwards, her lust turned into pangs of guilt, even moments of depression as she had submitted willingly, but not out of love. She had a contract to honor. Saisha was not sure Balvan really loved her. The words, "I love you" spoken in the moment of passion drifted away like wispy clouds passing over the camp. Additionally, the awful memories of the demeaning rape weighed on her heart.

Out of the shadows, she noticed Balvan quietly summoning her, ensuring he did not wake Anya, who slept with Saisha every night. She slipped out of bed, accompanying Balvan to another room. Balvan said, "Saisha, the warriors will return today from the battle at Desa. I am told we suffered many casualties, perhaps up to 1,000. You and Anya must be incredibly careful, especially Anya, as I cannot assure you of her safety."

Saisha could hardly believe what he was saying, "I thought you told me Anya would be safe in your home. I don't understand."

"Saisha, in these rare moments, when our forces suffer defeat and devastating losses, military law immediately empowers the local field commander with absolute authority. Dhanur could decide to banish all foreigners from the camp unless determined to be of direct military value. As a former unit commander, I can plea on your behalf, but normal protections afforded to me are -". Saisha aggressively interrupted. "What normal protections?"

Balvan did not want to answer, hoping Saisha would not persist. She demanded to know which normal protections. She would not relent, "tell me Balvan." Balvan sheepishly answered, "They consider you and Anya as property. They can seize you at will, without my approval."

Saisha slumped down, barely able to sit, her body devoid of life, as if all her blood had vanished, leaving a vacuous shell. She felt she would fall into unconsciousness from shock. Balvan reached to catch her, holding her in his arms, he gently gave life back to her, pulling her from her semi-conscious state.

"Saisha, I love you. I am sorry your fate brought you here. I am sorry the Assassins squandered your husband's life for ill reasons, and I am sorry I raped you, thinking only of myself with no regard for your feelings. Please forgive me. "She looked deeply into Balvan's eyes, peering into his soul. She saw truth and sincerity; she saw genuine sorrow, and she saw love arising from his spirit.

Balvan, still holding her, breathing new life into her body and spirit with the words she never thought she would hear, whispered,

"Saisha, please marry me and allow me to adopt Anya and Jai. I promise I will love you always and spill my blood to protect you, Anya, and Jai. Under the law, you and my adopted children will become part of our people. But there is one thing you must promise during the service."

Saisha stared at Balvan, concern, suspicion and curiosity blending into her words, probing, "What must I promise?"

"You must promise fidelity to me and the people, you must accept the ways of The Horse Warriors. If you renounce the Horse Warriors, they will condemn both of us to death and sell Anya into slavery."

Saisha released herself from his embrace, realizing she had to decide at that moment. Balvan looked at her, not saying a word of persuasion. This was her moment, he thought, this is her time to decide her fate. He turned to leave, thinking solace was best for both.

"Wait, come to me." Balvan turned and approached her, knowing she had never said those words before. She took his hand, her way of inviting him into her life, saying, "Balvan, I believe you are sorry, and I believe you love me. I trust you will protect my children, to the fullest extent of the law, and to the last breath of your life. I forgive you and will marry you. I promise fidelity to you."

Balvan was happy and relieved. The ceremony would take place immediately to ensure full legal protection. His joy was not unbounded. Balvan felt a tinge of sadness. The words Saisha spoke brought a sense of relief, happiness, and release from guilt, but the words not spoken plagued him. She did not say, "I love you." She also neglected to promise fidelity to the Horse Warrior people.

Saisha and Balvan wed a few hours later, a legal and administrative task, not celebratory, given the number of wounded warriors crossing the river into the somber camp. Since Jai and Anya were both under the age of 14, their consent was not required. Jai, now fully integrated into the ranks of other aspiring young warriors, aged thirteen to sixteen, was nonchalant as he knew nothing about Balvan except the brief encounter when captured. Perhaps Balvan was a lauded unit commander; a fact Jai cared nothing about. It made his life in the military even more difficult, facing the inevitable and continuous snide comments and comparisons.

On other hand, Anya was seething with hatred of Balvan. She did not view Balvan as her protector. Images of her mother intertwined and submitting to a stranger, tormented her; worse yet, someone from the wicked, uncouth people who murdered her father She also hatred the Horse Warriors for seizing her brother. She had not fully grasped what her fate would have been without Balvan's intervention, but it did not matter to her. She had a fiery and independent spirit like her cousin, Ekavir.

Her only words to Saisha were brief and ill-omened, "I hate these people and would rather die, before submitting to their culture." Anya did not speak again of this matter. Saisha hoped time would temper Anya's hatred.

The disciplined retreat from Desa offered countless hours of solitude for each man. Endless miles and days of travel provided the meditative opportunity for Dhanur and Axam to consider their futures. The wrath of Khander could strike either, both subject to endless questioning. Khander expected to know every detail of the battle. Axam, the youngest brother of Khander, did not seek refuge from the unrelenting probes by Khander and his senior strategists.

Axam well understood his familial status made him more exposed. The clan which comprised the leadership of the Horse Warriors did not accept failure. In fact, the judgment of Axam in some ways would be harsher as the clan leaders would tolerate no favoritism. Axam knew the best approach would be humility mixed with confidence. Khander wanted extensive knowledge of the enemy, above all their battle tactics, methods, and their character. He expected Axam to create a complete picture of the enemy's strengths and weaknesses. Khander demanded the same analysis of the Horse Warriors. Khander would judge Axam's value and future worthiness based on his contribution and resiliency.

The situation for Dhanur, although a brother of Khander, differed from that of Axam. Dhanur would be honorable in accepting his fate. Khander would be furious about the sheer number of dead and wounded, numbering well over 1,000. He deplored the fact these casualties did not result in victory. Dhanur understood the possibilities could range from execution to banishment to mere demotion. Khander would test him using a simple approach; he would look at Dhanur with a stoic, emotionless expression and ask, "Dhanur, what should your fate be?"

Balvan was prescient; the mood of the camp was extremely sullen. The crossing back to the camp took multiple days, although the river was shallower as the dry season was well underway. Balvan had served for forty years, most of the time as a unit commander, responsible for 100 men. He had his share of injuries, most of which were minor. He had never witnessed such carnage among the Horse Warriors, as they always won with minimal losses. The Horse Warriors predicated the entire on the personal success of each warrior and the collective success of the unit. Strict military discipline and fanatical fighting skills always resulted in conquest, along with the corresponding spoils of war.

Balvan was sure Khander would soon appear in the camp. Khander himself had been a phenomenal warrior possessing remarkable strength and a fanaticism to win, infectious among his subordinates. Khander demanded complete loyalty, which he returned in kind. He would listen to all the unit commanders and even have personal discussions with men chosen randomly from the ranks. Before taking any decisions on new tactics and strategies, he listened impassively for hours, as his will to win required extreme patience.

Legends abounded as to how Khander, under the supervision of an uncle known for extensive knowledge and experiences with large predatory cats, spent endless hours studying the leopard, an animal of strength, speed, versatility, and elusiveness, and, most of all, patience. His uncle was fond of telling young Khander the effectiveness of the leopard required all these skills, including excellent climbing skills; no one skill alone, no matter how well developed, would suffice.

Words are often useful to convey important information such as military organization or knowledge of the civil laws and spiritual beliefs, even practical information like identification of venomous insects and snakes. The ultimate survival skills, however, required challenging experiences.

To "celebrate" young Khander's birthday, his uncle blindfolded Khander and marched him into the deep forests, at least a full day's walk from home. He removed the blindfold, leaving Khander, with no food or water, to fend for himself. The immediate family, especially his parents, believed if Khander did not survive, whether from mistakes, lack of skill or failure to adapt, then death in the deep woods was best for all. The idea was plain; he would not be adroit or tough enough to succeed as Supreme Leader of the Horse Warriors. The uncle advised him to use all his senses and to develop a stealthy, patient, and methodical approach to survive. "Khander," the uncle said, "learn from the leopard the most important skill of all, patience and self-control." That is how Khander, at age ten, learned the art of patience!

As predicted, Khander arrived a few days later. With masterful poise, he walked around the camp, observing, exchanging small courtesies, asking questions of the men, and listening. Khander spoke few words. He dedicated his entire mental faculties to listening. Other foreign leaders such as Pratham, agitated by Jackal, would tear into the unit commanders and other senior officers. Khander would have no recrimination, no denunciations. Khander wanted to absorb every detail, especially descriptions of the chariots which interested him, a weapon pivotal against the Horse Warriors. Khander even invited Balvan to take part in the strategy discussions, as he was renowned among the Horse Warriors for battlefield ingenuity.

Following days of interminable discussions and unrelenting questioning, Khander convened a meeting of the senior leaders which included Dhanur, Axam and Balvan, to his surprise, along with six other unit commanders. Ten in all attended, a number fundamental to Warrior military organization. The only person not in jeopardy of execution or banishment was Balvan, every other commander was at risk. If Khander would have decreed a death sentence for the commanders responsible for the defeat, each man would have fully accepted his fate, and no Horse Warrior would have mourned them. Also, no one would question the decision by Khander to keep them all in their current positions.

Khander proceeded around the room, asking each man two questions. First, "What do you honor and cherish above all", and second, "What should your fate be?" Mere subservience of flattery or self- serving responses to protect or deny would not have entered the minds of these men. Khander decided Dhanur should answer first.

Dhanur, with no hesitation or anxiety, responded, "I live to serve the Horse Warriors and pledge my fidelity and life to Khander, Supreme Commander. My fate should be to do everything in my power, as a humble warrior, to complete my mission, avenge the dead, and to bring ultimate victory to the Supreme Commander. Otherwise, my life has no purpose." The answer satisfied Khander.

Khander ordered Dhanur to build an army of charioteers using the brilliance of Jung-Quo to construct a superior field weapon that would dominate any enemy chariots. He said, "Balvan, I want you to take charge of training our men to be as superior on chariots as we are on horses. Axam, you will assume overall command of the new invasion force while Dhanur trains the army in all new battle tactics. You will jointly be responsible for the mission, which is now the complete destruction of Desa, and the subjugation of these people called 'The Shore People'. If within one year, you fail in this task, all nine of you will commit suicide or I will banish your families to die in the desert. If you succeed, I will elevate each of you to the highest status. It is your duty to quench the lust for revenge which has afflicted my spirit. You must bring honor to yourselves and your families. I will assign 15,000 men to this mission. Do not fail." Ominous word, not unexpected.

PART 37
Threats to Rishaan

Rishaan, as ruler of the Shore People, wanted for nothing, possessing the absolute authority to secure anything he desired. However, he did not savor absolute power as with many other rulers with dictatorial supremacies. Perhaps his judicious use of authority was a weakness, since other men in the kingdom thirsted for absolute power and would do anything to achieve their ends. One such man was Viraj, the senior chief priest of the kingdom. Although Rishaan had absolute power in a civil sense, he would not challenge the religious authority of Viraj. Rishaan was wise enough to understand Viraj could declare him amoral to the oral scriptures, endangering his place in the echelon of ancestral spirits.

Viraj believed only complete devotion to religious doctrines and practices served the purpose of human destiny. He secretly despised Rishaan, judging the benevolent ruler stood for nothing. Rishaan was too tolerant of different interpretations of the sacred scriptures. Matters were much worse now with AO, who had poisoned the mind of Zeba and had propagated seditious ideas talking nonsense of the equality of all men and women.

AO and Kalpesh, both considered outsiders, had scuttled his devilish scheme to poison Zeba, who was emerging as the favorite of Rishaan. Rishaan was a man grown old and exhausted through tragedy including the long illness and final passing of his wife, Livia, the murder of his brother Kalpit by the Horse Warriors and now the death in battle of Ekavir, his nephew and heir apparent. Rishaan was close to the toppling point; Viraj could soon declare him as too mentally sick and distraught to continue as ruler. Viraj had it all planned; now the situation was muddled. In addition, Viraj assessed Daiwik as a potential threat, someone who was silent and respectful but never exhibiting the enthusiastic support, no matter how insincere, displayed by the other senior priests.

Normally, Rishaan would rise early each morning to celebrate the morning sun, but lately his motivation was lagging. His body was willing, but his spirit, fatigued by the loss of his brother and nephew, the near death of Zeba, preferred the dreamy state of despair. He sensed the rays of sun on his face gently urging him to rise from his sleepy doldrums. Thoughts of some warm milk and barley motivated Rishaan to shake himself from his depressive state.

Rishaan seemed to float into his garden, still not fully conscious. Perhaps he needed stimulation from the magnificent tropical flowers, the varied aromatic smells of spice plantings, the dazzling banana trees or the calm banyan trees. Rishaan's ancestors had built even grander and more impressive gardens with tiered hanging plantings, buttressed by sturdy rock foundations. Rishaan had long ago walled off the extensive garden into a public and private space, deeming a smaller garden with walled interiors less intrusive and more seductive to private moments.

A glimpse of a bullfrog caught his attention. Many varieties of frogs lived in the pooled fountains and rock-strewn garden ponds, but the golden bullfrog was one of the most unusual. The glance morphed into a trance-like gaze. Rishaan's mind emptied of any desires or thoughts. A long snout, a long green line running straight down its back, dozens of dark brown splotches and a golden teal gleaming skin painted a living portrait of nature, as beautiful in its own way as any other of nature's creatures. Nature did not discriminate, why did humans? *AO was right*, Rishaan thought, *there is equality in natural life, why not human life?*

Rishaan heard a rustling sound, a deliberate but subtle sound from his house guard, seeking Rishaan's attention in the most unobtrusive manner. "Sire, Daiwik, one of the chief priests is here to speak to you."

Most unusual, thought Rishaan. "Yes, ask him to join me here in the garden." Rishaan turned back to the frog, still fixed in its position, perhaps in its own trance. Rishaan wondered if the frog, so focused on some small edible target, would even respond to any external noise or movement. For a moment, Rishaan viewed the bullfrog from a slightly different angle; he was sure the golden teal subtly changed hues. Then the frog leaped into the water; a moment of serenity lost for Rishaan, an opportunity to eat, lost for the frog. "We both feel cheated", Rishaan mumbled to himself, not realizing the difference. The frog moved to the next opportunity to snatch a morsel for breakfast, while Rishaan remained trapped in a slice of time, lamenting his lost solitude with the frog.

Regret and mild irritation filled Rishaan's mind, a slice of time lost, a mere faint image in memory. With a wisp of sadness, Rishaan realized all memories are faint images of the mind, some joyful, while others are more painful, such as thoughts of Livia. Rishaan had joyful and sad thoughts of Livia, but last days of sadness seemed to overwhelm the previous memories of joy.

Morning greetings from Daiwik mercifully quelled his melancholy. "Lord Rishaan, I hope I have not disturbed your morning meditation."

Rishaan, with superficial politeness responded, "No, Daiwik, I am pleased to see you."

Daiwik, scanning the garden layout to find the quietest and most private spot, motioned to Rishaan, "Sire, please, if you don't mind, let us sit over here. I would like to ensure our privacy." Rishaan obliged, sensing Daiwik had important information for him.

Rishaan, now more than curious, sat next to Daiwik, leaning slightly closer to give the impression of increased concern with their privacy. "Yes, Daiwik, what is it you would like of me."

Daiwik replied, "I want to save you and your family from impending danger."

Rishaan stiffened and urged Daiwik to continue. Daiwik's explanations went into the differing view of the roles of religion, first outlining the views of Viraj which advocated a political theocracy, meaning the absolute rule by the senior chief priest and the elimination of the ruling family. Daiwik then espoused his view, which advocated a more broad-based political system, in which religion was critical but subservient to civil law.

Rishaan asked, "According to your views, Daiwik, what happens to the ruling family?"

Yes, thought Daiwik, *the crux of the matter for Rishaan*.

"The royal family would continue, although not with absolute power. The time is imminent for more equality in our society. The danger to your rule does not emanate from the people, the danger emanates from Viraj and his followers who seek to rule through dogma and rituals. Viraj believes he has the authority to declare you mentally unfit to rule. Do you understand what really happened to Zeba, and why they tried AO for religious and civil sedition?"

Rishaan was not confused. Now was the time to act on this information, but how? "What do you suggest, Daiwik?" The words spoken by both men were now inaudible to anyone who could be listening. Even the frogs, busy in their quest for breakfast, enjoyed the stillness, perfect conditions to snatch an unwary bug or spider or perhaps a tiny fish, vanishing with a flick of the tongue.

Daiwik, satisfied his conversation with Rishaan was private, started with his second task of the morning. He found AO sitting in a state of meditation, oblivious to the external world. "Good morning, AO, may I disturb your meditation?"

AO looked up, acknowledging Daiwik's presence with a slight smile, a twist of the neck, an awakening from the moment of reflection, a unique form of meditation. AO did not choose a subject for reflection which would defeat his purpose, which was no purpose, no thoughts, no expectations.

AO had only briefly met Daiwik, another face from the priesthood. "How may I assist you?" AO politely and sincerely inquired.

"I am Daiwik, one of the chief priests in the land. I heard your words at the trial."

These words triggered alarms within AO, like the barking of a watchdog as a wolf approaches a grazing sheep, not conscious of its vulnerability to the skulking predator. AO cared for his safety; he did not obsess about his safety. He proceeded through life motivated by his internal sense of correct behavior, which would keep him in harmony with the natural world. He could sense when danger lurked, like the mother leopard hovering over the newborn cubs. Instincts and senses spoke to him, not a reasoned mind, logically concluding Daiwik, a chief priest like Viraj, required caution.

"AO, I do not think your sentence as judged by Viraj was fair, nor was the trial anything more than a ruse. I would like to help you with the techniques the priests use for memorization of the poetic scriptures."

AO nodded, "Yes, thank you. Dumurkha recited the first book to me, about 500 verses, thousands of words. I believe the assigned task encompasses about 1500 verses. Dumurkha advised me it took him one year to complete the memorization, which was a monumental achievement."

Daiwik thought to himself, *Yes, extraordinary, even for a man whose mental capacities were quite limited except in his extraordinary mastering of memorization. It had taken me five years.*

AO explained Dumurkha arrived each morning, at precisely the same time. He recited the verses in the sequence required by oral tradition. At first, AO just listened to the entire set of verses which required an entire day to recite. Then AO asked for the recitation of just ten verses, repeated over and over, followed by another 10, until he had memorized 100 verses. This process went on for several days until AO having cleared his mind of any conflicting thoughts realized the correct technique required symbols to represent major ideas in each hymn. In addition, AO made a mark for each word to match up with the symbolic drawing.

Before long, he had mastered the first 500 verses in only a few days, having constructed a set of symbols or drawings. AO discovered he could repeat some symbols, allowing him to create a row of symbols, some repeating as each unique word or phrase had its own symbol. At first, the symbols were crude, but AO soon discovered techniques to change the symbols to comprehend a string of words, such as "from the sky and heavens", drawn as one symbol. It impressed Dumurkha as no one had previously attempted to draw such symbols, but the significance of translating to symbols was beyond him. Upon hearing about these symbols, it alarmed Viraj as this pictorial representation meant access to the poetic verses would be available to anyone, not just the purview of the priests.

PART 38
Civil Unrest in Desa

The death of Gandesh and Pratham offered an opportunity for people of unvarnished ambition to execute their visions, labeled as schemes by others. Both the Nivasi and the Varagans were now leaderless, although Devi and Arian were the practical leaders of their people. Arian had already announced he would not serve as Primary, a position Samarth deserved. It was Samarth who led the clan leaders to award full military dictatorial powers to Arian, bypassing the authority of Pratham and emasculating the pretense of power Jackal brandished.

The Varagans knew they could not return to their homeland, especially to their major city, which the Horse Warriors still occupied. No one doubted the current military status with the Horse Warriors was merely an interlude, a bitter setback for the Horse Warriors which would motivate an invading army with a more vengeful spirit. Everyone feared this development, above all Shanti.

Shanti believed in absolute adherence to tradition, principally the pacifist tradition engendered into every Nivasi for over a hundred years. Decades of peace followed The Terrible Conflict, fomenting the pacifist values of Desa. In addition, there had been virtually no conflicts of any nature with distanced neighbors, no military conflicts for hundreds of years. Shanti yearned for those tranquil days, interrupted by the Varagans. In her mind, all the unimaginable death and suffering directly resulted from the Varagans; people she held in low esteem, people who would contaminate Nivasi culture in the future.

One other development troubled her and many of her followers:

the intermarriage of Nivasi and Varagans, despoiling the purity of Nivasi blood. She believed in clear cultural separation between the Nivasi and the Varagans; better yet, banishment altogether from the land of Desa. Until, that time, Shanti would rally the people around pacifism, judging banning intermarriage would be a step too far, but others with more extremist views argued to save the purity of Nivasi blood, they would forbid intermarriage! Shanti naively believed the Horse Warriors would spare them if the Varagans disappeared from Desa.

To make matters worse, Mishka was also with child from the deceased Varagan warrior, Veer. More militant blood seeping into our culture, Shanti angrily mused. Although she did not advocate for the "blood purity" position, she was happy to announce her candidacy for the leadership position, representing a substantial number of Nivasi Council members both moderate and radical in their views.

The Varagans selected Samarth as Primary, a straightforward choice as Arian had disavowed interest and there were no legitimate heirs to Pratham, although two young men claimed they were the offspring of Pratham. True to form, one of the dubious sons, named Jaitra, inherited the worse traits of Pratham, seemingly a hybrid of Jackal and Pratham, a character with a devious soul but emboldened with a cleverer personality than Jackal. Unlike Jackal, Jaitra was a veteran of the battles with the Horse Warriors, although conniving methods to minimize personal harm.

The other young man, claiming direct lineage, was a very honorable warrior, in the best tradition of Pratham. Inesh was the opposite of Jaitra. People speculated the ancestral spirits had debated the fate of the two young men, choosing one to be the best of Pratham, while inherited the worst characteristics. Fate had already decided the outcomes for these men while still in the womb of their mothers. The ancestral spirits infused them with qualities true to their potentiality, one embracing virtuous values of bravery and honor, while the other gravitated to schemes and treachery.

Inesh admired Arian, fighting by his side at every opportunity. Arian respected young Inesh determined to develop him into a successor to himself and Veer. Now with the death of Veer and the passing of Primary to the Samarth, rivals to the Pratham clan, Inesh and Jaitra could vie for the future.

Inesh only thought of duty, preferring the soldier's life of honorable military leadership, while Jaitra obsessed with political power and all the material trappings possible as Primary. Neither envisioned life in Desa as permanent, the aim of returning to their homeland the only point of commonality.

Although women were equal in status in Desa, only men had served as Leader of the Nivasi Council. Mishka and Devi thought the time was ripe to change the dominance of males in that role. Devi announced she would stand as a candidate for the leadership position, which would require a majority of the 99 Nivasi Council members, meaning at least 50 votes for the winning candidate. Shanti also announced the same intentions. As Shanti was already a Nivasi Council member, she was not eligible to vote, leaving 98 members. No one was certain as to the procedures since it always was traditional for one male member of the Nivasi Council to gravitate to the leadership position based on universal concurrence.

No one objected when Mandeep assumed the organizational responsibility for the vote, as they highly respected his unbiased views. Mandeep permitted a week to pass before convening the Nivasi Council for the vote. There was no canvassing of ballots, no campaign rallies, not even small dinners to sway Nivasi Council members. At least, this was the theory.

Mandeep, betraying nothing of his personal views or offering words of wisdom, announced two candidates were present for selection by the Nivasi Council. Then, based upon age, he invited Shanti to make a brief statement to the assembly. No one, not even Mishka and Devi, doubted the sincerity of Shanti's beliefs, but Shanti's invectives against the impurity of the Nivasi peoples, expressly the views on intermarriage, shocked both.

Shanti drew murmurs from the assembly when she reminded the voters of the warnings of Mandeep, quoting his exact words," We do not know who these people are. We do not know their culture. We do not know their values."

Shanti pressed her point as Mandeep remained stoic, realizing she misconstrued his words. "Now, it is clear to all of us the Varagans brought misery and death to our lands. The Horse Warriors cared nothing about us; it was the Varagans they were seeking. We foolishly protected these people, led by a dishonorable and unethical leader. Mandeep said to observe the flow of truth. The Varagans must leave, and we should not permit any additional marriages between Nivasi and Varagans. The Varagans will destroy our culture and bring horrific destruction to our land. These are the truths!"

Devi, stunned by the virulent attack on her and Arian, questioned if she should even continue. Mishka whispered, "Devi, you must fight for our children conceived of true love between men and women who chose the universal value of freedom to be whoever they so desire. Shanti will destroy our destiny, our purpose in life, in the name of ethnic purity. Shanti, chasing pacifism, will surrender to all enemies including the Horse Warriors who thirst for our destruction."

The Assembly Hall was completely silent. There was no clapping or cheering for the words of Shanti, no jeers from the supporters of Devi. Shanti sat silently, her message of fear and cultural exclusion weighing heavily in the air like a morning mist, obscuring the mind's horizon. Devi also remained motionless, her body and mind in stillness.

She reflected on the wise advice of Mandeep who often said, "Our greatest moments are when we are still, our minds absent of the clutter of endless words, competing for a share of our minds, like the incessant exhortations to redemption of an itinerant mystic."

In contrast to Shanti, Devi had no prepared speech to stir the spirits of the Nivasi Council members, no over-riding message to motivate a desired outcome, like a street vendor hawking jewels of questionable value. Devi spoke from her soul or as some people like to say, from her heart, but there is a difference. Your heart speaks of emotion, like love, whereas your soul reveals your true character. The heart is often fickle, your soul the repository of the fundamental principles and values which anchor your life. Devi spoke from her soul, disregarding the implications of the vote.

"Shanti is a fine woman, a loyal and sincere citizen of our land. I know she believes her words are true. I will not try to refute anything she has spoken in this hall. Some of you may have already determined Shanti speaks the truth, which may even be self-evident in your minds. Perhaps, some of you may have already determined the truth based on your own observations or a yearning to restore the placid days of the past, free of conflict and the horrors of war.

"We did not wish for the Varagans, but it was clear they represented no threat to the Horse Warriors. Mandeep was correct. We did not understand their values, but I shall remind you Mandeep also said, 'Our ethical beliefs require us to welcome all people into Desa. This is our duty.' It was not a mistake to give shelter to these bedraggled people, clearly in desperate need, far from their homeland with virtually no possessions. And yes, Pratham and Jackal were not honorable, they shamelessly disregarded our deep respect for the Greenlands. Yes, I was the first to warn this Nivasi Council of the malevolent behavior of Pratham.

"Axam claimed to come in peace, but we know he was false in his words. The Horse Warriors had no reason to invade our land, no justification to lay siege to our city. We cannot predict the future, but we know the Horse Warriors will seek our complete destruction. You are not safe in pacifism; nativist seductions of ethnic purity will not save you. If you choose that path, they will slaughter you as pure Nivasi.

"We need the Varagans to help defend our freedom. We also need the Shore People to ally with us, as they too will be the object of subjugation. The only question before us is the survival of our civilization by facing the future with courage and confidence, not by yearning for the past and harboring fear. We must be free to pursue our purpose in life, free to follow our moral conscience."

Mandeep methodically ambled to the center of the Assembly Hall, observing the faces of the 98 voting members, providing the voting instructions with no additional comments. Oddly enough, the Nivasi Council faced the most consequential decision in centuries without further discussion or debate. Mandeep announced the procedure, "There will not be any further debate or comments in this hall; the only question before you pertain to the timing of the vote. You may choose to vote now or delay for any period you deem necessary."

Each Nivasi Council member vote announced for all to hear. The tally amounted to a clear preference to vote immediately for the leadership position; the vote being 90 to 8 in favor. Next, Mandeep required the oral vote of each member, again following the principle of age. As the voice vote proceeded, it was clear they would not decide the total tally until the very end. The oldest members voted in significant numbers for Shanti, but the momentum shifted to Devi as the voters descended in age. The last person to vote was Mandeep, the only voter not following the rule of voting in age sequence. It electrified the atmosphere as the vote was 49 for Shanti and 48 for Devi, with only Mandeep to vote. He cast his vote for Devi, creating a tie at 49 votes each, precipitating a political crisis, an outcome which no one had predicted. The Nivasi Council session ended in a bit of confusion, with Mandeep advising everyone to reconvene the next day.

At home that evening, Devi heard a faint rap at the door, the knock which shows the uncertainty or hesitancy of the knocker. Still aware of potential dangers, Arian answered the door, pushing Devi into another room with a secret escape door. Arian inquired," Who is knocking?"

The voice of Priya responded, "It is Priya, seeking to speak with Devi."

Arian judged it was safe to open the door, still wary of the circumstances which would motivate Priya, the Chief Administrator of Agriculture, to visit their home. Devi appeared, politely asking Priya to sit and partake of some water and milk. Then she remembered Priya had voted for Shanti, the recall of the vote causing Devi to stiffen, her warm embrace giving way to a more neutral stance.

"Devi, I don't need to remind you I voted for Shanti today."

Devi, still uncertain, becoming even more cautious, responded, "Yes, I remember."

Priya continued, "I had previously committed to vote for Shanti, a violation of our practices. Shanti has been vigorously recruiting supporters, whipping her supporters into a frenzy with rhetoric infused with virulence, her promises more outlandish each hour. I am not here to indict Shanti for her actions. I want to learn more from you, as to your vision for our people. What will happen to us?"

Accepting the questions as sincere, Devi said, "Our people and the Varagans have endured much suffering and pain. The deep scars of anxiety and emotional trauma are still fresh and oozing into our spirits. We dream of the past world, of the solitude and peace, harmony among our people. We cannot wish away the reality of the past months. We must live with the uncertainty, no matter how discomforting, how troubling, how disruptive to our hopes or preferences. We must proceed with courage, knowing the right actions faced with fear, comprise the correct path. If we wish freedom, we must accept equality, we must be just to the Varagans."

Devi continued, "The Horse Warriors will return to fulfill their oaths of revenge against all of us, including the Shore People and the Varagans. They will make no distinction among us. Axam will use his powers of persuasion to convince Shanti to isolate the Varagans. Axam sent assassins to kill Gandesh because he wanted to convince the pacifists of the futility of war, to show even the gentlest of men could die from aimless violence. Priya, listen to your soul. They can twist your mind with words, but your soul is the essence of your character, it is your true self."

The next day, all the Nivasi Council members reconvened as

directed by Mandeep. Peering at the assemblage, sensing the divisions would remain as entrenched as the preceding day, Mandeep urged a spirit of reconciliation, "Friends and citizens, despite the deep disparities in our sincere views, I am asking each of you to reflect on our future, not based on our differences, but bound by our love of ethics and our common heritage. Regardless of whether Shanti or Devi is the elected leader of the Nivasi Council, I beseech each of you to unite to build a future for all the people. This is our duty from the soul and your obligation as elected representatives of the people."

Mandeep began the roll call. Each Nivasi Council member orally cast their vote, signifying either Shanti or Devi. Tension rose as the previous pattern of voting, which resulted in a tie vote, appeared to lead to another deadlock. When the order of voting came to Priya, she deferred for the moment, signifying she would cast her vote at the end. The tally arrived at the same position as the prior vote, 48 in favor of Shanti, 48 in favor of Devi.

Mandeep then reverted to Priya, who previously had voted for Shanti. She stood confidently in the assembly room and pronounced, "Devi". It shocked the Shanti forces, their faces expressive of anger and betrayal. Mandeep stayed true to his prior support for Devi, providing the margin of victory with 50 affirmative votes. Fifty Nivasi Council members had cast their affirmative vote for Devi, but forty-eight other members had strongly supported Shanti's vision of a revisionist past.

Mandeep declared a fair election; Devi would serve as Leader. Devi thought it best to conclude the Nivasi Council session, allowing the inhibited frustrations and passions of the defeated pro-Shanti forces to subside. It was not a moment of celebration. The intense division had gouged a gaping wound in the body politic, spilling out prejudices and anxieties, hidden in people's souls. Devi approached Shanti, entreating her to stroll together in the park, hoping to promote the first steps in healing the deep divisions.

People in Desa could find moments of calm sitting under the banyan tree. Shanti was still seething from her stinging defeat.

They perched themselves on several rocks, situated as natural places of meditation under the sacred peepal tree, revered for spiritual and medicinal purposes. Devi hoped the peepal tree would provide a brief interlude of tranquility from the heated emotions of the Nivasi Council meeting. Devi believed the Nivasi had no hope if the leadership remained deeply divided.

Shanti started the discussion, "Devi, I genuinely believe we can only select the path of non-violence, any attempt to use military force causing the end of our civilization. However, I am sorry I insulted you and Mishka by repeating the extremist views of ethnic purity. These opinions belie the true values of our people."

Devi wore two necklaces, including the snake bone used to save Pratham's life from the poisonous bite. The other necklace was uniquely different. She removed the necklace made of tulsi beads symbolizing purity of mind, body, and emotions. She took Shanti's hand, passing the necklace into her grasp, saying, "Shanti, this necklace is special given to me by my mother. I would like you to accept these tulsi beads as a gift."

Shanti felt a soft wave of joy and calmness envelope her body. Tears welled up in her eyes, her spirit calm for the first time in weeks. "Thank you, Devi, it is an honor to accept this gift as any endowment from our parents is incredibly significant. It also means you would like me as your spiritual sister." Devi nodded, her tears streaming down her face, joining with Shanti's tears, the mixture of tears creating a union of friendship as strong as the bond between sisters.

"Shanti, I would like you to serve in a new position as vice-leader, which I will ask the Nivasi Council to ratify. Then, I would like you and Arian to travel to the land of the Shore People to seek the counsel of Rishaan as to our future cooperation."

The next day, the Nivasi Council overwhelmingly approved Shanti as vice-leader, and her mission, accompanied by Arian, to consult with Rishaan sanctioned as well. Not completely transformed in her views, Shanti wanted to give the new partnership a chance to succeed. She still believed the Varagans must adopt the cultural values of the Nivasi and commit to seeking a peaceful resolution with the Horse Warriors. Devi and Arian also abhorred war, so common ground was possible. Shanti genuinely appreciated the gift of the necklace, a token of sisterly friendship. *Yes,* she thought, *I can work with Devi to heal the divisions.*

Meanwhile, in the camps of the Horse Warriors, there were no such thoughts of reconciliation. The marching orders were unmistakably clear; there was no misunderstanding the consequences of failure. The entire camp was in war mobilization mode as the days were ebbing away and the sense of urgency growing with each passing week.

In Desa, Devi did not have to induce a vision to foretell the future. The strikingly clear image of Axam, shrewdly plotting revenge, never faded from her mind. Several days of travel to the north, in the camp of the Horse Warriors, sat Axam, his mind equally possessed with thoughts of Devi. Two different people of equivalent skill and talent, loathing the intentions of the other, each obsessed with defeating the other, each respecting the other in an odd, dangerous way, not unlike the battle of wits and killing methods between the red scorpion and the tarantula in which death is the fate of the loser.

PART 39
AO's Recitation of the Ancestral Hymns

AO passed many days learning the stanzas they would require him to recite in front of Viraj and the other chief priests. His new technique of matching symbolic pictures with each key phase reduced the sheer number of words he had to memorize by a factor of ten. Using markings to note the number of symbols proved to very fruitful as an additional memorization technique.

AO believed non-experiential forms of learning through teachings and lectures were of limited value, the mind subject to external pressures like the rantings and exhortations of itinerant teachers or even the thoughtful advice of a doting parent. Students expecting the gift of wisdom and knowledge received instead a deluge of words, flooding a chaotic and cluttered mind. AO learned at an early age truth is elusive, wisdom unattainable, when sourced from another person's beliefs.

The priests who raised him taught him little through the device of words. The priests reflected the lessons of nature when the mother bird pushes her babies out of the nest to survive on their own. Nature provides no flight instructions, no hunting clues, no warnings of predators; the babies learn from instinct, driven by the desire to survive. The priests instilled in AO, the meditative methods to master the inner mind. They lived from their souls, their spirits providing the natural glues between mind and soul. AO harbored the primordial principle: a life in harmony with nature was a life filled with promise.

Dumurkha had the genius of memory combined with the skillful use of a self-induced trance which opened the recesses of his mind, letting the stored stanzas glide out in exactly the correct order, each word perfectly pronounced according to the oral traditions. The hymnal chanting of Dumurkha flowed into AO's perfectly still and absorbing mind.

The 90th day arrived for the recitation. A quiet hush of anticipation permeated through the crowd. No one including Daiwik, Rishaan, Zeba and Kalpesh had any idea as to the outcome. AO had not spoken to anyone as to his progress. Viraj had pressed Dumurkha for any insight into the progress being made by AO, but the recitation master, numbed by his own trances, could recall nothing of the progress of AO. The forum for the recitation was so quiet some people said they heard the imaginary sounds of passing clouds! Viraj summoned AO to begin his recitation.

AO took a seat at the designated place, considered blessed by the ancestral spirits because of frequent sightings of the Indian Owl. AO did not utter a sound for an interminable period. A slight smirk appeared as Viraj thought a mental block afflicted AO. Then, AO began his recitation, continuing through morning into mid-day, not hesitating until he completed the task as mandated.

Beaming with pride, Zeba approached with a smile, a certain inviting openness extended beyond politeness. She gently grasped the hand of AO, as if congratulatory in manner, but the eyes communicated this touch was no mere passing moment. The first sparks are the easiest to detect, igniting the embryonic embers of love. As evening arrived, AO rested quietly, his spirit in the wake state, calm, even a bit excited, reflecting on Zeba, daring to imagine what could be. He had never met a woman who so enthralled him.

AO fully understood no one can control their dreams. Dream, nested within a dream, are typical for people with highly imaginative minds. That night, his subconscious spirit dominated his sleep, marked by continual dreams of peoples in conflict, images of war and love. AO's dreams reverberated each hour as he lay in semi-conscious sleep, a time of confusion when the sleep state and the wake state blur, the time when reality is the dream.

AO's dream was extremely vivid, hallucinations of wicked and violent people, horrible destructive events, traitors, but also images of people pursuing friendship. In his sleep, he saw Rishaan planning military plans with Arian and Shanti. He saw himself listening and advising them. AO dreamed Shanti noddingly approving of his vision of peace but frowning when Arian also advised freedom is not a universal gift given without defense. In his dream, AO saw Daiwik and all the chief priests holding court with Rishaan with Viraj standing near the back of the room glaring with hatred. He witnessed thousands of warriors on horses streaming into Desa. AO saw the clash of armies, blood spilled in the name of revenge.

He was certain he was awake, perhaps he was only dreaming he was awake. How would he know for sure? From his bed, AO realized it was still the time when the moon ruled the heaven, and most people locked in sleep. Still, he pondered his dream, picking through some details. He tried to rouse himself but became fixated on the clouds passing over the moon, obscuring most of the lunar image, like a winter blanket strewed partially over his body. He noticed darkness dominated his room except for the brief episodes of moonlight. The faintly visible figure of an octopus appeared, a sliver of moonlight illuminating a beckoning image. AO tried to fight the attraction, his last thoughts he must wake.

Back in his dream state, images of Devi, Arian, Zeba, Shanti and Rishaan and dozens of others, including a splendid black war horse, occupied his mind. The dream became more pleasurable as his thoughts drifted to a garden, sitting with Zeba, their hands now touching without the pretense of an unintended or polite grasp, their bodies slowly merging to exchange soft kisses of a budding love.

PART 40
Anya's Anguish

Weeks, perhaps months, passed since her family's kidnapping. Anya stopped counting the days, content to live in her secluded dream world, which she entered every evening. She had become psychologically addicted to a sleep inducement herb called ashwagandha, which also amplified dreams. Balvan had overheard Anya complaining to her mother, Saisha, of sleep disturbances and seizing on any opportunity to gain even a sliver of favor with Anya, he provided her with these herbs. Balvan bought Ashwagandha from medicinal healers who were part of the Horse Warrior's entourage, although not native to the many tribes that comprised the bulk of the Horse Warrior population. Like the builders from the East, the Horse Warriors welcomed these local people from regions further south for their specific knowledge of all forms of folk remedies, and a cache of plants to provide hallucinogenic benefits.

Balvan realized Anya had not lost her sullen demeanor, but the herbal tea treatment seemed to quell her rebellious spirit, at least the outward anger; however, Balvan was mistaken. The resentment and anger had not abated, in fact, each day seemed to swell the hatred for everything around her. She was even contemptuous of her mother, who willingly shared the bed of an uncivilized killer. The mere thought of Balvan and her mother in a sexual embrace was repulsive. She vowed no disgusting male from these vile people would ever touch her.

So she dreamed. She despised the days, eagerly awaiting her nightly escape. Anya practiced every meditative technique to induce pleasurable dreams, images of her friends and family from the land of the Shore People. She was momentarily safe and happy in her stately home in the kingdom. Life was perfect again. A clap of thunder awoke her. The torrential rains assaulted the elaborate tents where they slept.

The idea to escape was a spark of insight, like the flash of a lightning bolt. *Yes*, she mused, *I can escape to the river and summon a passing boat to take me to my uncle, Lord Rishaan, the ruler of the kingdom who would richly reward my enablers.* Aided by the delusional properties of the ashwagandha herbs, it all seemed like a good idea. What could go wrong?

Anya packed a small amount of food, not thinking she would need to travel far before finding willing helpers. It did not occur to her the night has its own life, foreign and dangerous to a young thirteen-year-old girl, who would appear to some men, as well as to wild animals, as a prize available for pleasure or food.

Anya stealthily maneuvered through the narrow passages of the camp, pretending to be seeking water or to use the night facilities. Men from the camp were still raw from the previous weeks' battles, some without female companionships for months. She deceived himself imagining she was as cunning as a fox, but countless eyes noticed her odd movements.

Within minutes, she reached the outer perimeter; she felt free for the first time in months. It was a glorious sensation; then she disappeared into the night, off course from the direction to the river as swirling winds and rain disoriented her. Her pace quickened as she advanced further into the night thinking she was close to the river; in fact, she was miles away, headed in the opposite direction, straight into the heart of arid and wild lands. Thoughts of freedom quickly turned to abject fear and panic.

Balvan tapped Saisha on the shoulder waking her, "Saisha, wake up, Anya left, she fled into the desert."

Saisha screamed in absolute shock, "What? Balvan, you must find her! You must go now." Balvan tried to console her, arguing a search party would leave in the morning. "No Balvan, you cannot wait. Please bring her back to me. I beg of you."

Balvan figured Anya had about three hours' head start, but which direction? Several warriors approached him with critical information proving to be decisive. They did not stop her as any person of age thirteen is free to wander as they wish if no foul deeds were clear. Balvan departed with the benefit of a sturdy horse, but with only a limited idea which direction Anya may have headed. Of course, she would have tried to find the river, no easy task in the middle of a storm in complete darkness. At least the rain had stopped, which would help with tracking her steps when morning light arrived.

Morning normally brings rays of sunshine and hope, not the case for Anya. She had fallen asleep about two hours before daybreak. At the first hues of light, she awoke to a horrific sight; a pack of hyenas surrounded her. Although not normally dangerous to humans, more curious than threatening, in Anya's distorted mind, they appeared as vicious creatures. Total fright seized her. She imagined the worst. As one of the larger hyenas approached, Anya began screaming, causing the entire pack to back off.

Like a miracle, a strange voice pierced the morning stillness, instigating the pack of hyenas to scatter quickly. Anya could scarcely believe her eyes as she saw a man on a horse approach her. The "savior" signaled Anya to mount the horse, assisting her to jump up and sit behind him. Anya held on tightly, jubilant, thinking her problems were over. She was mistaken, her nightmare was about to get a lot worse.

The mounted rider trotted off for a few minutes, arriving at a small campsite with two tents. Both the rider and Anya dismounted in front of one of the tents. Another man emerged with a big smile as both men bantered in a dialect difficult for Anya to comprehend, but Anya was sure she heard her defender mention he had a gift for the other man, words which sounded like "virgin lamb".

Anya still not grasping the actual situation was still smiling, profusely thanking them both for her rescue and promising big rewards for her eventual release. The situation turned ugly when the man from the tent grabbed Anya and dragged her into the tent. Anya started screaming again while the two men laughed, making obscene gestures with their hands. One man ripped the shirt off from Anya's back, partially exposing her naked body. Again, the sounds of more salacious laughter; Anya recoiled, knowing full well her fate. The man dragged her into the tent, savagely yanking at Anya's clothes while pulling off his pants.

The other man waited outside for his turn; his thoughts fixated on a delightful encounter with a young girl. She would satisfy his lust for many days to come. Somewhat distracted by his aroused state, he failed to notice his assailant. His parting memory was the knife to his throat, which deftly sliced across his primary artery while the other hand covered his mouth. Without a sound, the man dropped slowly, led to the ground by Balvan, now mobilized for his task to eliminate the second man.

Balvan heard Anya screaming, begging her rapist to stop. The rapist was taunting Anya, laughing, promising he would be gentle. He slapped her across her face several times. Anya, dazed, just laid on her back as the ugly hulk of the grinning man with filthy hands grabbed her thighs. He anticipated wonderful pleasures with his helpless victim.

Tactically, it would have been better for Balvan to wait for him to emerge, satisfied with his deed, but her screams made Balvan realize he had to intervene immediately. Balvan barged into the tent, giving the rapist valuable reaction time as he was just about to mount Anya. The rapist jumped up and withdrew a sharp knife. Balvan knew the rapist was a trained, ruthless mercenary who would fight for any side if the money was sufficient or be content to engage in thievery and murder when not employed.

Both men squared off. Knives flashed as both men jockeyed for position. Usually, the first stroke was decisive, if properly timed. Meanwhile, Anya scampered off to the side of the tent, covering herself with blankets which smelled of urine. The rapist feigned an attack with the knife while using a drop kick to land a heavy blow to Balvan's leg. This strike knocked Balvan off balance, which gave the rapist the opportunity to land a slicing blow to Balvan's face, drawing blood with a gaping wound. Balvan slumped, exaggerating fatal wounds. The rapist laughed and swiftly approached shouting, "This is my lucky day." Balvan lurched up, landing his knife squarely in the rapist's throat. Both men tottered and collapsed.

Balvan did not want to use any of the rapist's clothes as a dressing, fearing contamination. He yelled to Anya, "Quick, give me your shirt. I must wrap my wounds. Wrap yourself in the blanket." He snatched Anya from the tent floor and quickly mounted his horse, uncertain as to the number of companions possibly lurking nearby. He rode rapidly back to the camp of the Horse Warriors, barely holding on to his horse and his life. Anya held onto Balvan's waist, a feeling of overwhelming joy and relief never repeated in her life.

Several Horse Warriors mobilized to assist Balvan as he slumped off his horse, more dead than alive, in a transitional state where a few more seconds of lost blood would cause fate to choose death. Saisha was both overjoyed and shocked when she saw both Balvan and Anya. The mother's instinct turned to Anya, who assured Saisha although not injured, she had come within seconds of being brutally raped. She sheepishly said, "Mama, Balvan saved my life and prevented me from being hideously raped by a savage man. He is a good man. I am so grateful."

Saisha turned her attention to Balvan, who was being treated by the camp doctors and herbalist. The wounds to his face were serious but not fatal; however, Balvan would wear the scars for life. Saisha tended to Balvan's wounds, reflecting on Balvan's bravery and deep commitment to her and Anya. As Balvan entered a deep recuperative sleep aided by many herbs, principally the ashwagandha plant, soothing and loving words trickled into his subconscious mind. Balvan hallucinated, dreaming Saisha was at his side, saying, "I love you."

The Dream of AO

The next morning, Saisha changed the dressings on the wound, asking if Balvan had any recollection of dreams. Balvan played coy, claiming incoherent dreams and memories. Saisha leaned over, kissing him on his face softly said, "I was hoping you heard me say, I love you." Balvan smiled, falling back into a deep sleep.

PART 41
War Plans and the Delights of Rishaan

The delegation from Desa, composed of Arian, Shanti, Mandeep and Simran, arrived two weeks following Devi's election as Leader of the Nivasi Council. Uncertain expectations were ripe, although Arian strongly believed they would require the military intervention of the Shore People to save Desa from an apocalyptic fate at the hands of the Horse Warriors. Arian requested Mandeep to attend, bypassing Amura, as the most uncertain person was Shanti, still holding firm to her naïve belief in a peaceful with the Horse Warriors. Perhaps he wishfully hoped the influence of Mandeep could sway Shanti to at least stay neutral in the war deliberations. Arian had wisely invited Simran, as he was the most knowledgeable of the land on the banks of the river opposite the Horse Warrior's camp.

They had sent solicitous messages to Rishaan requesting his counsel as to the threat from the Horse Warriors. Arian and Mandeep feared Rishaan would decide not to engage any additional forces as far north as Desa, calculating better defense lines were closer to his borders. Either through intent or loose conversation, Tarak had confided in Arian as to the revenge oath of Rishaan. Arian believed those deep seeds of anger intensified with the loss of Ekavir, the heir apparent to Rishaan.

Arian had to conceive of a way to secure the release of Saisha, Anya and Jai while providing Rishaan with the skull fragments of Kalpit's assassin. *Strange custom*, mused Arian. *How could anyone, especially from the Shore People, determine the exact bones of Kalpit's murderer?*

Devi had shrewdly devised a plan to accomplish that very

strategic objective, relying on her instincts of the guile of Axam. Devi confidently outlined the plan, daring and brilliant in concept, although exceedingly difficult to execute. Simran added additional tactical elements to Devi's plan, which added more credibility and increased the odds of execution. Arian exclaimed, "This plan can succeed, but Rishaan must fully endorse it and commit a massive force to march north in the next few weeks."

Rishaan welcomed the delegation from Desa, hosting his guests with a lavish mid-day banquet. The vast variety of foods, including new types of fruit and fish from the bordering sea, amazed the diplomats from Desa. In addition, an endless bounty of wine of several varieties graced each table. Rishaan spared no effort to impress his guests. Soon enough, Shanti began exhibiting the expected behavior of persons unaccustomed to this form of alcohol. The wine did the trick; any lingering tension soon evaporated.

Rishaan carefully considered the attendance from his side, quickly discarding Viraj, although it would have been customary for him to attend such a function. Instead, he chose Vedant, knowing full well the role he had played in the poisoning of Zeba. *Yes,* Rishaan ruminated in his mind, *I know exactly what evil deeds Vedant did in the service of Viraj.*

Craftily, he assigned Vedant the position to his left, a position of high honor normally reserved for Viraj. Vedant's discomfort was easy to discern as he was unsure as to the intentions of Rishaan. To Rishaan's right sat Zeba. An unusual decision since only Ekavir could occupy that chair, normally reserved for the person second in power to Rishaan. Her seating position surprised Zeba, protesting it was too soon after Ekavir's death; besides, no female had ever served as ruler of the Shore People.

Rishaan selected three other participants to this historic feast: Tarak as the new commander of the military, Harnish in his role as chief military strategist and AO. If the addition of AO to the main table pleased Zeba beyond her fondest hopes, it was extremely unsettling to Vedant, practically shattering his nerves. Subtle beads of sweat appeared on Vedant's face, noticeable only to Rishaan, delighting in the chief priest's anxiety.

Rishaan, comprehending the guests did not share the same spiritual beliefs as the Shore People, explained the morsels of food, scattered on the table, symbolically offering deference to the ancestral spirits. Water sprinkled around the table symbolized the purity of the gathering. Each person prayed in their own manner, most maintaining silence as several of the participants, including Zeba, believed only the soul could reach the nether world of spirits.

Rishaan briefly introduced AO as an honored guest in his kingdom, referring to him as a wise spiritual master of natural harmony, meaning the human interaction with the universe in the broadest sense. The delegation, interpreting AO as a person like Mandeep and Amura, thought nothing unusual of the role of AO. To a certain degree, these perceptions were true, although neither Mandeep nor Amura possessed the extraordinary talents of AO.

Rishaan heaped lavish praise on his guests, assuring them their journey to his land would be fruitful. He shifted his attention to Arian, showering him with the highest accolades as Arian had in fact saved the vast majority of Shore People cavalry from certain slaughter. "Arian, our people owe you a tremendous debt. My military leaders on the battlefield with Ekavir bear witness to your extraordinary heroism and daring tactics to cutoff the attack by the Horse Warriors. Everyone extols your courage asserting you led the counterattack, the first to engage the vicious enemy, the first to risk your own life for my soldiers."

Arian bowed to Rishaan and rejoined, "Lord Rishaan, we the Varagans and the Nivasi owe you our lives. Without your forces and the brilliant, noble leadership of Ekavir, our forces would have succumbed to the maniacal onslaughts of the Horse Warriors. Unfortunately, their defeat was only tactical; we can be sure of their return within the next six months with forces triple the original invasion force. They will build chariots in vast numbers. Their senior leaders will enter battle with the clear mandate for victory, the only other option being execution, as no Horse Warrior can live in defeat."

The evening concluded with the directive to the military leaders to devise a war plan within the next few days. Rishaan then turned to Shanti, asking reverently if she would honor him by accepting a tour of his city he personally would lead. Of course, Shanti gladly accepted the invitation, her face expressing a tinge of blush, intoxicated from wine and the charms of Rishaan.

As the guests departed, Rishaan directed Vedant to remain for some personal consultation. Rishaan wasted no time, now showing his contempt. "Vedant, I assume you are aware of the various means at my disposal to end your life. You could simply disappear or fall victim to some illness, not unlike the fate which Zeba experienced. A worse fate would be death in the 'hole', reserved for only the most wicked of men, diabolical creatures who would poison the daughter of the ruler."

Vedant's worst fears came to fruition. Rishaan continued, "Redemption is possible, perhaps even a luxurious retirement with your own house servants."

Swooning from sheer fear, Vedant fell on the floor kissing Rishaan's feet, imploring forgiveness. Rishaan placed his hands on Vedant's trembling shoulders, "Relax, Vedant, this is what I need you to do." Secretive conversations of revenge and ambition ensued.

The next day, Rishaan and Shanti indulged in walks and carriage rides throughout the city. Shanti fell in love with the magnificent gardens, the myriad of tropical flowers and bushes. Rishaan's endless stories of folktales held Shanti in a state of enchantment, especially the allusion to the wild peacocks, their symbolism for beauty and romance stirring Shanti's heart. Both Rishaan and Shanti were of the same age, both floundering in an emotionally debilitated state of persistent depression. Their presence together unleashed both their spirits, one of those rare intersections of two vastly different people, destined for union. The more Rishaan gazed into Shanti's green eyes, the more infatuated he became.

As Rishaan and Shanti grew more emotionally entangled with the passing hours, the military planners feverishly studied maps, devising various plans. The logical conclusion emerged; prevent the

Horse Warriors from crossing the wide river in massive numbers. Arian knew any delays in new battle engagements was to the advantage of the Horse Warriors as assembling 15,000 warriors with a fleet of chariots would consume months.

To the delight of Arian, Rishaan enthusiastically approved the final war plan.

"Arian", implored Rishaan, "do not forget to bring me the bones of Kalpit's killer. I must fulfill my oath and liberate my brother's ashes into the ocean."

With imperial direction, Rishaan ended the war strategy meeting as he had other matters on his mind. Rishaan and Shanti strolled off into Rishaan's private chambers, both charged with an energy neither had experienced in years.

AO and Zeba did not hide their budding relationship. They openly walked through the gardens and spent hours on nature walks. Spies reported to Rishaan the suspicion of a romantic relationship between Zeba and AO, certain Rishaan would object to his royal daughter marrying a mystic with an unknown family lineage from some sleepy tiny village at the distant corner of his kingdom.

AO's extraordinary personality had long ago captivated Rishaan, having saved Zeba's life and interpreted his dream brilliantly. Besides, AO had demolished Viraj's devilish plan by perfectly reciting the spiritual hymns in record time, a feat not even Dumurkha had accomplished. Best of all, AO was not ambitious, content to provide complete loyalty to him and his family and providing spiritual ballast against the religious intolerance of the chief priests.

Shanti informed Arian and Mandeep her visit to Rishaan's kingdom would extend for an unspecified period, ostensibly to work out the details of the new trade partnership. *Yes,* thought Arian, *there will be a new partnership which will keep Shanti busy for quite a while. Shanti will probably adopt a new attitude toward mixing the blood of two distinct peoples.*

PART 42
Jai's Terrible Fate

Several days had elapsed since Balvan suffered gruesome facial wounds in the rescue of Anya. He was fortunate, as the camp healers had properly cleansed the deep gashes to prevent infections, the primary concern for all wounded warriors. A messenger from Dhanur disturbed Balvan's recuperation, ordering him to the headquarters of the Horse Warriors. Without question, Balvan obeyed, although he was still weak from his injuries.

Dhanur greeted Balvan with humor typical of the warrior cult asking, "So Balvan, how are your facial scratches healing?"

Balvan responded in kind, "Scratches? You are the first person to mention something about scratches on my face. I noticed nothing." Both men laughed.

"Still one of the greatest Horse Warriors in our midst," remarked Dhanur.

Axam, silent, smiled slightly, always of a more subdued expression than his brother. Dhanur continued, "Balvan, the progress of military training of your adopted son, Jai, is not good. He is soft from his upbringing in the palace comforts of his previous home. No question, he has a fighting spirit, not unafraid to stare down opponents, but he lacks the physical development required to compete with the other boys. He has already lost several fights with the more aggressive boys."

Balvan stayed silent, fully comprehending the reality, understanding that young boys in this situation rarely survive the rigorous training. He recalled the violent meanness of the young warrior's mentality, unrelentingly targeting weaker boys.

"I have been discussing this matter with Axam. It is quite a dilemma, as young Jai will always bear dishonor with our soldiers if we grant any concessions. Plus, the other boys will beat him, surely causing serious, possibly life-threatening injuries."

Balvan thought about the severe disadvantage Jai had considering the other boys from the youngest ages grew up to be soldiers. *True,* he thought, *Jai is still five years from reaching combat status but Dhanur is telling me this now as the situation must be grave.*

"How can I be of help?" Balvan asked.

Dhanur nodded to Axam, who interjected, "Jai is of high intelligence with sharp wits and a resilient spirit. With the right training, he could join my secret forces, requiring different, more cunning skills."

Balvan understood the implications. These men were professional spies and assassins. They also suffered the highest casualty rates of the Horse Warriors, often their lives ended in hideous torture when captured.

Balvan answered, "Axam, thank you for your confidence in Jai as everyone knows this profession requires the most skill, especially stoic courage under stress." Balvan understood no other viable option existed except a lifetime of ridicule and subjugation, as every male had to serve in the military or face servitude.

Balvan said nothing other than, "I accept your judgment and thank you for the confidence in Jai's future potential." This statement was not as solicitous as it appeared; the elite commanders handpicked the men in this unique profession based on qualifications demanding superior personal and emotional sophistication, including skills in lying and acting. The art of murder, using any means, topped the list of required skills. Balvan understood the immediate downside; about half of the candidates failed to survive the multiyear training regimen, which required long, difficult solitary periods in every extreme condition.

There was another consideration striking terror in his heart. Balvan realized boys selected for Axam's elite team suffered cruel beatings. Such an appointment engendered tremendous jealousy and hatred. Ultimately, these uniquely skilled men enjoyed immense respect by veteran warriors, but the young recruits, jealous of any special privilege, thought of them differently. Balvan kept this information from Saisha and Anya, hoping time would improve the situation for Jai.

Nearly a month had passed since the Desa battles. Another 5,000 Horse Warriors arrived, increasing the logistical complexity of feeding thousands of soldiers and horses. The total fighting force increased to 8,000, on track to reach the required number to launch the second invasion of Desa. New chariots were being designed and tested.

Dhanur and Axam were aware of the need for improved methods to move large numbers of soldiers and horses rapidly across the treacherous river. True, the periodic rains had subsided, causing the river width to narrow, and decreasing the river turbulence to manageable levels. With luck, Dhanur thought, the heavy cavalry horses could cross in certain spots without difficulty. Of course, there were the occasional flash rainstorms causing turbulence and increased river depth.

The ever cautious and inventive Jung-Guo offered a more permanent solution than utilizing a fleet of rafts. He pictured for Axam and Dhanur a series of rafts connected, forming a long floating bridge capable of continuous troop movement across the Great Stars River. Axam inquired about flash floods to which Jung-Guo responded the construction would be strong enough to withstand the occasional storm of any intensity. This answer pleased Axam. The new design solved the nightmarish challenge which was the placement of insufficient troops on the south side of the river should an invading force attack from that direction.

Jung-Guo estimated only a few weeks to complete the floating bridge. Until they finished the bridge, Axam stationed several hundred Horse Warriors on the southern side across from the base camp. These soldiers would provide permanent reconnaissance forces providing at least three days' warning of any advancing enemy troops.

As the days passed, the river became shallower and calmer as the seasonal rains diminished, transitioning to a drier weather pattern. Axam, staring across the wide river, deep in thought, ruminated in his mind the various battle tactics he would use if he were in the shoes of Arian and Devi. His biggest unknown was the potential size of the military forces provided by the Shore People. The genius of strategy depended on one's skill in assessing all potential outcomes and preparing for each.

Sometimes Nature presents armies with freakish outcomes which defy prediction, no matter the genius of the strategist.

The day arrived, as Balvan had feared. An urgent message from Axam summoned Balvan to his headquarters. As he rapidly walked to meet Axam, Balvan tried to convince himself some other reason not involving Jai was the purpose of the requested appearance. The sight of Axam's face, messaging lines of sad news, greeted Balvan.

"Balvan, I have terrible news for you and your wife, Saisha. Your adopted son, Jai, is dead." Axam offered no explanation; both understood what had occurred. The mean spirited and envious boys in his unit had given Jai the proverbial "good luck" sendoff. A beating by several of the boys was not unusual, considered a sign of toughness expected of all young men. Fighting back was taboo, the victim simply endured the punishment, instinctively knowing how to protect his vital organs.

Balvan declared death should never occur in these situations. Something terrible had gone wrong. Axam mumbled, "Jai tried to fight back, striking one boy breaking his nose. The incensed boy grabbed a rock and smashed Jai's head, causing severe head injuries and bleeding. Jai died a few hours later."

Balvan asked Axam, "What will happen to the boy who killed Jai?"

"According to our laws, deathly blows against other fellow soldiers, regardless of age, violate the military codes. Execution is the only option for his commander" Axam answered somewhat defensively. "The other boys treated Jai as a foreigner even though, as your adopted son and an honorable member of the military, he had citizen rights."

Balvan understood the logic of Axam's words, but in his heart, he believed the treatment of Jai was wrong, exposing a defect in the moral fiber of the Horse Warriors. Saisha would be inconsolable, reenforcing deep irreconcilable hatred. Their future was never darker.

PART 43
Beautiful Revenge

Arian and Tarak were receiving disconcerting news from the various boat people who traversed the entire length of the river, conducting trade as neutral citizens of the river with no allegiance to any tribes or peoples. Some of these "neutral" boatsmen were spies working for Tarak but toiling away year by year, deeply embedded in the culture of the boat people. In fact, one of the four men accosted by Ekavir months earlier was a spy well known to senior Shore People military. His three companions had no inkling. He did nothing out of the ordinary; he also endured the "wheel" suffering the same fate as the others. He laughed later about his "ordeal" with Tarak and Harnish, thankful the only bad after-effects were nagging headaches and vomiting.

The spies informed Tarak and Arian the Horse Warriors had blockaded the entire section of the river, both downstream and upstream from the Horse Warrior Camp. All movement on the river had ceased. The last sighting of the camp showed unusual construction, the beginning of a series of rafts, lashed together to form a type of floating bridge. This information sent electrifying shocks throughout the senior leaders. The bridge, never constructed on the river, would allow a continuous flow of men, horses and supplies across the river, a true breakthrough advantage for the Horse Warriors.

While Rishaan continued heavy negotiations with Shanti, the holy man Viraj spent considerable time in all forms of meditation, normally assisted by beautiful young girls, sometimes not even one third his age. Viraj believed it was his spiritual duty to sleep with young women, all of whom were certified as virgins, claiming his pure holiness would bring good fortunes to these young girls in future years.

Viraj conveniently believed sexual encounters with young girls enhanced his spirituality. His assistants invested considerable time searching for suitable candidates. Most of the time, superstitious and gullible parents gladly nominated their daughters for this honor; occasionally politically ambitious parents spotted an opportunity to advance their family's fortunes.

Vedant approached Viraj, bragging of a young girl, barely of age, who defied all standards of beauty. Very exotic in appearance, this maiden was from a remote village reputed to raise the most beautiful women in the land. Viraj could hardly restrain himself, demanding Vedant send the young girl to his meditation chambers right away.

An hour later, a beautiful young woman, an image of sheer innocence, quietly appeared at the entrance to Viraj's lounging chambers. She seemed shy, a bit coy, but not afraid. Viraj slowly maneuvered her to the bed, not even bothering to ask her name. He slid off her top clothes revealing a sheer lacy undergarment which did not value modesty. Viraj laid down on the bed, motioning the young girl to approach. Clearly aroused with overwhelming anticipation, his eyes closed, swimming in pure lust, he awaited his prize. Slowly she slid onto him and deftly burst a foxglove pod, a deadly poison, with one hand into his nostrils while the other hand deftly stimulated Viraj.

People often say one should die doing what they loved most; such was the case for the holy man, Viraj. The "virgin", a very well-paid assassin, cleansed Viraj's face for any evidence of foxglove residue which moments earlier caused heart failure as Viraj in his moment of ecstasy inhaled deadly poisons into his lungs. Then she screamed, crying hysterically, provoking Vedant and other attendants to rush into the room.

"Quickly, call the doctors. Viraj has suffered a heart attack." The attendant ran for help, while Vedant took a pillow, pressing firmly on Viraj's mouth, ensuring his last memories would be the image of a beautiful young maiden endowed with all the virtues Viraj cherished. Moments later, the top physician confirmed Viraj had died from heart failure. On the way out, the confirming physician snatched a small purse discretely handed to him by Vedant. *Services perfectly rendered,* mused Vedant, a sly smile, barely discernible.

An hour later, Vedant informed Rishaan of the incredibly sad news; Viraj, the most holy of all people in the kingdom, had succumbed to heart failure. Rishaan responded, "This is sad news. We must honor Viraj with a magnificent funeral, befitting a man of his spiritual perfection."

PART 44
Nature Intervenes

Time was now of the essence. The war plan sped up, advancing soldiers in multiple waves. A critical cornerstone of the plan was to place at least five hundred Nivasi archers in strategic positions overlooking the crossing bridge. The archers departed on foot, covering about twenty miles per day accompanied by the Varagan cavalry. The bulk of the forces would depart from the kingdom with 1,000 light cavalry warriors with another 4,000 mounted soldiers and a massive number of supply wagons a few days behind.

This was a daring and risky plan, as the full complement of soldiers would not be in place to withstand an all-out assault from the Horse Warriors, if an enormous mass of their fighters had already crossed the river.

Within a few days, reconnaissance fighters spotted the forces heading north toward the Horse Warriors. Reports flooded back to Axam of several sizeable forces approaching from two separate directions. Axam had less than three hundred fighters on the south side of the river. Axam ordered Jung-Guo to complete the bridge within twenty-four hours, regardless of the number of laborers needed. The only option was to work through the night, making a treacherous task all but impossible.

Good fortune literally shone on the Horse Warriors and the construction crews that night as a full moon in a cloudless sky provided sufficient light. The last plank was lashed just as the morning sun began its daily journey. Axam marveled at his good luck. Perfect conditions for construction through the night and a fine day to begin the mass crossing of men and horses.

Axam was contented to see a long line of men and horses begin the crossing. Axam watched as the bridge performed brilliantly, supporting over a hundred warriors slowly leading their horses over the tightly bound rafts. A beautiful sight sighed Axam, the genius of Jung-Guo clear in the sturdy, steady design.

Dhanur nudged Axam, interrupting his dreamy vision of complete domination of Devi and her ragged army. *Would he allow her to live?* He wondered. *Arian would be one of the first executed, assuming he survived the vicious battles. Yes, he could have fun with Devi.*

"Axam, we will get a surprise visit from Khander. He will be here within a few hours."

Also arriving in full force by midday were the combined forces of the Nivasi, Varagan and Shore People. At noon, the Horse Warriors had nearly five hundred warriors on the south side of the river, with another hundred crossing each hour.

Far north in the vast mountains permanently encased in ice and snow, Nature's power unleashed an earthquake of epic proportions. Legends abound among the local people passed down from generation to generation of the day when the gods fought a terrible battle for mastery of the heavy dominions. Legend claims the victorious gods threw the evil gods from the top of the mountain, landing with such force the earth split open. It destroyed houses, swallowed up people in giant fissures, even the large rivers changed course at the direction of the victorious god. Some people said they had failed to worship the righteous gods; now their land became hell.

Today's massive earthquake, a mere rumbling in the Horse Warrior camp, lifted huge tracts of land, shifting with sudden force the normal flow of rivers. A river previously flowing away in an opposite direction altered course and now emptied directly into the Great Stars River. The effect was terrifying as a wall of water built up with no place to rush other than by joining with the Great Stars, a significant distance upstream from the floating bridge. The river was transformed into a massive wall of churning turbulence.

Dhanur had directed Axam to join the crossing to command the forces on the south side. Dhanur correctly judged he should greet Khander, who would soon appear. Within an hour, Khander entered the base camp, catching sight of the long floating bridge bearing hundreds of men and horses. He was absolutely delighted, his face beaming with pride and joy.

Axam completed the crossing just in time to receive reports of the advancing army. Axam reasoned a defensive perimeter would suffice until all the required warriors crossed. Within twenty-four hours, another 1,000 men would supplement his forces; three days later, his forces would top 5,000 well on the way to 10,000 fighters.

Before the wall of water was visible, warriors on both sides of the river heard the deafening sounds building in intensity. Horses on the floating bridge became agitated, causing the crossing pace to quicken. The river flow was extremely calm, but the roar increased in intensity like a violent storm approaching. But this could not be true, as the day was cloudless and calm. Just as the sound became unbearable, an immense wall of water swept down, smashing the bridge like dry twigs, snapped for kindling. Within seconds, all traces of the bridge vanished along with countless men and horses.

It also swept away any soldiers near the riverbank along with vast amounts of supplies and weapons, including the first ten chariots waiting for transport. Dhanur and Khander watched, completely stunned. The entire camp in absolute terror. The river widened and deepened with turbulence unseen in years.

The attacking forces led by Arian and Tarak could not believe the scene, watching in amazement as thousands of logs passed by at incredible speeds, with bodies of men and horses interspersed. The Horse Warriors on the south side were in complete disarray. Arian and Tarak quickly seized the opportunity, launching nearly a thousand arrows. Death and panic rained down on the Horse Warriors, scattering the men, leaving gaping holes in the defenses which permitted easy breaches by the various attacking cavalry units. Dead Horse Warriors lie everywhere, a complete breakdown of the entire defensive force.

Within minutes, half the Horse Warriors lay dead or gravely wounded. Arian halted the attack, asking for the Horse Warrior commander to meet for truce talks. To his pleasure, just as Devi had predicted, Axam emerged, his arm bleeding profusely from an arrow strike.

Arian began the engagement, saying, "Axam, we will soon have a force exceeding 10,000 in number. The river is now uncrossable. It would be complete suicide not to surrender."

Axam, obviously could not deny the facts nor conceive of any way to prevent outright annihilation, responded, "Yes, the foolish battles between our peoples should cease. We only want peace."

Arian laughed, "You may know the two fools to swallow your lies are now dead. Let me help you save your life and those of your men still lucky to be alive. I demand the release of Saisha, Anya and Jai plus the handmaiden and the corpse of the man who killed Kalpit. Do our bidding and we will permit you and the rest of your men to cross back to your encampment. Oh yes, I forgot, we also require fifteen bars of gold."

"How much time do I have to consider your demands?"

Arian shrugged, "Why would you need more time?" He signaled to Tarak, who summoned two thousand fighters and archers to advance into full sight. Arian added, "another 8,000 are behind them."

Axam, shocked at the sight of these men, fully convinced another 8,000 were likely in reserve, quickly agreed to the terms set by Arian.

"Where is the killer of Kalpit?" Arian demanded.

Axam departed for a few minutes, returning shortly with a dead man whose injuries seemed to suggest his death was very recent, as in the last few minutes. "This is your man", Axam pronounced.

Suspicious, Arian objected, saying, "How can I be sure?"

Axam ripped off his shirt, exposing a strange tattoo, illustrating a skull sitting on a dagger. "This man was a member of our secret forces, trained in assassinations. He is the man who killed Kalpit."

Arian had seen the same tattoo, mulling in his mind the circumstances. "Yes, I recognize the tattoo. You sent assassins with the same tattoo to kill me, is that right?"

Yes, Axam replied. The dead man dropped to the ground in front of Arian and Tarak. He was immediately picked up by Tarak's men and sent to the back lines for wrapping in funeral linens. The dead assassin would have an unusual funeral.

"Now we are making progress. All your men must disarm. As soon as Saisha, the handmaid and the children are secure in our custody along with fifteen bars of gold, we will begin the release of your men. Axam, you will remain as our prisoner, until you satisfy all conditions. Send a messenger to Dhanur."

Arian turned to Tarak, promising five gold bars would repay his monetary debt to Rishaan, while the other ten would secure a huge surplus of wheat and barley for the people of Desa.

The river was still raging from the massive wave, so they delayed the crossing by one day. Arian's men collected the weapons from the Horse Warriors, all of whom would have battled to the last man but Axam convinced them of the need for common sense, arguing bravery is knowing when to concede ground to fight another day. Even if discontented, the unit commanders ensured complete obedience as Axam's word was final.

The deal negotiated by Adam may have extremely displeased Khander; neither he nor Dhanur uttered a word. Khander, a man of deep superstition, interpreted the sudden surge of water as an ominous sign from his ancestral spirits. Then the unthinkable happened. Saisha demanded Balvan join him and Anya. Dhanur questioned Balvan as to his intentions. Balvan's reply was simple enough, "I pledged to never leave my wife, I will honor her."

He refused to say more, hiding his feelings. The senseless killing of Jai, another pointless murder which proved to him the values of the Horse Warriors lacked any sense of human decency. Saisha had also persuaded him the basic values of the Horse Warriors conflicted with the universal sanctity of life, a violent culture whose primary purpose in life was domination over all other people.

Above all, he genuinely loved Saisha and desired to spend his remaining life with her.

The reunion with Tarak was joyous beyond words. Anya dreamt of this moment from the first second of captivity. The bitterness within Saisha at the loss of Jai meant she could not live in the Horse Warrior culture. Both Saisha and Balvan realized in retrospect once Jai joined the army, his personality would change, transforming into a Horse Warrior, detesting the weakness of his previous life, denouncing any emotional attachment to his family.

After the last Horse Warrior departed in small boats, leaving behind their horses and weapons, Arian and Tarak began constructing a defensive fortification which would forever prevent significant troop movement across to the south bank of the river.

PART 45
Love Fulfilled

Sunrise ushered in another day, the melodic calls of birds sounding the reveille to begin another cycle in the ritualistic recurrence of light and darkness. Whether life spins in eternal repetitions or progresses through time is a mystery whose correct answer is unknowable, the only insight provided by the facade of beliefs. AO chose not to litter his mind with speculations. He savored the simplicity of the moment, filled with anticipation for his morning stroll with Zeba.

Today would be different. Kalpit's ashes would return home to the ocean, Rishaan faithfully executed his solemn oath. Shanti would join Rishaan in the dignified ceremony, as custom dictated new love should follow old bitterness, buried in the evil pot bearing the crushed skull bones of Kalpit's assassin. Daiwik the new senior chief priest would soon officiate the auspicious event of marriage between Rishaan and Shanti.

Absent from the ceremony was Vedant, happily ensconced in his new retirement home in the hills, surrounded by handmaidens, beautiful and youthful, perfect assistants for a long virile life.

Most prominent in attendance were Saisha and Anya, paying sad homage to the man murdered by thugs with no purpose worthy of humanity. Saisha lovingly invited Balvan to attend the service. She wanted the world to know the power of redemption and to prove love can persist even in the face of tragedy.

Anya kept her word, recounting the heroism of Balvan who saved her from a hellish slavery far worse than anything she could have imagined with the Horse Warriors. Rishaan joked about Balvan's scars, remarking it gave him a dashing, daring facade which made him the envy of all his senior military staff.

To the side of the burial ceremony stood Zeba and AO. He gently grasped her hand and whispered, "Zeba, I love you. Please honor me with marriage. You are my soul, my only love."

Zeba turned slowly to AO, a small tear of joy dripping down her face. "Yes, I will marry you and commit my soul to our lives together. My love for you is eternal."

Postlude: The Legacy of AO

I have now completed my duty to record the "Dream of AO "enshrined for future generations, a beacon for the moral choices of a harmonious life. I would be remiss if I failed to inform you of the authentic life of AO, his influence beyond the storyteller's tale.

AO retold the "dream" countless times, traveling from village to village. Admittedly, AO converted his dream into an elaborate fable, highly adorned with his personal wisdom. The dream was his device to preach his messages of equality, harmony, and purpose.

Countless children named Devi, Arian, Ekavir, Veer, Mishka, and Zeba populated babies' names through the ages. Some people refused to believe the tale was a dream; all wanted to embrace the teachings of AO as told in his dream.

Sometimes dreams come true, as with AO, extremely gifted, a dreamer and visionary. His reputation preceded him everywhere he traveled. People expected his arrival, waiting for hours to occupy a seat close enough to be in the aura of AO. Such was the case with a young woman from a powerful family. She was searching for greater truth in life; she believed AO would unleash her true purpose in life. One could imagine AO was also seeking to fill the emptiness of long, solitary nights.

As he entered the Assembly Hall, his eye caught the image of a young woman sitting in the first row. He bowed, gently grasping her hand saying, "I am AO."

The young woman's face sparkled with joy, replying, "My name is Zeba. May I show you our city after the telling of your tale, I think you would enjoy my garden."

AO, finding it difficult to move his eyes from her, answered, "I would love to spend the day with you and to find enchantment in your garden." As he slowly released her hand, their eyes remained fixed, tingles of attraction subtly provoking those rare stirrings of the heart.

Neither AO nor Zeba could think of anything else. That night AO fell into a deep dream. The octopus never appeared. Only the loving, perfect image of Zeba lingered throughout the night.

"The Dream of AO" chronicled by Akshay, the descendant of AO, a faithful written reproduction of the greatest tale ever told in these lands.

Copyright registration number: TXu 2-223-081
December 13, 2020

Characters

Description of the Four Peoples: Setting is Indus Valley around 1900BC in an area currently in Pakistan and India.

The Varagans: People of a feudal, clan-based kingdom, Northwest Indus Valley, defeated in battle by the Horse Warriors, they flee into Desa, land of the Nivasi and the Forest Dwellers. Key leaders are Pratham, Arian, Amura

The Nivasi: Pacifist, democratic society occupying major region in East Indus Valley. Believers in universal humanism. Key leaders are Gandesh, Mandeep, Devi and Shanti

The Horse Warriors: Collection of nomadic tribes from the steppes. North of the Indus Valley. Tribes are united under Khander, Supreme Ruler. And adhere to strict legal codes set by Khander. Warlike and aggressive in nature, the key leaders are Dhanur and Axam

The Shore People: People of a benevolent kingdom, highly religious in nature, occupying the southern part of the Indus Valley. Key leaders are Rishaan, Ekavir, Viraj, Zeba

General:

AO: an itinerant, storytelling mystic deeply endowed in wisdom, purveyor of the "dream".
Akshay: Translates the "dream" into the first written manuscript; serves as the narrator of the story.

From the Nivasi:

    Gandesh: Leader of the Council
    Mandeep: Senior philosopher and wise man
    Devi: Female leader of the Nivasi
    Shanti: Senior Council leader and chief peace advocate
    Vidya: Wise man/ leader of the Forest Dwellers
    Dhira: Male leader of the "Elite" military unit
    Mishka: Female leader of the "Elite" military unit
    Simran: Lead Scout
    Priya: Female leader of Farming and Grazing administration
    Lajita: First Female Elite archer killed in battle
    Dharma: Citizen killed in the Great Conflict
    Ponmudi: Inventor of the chariot

From the Varagans:

    Pratham: Ruler of the Varagans
    Jackal: Cowardly brother of Pratham
    Amura: senior philosopher and wise man
    Arian: Chief of the military
    Veer: Second in command to Aryan
    Samarth: Senior leader of second largest clan
    Manbir: Selected to be a leader of the "Elites"
    Inesh: Honorable illegitimate son of Pratham, admirer of Arian
    Jaitra: Dishonorable illegitimate son of Pratham, admirer of Jackal

From the Horse Warriors

    Khander: Ruler of the Horse Warriors
    Axam: Chief Emissary and Intelligence chief, younger brother of Khander
    Jangi: Second in command to Axam and nephew of Khander

Dhanur: Senior commander in charge and older brother of Khander
Jung-Guo: Chief Builder originally from the tribes of the East
Balashur: Heralded warrior and Husband of Omisha
Sudhir: Unit commander responsible for Balashur
Omisha: Woman sexually assaulted by Balashur
Balvan: Elder warrior, keeper of Saisha
Savita: Wife of Balvan

From the Shore People:

Rishaan: Ruler of the Shore People
Livia: Deceased wife of Rishaan
Kalpit: Slain brother of Rishaan
Zeba: Youngest daughter of Rishaan
Ekavir: Commander of the military, nephew of Rishaan
Tarak: second in command to Ekavir
Saisha: Wife of Kalpit captured by the Horse Warriors
Harnish: Chief of military strategy
Jai: Son of Saisha
Anya: daughter of Saisha
Vedant: High Priest and Spiritual Adviser to Rishaan
Viraj: Senior High Priest and Advocate for Theocracy
Dumurkha: High Priest, Poetic Hymns memorization genius
Kalpesh: Priest from the AO's monastery with excellent medicinal skills
Sachiv (Manan): Young assassin turned devoted disciple of AO
Daiwik: High Priest advocating Human Equality